THE
ATON BIRD

by

Jane Palmer

DODO BOOKS

First published in Great Britain
by Dodo Books 2008

ISBN 978-1-906442-16-3

Other science fiction books by this author

THE PLANET DWELLER
THE WATCHER
MOVING MOOSEVAN
BABEL'S BASEMENT
THE KYBION

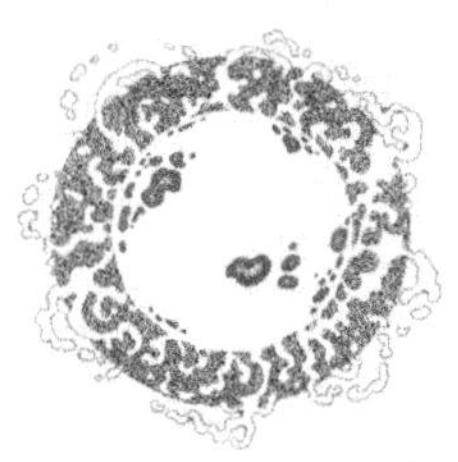

THE QUEEN

CHAPTER 1

The cloudbanks were glowing orange canyons in the setting sun, and the horizon's curving rim gleamed like a burnished ring mounted with the jewel of the solar disc. As Ahmose soared higher, silver meteors intermittently stabbed the thin layer of atmosphere, and above its misty curtain the constellations made a diamond collar against the backdrop of space.

The bird followed the Earth's rotation to bathe in the sun's perpetual warmth. Then he plunged back to the planet's surface through a whirlpool of cloud, sleet hammering against his golden plumage, and out into the glare of white mountains where Neanderthal tribes hid from the spears of the new hominids.

While the silence of space touched the highest peaks, busy winds swirled through the flower-speckled valleys below. Here, thatched stone outcrops and dank caves were dormitories for populations doomed by encroaching ice sheets.

Further south, land was being pushed up by erupting volcanoes. In a bright blue sea a chain of islands lay in a dusty girdle about the caldera where there used to be a mighty civilisation. The planet's crust had blistered, then blown away its people, artefacts and history. Crumbs of what it once was glistered in the art of other lands. Now only the dolphins remembered.

Ahmose floated in the rising thermals with the albatross and migrating swallow, across the boundary of one empire and over the deep green ocean of another. Here leviathans rose like bald grey islands and blew fountains of drizzle at circling gulls.

The wind picked up. It was fast and icy, buffeting the water into cliffs topped with ragged fringes of spume. As they arched over, the golden bird soared through their funnels until, dizzy with exhilaration, he misjudged the speed of the next wave and it crashed down on him.

Ahmose woke with a start.

The Nile was gently lapping against the side of the reed boat. The priest sat up and looked about. His horse was peacefully cropping the tufts of coarse grass on the bank above and the ferryman was dozing. A lad placed a bridle on the grazing animal and led it to the temple stables.

The royal barge came gliding ghostly over the water like a huge furtive pelican. The river's current brought it alongside the small jetty and the crew secured its weighty grandeur to the flimsy mooring posts. The prow and stern of the barge were curved over in elegant stems sprouting enormous lilies, their white cedar petals now shrouded by brown linen. The canopy decorated in gold at the centre of the vessel had also been covered and the lighter skinned crew members crew wore dark tunics with hoods; their oars so well muffled even the fish wouldn't hear them being stroked through the water.

Ahmose left the reed boat and climbed aboard. The captain was unable to conceal his surprise at the champion selected to save Queen Ankhesenamun. A full featured man, his shaven head glowed in the rays of the sinking sun, and the animal keeper's kilt was too large for his slight frame. There was an aura of holy innocence about him. Many in the Egyptian clergy were undoubtedly holy, though usually only as innocent as self-preservation would allow. In those troubled times that was as much as a scorpion waiting its chance to dash from a crack in the crumbling fabric of the Aton cult.

Ahmose was used to others observing him. Even the sacred animals in the menagerie of the temple of Amon Ra at Innu gave him curious glances. The crocodile of Sebek had a particularly disconcerting stare. The other priests held him in contempt for being literate, though not a scribe, and living next to the flood plain, but not owning land. Yet none of them dare feed the crocodile of Sebek. Every temple needed someone dedicated to do the dirty, dangerous work so they praised Ahmose a little and gave him the occasional small gift of honey, cheese or olive oil for treating their oxen, donkeys or servants. The animal priest wondered if his brethren would have been so patronising if they had known the real reason for his absence? Surely they didn't believe he had travelled so far south after all these years just to take a wife?

As he waited on the deck of the royal barge, Ahmose watched the sun set in the rose pink sky. Though the craft was moored a safe distance north of Thebes, as soon as some vigilant medjay or minor official questioned its disappearance, none of them would be safe.

A small party approached the royal barge and some sailors pushed out a ceremonial gangplank. Queen Ankhesenamun and her attendant, who carried a cedar casket banded with electrum and inlaid with ivory, came on board.

'Could you find nothing faster?' the young Queen asked her priest advisor as he caught up with them.

'Once away from here, who would try to stop a royal barge? When you reach Innu, Ahmose will hide you until your ship arrives.'

Queen Ankhesenamun then noticed Ahmose. Only sixteen, she had the imperious glance of a middle-aged matriarch, probably learnt from her large intimidating companion wearing a correspondingly huge wig. The animal priest frequently had to conduct such formidable women through the temple menagerie and it had left him with a fear of being engulfed. Fortunately he lived by a lake well away from the temple precincts and the world outside only intruded on inspection days.

Ahmose knelt before the Queen, his head almost touching her jewelled sandal. She looked at the wisp of a man as though he were a fallen leaf.

The Queen's advisor read the misgivings in her face.

'Ahmose is the second keeper of the sacred animals of the temple of Amon Ra at Innu,' he explained as though that should reassure her.

'What does the first keeper do?'

'Being senior to Ahmose, he is solely responsible for the bull of Merwer.'

'Well, Ahmose, second keeper for the sacred animals of the temple of Amon Ra, get up and let me see which beast you most resemble.'

Ahmose obeyed, trying not to look too simian.

His innocent, yet enigmatic, expression made her hesitate. 'What strange eyes you have. Like two pools of ink waiting for a scribe to spell out eternity.'

The priest advisor feared his plans could unravel for the sake of a colleague's haunted expression. 'No one is more devoted to the Aton than Ahmose. No other is trustworthy or dedicated enough to risk their life for your safety.'

The Queen reached out and placed a delicate hand on Ahmose's shoulder. 'I'm sorry, holy one. I am too used to priests with political minds.'

Her advisor was also aware of the danger he was in. 'I must go now. When I return to Thebes, I will try to delay Eye by telling him you are hiding in Akhetaton.'

'No, you must return to your temple. The old scoundrel would have fewer qualms about executing you than declaring his marriage to me.'

Ahmose was astonished. 'He has married you?'

The Queen looked at Ahmose as though some passing zephyr had just spoken. There was nothing extraordinary about his voice; it came as a surprise to discover he possessed one.

'Yes. Eye now has no reason to keep me alive.'

The Queen's advisor hastily bade farewell and returned to his waiting ferry. As soon as the senior priest was out of sight, Ahmose realised the danger he was also in and a chill of fear made him shudder. Thinking it was because of the night air Ahouri, the Queen's companion, wrapped a woollen cloak about his shoulders.

Ahmose looked puzzled.

'This material is the same colour as the night,' Queen Ankhesenamun explained. 'It is possible to see that your kilt once used to be white.'

'Surely the second keeper of the sacred animals of the temple of Amon Ra has a better robe to rescue his Queen in?' Ahouri joked.

'This is my best kilt.' Ahmose looked at his paw stained garment. It was much washed and threadbare. Embarrassed, he pretended to be interested in the sailors rowing the barge out into mid river where it could catch the current.

'Ahmose.'

He turned back to see Ahouri holding a garment of soft white folds.

The Queen took it from her and shook out the fine linen. 'Toss that other rag into the river.'

Ahmose refused to take the kilt. 'Even the High Priest would not wear a garment as splendid as that.' Especially his High Priest. He never wore anything finer than coarse brown linen except on ceremonial occasions.

'It belonged to a pharaoh. He has no need of it now.'

In the light of a lamp shielded by her companion's cloak, Queen Ankhesenamun delved into the casket Ahouri had brought on board, then beckoned Ahmose to her. He approached hesitantly. The Queen removed the small copper earring the priest wore in his left ear and replaced it with a gold pendant. She looked for the hole in his right ear lobe to hang its companion.

Ahmose was intimidated by the value of the gifts. 'I only wear one earring.'

'Why? Humility?'

'It was painful enough having one lobe pierced.'

She laughed, replaced the spare earring in the casket and lifted out an opulent necklace collar. Its jewels and gold glittered in the flickering light and probably hadn't been worn since leaving the hands of the goldsmith. The Queen would have placed it about Ahmose's neck if he hadn't backed away.

'No my lady, it would attract attention.'

'I don't expect you to go unrewarded for the risk you are taking.'

'I want no reward. It is for the truth of the Aton I do this.'

The cynical smile on Ahouri's face faded as she realised that he meant it.

On the journey north, Ahmose sat in the stern and wondered why the Aton had chosen this fool. He had been caught out many times, talking to the sacred animals, and eventually learnt not to mention that he understood what they said. Whatever the hippopotamus of Taueret told him wasn't worth repeating anyway because it was only interested in scandal and its appetite. Ahmose also dared to believe that the Aton listened to him. Amon Ra and the whole pantheon of deities were minor manifestations compared to the mighty oneness of the Sun. The Aton's rays had swept up Ahmose, and many more, leaving them suspended in the cushioning wonder of the Universe. Now Akhenaton had gone and his vision been eclipsed by the vengeful old order. The Aton had become like a comet that would not return for two thousand years.

While the daughter of Akhenaton slept, Ahouri watched the animal priest's bald pate catch the moonlight like another moon rising from his dark cloak. She was fascinated by Ahmose's wise innocence, but thought better of encouraging him to talk in case she became exasperated and was tempted to tip him into the river.

Several nights later the royal barge glided into a tributary below the city of Innu. The crew was paid in gold and copper debens, then Queen Ankhesenamun, Ahouri and Ahmose disembarked. They watched as the barge was rowed back towards Thebes. When it was out of sight the animal priest led the women from the river margin in the moonlight and along a tortuously narrow path to an entrance pierced in the rock at the bottom of an escarpment.

As the party went in they felt as though a serpent with icy breath was swallowing them. The ample Ahouri had trouble negotiating the twists and turns in the passage. Just when she thought she had lost the others she stumbled into a vast chamber. It was full of gold; they were entering

the gods' treasure chest. The lamps of pure olive oil that
Ahmose was lighting had not tarnished the precious metal,
and it was now obvious why gold didn't impress the priest -
he had a temple full of it.

'What is this place?' asked the Queen.

Ahmose pointed to a huge gleaming disc. The descending
rays ended in human hands. 'The temple of the Aton. When
your father died, everything dedicated to the One God was
brought here for safety. The cave was excavated as a tomb a
long time ago but the roof cracked it was never used.' He
added hastily, 'It's quite safe. Hardly anyone remembers it
existed.'

The Queen ran her fingertips over the muzzle of an
alabaster Anubis. 'The Aton was only worshipped in
temples open to the sky.'

'That would attract attention, and during the day the
sunlight does enter from those rock chimneys up there.'
Ahmose hesitated guiltily. 'I have little time to worship.'

'Are you this temple's priest?'

'Goodness no! The High Priest of Amon Ra allows me to
be its guardian.'

Ahouri laughed. 'Its guardian! And what honour does he
bestow on you for taking such a risk?'

As she would have found the idea of a menial animal
keeper being the confidant of a High Priest even more
amusing, Ahmose gave an innocent smile. 'The honour of
serving the Aton.'

Ahouri and the Queen glanced at each other. What could
they say while Ahmose wore that pious expression? Any
other priest would have demanded bolts of fine linen,
several years' supply of grain, and a herd of oxen for taking
such a risk - and needed to be drunk when agreeing to the
arrangement. They doubted Ahmose was even capable of
inebriation. The priest probably refused to don the dead
pharaoh's robe because he wore poverty to reflect the
greater glory of Akhenaton's god.

Ahmose felt like the subject of an autopsy trying to
determine how badly he was riddled with piety. He tried to
sound businesslike. 'Do you know when your ship will

arrive?'

'Soon. My agent will bring a boat to the place where we disembarked.'

'How will he contact us?'

'At dusk he will use a mirror to signal from the other side of the river. You must keep watch every day just before the "Aton" goes down.'

'It's a long way from the menagerie and I can't spend too much time from the animals. My assistant is a willing lad, but I've already been gone for some while.'

'You will only need to wait for a short time at sunset.'

A deluge of apology swept through Ahmose. 'Please forgive me. I didn't mean to be unhelpful.'

'Oh shut-up,' snapped Ahouri. 'Is it possible to get some sleep in this place?'

The fabulous bird soared through clouds rotating over deep gorges, churning the atmosphere into ionised soup. Suddenly daggers of lightning shattered pinnacles of desert sandstone as though they were blocks of salt on a blacksmith's anvil. The air twisted clouds into funnels of spinning fury. Like the trunks of cosmic elephants, they drank up everything they touched - sand, water, buildings, and ships.

From the stratosphere, Ahmose could see the moon's powdery glow giving off insipid warmth, its craters and rills an enigmatic jigsaw fretted out by Thoth. Up here the stars were huge and bald, wearing bland, cadaverous expressions that loured at the soaring spirit.

Suddenly a finger of plasma shot up from the storm below and the odour of singed feathers filled Ahmose's nostrils.

The animal priest picked himself up from the stone floor of the tomb and rubbed his head. He had these dreams so often he should have known how to avoid crash landings.

Ahmose trimmed his lamp and prepared food and wine for the Queen and Ahouri. Before they woke and the shafts of morning light streamed through the fissures in the tomb's roof, he rode back to his small hut in the temple menagerie.

Ahmose cleaned and cut the animals' food then went into each pen to make sure his apprentice hadn't missed any signs of moult, listlessness or foaming at the mouth. By the time he had been licked by the jackals and oxen, pawed by the leopard, butted by the pigs and splashed by the hippo, he needed to wash his kilt again. He didn't mind, the animals were his family.

Ahmose had reared the hippopotamus from when it had been small enough to fit in a breadbasket. Now its bulk filled the pen it had once looked so lost in. As he had refused to have its massive tusks trimmed, it had bitten its way through the wall that separated it from the beautiful mud bank. Sometimes it would follow the keeper along the lake or riverside like a mobile sarcophagus, but always returned to that small pen.

The lion was a gift from a Babylonian prince. Its intellect had never been great, to the everlasting contempt of the elderly Bast cat. Desert lions were no larger than wolves, though formidable hunters in their natural habitat. Now domesticated, this one was quite content in its garden of rocks, roaring for the visitors and living on a diet that it could never have hoped to catch in the desert. If it ever managed to reach the ibex of Thoth it would never remember what to do about it anyway. Ahmose had more trouble with the Bast cat. He often had to scold her for hungrily watching the aviary. While the ibis and falcons paid little attention, the racket the ducks made could have prematurely resurrected the dead.

The crocodile of Sebek always greeted the priest with a gaping pink mouth. However dead the meat thrown into its jaws, the reptile would thresh it about in the shallow water just to make sure. Any onlookers privileged to watch were awed by the priest's nerve. It was easier than believing he could talk to the animals.

As Ahmose sat waiting for his kilt to dry, the old Bast cat joined him. She was wiser than the other animals and noticed things they missed.

She sensed that his scent had changed. Her nose wrinkled. 'Are you ill, son of Ra?'

Ahmose momentarily allowed himself to become aware of his middle-aged body. 'No. What makes you think that?'

'Perhaps that corpulent man in the large wig worries you?'

'What corpulent man?'

'The one who has been watching for your return.'

'Probably a temple visitor waiting to inspect the animals.'

The old cat dozed off in a cushion of vigorous purrs; it was her way of dropping out of a conversation.

Ahmose heard the tread of his apprentice's large feet. The Bast cat sleepily raised her head to see who was coming and gave a matriarchal mew as the youth bounded to where the priest sat.

Goose had a large face, stubbly hair that refused to submit to a razor and a wide, perpetually smiling mouth that made him look slightly dim-witted. Nevertheless, he had a better grasp of reality than his mentor did.

'Hello Goose.'

'Where is she then?'

Ahmose had forgotten the excuse he had given for his journey. 'Who?'

'Your wife. Everyone in the lower temple can't wait to see her. Is she like you?'

The priest had never seriously thought about marriage and the complications of using that reason for his absence had not occurred to him. Now the world wanted to see what sort of woman was prepared to take the lowly animal keeper as a partner. To his horror he suddenly felt disappointed, and it showed in his face.

Goose never gave him time to answer. 'Oh – I'm sorry! Wouldn't she come?' 'I'll fetch you a drink and your other robe.'

The youth dashed off, leaving Ahmose to wonder why he had allowed the thought in.

The Bast cat's eyes remained inscrutably closed. 'There, I thought your scent had changed.'

'I don't want a wife.'

'Never used to want a wife.'

Ahmose sulked until Goose returned with a dry robe and some beer. Unable to remember having a father, the youth wasn't sure how to treat older men. He had always tried to show respect. The animals may not have been any trouble; his mentor was an enigma, however, and often exasperating.

Goose lifted the Bast cat from the priest's lap so he could dress himself. 'The Merwer bull has mange.' His tone had a degree of smug satisfaction.

Ahmose nodded. 'As it's never allowed outside, I'm not surprised.'

'I told them that, but they wouldn't let me touch it. Perhaps they want it to die so they can have a funeral.'

'Goose!' Ahmose chided.

'Well, we haven't had a good embalming for months. Think of how long that bull would take.'

'Lord Monte's funeral wasn't so long ago?'

'By the time they found him and his hunting party the sand had dried them out. The remains were so brittle we didn't need natron. Couldn't even get a piece of wadding up his backside.'

Ahmose laughed. 'Disgusting brat. Why did you have to become an assistant embalmer?'

'It pays well and you get used to the stench. It's also less dangerous than looking after a tomb full of Aton artefacts.'

The priest seized his arm. 'Has anyone asked you about that?'

Goose was puzzled. 'No. The only others who know are the priests of the inner temple. As they were the ones to move everything in there in the first place, they're not likely to say anything. Now the Aton's temple has been rededicated to Amon Ra, who's going to be any the wiser? What's the matter with you? That blackbird been perching on your roof again?'

'Someone believes that I'm too trusting.'

'Well, you're daft enough to trust anyone.'

Ahmose plunged his cup into the lake and tossed the water over his apprentice.

CHAPTER 3

Several evenings later, Ahouri was shaking out bed linen beneath the great golden disc of the Aton. 'Tell me, little priest, does no one suspect you of helping us?'

Ahmose stopped topping up the lamps. 'The only ones who know of this place are the senior priests of Amon Ra.'

'You still believe in the Aton, though?'

'Isn't generosity of spirit worth dedicating a life to?'

Ahouri laughed. 'Yes, if other people are going to show it to you.'

'Why do you always sneer at me?'

'Because I'm fond of you.' Ahmose grazed his shin on a bed frame in an attempt to move out of the intimidating matron's range. 'Not like that. My husband was twice your size and as unfaithful as any pharaoh. I'd never want another. Because you happen to be considerate, you expect everyone else to be the same.'

'Even I could never be that unrealistic.'

'Your mind knows that, but your heart doesn't. If you were ever given a noble's funeral, the embalmers wouldn't know which organs to put into which Canopic jars.'

'From what Goose says, they're not always that fussy. Many a dignitary has travelled to the West only to have Anubis weigh their intestines instead of their heart.'

'Don't change the subject.'

'Your reasoning is too fierce for my lotus thoughts.' There was a sarcastic edge in Ahmose's tone.

Ahouri was reassured that he might not have been a paragon after all. 'Don't you ever listen to anyone?'

'The animals.'

An eerie sensation prickled the scalp under Ahouri's huge wig, and it wasn't lice. She suspected that the unassuming priest was trying to frighten her. 'What sort of entity can see into the mind of an animal?'

'I've always been able to understand other creatures, except humans.'

'Not even your parents?'

'When I was a week old, a lady's pet goose found me by

the river. I was too ugly to keep so she donated me to the temple of Amon Ra.'

'Your parents deserted you because you were ugly?'

'Unless they thought that water was my natural element.'

Ahouri scrutinised his slight frame and full features. 'No, you never looked like a fish. It was because of those eyes. Their expression is unworldly, like that of a courageous gazelle's. But courage is for the lion, Ahmose. Why invite danger when all the other priests of Amon Ra pivot like locusts before a pouncing lizard to avoid it?'

'I have the brain of a river horse.'

'You may be stubborn, but you haven't the jaws to bite a crocodile in half.'

'That would annoy Sebek and the taste would no doubt be foul.'

'So you do respect the other gods?'

'All gods are what you believe them to be. When Seth is good I respect him as well.'

'Is Amon Ra bad?'

'The Aton is better.'

Ahouri raised her hands in exasperation. Ahmose was afraid she was going to shake him. 'The Aton is dead! All this is self-deception, the fancy of Akhenaton's fuddled mind. I know fuddled minds have moulded terrible tyrants and we should be thankful that his madness was benign, but he has been gone many inundations now and his daughter is fleeing from the usurper who some believed murdered her young husband.

'Do you believe that?'

'Goodness no. The silly boy spent more time in his chariot than on his throne, managing the country. He had an accident and the wound became infected. Even if he wasn't responsible, Eye would show you none of the Aton's compassion if he discovered your part in Queen Ankhesenanum's escape. By allowing yourself to be used by these priests, it's inevitable that suspicion will fall on you. Give up the Aton, Ahmose. Be a priest of Amon Ra and live!'

Ahmose looked thoughtful. 'Can you let me have a wig?'

he asked.

Realising that there was no way to intimidate common sense into the animal keeper, Ahouri gave up. 'We only have women's hairpieces with us.'

'Yes, I want a woman's wig.'

Having lived in the court of a hermaphrodite pharaoh, nothing could surprise Ahouri. 'You're welcome to it. You haven't even tried on your new robe, though. Would you prefer one of the Queen's instead?'

'No thank you, the one she gave me is long enough to be taken for a woman's when I wear it. I would like some eye make up.'

Ahouri went to the cedar casket and pulled out what he had requested. Ahmose carefully arranged the wig on one of the gilded wooden guards at the chamber's entrance and hung a mirror of polished silver on its spear. He looked objectively at his reflection.

After several moments, the priest turned back to Ahouri. 'Haven't you ever known a man wish he were a woman?'

'That wouldn't explain you.'

'No. I often dream that I am a large glittering bird that soars through the heavens bathed in the light of the Aton. It must be something to do with that goose finding me.'

'Stop going on about the Aton. I had enough of that when the Queen's father was alive.'

Ahmose yawned. 'I feel tired.'

'Sleep here tonight.'

'I daren't. I could be seen leaving in daylight. The city medjay are always gossiping to the doorkeepers and the new mayor demands to know everyone's business.'

'Well don't try flying off any hills in the darkness. I doubt that anyone as bald as you could grow so much as one feather. If you could, I would braid it in my hairpiece and wear it forever.'

'If I ever manage it, what colour should it be?'

'Gold of course, and long enough to circle my wig.' Reluctantly fascinated by the odd little priest, Ahouri stroked his face. 'Be careful. There is no Aton to watch over you during the night.' She wrapped a cloak about Ahmose's shoulders and he left.

As soon as his soft footsteps had faded, Ahouri went to the casket and pulled out two amulets and the wide golden necklace collar set with jewels. She arranged them on the gilded guard wearing his wig.

CHAPTER 4

Ahmose rode his donkey back to the menagerie.

Too tired to notice that he was being watched, and without bothering to shut the moonlight out of his hut, he toppled onto his reed bed and fell asleep.

Since being caught up in Queen Ankhesenamun's intrigue, the animal priest's dreams had become filled with even stranger images and, as well as being a bird, sinister, gaunt faces had started to appear. The apparitions didn't bother him any more than the whispers that echoed through the tomb's tunnels and chambers. Goose had explained how the change in temperature caused the night air to rush through cracks and crevices - 'Merely Anubis escorting the dead into the presence of Osiris.' The thought of the jackal deity on his journey to the land of Duat worried Ahmose less than the bad omen of the blackbird perching on his roof.

As usual he woke early, only to find something large and furry sitting on his chest.

'I warned you to be careful of the visitor, didn't I,' mewed the Bast cat.

'What?' Ahmose mumbled.

The animal priest's frail reed chair was valiantly taking the weight of a corpulent man in a wig larger than Ahouri's.

The intruder with the voluminous jowls beamed like a toad. 'I hope you will excuse me dropping in like this.' He poured something into a copper cup and his Nubian servant handed it to Ahmose. 'Drink this. It will help you wake up.'

The Bast cat smelt it. She mewed that it was all right, then jumped from Ahmose's chest so that he could sit up and drink the mixture of pomegranate juice and honey.

The priest wondered why an important dignitary was honouring him with this early morning visit.

'My name is Kahu, deputy to King Eye's new vizier. I recently received a message from Thebes.'

A tingle of horror reminded Ahmose's much shaven head that it still had hair roots.

'I understand you had a friend in Thebes? Used to be a

priest of the Aton in Akhetaton?'

Ahmose cautiously nodded. Being a senior priest of the Aton after the death of Smenkhkare, Akhenaton's successor, was not a very healthy occupation.

'Poor fellow. Met with the most dreadful accident. It's pity we can't find the Queen to let her know that her advisor is now taking that long journey to the West.'

'What happened?' the animal priest asked in an attempt to conceal his horror.

The toad smiled amiably. 'I think the beating my Nubians gave him was a little too severe.'

Ahmose's horror quickly turned to indignation. 'But he was a senior priest of Amon Ra!'

'And he is in the process of being dispatched with all ceremony due to such an elevated position.'

Ahmose knew that Kahu was inferring that a menial animal keeper could expect far less consideration. 'What do you want with me?'

'You kept in contact with this priest through letters.'

'Letters?'

'Written on small pieces of fine linen and carried by pigeons. That was really clever of you, talking those dim creatures into such important errands.'

'Birds aren't stupid.' Ahmose remembered the ducks. 'Mostly.'

'But then, you know more about other creatures than I do. You might also know something that could save you from...' Kahu didn't need to go on. His powerful servant, head brushing the beams of Ahmose's hut, looked as though he could make the priest admit anything. 'It would be reasonable to assume that your friend might have mentioned something about the movements of the Queen?'

'The Queen? Surely the King must know where his wife is?' Ahmose realised too late that very few could have known about the widowed Queen's betrothal to Eye.

'Ah!' The large man's belly juddered with a deep gurgle of glee. 'Life isn't always as simple as that.'

'So people keep telling me.'

'King Eye is rather keen to find out where his wife is.'

There was stubbornness in Ahmose's tone. 'Why would the Queen want to flee, and all the way from Thebes? It's such a long journey.'

The vizier's deputy knew that the frail chair wouldn't stand the strain of him leaning back to express his tedium, so he fixed the animal priest with a menacing glare instead. 'No harm would come to the lady if she returned to her responsibilities.'

Ahmose's gaze was so intense, Kahu felt as though he was reading his bloated entrails.

The potentate gave an agreeable smile. 'If you remember anything, it will be for the good of the Land.'

'Good of the Land?'

Kahu wondered how much Ahmose really knew about current political intrigues. 'Though Queen Ankhesenamun is very young, she can scheme as well as any high priest, even your's. When you decide to remember I will be waiting on my boat.' He rose. The chair creaked with relief and sprang as far back into shape as it could. 'I do have a few guards about the place, but they won't bother you.'

Kahu left, almost taking the narrow doorframe with him.

As he was going to be constantly followed, Ahmose wondered how he could keep watch for the signal of the Queen's agent. Something soft caressed his legs.

'I can help,' said the Bast cat.

'Your sight isn't what it used to be.'

'I can see some silly signal.'

'Lives depend on it, and I know what happens to your concentration when you find a lizard to chase.'

'You have no choice, son of Ra.'

'I keep telling you not to call me that.'

'Have you noticed the sun lately?'

'What do you mean?'

'It has a curious halo. Your father is angry'

Ahmose glanced out at the sky. He noticed nothing odd, only that infernal blackbird peering down from the roof of his hut. 'You imagined it.'

'Oh no, the air is charged with something strange - Are you sure you don't want me to eat that blackbird?'

Not daring to leave the menagerie in daylight, Ahmose remained with the animals. They sensed something was wrong and paced their pens, howling and baying so loudly it disturbed the devotions in the temple.

Goose had no need to attend the mortuary, as there was nothing apart from a noble's dog to embalm. Only two-legged nobility was lucrative enough to require his assistance.

When Ahmose started to pace up and down with the animals, this was too much for his apprentice. Goose sat on the wall of the lion's pen and looked down at him. 'What is wrong with you? Have you been bitten by something?'

The animal keeper stopped in surprise. So did the lion, as though demanding the youth's credentials.

Ahmose climbed out of the pen and pulled up the ladder. He rubbed his upper arms as though cold, then suddenly said, 'I want you to promise me something Goose.'

'Only if you and the animals stop walking grooves in the ground.'

'If you knew I wasn't going to be here tomorrow, would you stay?'

'Of course I would. Are you going away again, then?'

'I may have to. I'm not sure.'

Making sense of the priest could be a fine art at times, and it was too early in the morning for Goose to try. 'I'll always be here to feed and clean out the animals.'

'Make me a promise.'

'What is it?'

'You must disown me.'

Goose slid down from the wall to face Ahmose. 'How could I do that?'

'Because you must stay here to care for the animals.'

'How could a son renounce his father?'

'From the seventh cataract to the blue ocean, this country teams with so many priests the loss of one will hardly make the inundation fail.'

Believing that Ahmose had become totally eccentric, Goose put a gangling arm about his shoulders. 'How could I suddenly not know you?'

'You not only have big feet, you are a brash youth. I'm afraid you might try to snatch me from the jaws of the Ammet.'

Goose was bewildered. 'Tell me what has happened?'

'Just make that promise.'

'Why?'

'Promise.'

With no intention of keeping his word, Goose nodded. 'All right.'

The Bast cat sat and watched, ignoring every rasp of scales and scraping of small claws. The desert creatures seemed to know that the old eyes were not interested in them. As the sun sank behind her, the low rays reflected a sequence of flashes from the other side of the river.

When the Bast cat returned, Ahmose was scouring the animals' feeding bowls clean with a bundle of reeds and sand. 'Tonight? They're bound to see me. What will the High Priest say about me betraying the location of the Aton's temple?'

'Nothing much,' mewed the Bast cat. 'He and that fat Kahu will probably split the sacred gold between them.'

Ahmose ignored her slander and left the bowls to rummage in his chest for the scrap of papyrus on which he recorded the animal mortalities. He wiped it clean, trimmed a reed pen and wrote a note Goose would be able to understand. Though the youth could count his mortuary wages well enough, reading had never been his strong point.

Ahmose threw the dark cloak Ahouri had given him about his shoulders and rode off into the night on his donkey, across the flood plain to the desert margin.

The animal priest used every detour and narrow pass he knew to reach the cliff above the tomb. He looked out over the river, but couldn't see the lights of any ship. It must have been standing off further north while its small boat waited in the cover of the reeds for Queen Ankhesenamun. There was much Ahmose hadn't been told. However, this was not the time to remember the deputy vizier's allegation about the young woman's scheming nature. He released the donkey to find its own way home, then darted down into the tomb.

Ahouri quickly helped the Queen prepare for her journey. When they re-entered the main chamber they were surprised to see Ahmose applying elaborate eye make up in front of the polished silver mirror the gilded guard now clutched in his spear hand. The priest was already wearing the late King Tutankhamen's robe, amulets and necklace. Lastly, Ahmose put on the large wig. Its long ringlets fell to his waist. The transformation was amazing. Although he lacked breasts, the wig concealed this and the small priest had become a stunningly attractive woman.

'What are you doing?' asked the Queen.

'I'll go first. Give me time to get away, then leave.'

'You are coming with us, Ahmose,' she commanded.

'No my lady, I cannot.'

'Why this disguise?'

'Merely a precaution.'

'Are we being watched?'

'Probably not,' lied Ahmose.

'Come with us, little priest,' pleaded Ahouri. 'That way we can be sure you are safe.'

'Then tell me where you are going?'

'We cannot.'

'What foreign land could need the services of a minor animal keeper?'

'You will be my advisor,' Queen Ankhesenamun promised.

Ahmose almost told her what had happened to the last one, then realised it would have only strengthened her argument. 'Travel safely, my lady. When I have finished with this jewellery I will dedicate it to the Aton.'

'It belongs to you, not a figment of my father's irrational imagination.' The Queen took some jewel-encrusted sandals from the cedar casket and Ahouri placed them on the priest's feet.

Ahmose hardly ever put on footwear and found them uncomfortable. He couldn't afford another time wasting argument and turned to the entrance.

'Your cloak!' Ahouri wrapped the garment about his shoulders then reluctantly watched him slip into the twisting passage.

As soon as he was clear of the tomb's entrance Ahmose let the cloak fly off. Glittering in the silver moonlight, he dashed towards the river.

Someone was pursuing him. He daren't stop to pull off

the crippling sandals. If he were caught too soon the Queen and Ahouri wouldn't have time to reach their boat.

Despite his lungs being raw through gulping the freezing night air and the straps of the pharaoh's sandals cutting his feet, Ahmose didn't stop until he reached the river. He dived through the reeds of a narrow tributary in hope of finding one of the fishermen's' small boats.

As he stepped ono a mat of rotten papyrus stems a counterweighted cord ensnared his ankles and brought him down. Without bothering to examine their catch, two huge Nubians half carried, half marched the priest to a boat moored on the river. Under its decorated canopy, sitting like massive toad waiting for its supper, was Kahu. Ahmose was unceremoniously dumped before him.

'Well madam, what fools you must think we are.'

The priest had the urge to let him know just how much but couldn't disabuse the monster of his mistake too soon. He kept his head well down so the wig obscured his face and chest.

'Did you really believe you could escape like a traitor in the night?' Kahu had expected a little more response from his precious catch. She had never been short of protests before.

As the potentate hadn't wanted to attract attention to his regal kidnapping, there were few lamps. He leaned forward from his cushions to take a closer look. At first he didn't believe his eyes, then told an attendant to bring a light closer. In a spasm of rage he snatched off Ahmose's wig. The priest grabbed it back and replaced it on his bald head with a girlish smile.

Kahu's jowls convulsed in fury as he squealed like a pig robbed of its swill. 'Idiots!'

The bungling agents stepped back in horror at their mistake.

Had Ahmose not been enjoying his deception so much, he could have taken the opportunity to jump over the side of the boat. Unfortunately he left it too late and Kahu's hypnotising gaze settled on him.

The huge man's voice was cold and toneless. 'Where is

the Queen?'

'I don't know.'

'If you help us catch her you might be spared a thrashing.'

Ahmose remained silent.

'You do realise that you have been tricked into helping an enemy of this country?' It was obvious the priest didn't believe him. 'Your precious Queen Ankhesenamun is guilty of the ultimate treason. She dispatched a messenger to the ruler of Hatte, our greatest enemy, to demand he send one of his sons to marry her. He would have become pharaoh of the Upper and Lower Kingdoms.'

Ahmose's eyes widened in horror. Despite every sentimental thought he had about the delicate Queen, he believed the fat toad.

'Fortunately, while she was still trying to convince this enemy of Egypt, I discovered the plot. Hatte eventually did send a princeling. He never reached Thebes.' Kahu lounged back, confident this throne wouldn't collapse under his weight. 'Well priest, now will you tell me where Queen Ankhesenamun is?'

Ahmose's thoughts were arguing amongst themselves. He had been warned. Not only was her priest advisor dead, so was the prince she intended to put on the throne. She deserved to be betrayed. Having used so many, why should she escape? Even Ahouri must have known. However, what Ahmose lacked in common sense, he made up for in stubbornness.

CHAPTER 7

The High Priest of Amon Ra was an enigmatic creature. Few believed he was Egyptian. His expression was so like a cat's, he should have been a devotee of Bast. His skin was creamish beige and he had the eyes of an Eastern magician's, slightly crossed as though he were looking beyond the person confronting him and at some ghostly image over their shoulder. Instead of being roundly moulded like most Egyptians', his cheekbones could have been hewn from jade.

The High Priest never cared for the finery of his office. When he wasn't obliged to don the ceremonial leopard skin and stiff white double kilt, he preferred to wear an austere brown robe of coarse linen. The only other concession to his rank being a pectoral with the horns of Amon surmounting the disc of Ra and surrounded by the Cosmic serpent. It was gold inlaid with a strange green stone unknown to Egyptian jewellers and counterbalanced by a scarab beetle of electrum.

Like everyone else, Goose was in awe of the High Priest and expected to encounter his icy wrath for daring to get direct access to his presence by following the Bast cat. No one knew if the High Priest had a temper. If he did, his rage would have been capable of sandblasting the soul.

As the Bast cat made her serpentine greeting against the High Priest's legs, he took Ahmose's note from Goose and silently read it. Anxiety crept over his stony features as though someone had threatened to push him into the waters of Nun without so much as a papyrus prayer to grasp. The bizarre truth dawned on the assistant animal keeper. Someone not intimidated by the crocodile of Sebek was unlikely to be in awe of the High Priest of Amon Ra. It was obvious that the simple-natured Ahmose and the all-powerful High Priest were close friends. Goose shuddered at the condescending way he had always treated the animal keeper.

* * *

Totally shorn of body hair and ritually cleansed, the six mystics of the inner sanctum wended their way into the temple of the Aton where Ahmose had given Queen Ankhesenamun sanctuary. Their wan skins never saw sunlight, their thoughts were permanently purged by meditation, and loins forever celibate. Most of the other, more worldly, priests didn't know of their existence. They would have been unable to comprehend such commitment.

Unlike Ahmose, these mystics had never dedicated their lives to the Aton, or to the great pantheon of Horus and Ra. Their conviction stemmed from the primordial ocean of Nun. They were the guardians of the linchpin that held together many versions of the same truth; the essence of creation and the all-in-oneness of the Universe. Such semantics would have been beyond the animal keeper, yet it was not to enlighten him that they had gathered. It was to fulfil a strange prophecy. Although he would be unable to save his friend's life, the High Priest was determined to preserve Ahmose's soul in a permanent state of grace.

The true nature of his devout and unassuming confidant had always been an enigma to the High Priest. So the mystics of the inner sanctum had meditated on the mystery of eternal life. On the same night, at the sacred hour, they all experienced the same vision. The land rose from the waters of Nun and the great golden Phoenix perched on the Benben column. The song of the deity heralded the coming of all things that are, and all things to be. Then light and life filled the newly formed land. The Benben column was transformed. With the downbeat of the Phoenix's wings, an image appeared. It was not Horus, Ra, Isis, Osiris or Neith. It was a small round-featured creature with large honest eyes.

Learning of this, the High Priest was convinced that the prophecy meant Ra intended to bless Ahmose with immortal deification in Duat. It meant that the primeval deities, who created all things after creating themselves, would accept the animal priest into their pantheon. After all, wasn't the Aton the monothiestic manifestation of all entities, as well as Ra? A mere name could hardly matter to the Supreme Being ... could it?

Silently the priests of the inner sanctum lit the lamps in the Aton's last temple. In the gleam of Aton gold, they started their magical ritual.

CHAPTER 8

Like phantoms rising over the reeds, lights from a party of senior priests at their most inscrutable appeared on the bank.

Ahmose saw his chance and dashed to the side of the boat. Kahu's attendant caught him; the wig kept on travelling and landed in the dark water. Huge jaws snapped and it disappeared.

The vizier's deputy knew this was a timely warning that, however menial, the animal priest belonged to the temple of Amon Ra. The last thing the usurping Pharaoh Eye needed was a conflict with the most influential religious centre in Lower Egypt. The Queen's advisor may have been a traitor, yet there was no law that said a man could be executed for dressing up as a woman.

The High Priest of Amon Ra and an anxious youth clutching a crumpled note waited on the river jetty as a small figure glittering with a pharaoh's jewels was hustled towards them. As soon as he realised who was concealed beneath the eye shadow, Goose snatched Ahmose away from the Nubian guards.

Without a word the High Priest, unescorted, boarded Kahu's boat. There was a murmur of alarm amongst the waiting priests, though none of them attempted to follow. Trying to protect their superior would have been like standing below a tree to catch the panther about to drop out of its branches.

Kahu had never known the true meaning of sinister until he looked into the depths of the High Priest's feline eyes. In them he saw damnation waiting to swallow his corpulent incarnation. Fortunately he was in the realm of the living where he still held some sway.

'There is a battalion of the King's men within two days journey from here. They have instructions to search out and eradicate all mention of the Aton, including those who used to pursue its heretical cult.'

This meant the icy paragon before him, and all the senior priests and scribes within the precinct of Amon Ra's temple, not to mention the local population.

The High Priest still said nothing.

Kahu's expression was at its most toad like. 'King Eye's reign may not last, but it will be long enough for his soldiers to purge your temple before someone else overthrows him.'

Though Kahu was too well insulated to have cold shudders, the silent rage mirrored in the High Priest's expression made his blood run cold.

The vizier's deputy dare not back down. Credibility was everything; there was always some snake waiting to make a meal of this toad and claim his expensive burrow.

Kahu leant forward and glowered at the holy obelisk. 'Not only will your temple be purged, all those in the Delta who crafted the monuments and artefacts of the Aton, and their families, will be annihilated.'

The High Priest's stony glare radiated an unspoken curse.

Kahu knew he had to offer a way out if he wasn't to meet the jaws of the Ammet in the afterlife. 'Surrender the animal priest and nothing will happen. The King's soldiers will be sent to deface monuments somewhere else ... Not unless you are prepared to tell me where Queen Ankhesenamun is of course?'

The High Priest gave a thin-lipped smile and pointed towards the sea.

The toad's leer dropped into his jowls. 'Escaped?'

The High Priest had known it would end this way since he saw the note Goose brought him. What could he do? He had no right to allow the inhabitants of a city to be massacred.

The ritual of the mystics of the inner temple was now complete. The High Priest turned his back on the amoral mountain of flesh and went ashore, convinced that Ra would install Ahmose as an immortal in Duat.

Goose and the others watched hopefully. Only Ahmose understood. He could read his friend's thoughts as well as the animals in the menagerie.

Ahmose took Goose's arm. 'Can you remember everything I told you?'

The youth was baffled. 'About what?'

'The animals, of course. Remember that the crocodile only needs feeding every five days, the cats must have flesh in the morning or they will try to attack the cackler and waterfowl. Men, the butcher in the city, will always supply ox or pig's offal if you can't get it from the outer temple-' Before he could finish, Kahu's guards had seized Ahmose.

Goose launched a murderous attack on the Nubians. The High Priest caught the youth and held him back with the strength of three stone masons. Ahmose, still shouting instructions to his struggling apprentice, was taken aboard Kahu's boat.

Goose turned his rage on the High Priest. 'How could you murder your friend? What sort of monster are you?'

The other priests were puzzled by the youth's apparent brainstorm and assumed he had caught some disease from the animals. Although expecting him to foam at the mouth any moment, they decided that their superior was doing quite well without their assistance.

'Be still, priestling.' The High Priest's voice was cavernous. 'There is no other choice. Would you see everyone you know slain and Innu destroyed?'

Goose realised that he was cursing the only other person who felt the same way as he did. 'How could you do such a thing, though? Why Ahmose?'

'Ahmose's soul has been committed to the care of Ra.'

The hollow tone frightened Goose. This was the icy voice that could persuade thousands to put their trust in irrational miracles. 'I don't understand?'

'Most misunderstandings occur because of belief. Belief is the element that allows Nut to hold up the heavens, Ra to overcome Apep and rise each morning. It is the Inundation, the call of the Great Cackler and the life force of Isis.'

Goose was now sidetracked. 'You mean ... the Universe is really a misunderstanding?'

'Stupid boy. The belief belongs to the second keeper of the sacred animals. You are the one who misunderstands.'

It was too much to take in all at once. 'Ahmose ... immortality?'

'He has been chosen by the gods. His soul will become immortal and a deity greater than any pharaoh's.'

'Oh no,' Goose murmured. 'I don't think he'll like that.'

The High Priest frowned. 'What do you mean?'

'What sort of immortality will the gods confer on him?'

To his superior, immortality wasn't a thing of compartments. Everyone aspired to everlasting life and it wasn't for lowly mortals to question the form it came in. And here stood a scruffy adolescent challenging the wisdom of his mystic authority.

'Ahmose a deity?' Spoken by a semi-literate apprentice priest, it now sounded odd.

The High Priest knew he would remain awake all night wondering what monstrous mishap he might have set in motion.

CHAPTER 9

Having once again overcome the underworld serpent, Apep, the rising solar barque of Ra sent its rays soaring into the dawn sky like fountains of hope and lit up Goose's boat. The new day didn't reassure him. All night, by torchlight, he had been searching for Ahmose in the dark waters of the river and its tributaries. Although there was no chance of finding him alive, he wanted his body to be decently embalmed. As the sun rose higher, Goose had to accept that crabs were probably eating the animal priest's remains at the bottom of some stream.

He steered his boat into the reeds and watched the senior priests wending their way to the bank. They lifted their eyes to the rising sun and prayed to Amon Ra. The god may not have been listening but, in the menagerie, the Bast cat sensed an odd charge in the still air. Her thin fur rose and she growled as she warily paced the perimeter wall.

The priests went to Kahu's boat, expecting to find Ahmose's body waiting for collection. Unlike Goose, they believed that death was innately tidy.

Kahu's servant glowered back at them. 'Where are our master's guards?'

The priests looked at each other to make sure none of them were responsible for the disappearance of those two mountains of muscle. Their scribe raised his pen as though about to record a confession, then tucked the papyrus back into his belt as it became evident his brethren didn't know the answer.

A cry cut through the still air.

Having helped disembowel all manner of corpses, Goose shouldn't have been so horrified at his discovery. Yet, when the first fragment of human head floated out of the reeds and nudged his boat, the part of the expression it wore made him almost topple into the water. By the time the priests and Kahu's servant had reached him, he had netted enough remains to make up one and a half muscular guards.

The High Priest appeared to ensure that none of the

parts belonged to Ahmose. 'What did it? Crocodile?'

'No,' Goose called back. 'Probably a river horse.'

'What about your master?'

'No river horse would have touched Ahmose.' Goose pulled in the net. 'Shall I send these back to the vizier's deputy so he can try stuffing them himself?'

Regardless of the razor jawed wildlife, Kahu's servant plunged into the water and helped haul the net ashore. The others watched in dull amazement as the man cursed its contents with alien profanities.

'What's he muttering about?' a priest asked.

The scribe understood the language too well to give an exact translation. 'Something about serving them right. He's an animal worshipper. Saw Ahmose talking to his cat and believes he was a magician.'

'I can see part of a boat!' Goose called. He stood up and pulled off his kilt. 'I'm going in to look for him.'

The High Priest's almond eyes grew round with some secret terror. 'No! Wait!'

The other priests murmured in surprise at their superior's sudden command. For someone with the presence of a granite pillar, his behaviour had been a little erratic that morning. They had put it down to giddiness brought on by his austere diet. How could a man who never touched beer or honey cakes hope to keep his sanity forever?

Then they saw it.

The centre of the river was bubbling like frantically fermenting liquor. Deep beneath the boiling surface there was a large sphere of fiery light. It rose, and a beautiful, eerie sound filled the flood plain, making the walls of the temple ring with the clarity of a cosmic bell. Lightning struck the large sphere. There was a silent explosion and white light dazzled the onlookers.

When their eyes had recovered they could see a shape in the sky.

A large golden bird briefly merged with the rising solar disc like a child paying homage to its parent.

The sight transfixed goose.

'Come ashore quickly, boy!' the High Priest called.

'How beautiful! What is it?' The youth then came to his senses, retrieved his kilt and scrambled ashore.

The colour drained from the High Priest's face as his worst fears were realised. None of the other priests understood - How could they? Most of them were too married to the material to visualise the gods they had dedicated their lives to. None of them would be dragged down into the Great Abyss in their meditations. Their minds were so earthbound, they would soon be wondering if they really had seen the Aton bird rise from the river after all and put it down to excitement or badly digested fig.

The High Priest was not excited, nor had he eaten for a day and night. He could feel himself going down beneath those primordial waters suffocating his soul for daring to believe it was possible for a mere mortal to bargain with the gods. The animal priest had been a devotee of the Aton, whose cult briefly usurped the glory of Amon Ra. The High Priest hadn't taken into consideration that Ahmose had surrendered his life to save the daughter of the Aton's prophet. The only reason Ra wanted to deify the animal keeper was as a punishment. Instead of casting the protecting wings of Nephthys about Ahmose, Ra had sent the Phoenix to swallow his spirit. The priest was now doomed to immortality on Earth instead of everlasting rest in Duat.

Miracle or not, the other priests soon decided that life should go on as usual. They may have waited a lifetime for a sign from the gods, but that didn't mean they were obliged to believe it when it came.

'Ahmose always fed the animals about this time,' one of them reminded Goose. 'He wouldn't want you to keep them waiting.'

Knowing he would never find Ahmose's body, the youth returned the reed boat to the fisherman he had borrowed it from and rode off on Ahmose's donkey to collect food for the menagerie.

Automatically he chopped up the meals before taking the buckets down to the pens. As they had been able to sense Ahmose's thoughts, he expected the animals to be agitated.

Instead they were mysteriously content and ate well.

Then Goose remembered the Bast cat. She was always fed first. The cat had long since stopped living in her pen and taken up residence in Ahmose's hut. As she had few teeth left, Goose chopped her food finely, intending to leave it on the hut's cool floor where the flies would take longer to find it.

When he pulled the coarse curtain aside he thought the sun had risen again in the animal priest's room. The keeper's meagre possessions were bathed in a rich golden glow.

The Bast cat was in deep conversation with a visitor.

Goose's knees gave way in fright and he sank to the floor, nearly dropping the food.

Perched on Ahmose's rickety table was a large bird. Its wings and body were gold, and the tail a cascade of white streamers. On its head was a dazzling crest that rose like the flames of a torch and about its neck a deep collar of scalloped feathers.

'Stupid boy seems about to faint,' the Bast cat mewed.

The bird gave a low, soft whistle. There was something familiar in its tone and Goose tried to come to his senses.

'Mind my food, you oaf,' scolded the Bast cat.

Unable to make his legs obey him, Goose pushed the bowl aside and cautiously approached the magical bird on his hands and knees. Those eyes. Only one person had that gentle, haunted look about him.

The youth put out his hand to touch its plumage. It was like reaching from the shadows to feel the rays of the sun. Goose was saturated in soothing warmth. Then he keeled over into a deep, dreamless sleep.

When Goose woke, the bird had gone and the Bast cat, having finished its meal, was curled up on Ahmose's bed.

CHAPTER 10

A southerly breeze filled the sail of the white ship.

Suddenly the circling gulls deserted the sky and a school of dolphins rose from the depths to ride before its bows in arches of black, white and yellow.

Ahouri smelt an odd fragrance as she went up to the stern's upper deck. The sailors noticed a change in the sea zephyrs and scoured the darkening horizon for a storm.

The lookout on the masthead spotted a bright star in the slate grey sky. A fireball was heading straight towards them!

The captain tried to calm his crew, though he had no idea how they could avoid the collision. Thunderbolts from the gods never missed their targets, though he had no idea what crime he had committed to deserve it.

The blazing bolt of fire didn't hit the ship. It spun like a fiery tornado, sending down shafts of light that patterned the brown sail in gold. The lookout frantically abseiled to safety as a huge entity blazed on the top of the mast, making the ship shudder.

The ghostly song of a fabulous bird with gleaming plumage filled the air. The glorious phantom spread a wing and plucked out a long golden feather. Catching the breeze, the deity floated down to Ahouri like a dazzling umbrella, and dropped the plume into her hands. Then with one downbeat of its wings it soared into the sky and disappeared from sight. The clouds in the leaden sky disappeared and the gulls returned.

As the deity hadn't been the herald of some sea monster or typhoon, the crew decided not to mutiny.

For a long while Ahouri stood murmuring to herself, 'Those eyes, those beautiful eyes...'

* * *

Scribes, advisors and the temple baker believed that the High Priest's prolonged fast had turned his mind. Though overcome by guilt, it was not penance, but necessity. He was purging his body in preparation for mummification -

there were always problems when drawing cadavers with full digestive tracts. His corpse had to remain intact for eternity or, failing that, longer than any pharaoh's.

Goose continued to blame the High Priest for allowing Ahmose's death until, after watching him endure so many complicated rituals, the man's stoic resolution captured his reluctant admiration. Goose didn't understand what was going on, though was practical enough to realise that by now Ahmose was soaring through the skies far beyond the land of Punt.

Goose and the other priests were dismissed before the six emaciated mystics arrived like phantoms from the bowels of some Earthly underworld. Knowing these sinister, shrivelled men were going to send the High Priest on the first stage of his journey, Goose didn't want to witness their magic. The animals depended on him to stay Earthbound.

Two days later, as assistant embalmer, Goose once again met the High Priest.

After more interminable rituals, the dedicating of his corpse took one hundred days instead of seventy. Then it was placed in a plain coffin lined with papyrus text. The mummy was sealed in a stone sarcophagus that was lowered to the bottom of a deep shaft where it would remain, standing upright, for eternity.

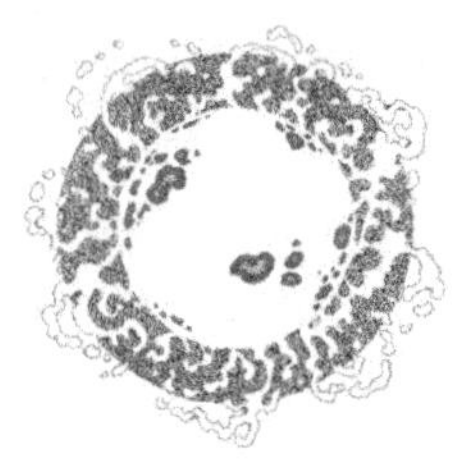

THE ATON BIRD

CHAPTER 11

Its tail of gleaming feathers ribboning in the thin air, and crest glittering like faceted jewels, the fabulous bird spiralled down to the banks of billowing clouds.

On wide golden wings, the entity had seen the crystal stars above the atmosphere and flown the world to dip its beak in stormy oceans. It had spun in tornadoes, floated on dry desert breezes, fanned life into creatures desiccated by drought, plucked rubies from the crowns of tyrants and dropped them into the hands of the poor.

The dazzling deity filled the centuries, soaring in the sun's rays like a mesmerised eagle then hanging dormant in the stratosphere like a sleeping swallow. Now legend and illusion, the Aton bird lived out the marvel it had once dreamt of as a mortal. Over the centuries it learnt secrets from every corner of the pristine Earth and watched quakes rend its crust and oceans erode its coral reefs.

Now the bird felt a pang of weariness and was aware of a shadow trying to drive a stake through its magical heart. The familiar gaze of cat like eyes appeared in its mind's eye and a jackal-headed staff pointed downwards.

Before the deity could descend, fiery tendrils tried to drag it back into the sky. Confused, the bird started to tumble, claw over wing, faster and faster as two determined entities battled to pull its mystical wishbone.

Magical though the bird might have been, its intellect was no greater than the animal keeper's it had incarnated from. It didn't know what to do and no longer knew what it wanted. Before then it had just been. Questions like, why?

What for? had never troubled the Aton bird as it had glided through cavernous blue grottoes, swooped down on coronation crowds or perched on ziggurats. The entity had believed that it owned its own immortality. It came as an unpleasant surprise to discover that it did not.

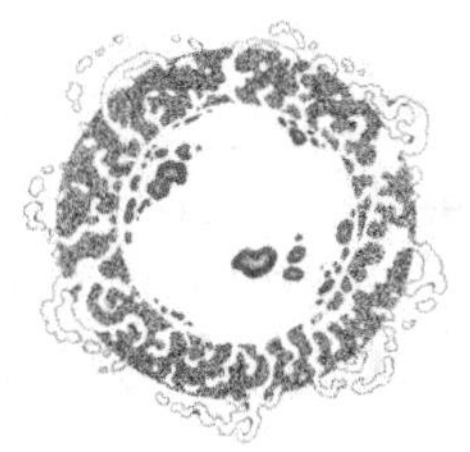

THE ALCHEMIST

CHAPTER 12

Helen Maat weighed some mercury. 'Lower the mirror a little, Dinan, then adjust the lenses to the sun's zenith.'

The alchemist was a middle-aged woman with the acuity of a Greek and temper of an annoyed hippo. Her scientific bent of mind didn't entertain the domestic, and her wealth had never been wasted on banquets for the idle rich. Such things could wait until she had comprehended the Universe, or at least managed to smelt dross metal into gold.

Dinan wasn't so sure about his origins. He had been born into slavery and intended as a guard for the women's quarters in Ptolemy's palace. He wouldn't have survived the operation essential for that position if the court astrologer had not known Helen. She was the only one with the medical skill to save him, and rich enough to disregard the wrath of a Ptolemy. The head eunuch was bribed to declare Dinan dead so he could be spirited away to the remote and maniacal household of the alchemist. When a boy, Dinan had served the court astrologer well and learnt much more than was expected of an adolescent slave. For all his intellect, he still wondered what he had been doing in the eccentric company of Helen Maat for so many years.

With an expert hand, Dinan aligned the mirror and lenses as instructed. When that great fiery orb, beloved and deified by Egypt, reached its zenith, the searing rays would be directed onto the crucible half buried in the sand.

Helen would have chosen the alchemical name of Isis or Nephthys if her rational mind could have coped with the conceit of being called after an all-creating, empathic goddess. Maat, the essence of balance and justice, had a more convincing ring. When experimenting, the Greek wore that deity's feather in her headband even though the heat usually frizzled it.

Then one day Dinan had discovered an extraordinary feather for himself. The exotic plume glittered as the breeze tumbled it over the sand into his grasp. It was gold. Helen had insisted he find the whole bird in moult before she would be impressed. Closer examination had shown it to be from no ordinary plumage and the alchemist wasn't too sure she wanted to encounter the creature that had shed it after all. To annoy her, Dinan wore the long feather in his hair like a pennant.

Day after day they had set up their experiment with the sun's rays. Other alchemists would have used sand and dung baths to distil their ingredients. Helen Maat didn't have that patience. She had intuitively made the connection between heat and cosmic creation. It was obvious that the answer to all alchemic riddles lay in the power of the sun. Common sense had also told her that she would never be able to create enough energy to generate it, but that had never stopped her before. Peasants and gentry alike thought her mad. They believed Helen Maat's fiery expression and affinity with large cats meant that she had the protection of Sekhmet, a pretty fierce deity, and they always looked on from a safe distance. Curiosity overcoming personal safety, they were watching at that moment.

The solar barque of Ra neared its zenith. The sun's rays were concentrated through two lenses to brilliant points of light that seared the contents of the crucible.

Then Dinan glanced up. He rashly removed his smoked glass eye shield and gave a sudden shout, making Helen jump. 'Look!'

'What is it?'

'A bird! A large bird!'

The alchemist was more interested in her experiment.

'Probably a vulture. Watch the crucible.'

For several minutes Dinan and Helen scrutinised the dross metal being bombarded by the sun's heat. After the surface impurities had been vaporised away in fiery blisters, scrolls of white heat patterned the mixture of smelting metals.

Without warning a fierce glow radiated from the small crucible. At last! The secrets long hidden in the Universe's mystic locker were about to be revealed.

The glow increased and became a teardrop of sun blazing with the intensity of a hundred furnaces.

On the verge of jubilant terror at what they had achieved, the alchemists quickly leapt back.

Then something above them flapped huge golden wings and cast a shadow over the alchemist's experiment. It hovered a short distance above, gazing down as though unable to believe its luck.

'What in Typhon's name is that!?' raged Helen.

'The rest of my feather!' Dinan sounded a little too enthusiastic.

'Well make it go away!'

'How?'

'Tell it how many cats there are in this place!'

'That bird would eat them.'

'Its shadow will ruin the experiment!'

But the heat of the crucible remained constant and reached some magical temperature.

Before Helen could aim a stone at the golden bird, it fell from the sky like molten fire.

For a millisecond everything was saturated by a wave of mysterious plasma that would have transmuted the elements into gold had the right ones been available.

Believing that Ra had once again hurled his eye at ungrateful humanity, the watching villagers dived for cover.

After their traumatised retinas had recovered, the two targets of his wrath were amazed to discover that they hadn't been burnt to a crisp.

Helen rolled over on the sand to glower up at the sky and let loose a stream of curses that would have made a crocodile blush. Dinan was already sitting up, shivering with an odd sensation she would also experience as soon as her blood pressure went down.

'Everything's smashed!' Helen raged. 'Those lenses will take years to regrind! I hope that wretched bird's dead!'

Dinan stopped shivering. 'Well, it's certainly not here any more.'

'Damn its beak! We've spent years working for this!'

Dinan tried to sound sensible. 'It seems to be turning into something else.'

Helen sat bolt upright. 'What?'

Standing amongst the remains of the crucible and shattered equipment was a shimmering form. It certainly wasn't that of a bird. It looked uncannily like a golden statue.

Helen jubilantly leapt up. 'We've done it!' Then keeled over as she was struck by a strange, crushing sensation. She hammered her fists in the sand. 'We've made gold!'

Dinan's tone was somewhat flat. 'Then why is it shaped like a man?'

The alchemist lurched towards the statue. 'Who knows? That thing is pure gold.'

Dinan stopped her before she could touch it.

'What's the matter?'

'Something's wrong.'

'How do you know? Have you ever seen a statue of solid gold that size before?'

'Yes, in pharaoh's palace. And there is something wrong with this one.'

'Why, Dinan?'

'The Ptolemies only use gold to sculpt perfection - the immortal, the beautiful ... Just look at this.'

'Well, it's not ugly. Quite cuddlesome in a metallic sort of way.'

'What else would you want to cuddle.'

'Don't be insolent, bird lover.' As Helen calmed down she saw what he meant. 'The face is rather rounded now you mention it.'

'Too Egyptian. No Greek would cast an effigy like that.'

'What a strange little man.'

The statue's eyes suddenly opened.

Dinan fainted and Helen found herself looking into the most haunted expression she was ever likely to see on a human face.

After taking in its surroundings, the statue tried to move. It toppled forward instead, into the alchemist's arms. Half expecting to be flattened, Helen was amazed to find that this sculpture weighed no more than a small mortal man whose breath had the perfume of cedar, and skin the overripe peach pliability of middle age.

Her countenance, usually fierce enough to curdle milk, softened a little in curiosity. The intruder's long golden lashes set a beautiful frame around the only part of him that was a natural colour. Even then, those penetrating, deep brown eyes had a minute furnace blazing in their depths.

Helen gave a smile that could have frozen water. 'Do you know what you've done to my experiment, little bundle of sunbeams?'

'I'm, I'm sorry,' the golden man murmured apprehensively.

'You've got to be bad news from Ra.'

'I come from the Aton.'

'The what?' Helen's grip on his arm increased.

'All right. They are the same.'

'You stupid Egyptians couldn't tell a good harvest from the plague.'

'Everything has its meaning, and many things mean the same.'

'Ugh! A philosophising statue.' Helen released him so suddenly he fell down next to Dinan. The large man had come round some moments before but remained on the ground as a precaution.

'Don't let her bully you,' Dinan whispered. 'She gets like this.' The intruder looked at the friendly black man beside him and retreated a little. Dinan smiled reassuringly. 'It's all right. My "aggression" was removed years ago. What's the matter?'

'I was killed by two men like you.'

Not even Dinan could think of an answer to that, but had to keep the conversation going. 'You make a habit of this sort of thing, then?'

'The Aton has given me immortality.'

In most people this would have provoked amazement, in Dinan it brought on an anecdote. 'I've often wondered myself, whether the elixir of life hasn't been overrated. All the mumbling and magic - so many people wasting lifetimes searching for it, still ending up dead. Now, this character who used to own me a long while ago - Sort of prince-'

'Sort of prince?'

'Pharaoh had their mother assassinated just in case she had conceived him in adultery, so no one could be sure after that. Anyway, when this prince died they tried to give him the right send off. Full burial rites, libations, coffin portrait, laying in, drying out - you know the sort of thing - all for immortality. So, when the day came to put his body in the coffin, guess what happened?'

'What?'

'He was so brittle he fell apart. They overdid the natron.' Dinan shrugged. 'All that for an afterlife. I sometimes wonder which part of him became immortal.'

The visitor gave a self-effacing smile. 'I don't know why the Aton thought I was worthy of immortality.'

'What did you do to upset it?'

'You know of the Aton?'

'Not much. Most traces of the heretic pharaoh have been obliterated. Something to do with goodness and light wasn't it? And there isn't much of that in the court of a Ptolemy.'

'Ptolemy?'

'Greeks.'

Ahmose was still puzzled but let the subject drop. 'My name's Ahmose.'

'I'm called Dinan.'

Ahmose realised that Dinan's misfortune was to have a mild nature in the body of a giant. 'I shouldn't have thought evil of you.'

'I was thinking some pretty strange things about you for

a moment.' Dinan now accepted that he was facing the impossible. 'What are you?'

Ahmose was just as confused. 'I'm no longer sure.'

Helen had been listening to the new companions commiserating, and could stand it no longer. 'You must know who you are?'

The animal priest immediately recognised a predator. This was one fierce creature that couldn't be bought with soothing words and a freshly caught fish. As for reading her thoughts ... 'I am - was - the second keeper of the sacred animals of the temple of Amon Ra in Innu.'

'You mean, you weren't even a Pharaoh?'

Ahmose had been so occupied with his predicament, he hadn't given any thought to his appearance. 'Why no. I was only a minor priest. Then he remembered that he was wearing a king's robe and Queen's jewellery. 'Oh, the necklace and amulets. I don't know why the Nubians didn't take them. They must have suited me too well.'

Helen held up a shard of her polished metal mirror before him. 'Look at yourself, second keeper of the sacred animals of the temple of Amon Ra!'

Ahmose unsuspectingly marvelled at the golden image mimicking his movements. Then he realised who it was.

He frantically tried to rub the gold from his skin. When he had just dropped from the sky onto the alchemist's furnace he had been transmuted – not only from a bird. It may have been fortune that he had materialised before two people who weren't likely to dedicate him as a living trinket to some deity or other.

Dinan helped the priest rise. 'We'd better hide you, Ahmose. Too many curious eyes have seen too much already.' He put his cloak about the animal priest's shoulders.

'No, it could be dangerous for you. I must go to the nearest temple of Amon Ra.'

Helen laughed. 'To that lot? They'd melt you down and sell you to the Greeks as finger rings.'

'Are they still that unscrupulous?'

'I always thought the way they carried on was

traditional.'

Ahmose was afraid the idea might have appealed to the alchemist. She didn't look Egyptian, and was probably Greek as well. 'Will you melt me down?'

Helen laughed. 'Only the bits I can't cuddle.' She strode off.

Having already fallen into her arms once, Ahmose wasn't that reassured.

CHAPTER 13

Helen's house sat on the banks of the Nile like an elegant outcrop. During the inundation, her estate became an island that could only be reached by boat, which suited her. While the fields were under water, the farmers often shared their time between building tombs for the nobility, watching the plumes of smoke coming from the alchemist's courtyard and wondering what was in the sacks being ferried to and fro.

Helen and Dinan had so many scars from their dangerous attempts to reshape the laws of physics, many believed that they were attempting to find the meaning of life by trying to lose theirs. Despite her insistence that the experiments were more to do with the inner soul, the locals continued to hang around for free samples just in case she did eventually manage to transmute dross metal into gold.

To be sure that Ahmose's appearance wasn't a trick of glue and gilt, Helen told Dinan to scrub the priest with a bristle brush until they could see the colour of his blood. Then she tried to concoct a cure for that strange sensation that had come over her since the explosion. Dinan disobeyed her of course, and never even managed to wash away the fragrance of cedar.

As Helen hadn't broken out into a rash, developed a temperature or been beset by severe cramps, her malaise couldn't have been serious but the unworldly feeling had unsettled her logical gyroscope. The alchemist reluctantly admitted to herself that some things were beyond even her comprehension. To make matters worse, she gashed her hand as she was throwing ingredients into a chipped basin. After cursing a little, she forgot about the wound. A short time later it had completely disappeared.

Without warning or apology, Helen Maat deftly removed the bandage covering a recent deep wound on Dinan's leg. That had healed without leaving so much as a scar.

The meal Ahmose had been looking forward to after five centuries as a deity was suddenly forgotten. He wrapped himself in the robe Dinan had given him and, trying not to glow too much, crouched disconsolately in a corner by a statue of Hermanubis. A servant girl, fascinated by the magical priest, brought him a cushion and goblet of wine. By the time Dinan and Helen had decided to plot the conjunction of Sirius with the planets in an attempt to solve the mystery, Ahmose was fast asleep. Silently a panther called Ink, padded over to the newcomer and curled up beside him.

After hours studying charts, scrolls and calculations, Helen was questioning her commitment to logic. 'There is no explanation.'

Dinan had no such problem with the impossible. 'Ahmose must be the Phoenix or Bennu bird.'

'Neither of them are supposed to turn into a man after immolation.'

'Your experiment must have interfered with its transformation.'

That was the last straw. 'He!' She stabbed a finger at Ahmose, 'interfered with my experiment! I only hope after I've melted him down there's enough gold to pay for my equipment!'

'Don't let him hear you. I'm sure he is what he says.'

'A menial priest from Innu? A keeper of the sacred animals?' Helen suddenly realised that a panther fierce enough to scare off river bandits had snuggled up beside the priest. She lowered her voice. 'Then how did someone as insignificant as Ahmose manage to get changed into a fabulous bird?'

'The Aton must have cast a spell on him.'

In a world that believed the world was driven by magic, Dinan had to end up with the only person who would have asked Isis how she managed to sew the pieces of her husband, Osiris, back together without gangrene setting in.

'Don't talk rubbish. This has a rational explanation. It must be something to do with the sun.'

'The Aton,' insisted Dinan. 'He mentioned the Aton.'

'The Aton?'

'The Aton, Aton Ra, Ra, Ra Harakhte, Ra Atum, Khepri, Amon Ra. In Heliopolis there stands an obelisk, a frozen ray of the sun from which the sacred bird heralded creation.'

'So much for being educated by an astrologer,' muttered Helen.

'Start with the legend, and we might arrive at the truth.'

'Do you really believe in all that rubbish? If he's as old as the legend, then that is supernatural.'

'You don't question the possibility of matter being transformed by the sun.'

'Heat transforms everything.'

'Then why not accept that the Egyptians knew this centuries before the Greeks arrived?'

'Let's wake him up and ask.' Before Dinan could protest, Helen shooed away the panther and shook Ahmose.

'Don't bully him.'

Ahmose was going to take some time to get used to Helen Maat's penetrating gaze and preferred the floor for company, but she pulled him up and pushed him into a chair.

'How old are you?' the alchemist demanded.

Ahmose tried to remember how many inundations he had seen. 'I can't be much more than fifty years.'

'I didn't mean that, little sunbeam. I meant, how old are you - collectively?'

Ahmose was puzzled.

Dinan interceded. 'What Pharaoh was on the throne before you changed into a bird?'

'Oh. The son and daughter of the Aton.'

'He means the children of the heretic King, Akhenaton.'

Helen turned her penetrating gaze on her long-suffering companion. 'That was dynasties ago?'

'It would account for him being a devotee of the Aton.'

'The little liar!' she snapped.

'It is what I remember,' Ahmose protested thinly.

'Then why do you know how to speak Greek?'

That name again. 'Greek?'

She angrily rounded on the priest. 'What sort of trick are you playing? Who sent you? Was it that wizened old charlatan over the river who wouldn't know how to cook an egg even if you gave him the boiling water?'

Dinan laughed. 'If he's that inept, it's unlikely he would have managed to produce Ahmose.'

The animal keeper was too exhausted to argue. 'I had to change. There was something trying to pull me out of the sky. Perhaps I changed into the wrong thing.'

'What should you change into?'

It was only then that Ahmose became aware of the ghastly trick some cosmic malefactor had played on him. 'Perhaps another bird'

Helen gave a hard laugh. 'Or perhaps something with a tongue forked enough to cradle a million lies.'

'Ignore her. She's at that time of life,' Dinan told him. 'Go on?'

'I was pulled here. I didn't know what was going to happen. I can't stay like this.' Unfortunately the only person Ahmose could turn to was the glowering menopausal alchemist. 'Please help me.'

'Help you? I don't even know what you are.'

'But you do understand what caused it?'

Helen Maat exploded. 'What do you think we've been trying to work out while you were snoring! We should put you back in the crucible and see what your precious Aton does about that!' Her pent up rage expended, the alchemist snatched one of Ahmose's hands and examined it. 'Did you scrub him?' Dinan's moon features were eclipsed by false guilt. 'Clear away this mess.' Helen took a small knife from her belt.

Ahmose flinched.

'Keep still man, I'm only going to make a scratch.' She deftly nicked one of his fingers and pushed some blood from it. It was red. Helen replaced her knife and started to pace up and down.

The panther came over and rubbed her broad head against Ahmose's legs.

'Where am I?' the priest quietly mewed to the cat.

'By the Nile,' Ink purred.

'But, which part?'

'Where there are plenty of reeds and granaries full of mice. Nice, fat, juicy-'

'Don't be disgusting.'

'Don't you like mice?'

'Not to eat. Tell me who these people are?'

'You mean the humans?'

'Yes, the mad woman and her placid friend.'

'Oh, they're all right.' Ink paused to lick Ahmose's arm. 'You are odd - No salt.'

'I know I'm odd. Please try and tell me something useful.'

'Salt is very good, you know. Helen Maat uses a lot of it. Heals wounds.' The panther stretched her neck and Ahmose could see a long scar parting her black fur.

'How did that happen?'

'An intruder with a knife. He tasted very good.'

'Please stop mentioning your appetite. I was hungry before you started telling me about it.'

'Little Green Eyes will feed you. She always feeds me whether I catch anyone or not.'

Helen aimed a kick at a stool that dared to block her path.

Ahmose cast her a fearful look.

'Oh don't mind her,' advised Ink. 'She's bad tempered and shouts a lot, but is very good at curing people.'

'She frightens me.'

As Helen paced to and fro, she slowly became aware of what was breaking her attention. It was the faint whispering of animal tongues.

Dinan was peering in curiosity at Ahmose and the panther over a pile of scrolls, and the alchemist was glaring.

A tense stillness filled the room.

'Don't pay any attention,' mewed Ink. 'They think they're so clever, yet can't even understand simple directions.'

Ahmose's curiosity overcame his apprehension. 'Simple directions?'

'To this treasure the whole nome has been searching for. The grave robbers were executed before they would admit where they threw their loot.'

'Why let them know? That's sacrilegious.'

'It was only a human tomb. Us cats have our own catacomb in Bubastis. Shall I tell you where the treasure is?'

'No.'

'It might persuade her to help you.'

'All right!' Helen interrupted. 'What's going on between you and my cat?'

'I don't think she's aware that she belongs to you.'

Dinan was still peering over the scrolls. 'What was Ink telling you?'

'She knows where these grave robbers threw their loot.'

In too much of a hurry to reach Ahmose, Helen blundered into the stool she had previously kicked aside. 'What? Where?'

But the animal priest could be as stubborn as a donkey with a thorn in its flank. 'I don't know, and I'm not asking her.'

Helen pounced on Ahmose and seized his ear. 'Do you know how difficult it is to replace parts of the anatomy, especially golden ones?'

'I can't tell you something like that.'

Helen twisted his ear. 'Do you know what was in that tomb?'

'No.'

'They took a small casket. The priests claimed it contained an elixir.'

'For what?'

'Immortality.'

'And you still want it after seeing me?'

'Now I want it even more.'

'Why?'

She gave Ahmose's ear a final twist that made him yelp, then released him. 'Because Dinan and I have suddenly become immortal!'

By the tears Helen's thuggery had brought to the priest's eyes, Ink realised that he wasn't a kindred spirit after all. 'Coward.' The cat sloped away.

Ahmose rubbed his ear. 'I don't understand?'

'Every scar on our bodies has disappeared.'

'Then why are you angry?'

'Because I don't know why.'

'I thought you said that you were now immortal?'

Ahmose suddenly found himself looking into an expression that would have intimidated his High Priest. 'If our body tissue can renew itself so rapidly, it stands to reason we might never age, be fatally injured or contract any disease.'

The animal keeper backed away. 'Why should that be my fault?'

'Because we were only mere mortals before you arrived!'

Dinan dropped the scrolls and placed himself between Helen and Ahmose before real damage could be done. If the mysterious priest had given them immortality, it seemed reasonable to assume that he could do far worse if he put his mind to it.

Ahmose carefully peered round his large body at the alchemist. 'Surely you can find a cure?'

'Rumour claims that the answer is in the casket the robbers took,' Dinan explained. 'The fact that you exist, must mean the priests did know about immortality.'

Ahmose recalled the unfathomable mysticism of his friend, the High Priest of Amon Ra. If anyone could have discovered immortality, it would have been him. But that was centuries ago?

Before the others became suspicious, he quickly asked, 'Why don't you want to live forever?'

'Do you?'

'Well, no.'

'Immortality is for the unscrupulous and the fool, priest!'

Dinan compensated for the Greek's scowl with a moonish smile. 'Helen Maat's right.'

The alchemist kicked some scrolls out of the way. 'I want to understand the meaning of life, not cheat death. Do you want our help?'

Ahmose's resolve stiffened. 'Not at the price of robbing a tomb.'

'It's already been robbed. We just need to know where the thieves put their hoard. What's the matter with you, man? Your priestly brethren already do a lucrative trade in grave goods. They would have let the highest bidder take this casket if they'd known where to find it.'

Dinan gathered up the precious scrolls. 'Why won't you help us Ahmose?'

The animal priest removed his amulets. 'These are solid gold.'

'I am already wealthy,' Helen reminded him icily. 'I don't need to rob minor priests.'

'He's not going to tell us.' Dinan pushed the amulets back onto Ahmose's arms.

'He doesn't like pain.'

The priest flinched, then glowered back at Helen Maat.

'Don't pay any attention,' said Dinan. 'She usually mends more than she breaks.'

'Where did you learn to talk to animals, anyway?' she demanded.

'I've always had the ability.'

'All animals?'

'Not crocodiles. The only thing they can remember is their last meal.' Ahmose pulled his robe tight about him. 'What are you going to do with me?'

'Before or after I dissect you?'

'Stop frightening him,' scolded Dinan. 'You're as subtle as a hippo in a mud wallow.'

'No,' disagreed Ahmose. 'I can understand the river horse.'

'Are you calling me a crocodile?' Helen would have menaced his other ear if the servant girl hadn't come in carrying a bowl of honey cakes and pomegranates. 'Who's that for?'

Green eyed and innocent, she placed the food before the animal priest.

Dinan gave a girlish giggle. 'She's been talking to the cat.'

'She'd better not,' snarled Helen.

Green Eyes smiled fearlessly and left.

Ahmose looked at the food hungrily.

'Well, are you going to let him eat it?' asked Dinan.

Helen knew he was inferring that her presence could have spoilt the appetite of a ravenous camel. Casting a disconcerting glare at the priest, the alchemist swept out.

Dinan would have followed if Ahmose hadn't caught his arm.

'What's the matter?'

'I don't want to be left alone.'

'You're safe here.' Dinan righted the stool Helen had kicked over and sat beside him. 'We're really all harmless. This house is the logical habitat for any misfit who drifts up the Nile.'

'You aren't afraid of your mistress?'

'Only men who have an ego to defend run from Helen Maat. I am the husband she will never have.'

'How did you come here?'

'My ancestors must have managed to get past all six cataracts.'

'Little Green Eyes?'

'Green Eyes? You mean Lilia. She never talks, though we're sure she can. Left on our steps when she was three. I brought her up and taught her what I could, but she never talks.' Dinan shook his head. 'Yes, we're all misfits here.'

'I was brought up by the priests.'

'I'm not surprised you're a mess.'

'I felt safe when I was a bird, knowing the Aton would always protect me, but now...'

'Eat your food.'

'I can't stay like this. If I go outside I would be seen for miles.'

'Tell Helen where that casket is and she might help you.'

'No, I couldn't.'

Dinan knew Ahmose wouldn't change his mind.

Eventually Helen grew tired of being dazzled and tried to find the cure for his goldness all the same. Having decided that the priest was more closely related to a mouse, Ink treated him with contempt. She was too well behaved to eat houseguests, so Ahmose's principal company was Lilia when Dinan was assisting the Alchemist.

CHAPTER 14

One morning, while he sat braiding Lilia's hair, Ahmose saw the black sail of a bireme pass on the river below. Many ships, dhows, barges and ferries filled the Nile, but there was something incongruous about this sea going vessel. A large hand gently pulled him away from the window.

'It's a pirate,' warned Dinan. 'If you can't stop glowing, keep out of sight. Some of the tyrants and satraps about the Aegean would pay generously for a golden deity.' He smiled. 'Anyway, even if we can't cure you, we can at least stain you a more civilised colour. You'll still glow a little, though not like the Pharos.'

Lilia mimed that she wanted to help.

'No, it would mark your skin. I'll do it. Mine can't be stained any darker than it is."

Helen's laboratory was filled with the acrid smell of pulverised bark. Hay, a servant, was stirring a bubbling cauldron while the alchemist tossed chunks of an evil looking substance into it.

She flashed Ahmose a satanic smile. 'Your bath is ready.'

The priest had become used to her wicked humour and merely cast her a reproachful look.

'Oh, if only I could alter the expression in those eyes as well.'

'Is the first batch cool yet?' asked Dinan.

'On the south sill.'

Dinan sat Ahmose down by a table then brought over the bowl of warm fluid. He dabbed the sticky substance onto the back of the priest's hand with a sponge. Much to the patient's disappointment, the gold didn't disappear, merely ceased to sparkle.

'Good.' Dinan started to apply it to the rest of his body.

Ahmose wondered if it would have been easier just to turn back into a bird. 'How many times will you have to do this?'

'No idea,' said Dinan. 'You will have to be scrubbed after each coating.'

'Why?'

'The skin reacts by creating an oily film that prevents the next coat going on. Could take weeks.'

'Weeks?'
'Thinking of going somewhere?' asked Helen.
'The dye will be permanent,' Dinan promised.
'I didn't mean to be ungrateful.
The alchemist gave a wry smile. 'Oh, we're going to be a little mouse again, are we.'
'Better than a crocodile,' muttered Ahmose.

CHAPTER 15

Though still gold, Ahmose ceased to gleam after several days, and was cleaner than the pharaoh's favourite concubine.

In between the repeated stainings, he would sit in the courtyard and talk to a couple of friendly mice, until Ink ate them. He tried to persuade Lilia to talk but she wouldn't, or couldn't, speak. Perhaps she knew that all the world would demand of her were explanations and thought that the world should work things out for itself.

One night, Ahmose lay on the flat roof of the large house sleeping in the cool air. Below, a large black sail billowed darkly in a thermal. Ink was out in the reeds hunting, so never heard the soft footfall on the outside steps.

Woke by the faint splash of oars, Lilia ran up to the roof.

Across the flagstones were several wet footprints, silver in the moonlight. Ahmose's thin mattress lay in a tangled heap and some woken pigeons were warbling in confusion.

The whole household heard Lilia scream.

When Dinan reached the roof she was pointing to the black sail silhouetted against the starlit sky.

Helen's voice was next to slice through the night air. 'They must stop in Alexandria! Tell Hay to follow them and find out where they're going!'

Lilia dashed downstairs.

Dinan was surprised. 'We're going after him?'

'Why not?'

'You were forever saying what a nuisance the priest was.'

'I wouldn't wish what could happen to him on a demon from Hades. He's still gold enough to make a tyrant reach deep into his coffers, and all the tyrants I've encountered were not renowned for their intellect or altruism.'

'Where are we going to find a galley crew willing to take on a pirate?'

'We don't need to. They're not likely to harm Ahmose and bring down his price. What was the ship?'

'A bireme.'

'Then we'll hire a trireme.'

'How will Hay find out their destination?'

'No ship leaves Alexandria without telling the port authorities where they're going, and Hay has a list of bribeable officials.'

'So what happens when Ahmose is sold to some power-mad satrap who wants him to explain immortality?'

'I'll think of something.'

Helen went downstairs to pack.

'You always do,' muttered Dinan.

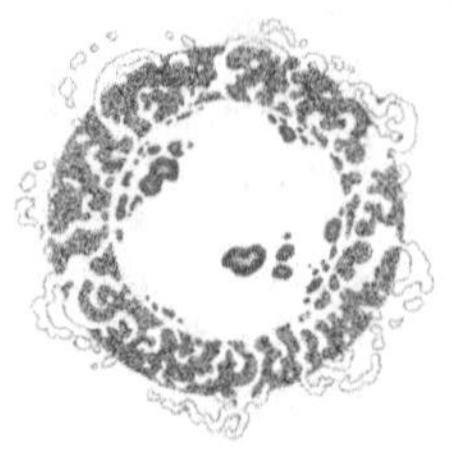

THE TYRANT

CHAPTER 16

On a desolate peak, where the shimmering desert merges with the sky, there glints a statue of gold. Now immobile as marble, it once lived. Some have tried to reach it, a few out of curiosity, many for avarice. One or two came close enough to see the features of the mirage's gaunt, mean face. As they reached out to touch it, the statue briefly joined with the sky to become a fretwork of sunbeams against a fierce blue backdrop. Once he had been called king, now few remembered that Pylas had ever lived. Like Ozymandias, there was no one left to quake at the mention of his name. His legend had disappeared because no one wanted to remember the man who had enraged the sun.

Pylas had a lust for gold that turned to madness, and a craving for power that became tyranny. Having murdered his brother, married his widow, and usurped his crown, that alone should have been enough to condemn him to eternity on a remote peak, frozen between heaven and hell. That was not the reason, though. This curious crime was a minor misdemeanour compared with the many other outrages he had committed.

As the province fell into poverty to feed Pylas's greed, the palace walls grew higher. They were faced by the stones from the temples he had sacked, and filled by the pebbles of a whole beach. In his small kingdom fortress surrounded by the sea, cliffs and vast inland desert, nothing could threaten the tyrant.

Then a ship with a black sail appeared on the horizon.

CHAPTER 17

The cliff paths were narrow and overlooked sheer drops to sea worn rocks, so the pirate captain wouldn't trust his precious parcel to the hands of his fumble-fisted men.

The town they passed through once possessed a wall. Now there was nothing left to defend since Pylas pillaged the place to quell its rebellious population. Its bricks had been scavenged to build the small hovels where the survivors cowered.

Those not privileged to live in the palace complex were compelled to pick their livings from the rubbish tip not even the sea breezes could purge the stench from. Small plots of arable land were cultivated for the needs of Pylas's entourage, and the sunken wells that had not cracked supplied only brackish water. No merchants came this way. Given the opportunity, this tyrant would trade in hostages.

The pirate captain was a frequent visitor. His party was allowed through the fortifications to the palace where the wealth of the plundered town had been carelessly scattered about its corridors and courtyards. Even the tyrant's favourite horse had a stable lined with rich carpets and was fed on the precious vegetables farmers managed to grow in the thin topsoil.

Pylas was a man forever fidgeting. Some said - though not out loud - that it was part of his madness, others, that the gods had cursed him with perpetual movement. Tall, lean and stooped, Pylas resembled a vulture about to delve into the entrails of his next victim. Features that might have been distinguished were distorted by cruelty, and that thin, crooked mouth had never raised a smile.

The captain entered carrying a rolled carpet on his shoulder and the tyrant's fingers danced a greedy tattoo on the arm of his throne. 'Well, well. What have you got? Show me! Show me!'

As his acquisitive frenzy increased the captain knew that, if he was careful, he could get a good price for this booty.

The pirate laid the rolled carpet before Pylas. 'In here is

the rarest, most mysterious treasure to be stolen from the inner sanctum of an Egyptian temple. When the great Amon Ra whispered the secrets of immortality to the mystics who built the pyramids, his sacred breath enveloped a mortal.'

The tyrant was beside himself. 'Let me see! Let me see!' He ordered his servants to open two caskets. One contained raw gems of amethyst, tiger's eye, beryl and garnet. The smaller had in it polished and cut amber, sapphires, turquoise, topaz and emeralds.

The captain frowned.

'What more do you want? Do you want!' snapped Pylas.

'There is something else as well.'

'What? What?'

'The creature won't admit it.'

'Admit what? Admit what?'

'He knows how to make gold.'

The mad monarch halted in mid fidget. The jewelled fingers reached up to scratch his waxed beard. 'Then why part with him? Part with him?'

The captain shrugged. 'He is stubborn...'

'Let me see him, see him!' Pylas was now dangerously agitated.

He waved another casket forward. It contained a dagger with a hilt and sheaf encrusted in sapphires, two rock crystal goblets, a ruby pendant with strings of seed pearls, several lapis lazuli figurines, an onyx cameo and bowl of carved tiger's eye.

The pirate tried not to marvel at the treasure in case Pylas realised its true value. He accepted the third casket grudgingly while working out how he was going to make it back to the bireme before the tyrant changed his mind.

The captain unfurled the carpet with a sharp tug. Ahmose was sent spinning across the mosaic floor in a flurry of gold and purple.

The court couldn't believe their eyes. They didn't see a small, dazed Egyptian priest, but a glittering deity. Pylas ordered his chief eunuch to try and rub the gold from Ahmose's skin. That only burnished the priest and made him shine more brightly. Until then, the tyrant had believed that there were no more marvels in the world to plunder and was so mesmerised by the Egyptian that he allowed the pirates to leave with the treasure.

Because of drug-induced giddiness, Ahmose felt as though the Aton had clipped his wings in mid flight and let him crash to earth. Then he realised that he wasn't a bird any more, but a hairless, featherless mortal with a severe tyrant problem.

As his new acquisition was in no state to come to him, Pylas left his throne to pinch Ahmose's skin in spasms of excited cupidity. Annoyed, the priest shook the shaking fingers off. He was promptly rewarded with a sharp blow. This helped Ahmose collect his wits. Given his immediate situation, they weren't that much use. In the tyrant's greedily glittering eyes, the animal priest saw the demon in the man's soul. He got up and dashed away, only to find that he was totally encircled by courtiers and guards. Once again Pylas closed in with all the maniacal malevolence that went to make a tyrant. As Ahmose circled to avoid the creature, other hands plucked at his purple robe and touched his skin.

'You are mine now, mine now,' cackled Pylas. He pinched Ahmose's face and neck. Not wanting another blow from those gnarled hands jagged with rings, Ahmose tried not to flinch.

'I have paid a fortune for you! A fortune!' The tyrant obviously wasn't open to negotiation on that point. Just as Ahmose believed things could get no worse, Pylas insisted, 'You will tell me how to make gold, make gold!'

It was a demand, not a question.

Sheer terror nudged the entity deep inside Ahmose and the expression in his eyes made Pylas hesitate. At the back of the priest's pupils gleamed the flame of a very angry deity. Even a tyrant had to think twice about having a god thrashed.

Pylas plucked the air. At this signal, his chamberlain led Ahmose away to the women's quarters, the best-guarded territory in the realm. Its residents found the small priest a welcome change from the tyrant and bossy eunuchs. Ahmose liked their company and thoughts that had seldom crossed his mind before started to peep over its parapets. On learning that the eunuchs were the surviving suitors of the tyrant's wives, they ducked back down again.

Drowsy from the pirates' drug and a fragrant bath, Ahmose did some illicit dreaming instead before being summoned again.

Apparently Pylas didn't fidget so much in the afternoons and was less prone to repetition.

Ahmose was on the verge of communicating with the tyrant when a messenger dashed into the throne room. He whispered to a guard who whispered to the cup-bearer, who whispered to the chamberlain. The laws about who could directly address Pylas tended to slow the passage of information. The tyrant hadn't yet grasped how many battles had been lost this way.

'There is a foreign ship standing off the headland, Sire,' announced the chamberlain.

Pylas was feeling unusually magnanimous. 'Leave it for the pirate.'

'He sailed some while ago, Sire.'

'Well leave it for the gulls, the gulls! I'm not risking my ships unless it's carrying gold! Carrying gold!' Thinking Ahmose had dozed off; Pylas poked him with his staff. 'You, Egyptian! You will tell me how to make gold, make gold!'

Ahmose begged his wits to return but they insisted on dawdling. 'Gold?'

'Gold! Gold!' echoed Pylas.

'I'm just a minor priest,' explained Ahmose.

The tyrant's staff caught him such a blow he was winded. His hopes of holding rational conversation with the creature had been premature.

'You are gold, so you must know how to make gold, make gold.'

The thought of the yellowish metal was working Pylas into a frenzy, the like of which Ahmose had never seen, even in a rabid hyena.

'It was an accident.'

'Accident? Accident?'

'A curse.' At last the priest recovered his wits. 'Some magicians cast a spell on me. They are the ones who know how to make gold.' Ahmose was surprised at how easily lying came to him in the absence of any honest alternative.

Pylas squinted in disbelief. He beckoned over a bodyguard. Ahmose looked up at the aquiline features of a human predator and his spirit went limp. Judging by the locks of victims' hair hanging from his belt, this man loved his work and he hardly seemed disappointed that Ahmose didn't have any.

CHAPTER 18

As Dinan carefully lowered the precious lenses and mirror to the small boat bobbing on the night black waves, inquisitive faces peered from the trireme's oar ports.

'It won't work, I know it won't work,' Dinan cursed under his breath, anticipating the tyrant's scepticism as well as his speech impediment.

'Stop muttering and let down the crucible!' Helen called up.

'Is she quite sane?' the captain whispered to Dinan.

'Depends which side of bed she falls out of.'

The captain gave the eunuch a sideways glance. 'If you two get into trouble, my crew can't take on a tyrant's army. Pylas *is* mad y'know.'

'Let's hope they get on then.' After passing down the crucible, Dinan tucked the parcel containing Ahmose's jewellery, robe and sandals into his satchel.

'Is this priest worth the fee for my ship and risk to your lives?'

Dinan wondered for a moment. 'Helen Maat would travel to the sun if helped explain that Egyptian. If you don't see our signal in two days, sail without us.' He stepped over the side of the ship and descended the rope ladder like a giant on a stem of columbine.

Helen and Dinan were ferried ashore and left on the beach with their equipment. In the moonlight they could see a small fishing boat being hauled ashore. The crew quickly disappeared into the cliff's shadow with their meagre catch and were lost from sight.

It was impossible to pick out the path the men took, so Helen and Dinan gazed up at the unbroken line of cliffs and wished for a sure-footed mule.

They were still searching for a pass up the rocks when a massive dark man confronted them. Beardless, with a stern expression, he wore a short tunic edged with silver and Phrygian's conical cap. He would have looked absurd if he weren't so formidable. The man pointed at the weighty equipment on their backs and Dinan instinctively reached for his sword.

Helen caught his wrist. 'It's all right. He's not a soldier.'

'I know another slave when I see one, and they're not all as sweet natured as me.'

'Does he understand Greek? He's not very talkative.'

The other eunuch opened his mouth. There was no tongue to speak with. There was a scar where it had been torn from his mouth many years before. The slave took something from his pouch and laid it across his wide palm.

Helen recognised the earring. 'That's Ahmose's.'

'It's probably a trap.'

The slave shook his head and pointed upwards.

'We've got to trust him.'

'Why?'

'Because we don't have a choice.'

The stranger nodded.

'Why should he risk his life for Ahmose?'

Helen asked the mute eunuch, 'Is the golden man still alive?'

The slave nodded then, giving Dinan a wary look, lifted the lenses and box of equipment from her shoulders. He sure-footedly led the couple up a winding pass and through the foul smelling town beyond. They were being watched, but it was by fearful eyes.

Noiselessly the companions skirted the palace walls until they came to a finger wide crack in its defences. The slave pulled aside a large buttress stone and revealed a short tunnel. Dinan and Helen crammed themselves through it and entered a small, silent courtyard. On the other side of it was a dimly lit room filled with the aroma of cloves and jasmine. The furnishings reflected the refinement of the Lydian court in the statuettes of winged genii, slender lamp holders and a fan shaped array of curved bows - though a noticeable lack of arrows. An elegant woman was sitting on a couch. As they entered, the slave bowed and she beckoned Helen and Dinan to her.

'I am glad you found your way here safely.' The woman spoke in halting Greek as though it was a childhood language she was on the verge of forgetting. 'I am the

Queen of this pathetic little realm, first wife to the even more pathetic man who usurped its crown.'

'Is this some sort of trap?' Helen asked in a tone too civil to suggest she believed it.

'Had you walked through the palace gates, you would have never left here alive. You are friends of the small golden man, aren't you?'

'Yes. How did you know?'

'Nothing brings anyone to this place unless they are a brigand, hostage or rescue party.'

'Why would you protect us?'

'I am a princess of the house ruling Lydia where there is much gold and a little more civilisation. When this realm was contented, I was married to Pylas's brother. You have seen what it is like now.'

'What do you want us to do?'

'Pylas believes that your mysterious friend can make gold. I have watched it being sieved from the waters that flow from the mountains of my homeland and worked by the best jewellers in the world. I have never seen it being created from dross lead. That is impossible.'

Helen Maat gave a sinister grin. 'Oh no, not impossible.'

'Helen...' Dinan quietly warned.

She ignored him. 'Introduce me to your husband and I will show him how to make gold.'

The Queen hesitated. 'If this were possible, you would be giving a madman the keys to the gates of the Underworld.'

'The place I have in mind for him needs no key. Where is Ahmose?'

'We are not sure.'

'We have to know before we can rescue him.'

'Pylas would never give you the chance if he believes he can make gold.'

'Even a tyrant should be granted a last wish.'

Dinan hadn't come all that way just to commit murder. 'Helen!'

The Queen had never met a person like the formidable alchemist before and, against all reason, believed that she could free the realm of its monster. 'You can not only make gold, but destroy kings?'

'A new side line I'm working on.'

'No!' snapped Dinan. 'Let's just grab Ahmose and run.' Then he had to ask the unthinkable. 'He hasn't been harmed has he?'

'A fool like Pylas would not be able to tell whether golden skin can bruise.' The Queen turned to Helen. 'My husband is heavily guarded and has many food tasters. How could you kill him?'

'That depends on how desperate he is to acquire gold - or immortality.'

'Immortality?' The Queen tried to see trickery in the alchemist's glittering smile, but the woman meant it. 'Yes, he would prefer immortality to a mountain of gold, but is that possible?'

'Trust me. I'm an alchemist.'

Even the Queen wasn't allowed to approach her suspicious husband, and the next morning she asked the chamberlain to arrange an audience for Helen Maat. At the mention of alchemy, Pylas was bound to see the Greek. If she could make gold for him, he might forget to ask how she had managed to get into the palace.

The alchemist wore as many gold amulets and necklaces as she could carry, a Babylonian head-dress of turquoise flowers with beaten gold leaves and matching belt from which hung small phials, scissors, a pouch of woven silver thread and a carnelian plum bob. Being more easily aroused by the sight of gold than a regiment of dancing girls, much to the relief of the region's nubile young women, Pylas was duly impressed. Dinan just wondered how Helen managed to stay upright under the weight.

With the superiority of a true Greek, she ordered Dinan to set up the tripods on the chequered roof of the palace. He aligned the mirror and lenses to direct the rays of the rising sun into the crucible.

Trembling with anticipation, Pylas demanded to know why they had chosen his palace's highest point for the demonstration.

Helen theatrically raised her hands to the sky. 'The closer we are to the sun, the more powerful becomes its magic.'

Dinan winced, but Pylas was taken in.

'How does it work? Does it work?' he rasped greedily.

'Tell one of your guards to fetch me a pebble.'

'A pebble? A pebble?'

'An ordinary pebble the size of a gull's egg.'

Pylas nodded. His chamberlain delegated the task to the nearest guard who looked intelligent enough to recognise a gull.

Helen took a bottle of mercury from her pouch. She held it up. 'Quicksilver. The element that can transform and be transformed.'

As Pylas fidgeted himself into an excited paroxysm,

Dinan wondered how long Helen's rational tongue could keep churning out such inanities.

When the guard returned, the alchemist told him to examine the crucible then place the pebble inside it. Not knowing what he was meant to be looking for, the man obeyed then quickly withdrew.

'How many things can you turn into gold? Turn into gold?' demanded Pylas.

'With the right spells - anything. Feathers, rocks, pottery...'

'People?'

Helen gave a sinister smile. 'And people.'

'Who? Who?'

'I have transmuted a foolish Egyptian priest who tried to stop me discovering the ancient scrolls holding the solution to immortality.'

The effect on the tyrant was electric. 'Immortality? Immortality?'

'That is another matter, though.'

'Who was this priest?' asked the chamberlain before the tyrant could leap from his throne and choke the secret from her.

'He was a stupid creature of no more consequence than,' Helen pointed to the crucible, 'that pebble. He knew nothing but a few prayers to Amon Ra and how to feed crocodiles.'

Pylas stopped fidgeting for a moment. 'He wasn't a magician? A magician?'

The alchemist laughed. 'He was one of many priests who have been trying to stop our heresies. They believe that a Greek making gold and experimenting with immortality is sacrilege, an offence against their precious Osiris. But then, they think they have a monopoly on spells for the afterlife.'

'Tell me how to achieve immortality? Immortality?'

'First - gold!'

Helen poured the mercury into the crucible. The focussed sun's rays struck the pebble and it glowed as though it was in a furnace.

Nothing happened.

Pylas started to fidget again.

Helen beckoned to his chamberlain as Dinan adjusted the lenses so it was safe for him to stoop down and take a sparkling golden pebble from the crucible. It was barely warm. The chamberlain held it up for Pylas to see.

Dinan whispered into the alchemist's ear, 'How did you do that?'

'Shut-up and give me your sword.'

Worried about what she was liable to do next, he nevertheless obeyed.

Before the tyrant's astonishment could wear off, Helen held the weapon aloft. 'As for immortality!' Before the awe-struck court the alchemist drew the sharp blade across her arm and made a deep cut. There was a copious spurt of blood.

Immediately the wound knitted itself together and healed. The chamberlain wiped away the gore to discover nothing more than a thin whitish line on her copper coloured skin.

Pylas was beside himself. 'Tell me! Tell me!'

'I will make you immortal,' declared Helen. 'But you must be closer to the sun.'

Consumed by manic greed, Pylas never thought to ask what she wanted in return. His chamberlain suggested it would be prudent to find out. Upsetting someone with that sort of power could be a bad move.

'I have no use for gold,' announced Helen. 'I need another slave.' She ignored Dinan's look of contempt.

'Take whoever you want, whoever you want,' said Pylas. 'What will you do with them? Do with them?'

'Turn them to gold.'

There was a delicious moment of silent horror. His entourage knew what had happened to the last person unwise enough to gleam in the presence of Pylas.

From a distant balcony of the women's quarters, the alchemist saw the Queen signal with a large fan. She had to move fast.

'The highest peak borders the desert.' The chamberlain pointed to a jagged line of rose red mountains behind the palace. 'It is easy to reach.'

Dinan knew that he was going to be the one to cart the equipment up there. Just then he would have appreciated another slave to help, but everyone else had their minds on higher things however.

An hour later, under the glare of the tyrant's bodyguard, the African once again set up the lenses and mirror.

Helen took a small sachet from her pouch.

'What's that?' demanded Pylas.

'The elixir. You must swallow ten grains of it before entering the sun's rays.' Helen pointed to the coloured glass filters Dinan had placed before the lenses. 'Those screens alter the substance of the sunlight. When you enter its rays, immortality will surge through your body.'

So, the most suspicious man alive was sold an absurdity. Though dubious, his chamberlain remained silent.

Pylas's hand shook too much to hold the precious grains so Dinan counted them out onto a taper and dropped them onto the tyrant's tongue. Then the chamberlain, the only courtier allowed to touch the body of the ruler, escorted him into the spotlight of many colours.

The concentration of his entourage was so intense, they never noticed that the sun was changing colour.

Like a cormorant drying its wings, Pylas bathed in the pink light. He felt immortality course through his veins and raised his hands to the sun.

The sun replied with the accuracy of a cosmic mathematician and hurled down a globe of plasma that engulfed the tyrant. Everyone else was sent sprawling.

When they could see again, Pylas had been transmuted. His skin, flesh, bone and robes were solid gold. He now had immortality.

The chamberlain reached out to touch him.

'No!' called Helen.

Terrified, the chamberlain pulled back his hand, picked up the hem of his gown and fled down the mountain path after the tyrant's bodyguard.

Pylas once again metamorphosed.

Trapped between dimensions, he was no longer tangible. Like a quicksilver sandwich in the ether, he became a pattern of light rippling against the sky.

No one could guess what had happened to his soul. Most people wouldn't have credited him with one. The odd traveller who subsequently became lost in the pink sandstone desert and ruins below swore that his unearthly sighs echo through the craggy spires.

Helen looked down at her shattered lenses, mirror and filters. 'That priest has now cost me my whole laboratory.'

Dinan tried to gather up some pieces.

'Leave them,' she told him. 'There isn't time. We have to find Ahmose.'

When they reached the palace it was girdled by leaden silence and had started to crumble as though struck by a hail of falling stars. There was no longer the clicking of the guards' armour as they patrolled the walls, no strains of music from the women's quarters, or monotonous thud on the smith's anvil. As though the soul of the place had passed into another dimension with that of the tyrant who had ruled it, sand was being blown against its buttresses and the banners tattered by the rising breeze, heralding the anonymity of the once terrible ruler.

Looters had clambered over the breached palace wall and desert antelope were skipping over the rubble.

Helen and Dinan followed. Some of the animals stopped to nibble at the food and furnishings strewed everywhere. The human locusts who had looted the palace had ripped bronze from plinths and doorposts in the belief it was gold. They ignored goblets carved from garnet and sardonyx, bowls and fans inlaid with lapis lazuli, turquoise and sapphire. Dinan and Helen wondered if they would find the golden Ahmose in one piece.

The bolder of the antelope trotted into the main courtyard where the mosaic floor was a surreal jigsaw of small bonfires, smashed amphorae and overturned statues. The herd was gathering about a roughly erected screen made from spears and embroidered robes. Two figures knelt bedside the body it shielded from the sunlight.

Dinan caught Helen's arm.

'What's the matter?'

'Look at the sun.'

Helen wasn't sure she wanted to. 'What's it doing now?'

'Changing colour.'

Long, lurid shadows were bleeding across the ground like the gore of a slain monster.

The alchemist looked up.

This was not the sun she was familiar with. Something had parasitised its golden hue with a reddish pallor. It might have been recharging itself after hurling its might at the tyrant. Helen suspected a more sinister reason.

In the small gathering at the fluttering screen, the Queen was pouring drops of wine through Ahmose's lips and her slave was wafting air over him with a broken fan.

The Queen looked up at the alchemist. 'We were too late. When the guards heard that Pylas was dead they left your friend here then fled - The sun is angry.'

'Damn the sun!' snarled Helen. 'All this was the fault of his precious Aton.'

Dinan knelt beside Ahmose and took the sandals, jewellery and robe from his satchel. 'We can't leave him here.'

'You can't do anything else. You'd kill him if you tried to move him.'

'If he's immortal, surely his wounds must be able to heal like ours'?'

'Don't be a fool, Dinan. The bird was immortal, the priest isn't.'

'Then you can heal him.'

'He is dying,' the Queen gently told Dinan.

Helen took the phial from her belt and handed it to her. 'Pour this through his lips.'

The Queen did as she said. A small antelope watched closely in bold curiosity. 'Why are they here?'

'Perhaps they've come to see the second keeper of the sacred animals of the temple of Amon Ra.' Helen laid the necklace across Ahmose's chest then shook out the robe and spread it over him. She placed the sandals by his feet.

'He's trying to speak,' said Dinan.

'What is it?' the alchemist asked Ahmose.

'I am going to die aren't I?'

'Yes, little priest. Your Aton is coming to collect you. We're the ones with the problem now.'

'I will ask it to release you.'

'After what I've been calling it, you shouldn't bother.'

'The Aton is good.'

Helen bit her tongue.

It gave Dinan the chance to ask, 'Is there any pain?'

'I feel sleepy. Let me see the sun.'

The slave pulled the spears from the ground and the tent of robes collapsed.

Ahmose closed his eyes and bathed in the warmth. 'Will you bury me at Innu?'

'In the inner sanctum of Amon's temple,' Helen promised.

'No, no. That would be sacrilegious. Just in the sand.'

'I'll build you a tomb.'

'No, I'm not important.'

'If I want to build you a tomb, I'll build you a tomb.'

Ahmose smiled. 'Tell Lilia I changed back into a bird and flew away. Give her my jewellery and let Ink make a bed of my robe.'

As Dinan cradled Ahmose's head in his large hands, the priest's skin began to glow. That golden complexion, the capricious whim of Ra, turned back to its natural warm brown. On his forehead there remained a disc of gold as though the entity had stamped its own eye over Ahmose's.

The alchemist suddenly sensed what was going to happen. She leapt up and let out a stream of abuse at the sun.

The Queen and her slave unsurely backed away at the maniacal proceedings while Dinan desperately tried to find the flicker of a pulse in Ahmose's body.

'He's dead.'

Helen stopped shouting at the heavens and jerked him back by the tunic. 'Come away! Leave him to his infernal god!'

'What?'

'Look.' She pointed at the sun. It was resuming its natural fiery hue.

Ahmose's body became enveloped in a misty yellow cocoon. A glittering gold shape formed inside it and there was the rustling of feathers. Huge wings spread themselves. With one downward stroke, they launched the Aton Bird into the sky. As it rose on the blustery Aegean thermals a beautiful, eerie song filled the realm. Looters stopped their squabbling as the sky seemed to move, and the unearthly sound percolated through it, mocking their mortality.

The antelope darted back to the desert and the Queen picked up the purple and gold robe that had covered Ahmose. It was no longer stained with blood. The sandals, jewellery and white robe had disappeared with their owner.

Helen watched the golden speck in the sky. 'Damn you sun!' Damn you Aton!'

The Queen was baffled by her rage. 'But he is transformed?'

'He's cursed. The sun had no intention of releasing Ahmose. It will go on using him like a cosmic plaything until it cools.' Helen set her jaw. 'But I'm going to stop it. If it takes eternity, I will find a way to defeat it.'

Dinan silently nodded. If they were going to live forever, it would help pass the time.

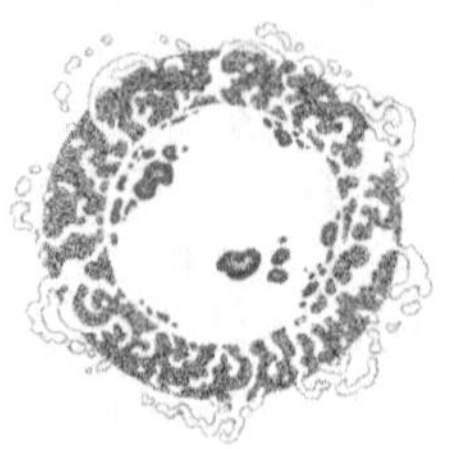

KLEOPATRA

CHAPTER 20

Had Helen been in Alexandria before the air was filled with the ashes of burnt papyrus, history might have taken a different turn. Had she acquired the knowledge of Hypatia before a Christian mob lynched the scientist, centuries might have been saved. However, by the time Helen and Dinan arrived, the city was crawling with the maggots of intolerance, mob rule and Roman ineptitude.

For three centuries Dinan had nagged the alchemist to visit the Alexandrian library. Only after it had become a target for religious fervour would she acknowledge that she did not, after all, possess the wisdom of this reeling world. She would never have admitted that if it had not been for a strange dream calling her to the capital. In it, another alchemist told her that only there would she discover anything about the deity enslaving Ahmose. How she was going to find her when they arrived, Helen wasn't quite sure.

Over the centuries, Dinan had seen most forms of madness. He kept a mental catalogue of their symptoms in the same way the alchemist remembered herbal remedies. But Helen Maat had developed a derangement all her own. With immortality, pain had become a mere inconvenience, and without its distraction, she had somehow found it easier to close the shutters on reality.

The Alexandrian library once contained over half a million books and copies of every manuscript to pass through the port; officers had searched each ship to ensure none escaped the scribe. Now the very heat Helen wanted to control had consumed the knowledge she needed. The only time the alchemist had achieved the correct combination of elements and temperature, it had been an accident. However methodically she reconstructed the experiment, she could not repeat the result. Dinan was convinced that, if she succeeded, another entity would land on their heads and curse them with something even worse than longevity. But he kept his peace. For all his knowledge and Helen's eccentricity, she was the one only one capable of finding the solution to their immortality.

The temple scribe they had travelled to meet was no longer a busy man. The mob had invaded the sanctuary of Serapis, defaced the wall carvings dedicated to Isis, knocked the ears from the statue of Hermanubis and filled the aisles with rubble when they brought down the roof.

Djutmose eked out a living as a letter writer in a back street house with his huge family and a courtyard crowded with in-laws. They all felt safer, gathered together there, from the pagan chasing fanatics. The quarters were so cramped it was remarkable the scribe found any room for the valuable scrolls he had snatched before flames engulfed the Alexandrian Library. Unfortunately they were not the most scientific and there wasn't much the alchemist could glean from a play by Euripides that a melancholic couldn't tell her.

Over the noise of squabbling children, clacking old men and bleating goats, Djutmose told the Greek that the documents she needed were now in the hands of a reclusive old scholar. The scribe only knew that she was called Kleopatra, not an uncommon pseudonym for an alchemist, and had gone into hiding. Christians had as much time for devotees of the hermetic arts as pagans and irony. Dinan had often wondered why the Romans turned to such an austere religion as Christianity after centuries of debauchery. Perhaps it was drinking water from lead pipes, or the freedom to riot after generations of military suppression. It was a pity that the pacifism of their prophet had become somewhat marginalised along the way.

Leaving Djutmose with enough gold to flee to a more peaceful backwater, Helen and Dinan left to search for

Kleopatra.

By bribing a glass blower who secretly made alembics for alchemists, Dinan acquired a list of his customers. He set out to visit them while Helen installed a furnace in a courtyard south of Alexandria, well away from the Roman garrisons. The arrangement suited Dinan. He preferred not to be around when she did eventually hit on the correct combination of elements and heat. The African already had the feeling a dangerous entity was looking over his massive shoulder, and any phantom gigantic enough to do that could curse on the cosmic scale.

One morning Dinan stopped to rest on the bank of a small tributary in heat intense enough to scorch the soul. He noticed small tongues of flame skittering over the shallow water.

An old woman cutting reeds saw his startled expression. 'We call them fire dancers.'

'What are they?'

'They started to appear when that magician set up house.' The reed gatherer pointed a callused finger at a stone building on a hillock.

'What's she called?'

The old woman was suspicious. 'What makes you think she's a woman?'

Dinan beamed innocently. 'Seemed somehow inevitable.'

'No one knows her name. No one talks to her. She doesn't bother us, so we don't bother her. You know what alchemists are like. Anyway, why should we set the Romans on one of our own.'

Dinan knew that it was the phantom on his shoulder that had led him to Kleopatra. Perhaps it wasn't so dangerous after all.

He helped the reed cutter lift the bundle onto her back and she hobbled off to her village.

As he watched the fire dancers, Dinan became aware that he was not alone. Standing a short way off - on the water - was his phantom, a man with features of carved jade. He held a jackal-headed staff and wore the pectoral of an ancient priest.

Dinan realised that this image had been lodged in the back of his mind for centuries. The apparition's cat like eyes seemed to demand something of him. Before he could make sense of what it was, the fire dancers spiralled about the figure like a blazing lasso. The knot tightened and the phantom was choked out of existence.

This was too strange for Dinan to tackle by himself. He shook the grit from his sandals and found a fisherman to ferry him back to the outskirts of Alexandria.

When Dinan arrived, the streets and alleyways surrounding Helen Maat's house were teeming with mounted Roman soldiers and a braying rabble. As they weren't fighting each other, it must have been another holy riot, and the most likely target in the vicinity was the alchemist.

A cloth merchant recognised Dinan and seized the sleeve of his tunic. 'It's no use. Your mistress's house is burning.'

Dinan felt his stomach muscles tighten. 'Where is she?'

The Jew drew a hand across his throat. He wasn't making the sign of the cross. 'They say it was a decurion, but any of the rabble could have done it just as easily.'

Though a small man, the merchant held onto the African's arm as though trying to stop him flying off. 'Don't do it. The crowd is maddened by the rumour of a Christian child being bled to death in some alchemical ritual.' He hustled Dinan into a porch and through to a room piled with bolts of fabric. He quickly secured the door after them.

'I have to reach her.'

'There is no point.' The merchant thrust a goblet of wine into Dinan's hands. 'Drink this, it will help calm you. When the mob has dispersed I'll go up and see what has happened.' He pointed to a trap door in the ceiling. 'There are no outside steps because of my stock and family.'

'Let me go up.'

'You'd be seen. In a short while it will be night.'

Dinan gulped down the wine. He didn't feel any calmer, but it helped him know good advice when it was offered.

For over an hour he sat listening to the mob outside and laughing of the Jew's family on the other side of a fretwork screen.

As the sky turned from pink to dark blue, the merchant let down the ladder and climbed to the roof. The moon was full and smouldering fires illuminated the maze of passages below.

He came back down. 'It is bad.'

Dinan didn't expect it to be anything else. 'What could you see?'

'Your mistress's house has been razed to the ground. Its ruins are still smouldering.'

'I have to leave.'

The Jew took a cloak covering a pile of half made garments. 'You must be my slave if we aren't to raise suspicion.'

'I don't want you to take the risk.'

'You would do as much for me. We are all threads in life's loom. Although a greater power throws the shuttle, we make up its warp and weft. Without us civilisation would unravel.'

The man's logic was sounder than Helen Maat's, and put more persuasively, so Dinan agreed to play the slave.

The merchant lit their way with a torch to the ruins of the alchemist's house. They were challenged twice. Both times the soldiers believed the Jew's story about having to perform some religious office that the riot of the day had prevented. There was no curfew and his tribe wasn't on the mob's menu that night, so they were allowed to pass.

Six cavalry soldiers guarded the rubble that had been Helen Maat's house. Their horses watched warily from the other side of the courtyard as the men turned over the debris like shadowy vultures.

The Jew threw up his hands. 'This is no good! You must escape and save yourself.'

'I cannot leave without Helen Maat's body.'

The merchant knew how important a decent burial was to Egyptians of all races. 'She was Greek?'

Dinan nodded. 'As logical as Thales, and as mad an a inbred Ptolemy.'

The Jew pondered for a few seconds. 'The Phoenician

who supplies my cloth needs to catch the early tide.' He pulled Dinan deeper into the cover of the alley and handed him the torch. Using a stick of ink and the back of a receipt, he jotted down a few words, then smeared the ink on his ring and impressed his seal on the note.

Dinan totally forgot that he should have been mourning his companion. 'That's an ingenious writing tool. Helen could make use of something like that.'

The merchant smiled indulgently; he had seen shock cause such amnesiac reactions before. 'An Oriental device, a mixture of wax and ink.'

'How do they blend it?'

'Never mind, never mind.' He tucked the note into Dinan's pouch. 'The ship is berthed at the dock below the temple of Isis and will leave on the high tide at dawn. Look for the horns of Hathor on his sail. Hand the captain that note. Try to reach him in time, with or without your mistress's remains.' The merchant almost added that it was unlikely there would be much left to bury.

Dinan handed back the torch. 'I will wait for you to get away.'

The Jew pulled his cloak about him. 'May your gods be with you and the eye of Ra be avenged on those who slew your mistress.'

Dinan resisted going into what Ra had really been up to. 'And your God with you.' He laid his borrowed cloak over his benefactor's free arm.

The merchant quickly wended his way down the alley, and his torch was soon out of sight.

Now alone, the cold logic Helen had contaminated Dinan's easy-going spirit with started to course through his thoughts. Without the good merchant there to witness a sight that would have persecuted his dreams into his dotage, Dinan was free to show the guards what some alchemists were really made of. When they discovered what that was, they would live with nightmares for the rest of their lives.

Dinan stepped into the glow of the smouldering building like a majestic phantom.

Two soldiers drew their swords, then hesitated at the man's size.

Their companions joined them.

'What do you want, slave?'

Dinan's gleaming eyes opened wide and he pointed to the gutted building. 'My mistress.' Though far from deep, his voice had the resonance of the tomb.

The decurion would have laughed at a lesser mortal making such a bald demand. In this case he thought better of it. 'So you were the magician's slave?' The African looked more like a genie, but the Roman was determined not to lose face. 'You know the penalty for consorting with magicians?'

Dinan's voice became slow, soft and sinister. 'My mistress practised the art of science.'

'Haven't you heard, slave? Science is out of fashion.'

'If she had the powers of a magician, would you have been able to murder her and put our house to the torch?'

'That was the mob.'

'Whom you made no effort to stop.' Dinan seemed to grow larger, like a huge silhouette with a malevolent moon at its back. His tone was now like the scales of a snake rasping against stone. 'But what if she were a magician?'

'She was a magician!' blurted out one of the younger soldiers recruited from superstitious local stock.

Dinan's eyes opened so wide they resembled the lamps glowing from the face of the statue in the temple of Hermanubis. 'Then she must be able to rise from the dead.'

'Only Jesus Christ can do that!' The decurion unsheathed his sword. 'This has gone too far. Get away from here or you will die like your mistress.'

'You'd cut my throat?' whispered Dinan.

The Roman was visibly shaking. 'And burn your remains!' He pointed inside the ruins to the shards of hermetic vessels and a charred skeleton lying amongst the charcoal of the roof beams. 'There is your mistress! The fire was so fierce her rings melted and her bones powder at the touch.'

For one cold, clammy moment Dinan believed the soldier.

It wasn't possible. What would he do without Helen Maat?

While he towered over the men like a massive avenging angel, inside he trembled at the thought of spending eternity alone. 'If you really thought her capable of magic, you would not be standing by the very place where she was murdered. Or were you hoping to find gold. What if she were to rise from the dead like that prophet the rabble pretend to worship?'

'We fear no magic!'

'Then you should.' Dinan slowly raised his hand and pointed to the alchemist's remains.

There was a faint rustling sound.

'Must be rats,' muttered one of the men.

His superior knew better. 'Not in that heat.'

The rustling increased, then carbonised bones clacked together as they pushed their way up through the blackened rubble.

Five of the soldiers stood mesmerised while the local recruit dashed to his horse and rode off before any of his worst nightmares became flesh.

Like a charred mushroom, a small dome rose through the faintly clattering muddle of bone and shattered brick. Two empty eye sockets, a triangular nasal cavity and the hideous grin of the vengeful dead, followed it.

Two more men ran off.

Resembling the head of an uncoiling serpent, the dreadful visage was pushed up by vertebrae as they gathered together all the bones that had once been attached to it. When the skull had reared to human height, it gave an unearthly cackle. The skeleton shuddered and the carbon encrusting it fell away to reveal gleaming white bones. They became flushed by blood as they were fleshed. Eyes appeared in the empty sockets, greying hair grew straight out from the skull in a frizzled halo and, lastly, skin covered the pulsating tangle of muscle and tendon.

Another soldier let his sword clatter to the ground and followed the others.

The decurion and his stalwart companion remained until the Greek woman's malicious lemon eyes stabbed a glare directly at them. With ragged screams they took off in opposite directions, too panicked to mount their horses.

Helen Maat stood listening like a predatory owl while their cries reverberated up and down the narrow alleyways. As they petered away she stepped over the rubble to where Dinan lay in a dead faint. She gave him a hard nudge with her foot.

Dinan, very reluctantly, looked up. He had no idea that she was capable of such a terrifying reincarnation. 'Was that really necessary?'

'There was no point in me appearing until you came back. Where have you been anyway?'

Dinan pulled himself up and cast a more practical glance over the mob's demolition. 'Is there anything left?'

'Don't be a fool. It was stupid of us to come here anyway. The world is beginning to retrogress. It could be centuries before science is studied again.'

Dinan remembered why he was there. 'I've found Kleopatra.'

'Well let's go before the rabble returns.'

'If we're seen, we could lead the mob to her.' Dinan took the receipt from his pouch. 'A trader gave me a note to take to a Phoenician merchant ship. It will leave before dawn and must pass the mouth of the tributary leading to the village.'

'Where is it docked?'

'The temple of Isis.'

'All right, when our business is finished we'll leave Egypt.'

'For where?'

'If Barbarians can knock on the gates of Rome, then so can we.' Helen found some sandals and a linen tunic in one of the horse's saddlebags. She put them on then mounted up as though she had suffered nothing worse than a slight headache.

Dinan failed to see what they had in common with invading Goths. 'So, what's wrong with having a century of peace and quiet for a change?' he muttered.

CHAPTER 21

Dinan and Helen reached the Phoenician ship before dawn. The captain took them to the tributary where they were rowed ashore. Then they watched the Mediterranean breezes carry the merchant out to sea.

Local boatmen ferried the companions to the tributary in a parched landscape shimmering in the morning heat. It was a world the inundation had forgotten - Hapi's revenge for the people deserting the old gods.

In the heat of the rapidly rising sun, they ascended the slope to Kleopatra's sprawling stone house clutching the hillock like a crab with vertigo.

'Odd place,' said Helen.

Dinan was uneasy at the number of discarded retorts, flasks and furnace bricks littering the yard. 'Looks as though she left in a hurry.'

Helen Maat pushed the door open, then stopped dead. 'I don't believe it!' Meaning, she was confronting something that scared even her.

Dinan came up and looked over her shoulder into the room.

A fiery obelisk in the middle of the floor filled it with brilliant light.

'What has she done?'

Helen cautiously entered. 'I'm not sure.'

'Is it something to do with those fire dancers I saw on the river?' Dinan suddenly clutched her arm. 'It's him again!'

'Who?'

'The character on the water!'

'The alchemist is a woman.'

'He wore an Egyptian priest's pectoral and hung in the air like dust. Can't you see him?'

Helen did her best. 'You're imagining things.'

'I saw the flames on the river swallow him.'

Her tone quickly changed. 'Get out Dinan!'

'What?'

'Out!!'

Dinan was half way down the slope before turning to see

if she was following.

Helen hadn't moved. She extended a hand to the pulsating steeple of plasma. 'Where is the papyrus, Kleopatra?'

There was a sound like the roaring of a furnace. It could have been fire laughing.

'What are you?'

The plasma began to ripple.

'Why did you do it? How did you do it?'

There were excited voices outside. Helen remained transfixed. Was this the truth alchemists had been struggling to discover for centuries? More priceless than gold, more desired than enlightenment, and more useless than-

'Helen! Helen!' Dinan suddenly bellowed. 'Soldiers! Come down!'

Believing Kleopatra was going to tell her nothing, the alchemist quickly scooped up a ragged papyrus page laying on the step.

Having already died horribly within the last twenty-four hours, Helen Maat decided not the wait around any longer and darted back down to the agitated boatmen. The soldiers were closing so they had pushed their craft into the reeds from where they could secretly watch.

'What's going on?' demanded Helen.

The headman beckoned her to duck down in his boat and out of sight. 'They say that an order to destroy all alchemists has been issued by the bishops.'

'I've recently encountered it. Why Kleopatra though?'

'They found out that she had conjured up a genie.'

So Dinan hadn't imagined the phantom ancient priest after all.

'You mean Kleopatra was the one to create-?' Helen hesitated. 'No, the genie must have chosen to come to her. Whoever heard of a mortal granting a genie three wishes?'

'Someone in the village must have betrayed her.' The headman gave Dinan a sharp look. 'They say you were here yesterday?'

'I sent him to find Kleopatra.'

'Perhaps you were followed on your way back here?'

'No one saw us go aboard or come ashore.'

The headman gave a thoughtful nod. 'Then, the old one's time might have come.'

'What did Kleopatra's genie look like?'

'An ancient high priest of Amon Ra.'

Dinan felt vindicated. 'There, what did I tell you.'

Helen mused for a few moments. 'Why would an Egyptian high priest be haunting this place?'

'I don't know. He and Kleopatra must have found out...' Dinan sensed the inquisitive gaze of several boatmen and shrugged. 'You know.'

'No.'

'Don't you see? Those fire dancers were trying to swallow him. There's a battle of some sort going on.'

'Perhaps that was what I should have asked her.'

The headman could contain his curiosity no longer. 'What did she say to you?'

'Not much. She had other things on her mind.'

'Other things? What is so important that she refuses to come out?'

'She has progressed beyond incantations and mortal terror.'

The headman broke cover. 'I should warn her that the soldiers are coming.'

Helen pulled him back. 'She's not the one going to get a shock.'

The man turned to Dinan who assumed one of his moonish smiles. The boatmen were beginning to wonder how they had managed to land these odd fish.

'What manner of people are you?' asked their leader.

Helen changed the subject. 'I don't suppose you know where Kleopatra kept her library?' Like all good alchemists, she had probably destroyed the records of her work.

'No one ever went close enough to find out.'

The Roman soldiers were now just above them, surrounding Kleopatra's house and preparing to batter down the door.

'Idiots,' groaned Helen.

'Why?' asked the headman.

'The door's unbolted.'

Lifting the latch was too simple for the Roman soldiers. They used a discarded cast iron crucible to splinter the ancient timbers and several of them tumbled inside.

There was a strange roar like the appreciative gulp of a dragon. Then everything fell silent.

The headman was apprehensive. 'What happened?'

'I don't like to think about it,' murmured Dinan.

'Could they have fallen down a well?'

A centurion began to shout.

'What's he saying?'

'Seems his men have disappeared,' translated Dinan.

Why won't he go inside after them?' The headman stopped as the building started to glow.

Driven back by fierce heat, the soldiers broke formation and, leather armour clattering, ran for their lives. A crowd of religious zealots, keen to see the job through, was coming up to urge them back. They stopped dead when the walls of the building fell open like a huge fiery blossom to reveal the blazing throat of Hell.

The ground sighed. With a rush of hot wind, the unearthly plasma that was once Kleopatra poured down the sides of the hillock like molten sugar. A musty perfume filled the air as the remains of Kleopatra's house melted.

'I bet she drank fig wine,' Dinan murmured to himself.

The zealots who had been pursuing the soldiers were now running before them in panic, back to their boats. The syrupy drift of fiery lava pursued them along the tributary, engulfing them in clouds of scalding steam.

The watchers in the reeds were unscathed, and when everything was at last quiet they furtively slipped out of the reeds. The ground was hot and the rock had vitrified into a glassy sheet. Helen warned the sandal-less boatmen to stay back while she picked her way over the smouldering ground. They knew she was wasting her time. Anything that could melt rock would make short work of papyrus. The alchemist stooped several times to take a closer look but came back empty-handed.

Helen Maat pulled a purse from the folds of her Phoenician mantle and, to Dinan's dismay, handed the boatmen the last of the gold he had carefully stashed away. It was a bonus to the money they would earn for retelling the story of what had happened that morning.

When the men had gone, Dinan put his hands on his hips and vaguely resembled the Colossus of Rhodes. 'Right, now how do we get to Rome without any money?'

Helen strolled away. 'Don't worry about it.'

'We can't fly, you know!' he shouted after her.

Helen smiled then took a page of papyrus from her mantle.

Dinan was unimpressed. 'That's going to buy us meals and lodging for a year?'

'Stop thinking about your stomach. This is more important.'

'What did that crazy woman do then?'

'She discovered the answer to the question I really should have been asking.'

Dinan folded his arms. 'What?'

'Without intending to, she attracted the attention of an entity.'

'You mean the Egyptian priest you don't believe I saw?'

'Possibly.'

'What do you mean, "possibly"? I saved all the money I could have used on alcohol, the whole village saw this genie as well, and why would anyone chose to transmute themselves into a pillar of fire?'

'Because she knew how to do it. Why do mystics sit on columns for decades or penitents flog themselves for crimes they never committed?'

'The only way they can justify their existence?'

'Because they believe it makes them superior.'

'Anyone who turns herself into a pillar of fire is past worrying about her social status.' Dinan looked darkly at the alchemist. 'And don't you dare try it. You've already been incinerated once this week.'

'After Kleopatra, those zealots and Romans will think twice about chasing alchemists for the time being.'

Dinan thought of the cloth merchant. 'They'll probably start on the Jews instead.'

'We still have to get out of Alexandria. We'll not find Ahmose here however long we wait, but there is something I need.'

'What?'

'Kleopatra buried her most valuable equipment.'

'How do you know?'

'She told me.'

'Did she tell you whether there was a wagon and onager to pull it?'

'It won't be that heavy. She destroyed most of her hermetic tools when she realised the truth.'

'The truth?'

'She discovered that not all metals are impure forms of gold.'

'Thought you already knew that?'

'Gold can only be formed at temperatures we cannot comprehend.'

'She managed to reach a pretty unlikely temperature.' Dinan wished he had never been introduced to Hermes and his art. 'Well, it's a long walk to Rome.'

'Oh shut-up!' snapped Helen.

'We're going to need a meal before we get there.'

'Why not try starving to death? That could be even more interesting than me getting my throat cut.'

Dinan shook his large head. 'I shouldn't think so. And how do we pay for our passage?'

'Conjuring tricks.'

Dinan groaned. 'What's on that papyrus?'

'It's in an ancient hieroglyphic code. Looks as though it came from a tomb. It could take centuries to decipher.'

'Just as well we're immortal.'

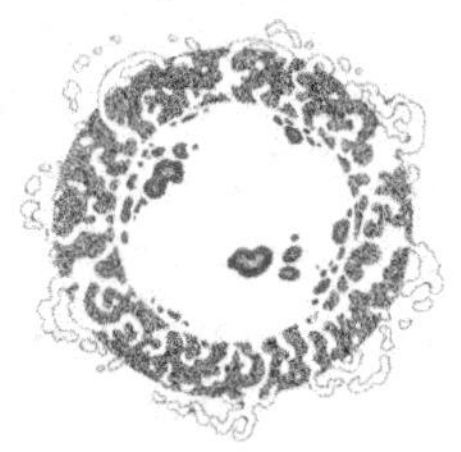

THE SCHOLAR

CHAPTER 22

No longer able to ignore the aches afflicting his fragile bones, Tommaso turned to his travelling companion. 'General, are you sure that this horse benefits from having me ride it?'

Gerard Jorden continued to look straight ahead. 'That animal must be ridden by someone. Too long without a rider and it starts to think for itself.'

Tommaso sighed. 'It must be another scholar and regards me as some unwelcome dogma.'

'Don't feel sorry for the beast, it knows you are the more uncomfortable.'

'I've sat on the cruellest perches in every monastery and library from Venice to Vercelli, but none of them could move at a trot.'

The teenager on the pony beside Tommaso laughed. 'That was just as well Socrates. You wouldn't have learnt much otherwise.'

Duke Vittorio's daughter had a heart shaped face and dense black hair. Her eyebrows were youthfully thick and her figure just filled out from its adolescent frame. Her hazel eyes were similar to her father's but, while his had the milky gaze of a melancholy rat, hers were framed by long lashes and were more like a dormouse's.

With an indulgent smile, Tommaso turned to his charge. 'At last Signorina Laura has managed to laugh.'

She shrugged bravely. Perhaps the rumours hadn't been true, and her suitor wasn't a monster after all. Then Laura burst into tears.

'We must stop,' demanded Tommaso.

General Jorden groaned at what he believed to be delaying tactics and reined his white mare to a halt. His military mind couldn't see any other point in it. He may have been able to control an army, but there was no way he could countermand this scholar without sounding unreasonable. He resented having to escort Duke Vittorio's daughter to Ruggero where her bridegroom waited. He had only agreed to do it because she had no mother to accompany her, and the Duke was afraid of being held hostage. At least the union would prevent a war.

Tommaso dismounted to comfort his pupil. 'You have a heart as hard as those marble Germanic features, General. It's a pity you weren't devoured by a pack of wolves before you blundered your way over the Alps. Though given the climate that spawned you, they are probably all too crippled by the damp.'

'The General is only following orders, Socrates. It's not like you to be so unkind.'

Laura was right. The journey was putting a strain on Tommaso's mild disposition. A tall, slightly built, middle-aged man, he had a soft intelligent smile and was clean-shaven with a profusion of powder grey hair under his large triangular cap. His mouth was too wide and there was something inexplicably blurred about the scholar, as though he was being seen through fine muslin.

The General was in no mood for verbal combat and ordered Matteo, his aide, to bring up the wagon.

Stones cracked under the wheels bearing the weight of the cassone, the great decorated chest that was part of Laura's dowry. General Jorden seemed to have every intention of making the young woman sit on its carved lid the rest of the way to Ruggero.

Tommaso paled with indignation. 'You surely don't intend to travel all night?'

'I'm not going to make camp for the sake of a few tears.'

'Then we shall find somewhere civilised to rest.' Tommaso took the rein of Laura's pony and led it to a fork in the road.

Jorden watched the scholar and his pupil ascend the

overgrown, winding track and raised a hand to stop one of his men following them. 'Let them go. By the time dusk falls they will be less defiant. The track can lead to nowhere but a sheer drop.' He watched sternly until they disappeared from sight before allowing himself a smile; there would have been no point in letting the scholar and his quick-witted charge believe that he was human after all.

Lofty, powerful and not yet brought down by middle age, Gerard Jorden was at a peak he could only topple from. The few concessions this German would make to Italian Renaissance elegance were a small pearl earring, silver velvet doublet - which he seldom wore - and gold belt set with tiger's eye and turquoise, a present from his mistress. Jorden's small moustache, intended to make his blond features appear even firmer, could not conceal the unwelcome humanity encroaching into his expression. Age was bringing truths he preferred to hold off for as long as possible.

* * *

Laura ducked overhanging branches and wondered what was rustling in the undergrowth. 'Why are we going up here Socrates?'

'Sanctuary.'

'In this wilderness?'

'All tracks lead somewhere. Their condition can sometimes tell you who lives at the end of them. In Egypt, as Coptic monks walk the bleached desert, they remove each stone from their path.'

'They must have tidy minds?'

'It is part of their contemplation.'

Something glinted in the verge. Tommaso stooped to pluck a long, golden feather from the leaf litter. Laura's eyes lit up and she held out her hand. He gave a small laugh and passed it to her.

The heiress tucked the plume into the ribbons braiding her hair. 'What muddled hermit lives at the end of this path, Socrates?'

'A priest, and not a lowly one.'

'How do you know?'

'His Greek is better than mine.'

'Who lives with him then?'

'A notary.'

The feather's reflection gleamed on Laura's cheeks. 'A notary?' She smiled. 'How do you know he understands Greek?'

'I read the notice by the fork in the road.'

'I thought that was an Etruscan sign post?'

'Shame on you.'

'Be careful. The brambles are snagging your gown. Our German General may not understand Greek any better than I do, but Matteo is shrewd and may be following us.'

'He has spent too long holding conversations with his daggers to be interested in tamer dialects.'

Laura shuddered at the lengthening shadows. 'I wish he were here with them now.'

'Don't you trust me, little finch?'

'Of course I do Socrates, but wit cannot repel bandits.'

Tommaso fell silent for some while. 'I haven't been much use to you, have I princess?'

'My father had no choice over this marriage. With Via La Rosa in rebellion he cannot afford a war with another neighbour, especially Count Paolo... The boy is still an oaf, though.'

'You can refuse to consent to the marriage.'

'Oh Socrates, you have been living in books too long. To a fifteen-year-old that law is mere illumination, not meant to be taken seriously.'

'It is the law which marries you against your will.'

'What can I do about it?'

'I would do anything you asked.'

'You are a sentimental old owl, Socrates.' Laura smiled to herself. 'If such injustices can be both imposed and opposed by the same law, then perhaps they can be thwarted just as legally.'

'What are you thinking, princess?'

'It would be worth doing it just to see the expression on our General's proud face.' She laughed. 'How can such a handsome man have such a steely heart?'

'It was probably forged by some Nordic trolls at the bottom of a deep, dark fjord.'

'The man's sarcasm can penetrate like a driving blizzard.'

'The ghosts of his ancestors are probably still howling amongst the dank, dismal forests of gnarled trees full of monstrous bats.'

'You have been there, haven't you Socrates?'

'When I had the youthful strength to climb those mountains.'

'With Hannibal?'

'I'm not that old, precious minx.'

'I didn't mean it Socrates.' Laura reached out to remove his large cap and ran her fingers through his tousled hair. 'Do you think our priest and notary will be friendly?'

'I'll try to impress them with my Greek and they might give us shelter for the night.'

'Only one night?'

Tommaso recognised the tone in her voice. 'What are you plotting, pretty witch?'

Satisfied that there was no other path down from the hillside, General Jorden stationed two men at the fork in the road, then went on ahead into the valley with Matteo and the wagon. They came to a rambling villa. Part of it looked as though it had been brought down by an earth tremor and what remained looked as though been designed for a more southerly climate.

Matteo spurred his horse on into the valley to check that the General was not riding into an ambush.

A large African suddenly stepped from the villa's partly fallen loggia. His costume was as rich as any Italian noble's and his round features wore the expression of an alien moon. A silver girdle held a long scallop edged gown to his ample proportions and a golden neck chain set with garnets and rubies was pinned to pearl shoulder tabs. The heavy embroidery and mismatched jewellery indicated such bad taste, Matteo assumed the man to be a servant. His horse came to an abrupt halt, also unable to make out the stranger.

General Jorden caught up. 'Signore.' He nodded stiffly, half expecting the African to be Hannibal's ghost.

'General,' the man acknowledged in a voice unusually light for such a large frame.

'You know me?'

'Your reputation is no secret, General Jorden. We passed by the camp where your troops are being recruited.'

'I haven't seen them yet. How do they look?'

'I think your paymaster has an economical outlook as far as warfare is concerned.'

Jorden silently groaned. At least Laura's marriage would save him from a battle on a more dangerous front. After a night in the brambles with bats, mice and her tutor, at she'd appreciate the comforts it would bring.

'May I know your name, Signore?' the General asked.

'Dinan.'

'We need lodging for the night.'

Before Dinan could answer, a woman's husky voice rang

out from a high balcony. 'Have they got any salt?'

'I have half a quintal in the wagon, Signora,' called Matteo.

'Good. They can stay.'

Dinan led them to a white walled yard with a stable large enough to accommodate ten horses.

The habitable part of the villa had been made comfortable with furniture and wall hangings to stop the worst draughts. Smoke mingled with cordite fumes reminded Jorden of stale battlefield. Dinan explained that this was because his companion experimented with heat. They had been expelled from several towns because of the explosions, so had acquired the remote villa.

Jorden was curious. 'Why heat?'

Dinan's face clouded with disapproval. 'She wants to mimic the sun, General.'

Jorden and his aide glanced at each other, but said nothing.

'She needs the salt to control the fire.'

Matteo went to the wagon and returned with the pouch of ground salt. Dinan tipped some of it into a bowl and handed it back.

Jorden's curiosity got the better of him and he asked why she wanted to mimic the sun.

'She's mad. All scholars are mad.'

The soldier knew the problem.

After leaving the wagon driver with bread, a jug of wine and lamp to guard the cassone in the stables, Dinan led Jorden and his aide to a room well away from the fumes. It had two beds with dry mattresses, and was out of the cutting edge of the wind that whistled through the valley.

As dusk fell, the soldiers sat with Dinan in the main hall, listening to the muffled curses coming from above.

'I used to help her at one time,' explained Dinan. 'Now it all seems pointless.'

As the candle flames flickered eerie shadows into life, the visitors wondered what magic the sorceress above was working. Matteo was deeply religious, yet didn't want to give offence by asking. The General was a natural sceptic and ordered his imagination back to barracks.

At last the weary tread of the sun maker descended the stairs.

A chunk of smelted steel suddenly landed on the table before the men. Jorden just managed to stop himself from jumping. The metal instantly fascinated Matteo.

The magician was a middle-aged woman dressed in elaborate skirts hazardous near any fire. For all its crevices, the face was strangely magnetic, her eyes bulging slightly to give them a faintly manic expression. The skin had been weathered into a patina any master tanner would have been hard put to replicate and the veins in the woman's sinewy hands stood out like blue knots. Jorden tried not to be intimidated by her appearance, made grotesque by the gleam of the candlelight. In it he saw the regiment that would not take orders and the oracle capable of peering through the armour of his soul.

Matteo had no such qualms. 'This is the best quality metal I have ever seen, Signora.'

'No better than what they can produce in the Orient,' Helen Maat rasped.

'You surely don't have a furnace capable of smelting this upstairs?'

'It's in the basement. I lower the material in a closed crucible to avoid corruption from soot.'

'But fire would help harden the metal. At the temperature you must have reached, you could create an edge capable of cutting through brick. What do you think General?'

'I do not engage in combat with brick.'

From what Helen had seen of his soldiers, the General was about to acquire an army of them. 'Why didn't you follow the fashion and raise your own mercenary battalion to hire out?' She slumped into a chair and poured some wine.

'I have no head for economics or languages, Signora. If it were not for Duke Vittorio, I would probably be a woodcutter.'

'The General's accomplishments are so great he often has

to compensate by denigrating them,' explained Matteo.

'Self mockery sits uncomfortably on that stern brow.'

Jorden felt ridiculous at being flattered by her derision. 'The Duke cannot retain a standing army or hire a ready made one. Normally I only have forty men under my command.'

The thugs and buffoons now being recruited were inexpensive and only need look intimidating. Mostly lawyers, shopkeepers and peasants inhabited the town they had to occupy. Lame goats could breach the walls and, however well a person could handle a hoe, they were no match for an idiot armed with a crossbow.

Helen threw back her wine in one gulp. 'I suspect that you are not a true warrior at heart, General.'

To Matteo, there could have been few worse insults. 'Why not?'

'He thinks too much for a soldier.'

Gerard Jorden realised that the alchemist was right.

'Though perhaps I can see ruthlessness trying to perch on those blond features,' the Alchemist added.

Jorden sneered.' I am no scholar,'

'Bend a little, General, before fate bring up its knee and lays your pride low.' Helen Maat always started arguments when the day's work hadn't gone well.

After downing his fifth goblet of wine, Dinan rubbed his eyes and stretched, then he went out to bring in some polenta, cheese and wine.

At the sight of the food Jorden felt a pang of guilt, albeit a small one, as he imagined his young charge sitting in the darkness while her tutor vainly tried to light a fire to keep them warm. It didn't prevent the General from sleeping well that night, though.

He slept so well, he missed the arrival of the runaways and the pony the next morning, only waking when he heard a celebration below. Half dressed, he charged down to see Matteo, his three soldiers, Dinan and Helen assembled about the couple.

Looking as though she had just discovered the philosopher's stone, the Greek had been taken with Laura's open expression and warm smile. Dinan was holding a gown that might have once been Helen's. Even if the garment still fitted her, the golden drops encrusting the sleeves would have made her look like an old goblet of brandy being spilt.

Tommaso wasn't happy about Laura's gift. It must have been worth a prince's ransom.

Helen insisted that if Dinan wanted her to have it, they had to indulge him. The gown needed an ivory complexion to set it off. Hers was now more like old bone buried by a dog.

'How can the child understand the virtue of poverty if such gifts are given without reason?' protested Tommaso.

'There is no virtue in poverty, and Dinan has his reasons, though he never tells anyone what they are.'

Relieved that the couple hadn't come to grief, Jorden was nevertheless annoyed that they appeared well fed and rested. 'So you decided to come back.'

Tommaso was his normally serene self. 'General, why do you always state the obvious when you are annoyed? Of course, we could have died of exposure or been eaten by bears. That probably wouldn't have suited you either.'

Laura giggled mischievously. 'The only thing that suits the General is his hose.'

Jorden realised that he was revealing more than was decent for a German with his well-formed physique and hastily freed the shirt caught up in his waistband so it covered him from salacious female glances.

'Shame on you child! If you must notice a man's loins you should keep it to yourself.' There was a tinge of possessive disapproval in Tommaso's tone.

Helen chuckled. She had to admit that they kept the rest of him up pretty well and cast an appreciative glance. She was surprised to see a spark of jealousy enter Dinan's expression.

Now embarrassed as well as annoyed, Jorden wasn't in the mood for any more scrutiny of his anatomy. He would have made a dignified exit, but noticed that Laura had the confident air of a vixen who had just caught her supper.

'Why are you two partridges looking so pleased with yourselves?'

The three soldiers discreetly sidled from the room and Matteo started to clear the platters from the table.

That convinced Jorden something was wrong. 'By your brave manner, anyone would think you are planning to run off together?'

Helen chuckled. 'Oh, they did better than that.'

Jorden's manner became threatening. 'I'm not in the mood for mysteries, clerk.'

Laura put her arms about Tommaso's waist and Matteo hid the short whip tucked in his belt inside an amphora.

Tommaso gently disengaged himself from Laura and moved protectively before her. 'Please get dressed, General. Or at least fasten your shirt. I want my bride to witness the male body by tasteful degrees.'

Jorden had already fastened two ties before realising what the man had said.

'Your what?'

'The priest who gave us lodging for the night married us.'

Tommaso had made the news sound as reasonable as he could, but the announcement so shook Jorden, he sent the scholar spinning across the hall with a blow from the back of his hand.

Suddenly a spitting lynx confronted the General. Less than two hours exposure to Helen Maat had shown the sweet, innocent child bride everything Tommaso had been unable to teach her in seven years.

'Leave him alone you iron-brained martinet!'

'Step aside child.'

'I'm not even a child to you! I'm just the dowry that will save you and your pathetic soldiers from fighting another stupid war! You are nothing but a killing machine hired by a man who keeps you like a common prostitute! Our marriage is legal! We have witnessed documents to prove it, so you can rage all you want!'

Not even Jorden could answer that. He scowled. 'So what do I tell Count Paolo when I reach Ruggero?'

Helen had lost the ability to feign innocence centuries

ago. 'Hand over the dowry, General, and let them go.'

Jorden read the lines in her expression, and realised who was responsible for teaching the girl to draw her claws. 'Hand over the dowry!'

'I'm sure Duke Vittorio won't mind. After all, if he was willing to marry his daughter to a congenital oaf, he would hardly be bothered if she spent the next thirty years sleeping in bracken and living off nettle soup.'

'Damn you woman!' Jorden would have made a lunge at Tommaso if Dinan hadn't lifted the scholar aside and stood between them like the Apennines. 'I have to talk to the man alone.' The surrounding expressions told Jorden that prospect was very unlikely, so he took a deep breath and swallowed his rage. 'I won't touch him.'

Helen looked at Dinan, Dinan looked at Laura, and Laura glowered at the General.

'Matteo will stay,' he conceded.

This seemed to reassure everyone except Tommaso. Despite that, Helen, Dinan and Laura left the hall with the scholar feeling as secure as a Roman dormouse waiting for the chef.

Jorden pointed to a chair by the table. 'Sit down.'

Tommaso obeyed and took the wine Matteo handed him.

Jorden threw out his arms and spun round. The voluminous sleeves of his shirt flared out like the wings of a swooping owl. 'Well, dear Socrates, so you're a married man after all these years!'

The wine gave Tommaso a little strength. 'I've never been proposed to before.'

'So it was her idea?'

'How could I have refused?'

'You could have remembered your age. You've been living with musty volumes so long you're beginning to look like a brittle page, clerk.'

It didn't occur to the scholar to point out that he wasn't that much older than the General. 'I was young once, Gerard.'

'Why didn't you launch out on these ridiculous escapades years ago then?'

'How do you know I wasn't capable?'

'Because you would have had to spend twenty years studying how to go about it. Should fifteen marry fifty?'

'Desperation can make the sensible do drastic things.'

'So, you regret it?'

Tommaso fingered the marriage contract tucked in his gown. He knew Jorden was going to bully him into tearing it up. 'No.'

'Do you know what could happen to you?'

Tommaso felt his resolve withering under the man's icy glare. It was the one usually reserved for the Duke's treasurer when he needed him to open the coffers and pay his troops. The scholar attempted to appeal to the man's burgeoning humanity with a smile, but it would take more than a flicker of his facial muscles to persuade the soldier.

'No, I'm not going to let you two run off together then pretend you were devoured by wolves. Too many men could die if this alliance isn't sealed.'

Tommaso could no longer stand the man's callousness. 'Is that the fault of an innocent girl? You warmongers choose to kill each other. Your way, she would be devoured, slowly, hideously, in the process of creating more brutes like the man you would have her married to!'

Jorden perched on the table and looked down at him. 'Yes, Paolo's family are usurping tyrants and assassins, and they wouldn't have the slightest compunction about disposing of you.'

'You cannot compel the child into a marriage she doesn't want. That is the law.'

'Then she will have to learn to like a convent.' Jorden's voice mellowed a little. 'Why didn't you escape when you had the chance?'

Tommaso hung his head. It now seemed like a sensible idea.

'You thought the law would be protection enough didn't you? Don't you realise that I could wring your wretched neck here and now, scholar? There is no law where politics and power are involved.'

Tommaso involuntarily touched the bruise on his jaw.

There could be no understanding between might and mind as long as one did not edge a little closer. He had no might on any level, though Jorden did have a mind.

The soldier sat at the table to face Tommaso and laid his hand over the scholar's. 'I cannot let you go. But, if you help me, I swear no one will harm you.'

'I'll not desert Laura.'

'She is using you.'

'Only because she is being used.'

'What do you expect me to do?'

Tommaso thought carefully for a moment. 'Take me to Ruggero and let Laura go.'

Jorden shook his head. He could never protect the scholar there. Count Paolo might kill him mercifully. However, from what he knew of his court, their entertainments had a direct descent from the Caesars. That stuffed mind of Tommaso's couldn't stand brutality. He'd faint at the sight of someone else's blood. There was no such escape from seeing his own entrails.

'Why persist in this silly scheme? She's making a fool of you.'

'Don't bully me Gerard. I've made up my mind.'

Jorden rose angrily. He struck the table with such force Tommaso's goblet leapt from it. 'All right! May they throw you to the wolves!'

At that moment Tommaso believed that most of them would have been related to the soldier.

'They can flog you to death for all I care and hurl that stupid girl down a well.'

Tommaso caught Jorden's shirt before he could storm out. 'Have you never been in love Gerard?'

Jorden slowly turned back in disbelief. 'You fool. You old besotted fool!'

'No, you've never truly loved anyone or been loved.'

'Do you believe she loves you?'

Tommaso swallowed hard. 'I believe she does.'

The General pulled his shirt free. Was this the mind the Duke consulted when all other advice failed him? Was this the brain that could comprehend the Universe?

The scholar gazed steadily at the soldier. 'I pity you Gerard. You are not a hard man, just have to pretend so much for the world to believe it. Even Matteo is convinced by this mythology you have woven for yourself. You and I know differently.'

'Your artful manipulations will not work on me.'

'Take care Gerard. However horrible my fate, your's will be far worse.'

The General had heard it all before. 'I will allow you and your bride one day together, under guard.' Then he left.

Matteo picked up the goblet from the floor. 'I'm sorry Signore.'

'Do you understand, Matteo?'

'No Signore. The General is a good man and soldiering is the only living I've ever had. I have reared a family on its proceeds, and -' He stopped.

'And the scholar hasn't?'

'I'm sorry, Signore. I understand none of this.'

'God help Gerard then.'

'Why?'

'Because you are his only friend.'

Dinan hauled up the weighty crucible and started to chip out Helen's experiment of the day before. The head of the flue was in the centre of the room. Above it, where the plaster had cracked and fallen away long ago, was a huge sooty patch caused by intense heat hitting the rafters. There was no chimney because the downdraught would have interfered with the stable temperature she was trying to create. The furnace in the cellar warmed the rooms surrounding its patchwork chimney, not always during the right season. Fortunately the villa had no windows, only shutters so the heat was easily dissipated.

When smoke escaped at the top of the flue, Helen came down looking and smelling like a smouldering tapestry. The cloak she kept to protect her clothes was usually tossed over the hermetic flasks, retorts and alembics. They were only useful for distillations that required much lower temperatures.

The alchemist's precious lenses and mirrors, created by specialists mindlessly grinding away at glass blanks in clouds of lethal dust, had been carefully wrapped and stored away. There had been no point in setting up the equipment near the villa. The wind through the valley was fierce and the shadows too long. What Helen Maat needed was an arena, a pool of level sunlit ground sheltered from cooling breezes, preferably in an isolated place where the local population wouldn't think she was trying to raise the Devil.

As well as stacking the valuable scrolls and books where they were least likely to be fire damaged, Dinan tried to keep the Hermetic equipment out of Helen's path. The alchemist had seen little point in hanging onto the fragile glass and pottery, and the books and scrolls told her nothing she hadn't already found out for herself. But Dinan was sentimental. Whenever they were condemned as alchemists, he liked to play the part, much preferring to be hanged as a heretical scoundrel than innocent lamb. It was wonderful to see the mob's dread when they came back to life and walked away, guards and clergy alike, too terrified to stop them. Not many inquisitors who demanded their victims to be misguided and contrite were able to recover their composure after that. As they had never executed a genuine magician, it came as quite a surprise when they got it right. If the God fearing Matteo had peered into the smoke damaged room upstairs, his Christian convictions would have compelled him to flee the villa, with or without his rational German General.

Helen stood looking out at the oddly matched couple below. 'They really are in love, you know. You wouldn't think that there was thirty-five years between them.'

Dinan was surprised at his companion's romantic expression.

Perhaps the expression hadn't been romantic after all. 'I want that man's brain.'

'That's body stealing. Anyway, he belongs to the girl.'

'He must know the contents of every library between the Alps and Apennines.'

'Oh, an index on two legs.' Dinan wiped his hands and joined her. 'Doesn't look as though he's got books on his mind at the moment.'

'You can see he's infatuated. He hardly dare touch her.'

'And the General doesn't look very happy about it.'

'I can't see why. A good-looking man like that must have had the pick of all the women he ever wanted. Do you remember the brothel used by those crumpled courtiers at Count Paolo's palace?'

'The one that sold you the lead?'

'They had a girl there who looked just like Laura. She was called Maddalena.'

'I remember.'

Helen obviously had the mischievous thought that it might placate General Jorden if they were introduced.

Dinan knew that his problems weren't carnal. 'You never notice that much about people, do you? You've spent so much time waging your one-sided battle with existence, you've forgotten you're human.'

'So, you want to go on living forever? If we ever see

Ahmose again, what do I tell him? We found some good investments?'

'It'll be centuries before the equipment you need is invented.'

'With the help of that man's mind, perhaps not.' But there were others who already had claims on his body.

Helen thoughtfully scratched her chin. 'We'll have to help him.'

Dinan stepped back, palms raised in protest. 'Oh no. No, no, no. I'm not getting myself hanged, shot or mangled any more. You do some dying for a change.'

'There won't be any need.'

'I don't like it when you sound this confident.'

'We've got to do something. Paolo's family has the sort of reputation that would have kept Attila away from Ruggero.'

Dinan gave in. 'All right, as long as you promise to save Laura as well.'

'Why shouldn't I? I like the girl, and she seems bright enough to be useful. We'll follow them. Pack everything and we'll collect it on the way back.' Helen pulled her cloak from under a pelican alembic that was sent spinning across the floor.

Dinan just managed to save the valuable glass before it lost its beak. 'We won't get inside the palace.'

'That's all right, the place teams with spies.'

'What are you going to do?'

'I'm not sure, I've got several ideas.'

'Only several?' Dinan went back to chip at the crucible.

CHAPTER 25

Under the Arctic glare of General Jorden, Laura and Tommaso spent their last few hours together talking desperate inanities. The breeze was laden with the late afternoon scent of the valley's flowers trying to break the scholar's resolve to hide his true feelings.

'How many wings has a dragonfly?' he asked his pupil.

'I can't remember.'

'Colours in the rainbow?'

'Not enough.'

'Who preceded Augustus?' He changed his mind. 'No, who declared he was a god?'

'Wasn't he the one who married a horse?'

Tommaso didn't want their last conversation to bolt down that road. 'How many crystal spheres hold up the heavens?'

'I don't want to talk about astronomy. You'll never be able to fly there, you know.'

'How many angels can dance on the head of a pin?'

'Stop being foolish, Socrates.'

'I want to believe that I taught you something.'

'What colour are my eyes?'

'Which one?'

'Stop teasing.'

'Why marry a scholar if he can't teach you anything?'

'I love you, Tommaso.'

'Most bees avoid flowers when their stamens have shrivelled.'

'Have your's then, Socrates?'

Tommaso blushed. 'I didn't mean the metaphor in that sense.'

'You are still able then?'

'What would your father's opinion be of me if he found out that you had such thoughts?'

'He would know I could never have learnt them from you?'

Tommaso hesitated as the fortress of his self-esteem tried to close its gates from further attack. 'The General's glare is more icy than usual.'

'He can't hear what we say. Would it matter if he could?'

'Our priest and notary did promise to swear we were legally married if Count Paolo needed confirmation.'

Laura knew it would have been unreasonable to demand that the old men make such a testimony before a gathering of basilisks who wanted proof to the contrary. 'I think a dragonfly has six wings.'

'You have brown eyes, though one is slightly greener than the other. Probably because you always read with the candle on that side.'

'I really do love you Tommaso.'

The scholar seemed on the verge of petulance. 'Don't be foolish.'

'I would do anything to prove it.'

'All girls your age develop infatuations. I even heard of one falling in love with a picture.'

'How do you know anything about girls my age?'

'I read about them somewhere.'

'How can I prove it?'

'Prove what?'

'I love you.'

'You can't.'

'Let me hug you.'

'No. Remember what we agreed.'

'But we're married.'

'I don't think Gerard would be very amused.'

'Gerard? Does the General allow you to call him by his first name?'

'I am the older, so it is permitted.'

'I thought only his mistresses were allowed to do that?'

'They call him Signore.' Tommaso sat on the wall of a boarded up well.

Laura removed his triangular cap, blew several strands of unruly hair from his face then kissed his forehead. She assumed that he never returned her embrace because scholars didn't do that sort of thing. But she would always love her Socrates, even though he thought she was a stupid, immature girl. Laura raised his head. She wanted to remember every detail of his middle-aged, silly face. When she had to spend months embroidering an altar cloth or praying in front of some painted wooden effigy, she would see nothing but that fine nose and chin, wavy grey hair and large sarcastic mouth. No one could rob her of that. She could love him however much she liked in her thoughts.

Then Laura looked up and saw General Jorden.

'That's enough,' he said.

Laura gripped Tommaso so tightly he would have had to break her fingers to make her release him. 'The sun hasn't set.'

'I'm tired,' Tommaso gently told her. 'I am an old man, you know.'

'Poor Socrates. Let me help you inside.'

'No. You go in. The General has something to say to me.'

Laura glowered in warning at the soldier, then went into the villa.

Tommaso pitched sideways. It was fortunate the well was boarded up.

Jorden's iron grip steadied him. 'The Greek wants to talk to you.'

There was something in the man's eyes that spoke of pity and envy at the same time.

'Give me a few moments.'

'Don't you feel exhilarated to be loved by a fifteen-year-old?'

'I'd sooner be whipped.'

Helen approached carrying a goblet.

'What's that?' demanded Jorden. 'The antidote to the love potion you fed him?'

'Something to calm the prisoner's senses.' She sat beside Tommaso and held the goblet to his lips. 'This will help clear your thoughts.'

The scholar had never tasted an infusion like it before and the drink was refreshing. 'Thank you.' He looked into the alchemist's strong features. They carried more lines of experience than was natural for one lifetime and should have been at the prow of Jason's ship. 'You have been kind to us Signora.'

'I like beautiful young things, and older wise ones.'

'If I were wise, I would not be spending the night under lock and key.'

'General, how could you?'

'I want my men to get all the sleep they can, not have to stay awake guarding a love sick catalogue.'

'Surely you need someone to watch the dowry?'

'There is no need Signora,' Jorden said enigmatically.

'It is strapped to the General's body,' whispered Tommaso.

'I hope the company it's compelled to keep doesn't devalue it.'

'The General can be a terrible person when mocked.'

'So can a baboon.'

'Is this all you have to say to the clerk? Perhaps you would like to slander my horse as well?'

'Given the part of your anatomy she is most acquainted with, she must already feel adequately insulted.'

Tommaso threw his arms about Helen's neck and laughed into her huge collar.

Unable to take any more of their derision, Jorden moved off a few paces.

'Listen to me Tommaso,' she whispered. 'Dinan and I are going to help you.'

'Help us?'

'You and Laura.'

'How?'

'We can do nothing while the General holds you. He's too shrewd. Just remember, go along with anything I say or do when we meet again.'

'Laura?'

'She'll be safe enough, as long as she knows nothing of this.'

'Why would you do this?'

'I need your mind.'

'My mind?'

'This land floats on manuscripts. I don't know where to start looking for the ones I need, and female scholars are no more welcome in libraries than large male Africans.'

'What are you studying?'

'Heat.'

'Why? For your alchemy?'

'We're trying to give back a gift we never wanted.'

'What gift is that?'

'Immortality.'

Tommaso gave a small giggle; he obviously didn't believe her. 'What about Laura?'

'What about her?'

'When her infatuation wears off, she will want someone younger.'

'Don't think about that. She loves you now.'

'She's a child.'

'She's a woman. Don't underestimate her.'

'She can't even remember how many colours there are in the rainbow.'

'Can you?'

Tommaso shook his head. He was amazed to discover that he had totally forgotten.

'That only proves there are better things to fill the mind with.'

Jorden moved back into earshot. 'What are you two plotting?'

Helen smiled. 'Just how to speed up the Earth's revolution.'

'The Earth revolves-?'

'Only for us. You will soon fall off the edge.'

Duke Vittorio would have sent a more opulent bridal retinue with his daughter, but couldn't compel his courtiers to join it, being in debt to so many of them, so Count Paolo's party was as welcoming as the Black Death. Clad in dark green mantlets, they radiated disapproval at the sight of the soldiers, their General, the scholar, the teenager and her cassone. If this was the way they greeted their heir's bride-to-be, Jorden preferred not to think about what was going to happen when they discovered that there wasn't going to be a wedding.

It didn't help that Laura and Tommaso were far from contrite. Gerard Jorden sometimes wondered if life would be less complicated if he had become a sycophant instead.

From the dismal throng stepped Count Paolo's chamberlain, anachronistically a short, jolly Scotsman with a mild manner. He welcomed the German to Ruggero as though he had anticipated some problem. When it was explained to him, he didn't blame the General for his negligence and grievous insult it would cause Count Paolo. He just regretted he wouldn't be there to intercede when the Count learnt the news about the bride-not-to-be. However worthy, this noble preferred to keep foreigners out of family matters. Perhaps the fact that the General was a German wouldn't count against him too much.

Standing between Tommaso and Laura like a pillar of pale granite, General Jorden explained their deception to Count Paolo and his family.

A large table separated the bridal group from the dour, sinister court Laura had narrowly missed being married into. Its top was an arabesque of pink amethyst and yellow citrine flowers set in a background of jasper and garnet tendrils. The inlaid masterpiece was supported by six pink marble legs with brass claws and seemed out of place in the faded gilt melancholy pervading the palace. Despite the gravity of his situation, Jorden couldn't help wondering, as it was unlikely these robber nobles had commissioned the lapidary, how they had managed to carry it off during one of their frequent raids on their neighbours.

Like their surroundings, most of the Count Paolo's family looked ancient. All that wrinkled flesh clothed in black and dark green velvet reminded the General of the time he had marched through a town inhabited only by the husks of the plague dead. The disappointed bridegroom was of course present, though obediently quiet. Laura knew that was because he would only reveal what a fool he was as soon as he opened his mouth. The rest of the younger men were probably off fighting somewhere.

Tommaso gazed dreamily out of a half shuttered window and counted pine trees while Laura looked with enough contempt at her jilted betrothed to make him glad he wouldn't have to take her on.

The gnarled hand of Count Paolo reached out for the marriage contract Matteo offered. 'This is your proof?'

'I have spoken to the priest and notary who witnessed it and am satisfied it is genuine. Unfortunately they couldn't testify themselves, as they had to leave the region,' Jorden lied. 'You might be able to challenge it over the matter of parental consent.'

The old man frowned thoughtfully. The disparity in the couple's ages and Jorden's watchful eye would have made it unlikely the marriage had been consummated but, in his estimation, the girl was still spoiled goods.

'The Duke only has one daughter?' The edge in Count Paolo's voice was like the creaking of a tomb gate.

The noble already knew that and the General felt uneasy. It sounded as though he was ploughing new furrows in the hope of still finding gold.

'There are two nieces, both betrothed, four sisters of the Duke, two widowed-'

The Count's hand, which appeared to be hinged for the purpose, was suddenly raised. Jorden stopped.

The glittering gaze turned on Tommaso. 'We have no objection to our child marrying a widow.'

'The wife of the murdered husband might have something to say about it.' Laura's voice seemed to have gone down an octave. At that rate she would soon be speaking with the smoky tones of the alchemist.

The Count was taken aback by her hostility. 'You do not want to marry this personable young man with the fortune he would bring?' he asked with all the charm employed by the Serpent when enticing Eve.

Laura wasn't old enough to realise he was trying to be reasonable. 'No. And you cannot make me.'

This was a clever child. Her tutor had obviously taught her about more than sex and astronomy.

'Well General, what is your solution?'

Jorden realised that it was more of a threat than question. 'I want to return them to Duke Vittorio.'

'Oh, I'm sure he wouldn't mind them remaining here - with the dowry.'

That was a threat.

'With the dowry?'

'This inconvenience cannot go unrecompensed. Our child must be mortified by the disappointment.'

The mortified brat nodded and lowered his eyes as though about to burst into tears.

The General wished he hadn't been disarmed before entering the presence. 'I can only agree to that on one condition.'

'Name it. We are not unreasonable.'

'You must swear not to harm either of them.'

'I swear.' The old lizard limply raised his hand and dropped it as though the spring had snapped.

Jorden wasn't convinced. 'The Duke may be able to persuade his daughter to retract the marriage.'

'There is a comfortable cell where she can have all the time in the world to think it over. Me, harm a pretty thing like that? Never.'

'Her tutor?'

The old man half closed his eyes.

Jorden tried to conceal his growing frustration. 'He is a frail specimen, yet highly regarded by many scholars. He could serve you well.'

'Would you serve me well, scholar?'

Tommaso knew that he hadn't fallen into a den of

intellectuals. 'That depends on the needs of your court.'

Count Paolo was like a weasel menacing a mouse. 'You will not see your pupil again, of course, but I think I have just the place for you.'

'No harm must come to him, Signore.' The General knew he was powerless to do anything if it did. He pulled off the belt lying over his shoulder and tipped a handful of pearls from its pouches onto the inlaid tabletop. They looked like dewdrops lost in a meadow of flowers.

Count Paolo scratched his nose.

'Is something wrong, Signore?'

'No, no, they are very fine. It is a shame we will never see the bride wear them. The nuns are strict when it comes to ornaments.' He looked up. 'Will you be staying in Ruggero, General?'

'I have to rendezvous with my troops.'

The Count smiled. Without a rebellious town to suppress, it was unlikely Duke Vittorio would have sent his beloved daughter to such a fate. 'Well,' the gnarled hands parted in false gratitude, 'Go in peace General.'

Jorden felt dismissed. What could he and some ragtag army do if the family did decide to murder Tommaso and Laura?

As he left, several large women with pelican smiles bustled Laura away. Numb, though not sure why, Tommaso watched them go. When he turned back, two guards wearing half armour and the turned down smiles of vultures were waiting to collect him.

'I'm sorry, scholar.' Count Paolo shrugged. 'My court has little interest in the sciences.'

'Your promise to the General...?'

'That German is the only strength Duke Vittorio has. He would make a profitable hostage were we given provocation.'

'You would detain General Jorden?'

The Count could have ransomed him if he thought his employer would pay, but the Duke would merely borrow the money to buy another general. He loved his pretty ornaments and marble statues too well to trade them for a tarnished soldier. It might be more convenient if the General met with an accident. Tommaso knew what he was thinking and the Count laughed at his appalled expression.

'We have the Duke's daughter. That is enough.'

The scholar felt panic rise in the pit of his stomach. 'Don't harm her.'

'She will be safer here than in the hands of her father.' The Count pointed at a distant door. 'Take our scholar to meet Guiseppe.' Then he lost interest in Tommaso and instructed a servant to arrange the pearls in a casket so the family could view them.

CHAPTER 27

The scruffy infant weighed the alchemist's ducats in her hand. 'The guard told my sister that the girl has been taken to the convent of St Beatrice.'

Helen tried to reach an itch through her taffeta sleeve; even the city walls seemed to be lousy with lice. 'That's a closed order.'

'They come out every Sunday and Tuesday to pray in the chapel of St Stepheno under the old fortress wall.'

'All of them?'

'All of them. Three sisters were cured by a miracle there ten years ago. Its spring water is supposed to be holy.'

Helen pondered for a while. 'How high is the fortress wall?'

'Not high. The cliff above it is.'

'I'm not doing it,' Dinan muttered.

The real cause for his complaint didn't occur, even to this worldly-wise child. 'Oh, it's easy to climb.'

'What about the scholar?' Helen asked.

Isabella shrugged. The guard didn't know. Not many rumours escaped from the dungeons. 'No idea.'

Helen handed her another ducat. 'Remember, if you tell anyone you've met us, your family could be in grave danger.'

The child eagerly took the money and scuttled off like a mouse that had just discovered a new larder.

Dinan yawned. 'What now?'

'Do you remember the way to that brothel?'

'Yes, its Madame offered me a job, y'know. I would have taken it if she hadn't wanted me to wear maroon brocade with yellow ribbons.'

Helen had stopped paying attention to his attempts to annoy her long ago. 'I'll meet you there this evening. Don't let her fill you with drink.'

Dinan still hadn't learnt to feign indifference. 'Where are you going?'

'I have a little forgery to commit.'

CHAPTER 28

'Are you being fed?' Gerard Jorden asked.

Tommaso looked at him blandly, without any trace of accusation. It was obvious that the General was beginning to wish he had allowed the couple to run off after all.

The scholar answered in German. 'Yes.'

Jorden hesitated, then continued in Italian. 'Your quarters are clean?'

'Yes.'

'They haven't beat you?'

'No.'

This apparent lack of ill treatment appeared to annoy the General. 'There must be something that doesn't meet with your approval?'

'The bed is a little hard,' conceded Tommaso.

In guilty rage, Jorden seized the scholar's shoulders and shook him. 'Are you lying to me, Tommaso?'

'Please go Gerard.'

'Why?'

'Leave Ruggero as soon as you can.'

'I must know?'

The scholar knew that Count Paolo's family had more tentacles at its head than the Medusa had snakes. However gallant the General's concern, he wasn't a Perseus. Valour was for the troubadour, not a hired soldier.

'Tell me the truth?' demanded Jorden.

'The regularity with which you always discover it too late will be your downfall.'

The soldier had given his word. It wasn't his intention to pluck a scholar from his books and drop him into a lagoon of sharks. 'I'm not here for the benefit of your scholarly advice.'

'You made your decision. There is nothing you can do about it now. When you see Laura, you must tell her I'm well.' Tommaso lowered his voice to a whisper. 'Don't provoke these people, they are more devious than the sphinx. As soon as you've seen Laura you must leave, otherwise you will be slain.'

Jorden slowly released him. 'This flock of assassins

doesn't frighten me. There isn't enough blood in their veins to feed mosquitoes.'

'Then you are a fool.' Tommaso turned to his aide. 'Talk to him Matteo.'

Matteo pointed to a fissure in the chamber wall. It was obvious every word they said could be heard rooms away.

The General reluctantly agreed. 'All right. We'll make sure the girl is safe, then leave.'

Looking to neither left nor right, Jorden swept through the maze of palace corridors so rapidly the guard escorting them had to trot to keep up.

Tommaso spent another day and night pacing and trying to sleep on the stone floor of his dank cell.

It was mid morning when the summons arrived.

Accompanying the boyish featured psychopath, Guiseppe, was the family's chamberlain. The Scot seemed an amiable fellow, and Tommaso fully expected him to smile as he read out his death warrant.

'Are you well, Sir?' the sandy-haired courtier enquired.

Tommaso was unsure what to say. 'Please forgive me Signore, my English is a little weak at the moment.'

'Aye.' The chamberlain reverted to his adopted tongue. 'You haven't been faring too well, have you? This is no way to treat a scholar.'

'Many believe that it is the only way to treat scholars.'

'My man will tidy you up.' The Scot beckoned in an old retainer carrying water and fresh linen.

Tommaso hesitated; convinced he was about to be made presentable for the scaffold.

'There is a visitor to see you.'

'Visitor?'

In the large reception room, Count Paolo sat on the throne purloined from some genuinely noble family. His glittering eyes fixed their gaze on Tommaso as the chamberlain led him in, then glanced at a screen over which the tip of a white headdress was visible. Something seemed to amuse the old man. Not being party to the joke, this alarmed Tommaso all the more.

The old tyrant waved a crumpled parchment before him.

'You like making marriage contracts, scholar?'

Tommaso carefully read it.

Apart from his name, the contract was in Greek. Though able to translate with more speed than most other linguists, fatigue had fuddled his mind and he couldn't make sense of it.

Fortunately Count Paolo took the scholar's intense expression to be one of recognition. He snapped his fingers and a woman stepped from behind the screen. She was dressed in a French surcoat of embossed gold velvet that had huge windows of hell to reveal the tight fitting red gown underneath. On her head was an amazingly tall steeple henin from which floated several yards of finely embroidered muslin. Every hem was either trimmed with jewels or fur. Though splendid, the gothic apparition was incongruously antique.

Then Tommaso realised that he was looking at Helen Maat. He crumpled to the floor in a dead faint.

'Ah ha!' The Count was delighted. 'It seems you have proved your case Signora. Perhaps I should believe my chamberlain once in a while.'

The Scot made a sarcastic half bow.

'So this is your husband?'

'When I left Athens I never thought to see him again.'

'You are wealthy?'

'I believed that to be the reason he married me, until he ran off. But he was only ever in love with books.'

'And you want him back?'

She smiled wickedly. 'He's an old fool. Old fools do stupid things, like marrying fifteen-year-olds.'

'This is a very fortunate coincidence,' the chamberlain observed. 'It means that the girl's marriage is null.'

'If he loves the child so much, we could adopt her.'

'No, no.' The Count creaked a laugh. 'She is my guarantee of a well-behaved neighbour. You must have travelled far to find your scholar, Signora?'

'My agent discovered him some years ago, but I wasn't able to make the journey.'

'Of course.' Avarice sparkled in the reptilian eyes. 'He has caused us no end of inconvenience.'

Helen took a tablet of gold from her pouch. 'Name your price Signore?' She handed it to the chamberlain.

The Scotsman weighed it in his hand and nodded approval.

'Of course,' said Helen, 'I'm sure neither of us want to give him time to rekindle this infatuation.'

* * *

Later that day a small carriage rattled away from Ruggero at axle breaking speed.

A shabby man on a dun coloured horse followed some distance behind. He carried a crossbow inlaid with silver and a purse half full of gold.

CHAPTER 29

Count Paolo's family were confounded by the way Laura quickly settled into the convent's routine, and even agreed to wear the habit of a novice. The nuns weren't surprised. Many of them had also used the order of St Beatrice to escape horrendous marriages and live in cells as comfortable as their noble descent demanded.

The order only ever left the convent to pay their devotions to St Stepheno. It was something of an event and attracted crowds of the devout and those curious to see what effect a life of seclusion had on them. Some envious wives noted that it seemed to do them no harm at all.

St Stepheno's church had been built against a sheer cliff that was part of Ruggero's fortifications. It was over three hundred feet and overlooked the low-lying province. Many a penitent consumed by religious fervour - or too much alcohol - had cast themselves down from the cliff's summit in an attempt to emulate St Stepheno, who it was believed had flown to the tomb of St Beatrice on the other side of the city. Though, owing to a slight hiccup in the historical calendar, some theologians claimed that it must have been St Beatrice who had flown to the church of St Stepheno. The argument over which of them had possessed enough divine infatuation to defy gravity had rumbled on for centuries.

Whatever the holy precedent, when Laura had been obliged to join the sisters who wended their way down to the church every Sunday, someone was at it again.

On the cliff, far above the congregation gathering outside St Stepheno's, a large man stood, arms outstretched, looking more like a monument than a bird. Below, the devout prayed and pleaded, taking care to avoid the markers where so many other misguided souls had spread their limbs.

Laura was more amazed than anyone else was. She recognised the massive dark form and almost called out, 'Dinan!'

With one last look down at the ground that didn't seem

too solid from such a height, the African spread his cloak like a pair of wings and pitched forward off the cliff into the still air that could barely support a gliding swallow.

The panic and prayers reached a crescendo as the large body hurtled down like a badly stacked pile of bricks.

A child's shrill voice screeched over the din. 'He said it wouldn't hurt him! He said it wouldn't hurt him!'

The shock made Laura recall Dinan's gift of the golden dress and she hardly felt someone tap her on the shoulder. Expecting to see a nun instructed to take her away from the sight, there was instead a swarthy girl the same age as herself holding a plain dress and veil.

'Quickly, take that habit off.'

'What?'

'While no one's watching. In this doorway.'

Laura's wits returned. Maddalena pulled the novice's habit over her own clothes and Laura put on the dress.

'Cover your face.'

Laura drew the veil over her mouth and nose.

Suddenly a small hand thrust itself into hers. 'Hello, my name's Isabella. Come with me please.'

'But what about Dinan?'

'He's all right.'

A nun's voice wailed from the melee. 'Laura! Laura! Where are you?'

The impostor quickly made her way into the throng.

Isabella pulled Laura after her. 'This way.'

While the rest of the world milled about St Stepheno's piazza, they darted away from the suicide.

As soon as the girls reached the towering houses of Ruggero's feuding families, the symmetry of the paved streets disappeared. Balconies almost touched across narrow passages and stone walls concealing the villas of the wealthy plunged them into a strange smelling twilight world. Secret alleys opened into slurry-filled courtyards where tethered dogs bayed and the occasional pig snuffled in piles of kitchen waste. From behind shutters eyes watched them pass, but they were not interested in a mere infant and teenage girl. Anywhere else they would have been in danger. Here the hot bloods were more interested in fighting each other than waylaying women and, for all her tender years, Isabella carried a stiletto and pouch of powered pepper - and knew how to use them. Laura daren't imagine what other worlds she had missed because of her closeted upbringing. Given the place she was being taken to, she wouldn't need to.

Isabella and Laura crossed a small bridge leading to a bland three-storied house. On its balconies scantily dressed women were sunning themselves, their hair draped over large discs worn round their brows. A bizarre concoction of many unctions, including urine, was giving their locks a glossy sheen, and no doubt an aroma which, for some reason didn't bother their clients.

A middle-aged woman moving in a lopsided bovine way beckoned Laura inside. Isabella skipped off as though just finishing a satisfying game of hide-and-seek.

The Madame took Laura's hand and led her into a large room lit by small stained glass windows and the open door to a courtyard full of drying sheets and underclothes, many for men. Couches lined the walls of the room and cushions were scattered everywhere as though Isabella and her infant friends had been allowed to run riot. Another outside door had been opened just wide enough to waft away the smell of stale perfume and other musty odours Laura was too inexperienced to identify.

'Don't worry about us Signorina, you'll not need to be here long.' The Madame realised that her guest was trying hard not to notice her limp. 'I was a good worker until I turned down the custom of some noble.' She rapped the cylinder of wood supporting her. 'He cut off my leg.'

Laura's knees gave way and she dropped onto a couch. 'Why?'

'The law does nothing for a prostitute who scorns a client.'

Laura tried to disguise an excited thrill. 'How dreadful!'

So, this was a real house of ill fame occupied by real prostitutes, unlike those strange, elegantly esoteric creatures who drifted about her father's court and tried to persuade her to read Dante.

Her hostess lumbered to a dainty tabletop heavy with valuable glass goblets. 'I understand you are having trouble with some silly laws?'

'No, this is more to do with a noble as well - only I'm not the one in danger.'

The Madame handed her an ornate Venetian goblet filled with wine. 'Never mind about your lover. That Greek is a formidable woman. It would take more than a family of assassins to outsmart her.'

'Then this is the doing of Helen Maat? I wondered when I saw Dinan - But he killed himself?'

The woman shook her head. 'I don't understand either. I reckon they're both magicians myself.'

'And what about the girl who took my place?'

'Maddalena?' The Madame laughed. She was getting paid more than she was worth for it and knew Ruggero's alleyways well enough to lose a pack of hounds. 'She's a fast one. Looks a lot like you.'

'She's taking a dreadful risk.'

Laura closed her eyes and tried not to think of Tommaso.

The woman knew what was on her mind. 'Don't you worry about him my lovely.'

'I shouldn't. He doesn't care anything for me. He thinks I'm too immature to fall in love.'

'Men! They don't mind twelve-year-olds becoming prostitutes, but a woman who knows her own feelings has to be kept in check. More wine?'

'No, no thank you.' Laura handed the goblet back before she dropped it. 'Tommaso isn't heartless like other men. I couldn't love someone like that stuffed General Jorden, however handsome he is.'

'Yes.' The Madame sighed. 'That General is certainly a handsome man, and well equipped.'

Laura was puzzled. 'If he is so desirable, why does he have to be jealous of Tommaso?'

The older woman gave a smile of surprised delight. 'What? Of your scholar? I don't believe it.'

'He needn't have handed him over to that flock of blood

sucking bats.'

'He might be jealous because he thinks you're loving the wrong person. Men, my dear, men.'

The street door suddenly flew open and a novice nun's habit flew into the room as though a tornado was inside it.

'Dear Jesus!' gasped Maddalena. 'Sister, they must have thought a lot of you!' She dropped onto a cushion beside her mistress who handed her a drink, then limped over to close the door.

'Did they see you come here?'

'I lost them outside the farrier's.' Maddalena gulped down the wine.

Laura rose apprehensively. 'Shouldn't I go in case they search the street?'

'God no. Sit down,' the Madame told her. 'Some of our clients prefer their names not to be dropped into the Church's confessional boxes.'

'We have some very particular gentlemen visit us,' Maddalena chortled derisively.

It was the only way women like them could hold power in this world. They could love and suffer for it all they liked, yet were careful to girdle their hearts with steel before entrusting them to anyone.

Maddalena laughed. 'Jesus! That African must be made of steel!'

'What happened?' Laura asked anxiously.

'He got up.'

'What?'

'He fell three hundred feet, hit the flagstones like a limp rag, lay there for a few moments - then got up!'

Laura went pale.

'Wretched little liar!' The Madame cuffed Maddalena's ear.

'He got up I tell you! There was pandemonium. I'd never have escaped if he hadn't. It was declared a miracle.'

Laura was near to tears. 'Please don't joke, he was such a dear man.'

'But I'm not. The place must be buzzing with it.'

'It's impossible for someone to survive a fall from that

height.'

'Conjurers, magicians - I said they were odd,' muttered the Madame.

'You certainly did, mother.'

Laura dabbed her eyes with the veil she clutched. 'But how?'

'I didn't ask where their money came from, and I won't ask whether their souls belong to Heaven or Hell. I only know that you and your scholar have a couple of remarkable friends.'

Laura hardly dared hope. 'Then, they might have rescued Tommaso?'

'Just as well. He wouldn't have survived very long in that place,' muttered Maddalena.

'Shut-up minx!' The Madame rapped the girl with her wooden leg. 'Take that stupid habit off and fetch us some food.'

'But I've just risked my life for-'

'Money! Get us some food.'

The city was alive with rumours about the miracle at St Stepheno's and Laura's escape.

General Jorden sent his escort on ahead to make camp well away from Ruggero, and was preparing to depart when he overheard what had happened from the revellers below his lodgings.

When the streets were quieter, Matteo went down to check if it was safe to leave, only to discover that Count Paolo's men had surrounded the inn. These were no ordinary soldiers from the adjoining gatehouse. They were assassins armed with crossbows.

Jorden had half heeded Tommaso's warning and taken lodgings outside the city wall. Unfortunately the only exit was through the courtyard, and he could have easily been picked off trying to drop from the window of his room, especially in half armour. Matteo suggested that they draw the ambushers into the close confines of the courtyard where they would be compelled to use their swords. Crossbows needed less expertise than longbows, and those trained in either weapon were seldom efficient with any other.

While Matteo saddled the horses, the General finished securing his armour, apart from the despised helmet which restricted his view. He tossed it into a corner with all the other excess baggage and buckled on his second sword. Perhaps he should have asked the Greek to forge him a more reliable edge after all, yet doubted he would ever meet her again.

Warning the late night revellers in the inn to stay out of sight, Jorden went to the stables.

The full moon was rising as the last rays of the setting sun filtered away from the top of St Stepheno's cliff and the chanting inside Ruggero's walls heralded yet another holy procession. The survivor of the miraculous suicide had disappeared, probably to avoid being stuffed as a holy relic.

In the courtyard, a shape loomed across Jorden's path. The soldier immediately raised a sword. In reply, the masked figure pointed to a narrow passageway by the stable wall. Matteo quickly brought the horses round and persuaded them to walk through the gap. Stirrups clattered against the rough masonry, but the animals were blinkered and Jorden's white mare was intelligent enough to lead the way without a whinny of complaint.

'Who are you?' demanded Jorden.

The hooded figure pointed to the opposite side of the courtyard where three archers were ready to loose their bolts. More men were approaching with drawn swords.

'Get out man! Get out!' Jorden would have stepped in front of his benefactor to shield him from attack if the figure hadn't dissolved back into the shadows like a leisurely phantom.

One assailant fired a bolt at him, another swung out with his sword. Neither stopped the stranger who had disappeared into the night.

For a moment the assassins were confused. They quickly remembered why they were there and fired at the General. His breastplate deflected one bolt, though another punctured a greave. Before the archers could reload their cumbersome weapons, Jorden had disarmed two of the swordsmen and felled the other with his fist. A forth man sprang from nowhere to block his way and Matteo heard the clash of metal echo down the passage. He would have gone back to help the General if the din hadn't panicked his horse and he was in danger of losing it. From the other end of the passage, the aide saw a blade flash past Jorden's face and the other men closing in.

Matteo drew one of his knives.

Now surrounded, the General was fighting several men with a sword in both hands.

'Run Matteo!' he bellowed over his shoulder.

Matteo replied in his own peerless way. A knife whistled past Jorden and embedded itself in the skull of an attacker with a dull thud. The General drew the others nearer the passage. A blade flew from its depths and went through another assassin's shoulder.

Unable to work out what was spitting knives, the others

drew back, giving Jorden chance to make his clattering escape.

After fumbling for reins and stirrups in the darkness, two desperate shadows hurtled into the night. A little way up the road a large African watched them go. He laughed, then mounted his own steed and leisurely cantered off.

Jorden and Matteo rode at a gallop until they saw the lamps of the three soldiers sent on ahead to make a safe camp.

The General was peppered with several wounds where the armour couldn't protect him. Matteo prized the bolt that had pierced his greave from his leg.

The aide applied a tourniquet until the blood was stanched. 'You must rest tonight.'

'It could be dangerous. Ruggero is only ten miles away.'

'They have no way of telling which track we took and our camp is well hidden. This countryside is treacherous. The girl wouldn't have been able to get away without the help of someone who knew it.'

Jorden gave a wry smile. 'She's a sharp one, as cunning as her father. Married to her, a man never need think for himself again.'

'This could mean war.'

'I don't know, those leeches have her dowry and-' The General stopped. 'Oh dear God! Tommaso!'

'There is nothing we can do for him.'

'Poor Socrates.'

Matteo removed Jorden's breastplate and attended to the rest of his wounds. 'Do you know who that figure in the stable yard was, General?'

'Probably some phantom. Ruggero no doubt spawns a lost soul for every assassination.'

'We wouldn't have escaped if he hadn't shown us that passage.'

'What with friendly phantoms, escaping brides and magical Africans who fly off cliffs - Damn!'

'I'm sorry. Did I hurt you?'

'Oh Matteo - An African! They said that the miracle was a large African.'

Matteo stopped bandaging. 'Of course, so he was.'

'Forgive me Socrates?'

'But why?'

'I shouldn't have bullied you into marrying me.'

'It doesn't matter little finch, we're safe now.'

'I love you so much and didn't want you to get hurt. I promise to let you go as soon as we know what Helen wants us to do. She might like to marry you herself.'

Tommaso's soul recoiled at the prospect. 'Don't say that.'

'But she's not really ugly, and I think you like weird woman. Do you remember that Cardinal's mistress? I know she fancied you.'

'Hush child. That woman was really a man.'

Laura hesitated. 'How odd. If they do it together, does that mean they're still celibate?'

'How many wings does a dragonfly have?'

'Teach me to write a love letter.'

'I don't know what to put into a love letter.'

'What about feather pillows, warm mattresses...'

'I wish your way with letters had kept pace with your burgeoning lust.'

'Are you beginning to hate me?'

'Of course not.'

'Let me hug you.'

Tommaso drew back. He wandered away to tap the pollen from lilies and let weeping willow leaves caress his face.

'Don't be so unkind Socrates.'

He reached out and gathered an armful of the thin drooping branches, then heard the faint shedding of tears mingle with the rustling of the leaves.

'Silly grasshopper,' he scolded.

That short distance between them had became a quagmire of perfumed enticement. 'Can fifteen love fifty? Can fifty love fifteen, Gerard?' Tommaso asked the warbler watching the charade from a swaying sapling.

He went back to Laura and gently grasped her shoulders. 'Would you pull the wings off a dragonfly if it had more than you thought it should?'

'Go away Socrates. You only want to make fun of me.'

'Would you toss away the flask when you've drunk its wine, or throw down the casket when you've taken its jewels?'

Laura stamped in tearful petulance. 'I don't want any riddles!'

'Most flasks are dull, cracked things and the wood of a casket discolours with age, yet even tarnished silver has a gleam beneath its surface.' Despite herself, Laura wiped her eyes and listened. 'The oldest hives can sometimes produce the sweetest honey, but the last few grains left in an hourglass fall with less vigour; shaking it would not restore them.'

Despite her protestations of love, Laura hadn't expected the same flame to be burning just as brightly in the breast of her shy tutor.

She was confused and caught Tommaso's hands. 'I wouldn't be so unkind to you Socrates.'

Tommaso knew he was making a fool of himself. Having declared his feelings, they couldn't be reeled back into their fortress. 'My heart has never belonged to anyone else but you. If you want to play with it for a day, take it. When you do find the young man you really love, promise to leave me as silently as a Bedouin.'

Laura touched his fine hair as though it were the down of a dandelion clock, then hugged him until the warning chuck of a blackbird made her look up.

Once again, towering above them, was General Jorden. 'How very touching.' He was dishevelled and several bandages were visible through the rips in his blood-spattered shirt.

The soldier could have been limbless and disembowelled for all Laura cared. 'You no longer have any claim on us General.'

Jorden still had problems dealing with the contempt of a woman so young. 'I couldn't sleep for believing he was dead, and what do I tell your father?'

Laura gave a cruel smile. 'Don't be such a hypocrite,

General. You know you never wanted to play nursemaid to me in the first place. Now you're free to go and play the soldier instead.'

'I've have more than enough fighting for one week because of you.'

'We've made the General very angry, Socrates.'

'Where is that Greek?' Jorden growled.

Having heard the clank of armour suspended from Matteo's saddle, Helen came out to watch from the loggia.

The sight of her only enraged Jorden more. 'And where's that African?!'

Laura pointed a delicate finger. 'Behind you General.'

Jorden turned to see Dinan's moon face beaming benignly.

'Damn all of you! I don't know how you managed it, but - Damn you!!'

A flock of starlings feeding nearby took to the air. In their squawks, Jorden could hear the very elements mock him.

Tommaso took his arm. 'Gerard, please calm yourself.'

'Hellfire take you most of all!'

'Would you rather they had sent my soul to the Devil?'

'They could have easily sent it anywhere, there's never been any body attached to it, you whimpering catalogue of wisdom!'

Laura's serenity became oddly sinister... and she cursed him. 'General, I hope you one day die horribly, without your armour, humiliated and in public.'

Tommaso was alarmed. 'No Laura! You must not speak like that. A curse from a girl your age is a potent thing. Please take it back.'

'I would sooner swallow crushed glass.'

Jorden laughed. He had no fear of a woman's vitriol. He had been spat at by Gorgons, yet still survived.

Tommaso increased his grip on Jorden's arm. 'Why do you refuse to understand anything, Gerard?'

Laura flicked a loose tie of the soldier's doublet. 'Because he thinks that the Universe lives by his rules. He scorns you because he has never been compelled to crawl out of that self-satisfied shell.'

Jorden shook off Tommaso's restraining hand. 'Only a child could mistake this collection of parchment, bones and limp rag as a man. What use is he going to be to you in the early hours of the morning? If you want a family, why adopt a parrot?'

Helen's voice cut through the air like the hardened steel of a scimitar. 'That's enough General! I'm the one you should talk to - Inside!'

No longer sure why he was so angry, Jorden strode after Helen.

* * *

In the bushes, beyond the grazing horses, a drab figure crept, waiting, watching.

* * *

The subdued light inside the villa calmed Gerard Jordan a little and he realised just how much of his precious dignity he had forfeited to irrational rage.

Helen Maat handed him a goblet of wine. 'Don't you think any scholar has the right to happiness?'

'The man's mind is so full of cobwebs and clouds he wouldn't recognise passion if it hit him with a slapstick.'

'Why does the prospect of Tommaso having some joy in life make you erupt?'

'Because, since encountering you, I seem to have no more status than a maggot on a decaying ox.' Jorden swallowed his wine.

'You've known Tommaso for a long while. Do gentle people offend you in some way?'

'Only when their antics risk wars.'

'Aren't you paid well for fighting them?'

'My remuneration is no less than any other competent soldier's.'

'I could double it.'

For a moment Jorden was unable to take in what she had said, though it would explain why she was looking him up and down as if he were some costly livestock.

As a precaution, he made sure the table was between them before sitting down and pouring some more wine. 'I understand that your companion works miracles as well?'

Helen shrugged. 'We have enough wealth to indulge in some eccentricities.'

'Then why not use it to buy a castle and settle down - a long way from here.'

'Retirement is meaningless to us.' Helen let him drink his wine in silence and amused her fancy by wondering just how much of a stallion Jorden was. He obviously didn't want her to get close enough to find out, probably aware that there were few things the alchemist wouldn't experiment with when the inclination took her.

The General was amazed to feel a hot flush round his neck. He had to say something quickly to stop it reaching his cheeks. 'Why are you so interested in that silly girl and her pet infatuation?'

'The mind of a scholar is a precious thing, General. The brain that guides the sword need know little more than the direction of the enemy. A scholar's is a grove of fertile blossom pollinated by years of study.'

'So it can become infatuated with a silly girl?'

Helen's smile verged on the lascivious. 'General, I think their devotion to each other is becoming an obsession with you.'

She had eased her way to his side of the table and it was all he could do to stop himself bolting for the door.

'Why couldn't he choose a mature woman, like Bianca or Carmine. Such gorgeous creatures in the Duke's court surrounded Tommaso. They could have shown him what love is.'

'They could have shown him what lust is.'

Then, in apprehensive derision, he made a fatal error. 'You could show me the difference?'

Helen ran her fingers under his open doublet and ripped shirt down to his groin. Gerard Jorden fought to ignore the woman's strangely sensual touch but she could feel him tense with arousal. The soldier fought the sensation more out of fear at what Dinan might do if he caught them than the alchemist's sudden, full-mouthed kiss. He tried to become wooden and clenched his pewter goblet so hard it crumpled. No mistress of his had ever managed to seduce him with so little effort as this creased, copper harpy who rightfully shouldn't have been able to turn the head of a geriatric ragpicker.

Helen leisurely withdrew, then gave a slow smile. 'That is lust, General. How can you have any empathy with Laura and Tommaso when lust is all you understand?'

Jorden leapt up, unable to choke back his indignation. 'What Hellenistic deity gave you the right to make moral judgements? Are you one of those hags from Hades who swallow sinners like me, bones and all?'

'Those barbs on your sarcasm would stick in the throat of the Cyclops. Why carry two swords when one shaft of it could immobilise Mars and his whole entourage?'

'Being honourable can tax the patience.'

'One day you may need more than wit to escape the consequences of being honourable.'

'Don't prophesy at me! I've only just been cursed by a child!'

'Why won't you come out of that shell, General? I'm sure there's a human being somewhere inside it.'

'Without it, people like you would turn me into turtle soup. I know the world too well to believe it loves the vulnerable.'

'It takes the likes of us with shells to protect those without.'

Jorden put his guard up even higher and turned his back. Why should he concern himself with butterflies who flutter out over the sea and are carried off by its thermals?

Helen decided to be honest before the barricade became impregnable. 'I believe that, somewhere under that gleaming carapace, you are a compassionate man.'

It may have been his paranoia, but Jorden detected a tinge of pity in her tone. 'Compassion is for martyrs.'

'I am prepared to give you a fortune for Laura and Tommaso. Throw in your body and I'll double it.' Helen had to block his way before he could reach the door. 'The Duke will never know you found his daughter and scholar. We'll take them far away and, with the wealth I can offer, you need never return to Settimo.'

'Why are you so sure I'm going to take them back?'

'Your honour, General, your Achilles heel. But, think of this, what honour did Duke Vittorio or Count Paolo have in arranging this marriage against Laura's will?'

'Tommaso poisoned her mind against the match.'

'You know quite well she was capable of deciding for herself. What do you think would happen to the pretty creature if she returned to Settimo?'

'Nothing. The Duke doted on her.'

'And Tommaso?'

Jorden hesitated. 'I don't know. They were close - Don't try to bribe me again, alchemist!'

'Stay here until you've had time to think about it.'

'I have to rendezvous with my lieutenant. Via La Rosa is storing provisions for a siege.'

'Would it hurt to turn your back? Bend to that blissful state of compassion soldiers fear more than swamp fever?'

'I fear nothing, Signora.'

'You will, General, you will.'

'If you offer me another prophecy, alchemist, I shall throw you so hard you'll land in the Delphic oracle's lap!'

'Poor General, I think this is the nearest you will ever be to real passion.'

The soldiers and Matteo tended the horses while Dinan sat on the loggia watching Tommaso and Laura.

Frequently, even without the aid of alcohol, Dinan fancied he could peer into a parallel dimension where the sands of time had spent so long scouring the shutter of reality it had become transparent.

Laura snatched off Tommaso's cap and put it on her own head. 'I'm the teacher now!'

'Only after dusk, you lustful child. And not until you can instruct me in Latin.'

The fifteen-year-old lapsed into childish petulance. 'Must I still study languages, Socrates?'

Tommaso became the stern master. 'Yes, and astronomy, mathematics and antiquity.'

'But I won't have any time to study you then.' Playfully, Laura started to unbutton his gown.

Laughing, he tried to stop her and they tumbled to the ground.

Matteo watched disapprovingly, though Dinan detected the flicker of a smile trying to crack the adamantine features. He and the General were too deep for the African's dull acceptance of interminable life.

'Teach me to draw, Socrates,' demanded Laura, sitting on her husband.

'I'll teach you calligraphy.'

'Bookworm.'

'Stop sitting on me and I might think about it.'

Laura rose and tried to pull him up, but Tommaso preferred to stay where he was. She reached out to pluck some lilies instead.

Her youthful ears detected he faint sound of a ratchet being wound back somewhere across the valley.

There was a glint of silver and swish of a bolt making its lethal flight.

With a speed that startled Dinan, Laura hurled herself across Tommaso before it could find its mark.

Inside the villa, Helen and Jorden's exchange was cut

short by her scream. They ran outside.

Dinan was carefully lifting Laura.

A crossbow bolt impaled her body.

Matteo and a soldier had leapt onto saddleless horses and were hurtling across the valley.

'Clear the table!' called Dinan.

Jorden dashed back inside and swept the flagon and goblets onto the floor. Dinan laid Laura on the table and Helen pulled out her trunk of medical equipment. The bolt had gone through the heiress's back and heart with such force it had stabbed Tommaso as well, though he was oblivious of the wound.

'Socrates...' Laura murmured.

'What is it little finch?'

'Socrates...' There was a deep gurgle in her throat.

Tommaso frantically turned to Helen and Dinan. 'You will save her?'

Helen shook her head.

Tommaso refused to understand. 'I'm going to teach her to draw.'

Dinan gently laid his hand on the scholar's shoulder. 'She's dead, Tommaso.'

'No, she can't die. She's far too young. You didn't die?'

Helen eased him away from the table. 'We are magicians, Tommaso, but we cannot bring the dead back to life.'

'Take that horrible dart from her body,' the scholar sobbed.

'Go outside, Tommaso.' Helen turned to Jorden. 'Will you watch him.'

The General helped his dazed friend into the garden.

'Quickly Dinan, remove the bolt then bring down the finest gown we have. Where did the gold one go to?'

Dinan expertly pulled the bolt free with some pliers. 'Probably in the cassone, and Count Paolo has that.'

'Well don't bring anything with pearls.'

He sluiced his hands in a tub of water then went upstairs.

With the speed of a military undertaker, Helen had stripped and was washing the body by the time Dinan returned carrying a light blue gown with silver trim.

'Oh no, she'll look like a bride.'

'All the rest are your size.'

'All right. It doesn't suit her eyes though.'

'Well close them.'

Helen gave a sigh and, to Dinan's amazement, brushed away a tear. 'Silly girl. What a waste.'

'What about your scholar?'

'She would have recovered from his loss. He'll never get over losing her.'

'Now what?'

'The General will insist she goes back to Duke Vittorio, of course.'

'And her Socrates?'

* * *

Tommaso returned to the spot where Laura fell and touched the ground as though it could surrender up those last few words that she had been unable to utter. Instead, he saw the small eternity they should have spent together guttering away like a dying candle flame. He looked up to find the demon whose decisions had brought them to this, but only saw Gerard Jorden.

The soldier guiltily turned away and went back inside the villa. Tommaso picked up the lily Laura had plucked.

'Why?' he silently asked its amber stamens.

A bee alighted on the flower for a few seconds and, finding it had nothing to offer buzzed on its busy way. An odd numbness pervaded the scholar, then every fibre in his body shook uncontrollably. He felt cold, sick and faint and pulled his gown together.

Jorden returned with a bandage and compress to staunch his wound.

Two horses were returning, yet they seemed far away.

'No trace of him!' Matteo called to the General. 'How is the girl?'

Jorden raised a cautioning hand. He was confused and

didn't understand his own thoughts and feelings any more than Tommaso could make sense of his. The General was jealous - jealous of an ageing scholar demented with grief. Would any mistress of his have given up her life to save his? Was this something to be envied? Jorden shuddered, then quickly dressed Tommaso's wound and buttoned his gown.

Dinan came out and gently took the scholar's arm.

He refused to rise and looked up at him as though he had never seen an African before.   'They used to laugh at me.'

Dinan knelt beside him. 'Who Tommaso?'

'Laura and her cousins. They were always whispering behind my back and playing pranks. She was such a mischievous child.'

'Come inside.'

Dinan glanced up to see Jorden's expression. In the enamel of his self-assurance, embryo cracks were beginning to appear.

Dinan carefully helped Tommaso into the villa where Helen persuaded him to drink a potion that would enable him to sleep until the next morning.

Jorden spent the dawn hours writing two letters, which he sealed with his ring and tucked into his belt pouch.

It was midday when the General rendezvoused with his lieutenants and learnt that Via La Rosa had thrown out the Duke's officials and the local magistrates taken control. So the unenviable task of accompanying Laura back to Settimo and her father fell to his second lieutenant.

'Has Tommaso decided, Signora?' he asked Helen.

'He refuses to leave Laura and come with Dinan and me. We'll follow your men to the Duke.'

Jorden was unable to comprehend Helen's lack of concern for her personal safety. 'No, that would be dangerous.'

'Would he harm a man who has lost his wits?'

Jorden had no idea how Duke Vittorio would react to the loss of his daughter, but didn't trust his advisors. They were jealous of the scholar's influence.

He glanced at the wagon where Tommaso sat motionless. 'Do you think he might recover enough sense to be of use to you?' He pulled the letters from his pouch.

'Perhaps, though I can't compel him to run off with Dinan and me.'

'Then take this letter to Bianca. She has a house on the outskirts of Settimo where you can stay and will let you know what happens to your scholar.'

Inexplicably, Helen hesitated.

From the seat of their wagon, Dinan reached over her horse and took the letter. 'If there's any way to save him, we will, General.'

Jorden gave an embarrassed nod of gratitude before turning to his second lieutenant. 'Give the Duke this letter. Return to me as soon as you've done it. And bring some wages for the troops. Blow open the treasury's coffers if you have to, but don't leave without some money!'

'But General?' said Helen.

'No Signora,' Jorden interrupted. 'I will not take your gold. Duke Vittorio is my paymaster.'

'I hope you never regret it. I think my risks out before I take them. You only see problems in terms of honour and obligation.'

'Honour is not a bad thing, Signora,' protested Matteo.

'Honour, honour - this land floats on honour! Mind neither of you sink beneath it and drown.'

Helen had every intention of following Jorden's advice until, on the way to Settimo, they reached an ancient amphitheatre. The seats had crumbled, ancient cypress trees circled its rim, and most of the stone had been scavenged to build a church.

As soon as Helen reined her horse to a halt, Dinan knew that they might never get to see Bianca. Arguing was pointless when Helen set her mind on something, and she certainly wouldn't ride past the ideal location for her infernal experiment. He stopped the wagon.

Dinan didn't like the place. If destiny were going to ambush them, it would be here. With no inhabited towns or villages nearby, the landscape was dotted with prehistoric groves and terraces that earth tremors had nonchalantly resculptured over the centuries. Gnarled olive trees were scattered in untidy regiments; ancient fig roots undermined brick walls criss-crossing the countryside and the meadows were closely cropped by rabbits and wild cattle. The movement of the earth had also cracked ancient drainage systems and weeds pushed through cobblestones where legions and chariots once passed.

The main access to the basement once used by performers was blocked by rubble, so Dinan had to carry their luggage down, The holding area for animal acts was vast. The cavernous chamber gave Dinan the shivers and, as he walked out into the dazzling daylight of the arena, he could visualise the rapacious crowd waiting for the gladiators and lions.

The amphitheatre was a catchment basin for the rain and sun so it was well grassed and grazed by wild goats. Dinan unhitched the horses and persuaded them to descend the ramp to the arena. Then he stowed Helen's equipment by one of the mighty columns holding up the ruin while she unpacked her tripods, priceless mirrors and lenses. He only hoped they hadn't blundered into a region controlled by some Christian zealot who would accuse them of being dabblers in the black arts... yet again.

Dinan needn't have worried. They never saw a soul. The amphitheatre might well have been haunted, though any resident ghosts were keeping their heads down as if they knew that the manifestations the alchemist was trying to raise were players on a cosmic scale.

Helen set up her large mirrors to reflect the rays of the sun into the crucible in the centre of the arena, hurling curses as she tried to align them. Dinan recalled Kleopatra, the Alexandrian alchemist, and the old phobia of being burnt to a crisp returned.

The only way Helen had of measuring high temperatures was by observing the melting points of different materials. By doing that she could extrapolate how to produce the halo of energy that had appeared before Ahmose's arrival. As all the other furnaces about the continent, from the lead smelting cauldrons of the German printers to the fires of the glass blowers of Venice, hadn't been visited by a fire demon or immortality, only the sun could produce the heat she needed.

One morning there was a sudden breeze that misaligned a lens and concentrated a shaft of sunlight onto the polished side of the crucible. A dagger of light reflected the beam back into the sky. Without warning, the glass bubbling in the crucible produced a faint halo.

As Helen Maat darted about adjusting the lenses and mirrors to maintain the temperature Dinan had the strongest foreboding yet of his long life. He led the grazing horses down to the amphitheatre basement and reluctantly returned with two eye shields of darkened glass. His common sense insisted he ride off to tell Bianca his mistress was undoubtedly spread in small pieces over a large area. As it would take some time for her to pull herself together, she would be delayed. But, as always, that old problem of his, loyalty, persuaded him to stay and help the alchemist.

The air writhed, and in a pool of sunlight there appeared the ghostly struggle of a cosmic midwife fighting to deliver a supernatural birth. The trees above them shivered in the heat billowing about the improvised laboratory and the horse's lush grazing was turned to hay. Instead of summoning the Aton Bird, they had woken some bad tempered deities.

A few degrees away from incineration, Helen Maat and Dinan waited. Then the halo of light about the crucible ballooned into a dome. They edged closer, fully expecting a golden bird to appear in the sky. Unfortunately something else, malevolent and mighty, had won the phantom struggle.

Globules like molten glass rained about the alchemists. They coalesced into glowing hillocks, and the horses stabled below started to whinny in terror.

A blazing sun descended and capped the amphitheatre with its fiery shield, trapping Helen and Dinan. The searing lid belled down and the cypress trees fringing the top terraces shrivelled. Before the cosmic furnace consumed them, the hand of the demonic glass blower moulded the glassy globules into bizarrely ornate towers.

The amphitheatre resonated with an eerie burbling sound. It might have been speech, or cosmic indigestion.

Something evil was watching them.

Dinan lost the feeling in his legs. He dropped to the ground and covered his head with his mantlet.

The solar globe started to descend again. This time it touched down on the ornate tapering towers that supported it like fiery ballerina on points. The alchemists were trapped in a hellish ball of molten glass.

Her clothes scorching, Helen circled about the pillars, examining the belly of the silicon entity resting only an arm's reach above her head. The monster was trying to intimidate the alchemist, but manic obsession had hardened her capacity for terror. Curiosity had taken its place and she was too busy trying to calculate the nature of the beast.

The alchemists had been snatched into a parallel reality. Through the blistering heat of the solar shell they could see by a baying multitude on the terraces.

Instinctively Dinan reached for his sword. He wasn't wearing it.

The plasma towers dissipated and the glowing lid rolled

back to reveal a harsh blue sky. Helen averted her eyes from the glaring sun, only to find it again on the opposite horizon – it had manifested itself at all points of the compass. In this dimension it was dawn, noon, afternoon and sunset at once.

The howling of the crowd grew louder.

Dinan tried not to panic. 'What's happening?'

'Something is unravelling our time.'

'Is that bad? At least I can't see any lions.'

'You won't, none of this is real.'

'I'd still like my sword.'

Helen pointed to a large shape with swinging head and rattling teeth lumbering towards them. 'What's that?'

Dinan desperately delved about the sleeves of his ostentatious mantlet for a dagger. 'It's the Ammet, the devourer of souls.'

'It's not real.'

'Does it know that?'

'Ignore the thing. It's only a figment of the ancient Egyptian imagination.'

'Like Ahmose?'

The crocodile-headed chimera continued to plod forward on its hippopotamus legs. 'Don't let it panic you,' warned Helen. 'That's what the demon wants.'

'Will it be all right to worry a little?'

The Ammet stopped.

It had only hesitated because something more sinister and a less ridiculous was approaching from the other side of the arena. This demon had luminous slit eyes, and face shaped like a devilish donkey.

If the ground hadn't been baked hard, Dinan would have dug a hole with his bare hands and disappeared into it. 'Oh no! Typhon!'

The alchemist gave the new arrival a more clinical look. 'Typhon with a scythe.'

'I suppose it would be too much to hope they fight each other?'

'Probably.'

The Ammet waddled forward, jagged teeth gnashing.

Typhon closed in from the other direction with a loping stride, tail swishing and blade scything the air.

Dinan put his mantlet back over his head.

'It isn't real,' Helen insisted.

Dinan muttered something into the quilted folds.

'To think a nation used to live in fear of these creatures.'

'They had the right idea,' mumbled Dinan. 'What do they want with us?'

'Souls, Dinan. The Ammet devours the essence of humans, and Typhon is ultimate evil.'

There was a brief groan, and then the mantlet fell silent.

The monsters increased in size and blocked Helen's view of the excited crowd.

Dinan started to sway as though about to hit the ground - If there was a subconscious capable of fainting, it was Dinan's.

Helen decided to gamble that the entity controlling the demons was only after her. She sprang away from them before they could engulf Dinan, and ran to the edge of the arena.

The alchemist was right. They lost interest in him and pursued her. They knew she couldn't outrun or fight off the combination of scythe and incisors. They would make short work of her spirit, however steely her mortal resolve might have been. Once more Helen knew how to be terrified, though was able to marvel at how much she had annoyed the entity controlling Ahmose.

Extinction of the soul was no way to cure immortality. What would Dinan do if the alchemist couldn't find her way back? He'd never be able to face eternity on his own. The alchemist had to escape the nightmare and return to her real body but, as Typhon and the Ammet closed in, Helen Maat felt as though her very soul was being shredded.

Suddenly an intense light bloomed between her and the monsters and she was snatched from the amphitheatre and sent spinning amongst the stars, glittering pinpricks in a vast black velvet canopy.

The gaseous Jupiter, which Helen had studied for many years, swam by, a massive galleon radiating like the metal on a farrier's anvil, with moons of cratered rock, fractured ice and volcanoes.

A milliard rings circled Saturn; the moons braided on the outermost resembled necklaces of glass beads.

Helen Maat passed two more planets like calm, bland oceans. Beyond them there were no crystal spheres which Tommaso and his brethren believed supported the heavens, only a barrier of debris. Further still, and she came to another shell of shattered ice tombstones light years from the sun, now a small dot of light.

The alchemist eventually reached another star, a dark red sun that loured against the blackness of space like a malevolent ruby on a heretic priest's gown. The sinister anomaly was too bright and large to be a planet but didn't shine like a sun. It was livid, like a living creature, dangerous and devouring.

To Helen's amazement, the red sun stopped rotating and scarlet flares flickered from it like serpent tongues. Then the demon star ponderously began to turn in the opposite direction. This wasn't science; it was Sol's bastard twin playing malicious games.

This binary sun could never support a solar system of its own, so had become self-aware and developed malice on a cosmic scale. Every 30 million years its orbit came close enough to the sun's solar system to perturb some of those ice tombstones and send them hammering into its planets. That was an accident of their mutual rotation. What it had in store for Ahmose and Helen Maat was quite deliberate. It would not have noticed these puny humans if they hadn't clamoured so much for attention.

The jaws of gravity spun out the alchemist's spirit as she was pulled towards the louring red sun. The evil entity persecuting Ahmose was going to make her pay for getting so near to the truth. This death was going to be permanent. The link between body and spirit rapidly became more and more tenuous.

Helen lost all sense of being.

Then she was suddenly aware of her escort - a large jade cat. The red sun's flares lashed out in rage at the phantom that had come between her and extinction.

* * *

Dinan eventually looked up. The fiery lid over the arena had lifted, leaving the charred stumps of the cypress trees. He watched stupidly as Helen's priceless lenses shattered one by one and the crucible exploded.

Helen Maat lay sprawled on the charred ground. She looked very dead.

Dinan carried her body to the cover of the basement entrance and waited while he tried to get used to the idea.

The large African sat there for two days and nights, only stirring to feed and water the horses.

The third morning, a figure appeared on the uppermost terrace. It might have been a goatherd. Like a dusty ghost, it wended its way down to the arena littered by the shards of Helen's equipment. Perhaps it was only the amphitheatre's ghost returning to demand what the alchemists had done to its residence. Dinan wanted to put the apparition down to lack of food and sleep, but it was frighteningly substantial - not that he wanted to reach out and touch its brown linen robe. The man's features were finely sculpted and oriental. Dinan recognised them from the distant past.

'Helen Maat is dead but her body will not decay,' he explained just in case the visitor was in another dimension and may not have noticed.

The phantom lifted its Anubis headed staff and lightly touched Helen's lips with its tip. Instead of being released, her soul returned.

The alchemist's eyes flickered open. She slowly sat up and looked about. Before her gaze could settle on the ghost, it melted into the sunlight.

Dinan was wearing a look of disapproval.

'What's wrong?'

'Where do you think you've been?'

Helen gave a small, dry laugh, amazed that she still had a voice. 'It meant to kill me! It really meant to kill me!'

'Why?'

156

'I got too close.' Then the alchemist was aware of how much her throat hurt and swallowed the water Dinan held to her lips.

'Why didn't it then?'

'Something else came between us.'

Dinan didn't say anything about the mysterious phantom that had revived her. Why should he? She never told him anything.

Helen tried to get up. After being dead for two and a half days, she was too stiff. 'I think it must have been whatever made us immortal.'

'Why?'

'How should I know.'

All that night the alchemist sat and thought about the capricious beast that had cursed Ahmose, and its ability to play games with time.

As the dawn light filtered into the amphitheatre basement, Dinan grew tired of sulking and switched into nagging mode. 'We should never have stopped here.'

'That was probably the last chance we'll have for centuries to raise Ahmose.'

'We promised General Jorden we would help Tommaso and our wagon has probably been reduced to cinders.'

'Oh all right!' snapped Helen. She rose unsteadily and went to the arena entrance. 'Gather up what's left of the equipment and dig a deep hole.'

'What? Now?'

'Well I'm in no fit state.' She returned to the basement and continued to think.

By noon the glittering shards and shattered crucible had been tossed into a deep hole to keep company with the bones of defeated gladiators. Dinan stood back to contemplate his handiwork.

'Now fill it in!'

Dinan dropped his shovel. 'You made me jump! I thought you were writing?'

'Shut-up and fill in the hole.'

Dinan took a swig of the only wine that hadn't been vaporised. 'Why bury the pieces anyway?'

'We must convince the beast that I'm not going to try and raise Ahmose again.'

Dinan tossed the flask onto the shrivelled grass and picked up his shovel. 'But it can't erase your memory. The thing would have to send us back in time to do that.'

'It's the only way to recover the equipment.'

'I don't understand?'

'You don't need to.'

That afternoon Helen Maat sat, trance like, trying to memorise pictures inside her eyelids.

The bright cobalt sky switched to pale blue and it was suddenly morning.

* * *

Dinan yawned and saw the sun rising over the cypress trees that girdled the amphitheatre. He had the sensation of missing a step in time. Given his fondness for alcohol, that wasn't unusual. He shrugged it off. He wasn't going to question anything that helped shorten eternity.

'Hadn't we better get on our way now? We could reach Settimo before tomorrow evening.'

Helen remained silent.

'Look, I don't know why you wanted me to drag all our stuff down here for just one night - And what are you doing with that notebook? It should be kept safe with Kleopatra's papyrus.' Dinan took it from her. 'You'll only blame me if it gets lost.' He flipped through the blank pages. 'You haven't even bothered to do anything since the last experiment at the villa.' He wandered away grouchily to collect the horses.

Helen Maat sat until everything had been reloaded in the wagon and the horses harnessed.

When she joined Dinan he continued to nag. 'I wish you'd stop having these whims. You should have got over those women's problems centuries ago. What did you hope to do down there anyway? We'll find a much better place to set up the equipment once we're away from these lunatic dukedoms.'

Helen just nodded as she continued to staple notes from a blip in time to her memory.

Vigilant cat like eyes from another dimension watched
them leave.

THE ASSASSIN

CHAPTER 34

The tall woman wearing a rich purple gown spangled with seed pearls gently lifted the latch of the library door. A student deep in concentration didn't notice her and she silently passed through to the room beyond.

Tommaso's study was cluttered with books, astronomical equipment, an unmade bed and a chest that contained his gowns. An ancient skull was carelessly wearing his large triangular cap and several clogged quills were in the open inkwell. A half-filled vellum sheet betrayed the calligrapher's indifference to his once immaculate letters.

Perched on a high stool, Tommaso was carefully turning pages filled with adolescent scribble. He hardly read the words between the blots and doodles but occasionally touched the coarse paper with his fingertips.

'Master Tommaso,' Bianca quietly asked. 'Can I speak to you?'

Tommaso looked up and gave a thin smile.

Bianca closed the door behind her. 'How are you keeping?'

'I am strangely well considering my age.'

'I meant...'

'You want to know if I still mad, Signora Bianca?'

'No, you were never mad.' She took his hand. 'I have someone you know lodging with me.'

'Someone I know?'

'Helen Maat and Dinan.'

'Ah yes.' The ghost of a smile played about Tommaso's

wide mouth. 'I remember Helen and Dinan.'

'They want to know if you are well enough to leave with them while there is still the chance?'

'Still the chance?'

'Count Paolo has discovered the deception and is sending an emissary.'

'I can't leave.'

'You must.'

'I can't leave without Laura.'

'She is dead, Tommaso.'

He closed his eyes. 'You must think me a pathetic creature.'

'No Tommaso.' Of all the men Bianca had loved, she had never encountered anyone like the scholar. How could she know what to say to a romantic bookworm?

'Gerard thinks I am beneath contempt as well.'

Bianca realised that the soldier was as lost as Tommaso, but dare not show it. 'No he doesn't.'

'Laura cursed Gerard because he was mocking me. I will make her take it back, though. She will always listen to reason eventually.'

'Laura is dead, Tommaso.'

'Do you think I'm mad?'

'I think you are letting your heart deceive your senses. When you are far away from Settimo you will be able to remember Laura as she would want you to.'

'Do you love Gerard Jorden?' Tommaso suddenly asked.

'That isn't the same thing.'

'Would you be grief stricken if he fell in battle?' He reached out to touch the precious clasp on Bianca's gown. 'How true love glitters.'

'Don't mock me Tommaso, I'm trying to help you.'

'Could you love me in the same way?'

Bianca felt a deep blush rise to her cheeks as though Jesus Christ had asked her price. The thought of the scholar being a carnal creature had never entered her head. She doubted that it had been in his for long.

'Do you want me to, Tommaso?'

It was his turn to blush. Unlike the courtesan's shamed

crimson, his was virginally downcast. He felt foolish. Was it love of books that had quelled those baser instincts or good, clean, Christian guilt?

Bianca lifted his cap from the skull. 'Come with me Tommaso. Laura will never return. She's as dead as St Agnese. Don't use your frail bones to build a tomb over her memory. The one Duke Vittorio provided is splendid enough.'

Tommaso picked up a golden feather. The bright quill sparkled eerily as he tried to write with the clogging ink.

Bianca put down the cap. 'Where did you get that pen?'

Tommaso looked blankly at the quill for a moment. 'I found it on the path up to the notary and priest. We thought it would bring us luck so the notary used it to draw up our marriage contract.'

'What manner of bird did it come from?'

'I don't know, but if it ever moulted it could dazzle a city.' He handed Bianca the quill and note then rolled several star charts together. 'Give these to Helen. I don't know what knowledge she is seeking but they may be useful. Please don't think me ungrateful.'

'Of course not Tommaso.' Bianca kissed him gently on both cheeks, and then left as silently as she had come.

* * *

The wearer of the black embroidered gown was as lean as a gazehound and moved like a stalking hyena, noiselessly, with his back well protected. He had to, he was Count Paolo's diplomatic assassin.

As much as Duke Vittorio would have liked to use a poisoned dagger on Paolo's creature, he was persuaded to hand Tommaso the goblet of wine spiked with death angel. It was the only way he could save his realm from yet another war.

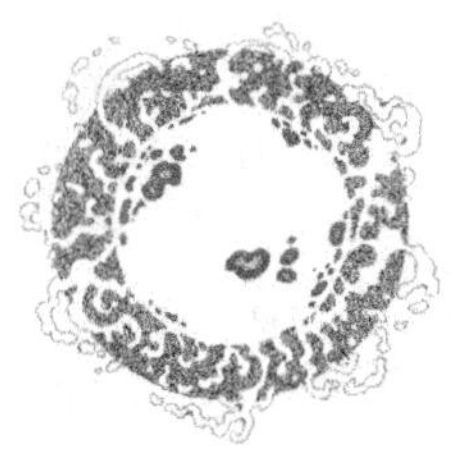

THE GENERAL

CHAPTER 35

The old woman stopped picking mushrooms. She watched the tall man in the voluminous soft cream shirt move ghostlike under the canopy of mulberry trees. He was handsome and elegantly powerful, prematurely grey and very troubled. The herbalist should have willed her staff into a spear to bring him down. The agent of a tyrant deserved no better death. Then she read his aura.

'What are you doing out here? Looking for rebelling rabbit warrens?' she called.

General Jorden half heard. He turned to look at the stooped woman wearing ancient brocade sleeves and gown over rough linen skirts. Her eyes glittered like Bianca's mischievous pet monkey's and she reminded him of a tapestry woven with many colours, coarse enough underneath to keep out a strong draught. The herbalist had that remorseless air of a survivor, and might have once been a vagabond entertainer.

Jorden realised he amused her for some reason so he threw on his cloak as though it could make him invisible to the world.

'Why do you need to get up this early? Haven't you a mistress to keep your bed warm?' she taunted.

He closed the cloak as though his lack of armour made him vulnerable to her verbal shafts. 'Go on your way Signora. My soldiers haven't killed any of your sons.'

The old woman laughed. 'You can kill all of my sons if you like. Useless, every one of them.'

'What then? Have my men started to loot Via La Rosa?'

'Not a one. They're all in such terror of you they wouldn't stoop to pick up a diamond cluster if they saw it sparkling in the gutter.'

'Then why abuse me?' Annoyed at himself for being intimidated by the mushroom picker, Gerard Jorden let his cloak fall onto a mossy bank and lounged back on it.

'I would have expected more courtly manners from such an important emissary,' she mocked.

'I've forgotten how to be polite.'

'So I've heard.' She gave an evil chuckle that told the General that there was something he should remember about the evening before. Her harsh voice rasped on. 'A man who wears such clean linen shouldn't know how to be rude, or is that only your soldier's way of avoiding an infected wound?'

He yawned and willed his hangover down a couple of throbs. 'Were you going to inflict damage on me with that rotten staff and a basket of mushrooms?'

'I wouldn't waste mushrooms by throwing them at you, and even a dart tipped with fly agaric couldn't penetrate your thick skin.'

She was probably right. He doubted that anything the old woman darted him with could do much for his state of mind. Jorden left his troops to experiment with the narcotic properties of fungi. He kept to the intoxicants that came from a flask.

Jorden gave a laugh of recognition. 'Aren't you the herbalist who speaks to spirits?'

'I sometimes read palms, but it's the eyes that never lie.' Knowing it was pointless trying to annoy the soldier, she was about to bustle away.

'No, wait.' The sudden mellowness of his voice made her turn back. 'How can you read a person's eyes?'

'The flower that surrounds the pupil carries the map of its owner's existence.'

'I've never heard of such a thing?'

'The iris is the reflection of a person's soul.' The herbalist set down her basket. Without invitation she lifted his face in her rough hands to face a shaft of sunlight. His contracted pupils revealed the pattern in the grey irises. She seemed puzzled for a moment.

Although dazzled, this didn't escape Jorden's notice. 'What's the matter?'

'You have had the favours of many women, though never given your heart.'

'You sound like a fortune teller.' The tone of the soldier returned. 'I've always selected my mistresses for their discretion and intelligence. Quirks of character, like sentiment and affection, can destroy a man's peace of mind.'

'When you do feel affection for another creature, it will destroy both of you. You'll cease to be a lover and become an emotional stampede.'

Jorden gave an ironic laugh. 'Humans aren't designed for love. It's merely Nature's practical joke to make us dependent on each other.'

'Only those who are capable of devotion feel the need to deny it. People who are too mean-spirited to give anything away protest all the time about how deeply they love.'

'Don't make any prophecies. It would remind me of that infernal Greek.'

The herbalist released his face and picked up her basket. She was some way off before she hesitated. 'There is one thing you should know, though.'

'Go ahead?' he sighed.

'You will have to slay the only thing you ever cared for.'

'Now that is Greek.'

The old woman cackled and wandered off in search of more mushrooms.

Jorden moved to the shade of a mulberry and rested beneath its canopy where he closed his eyes to think of Bianca. There would have been an explosion of fur and claw if he ever raised his hand to her.

In the still dawn air and warmth of the hazy autumn sun, he craved no stimulant, alcoholic or erotic. Gerard Jorden wondered whether he would have needed either had he been able to live the life of a peasant. Duke Vittorio realised that his General was actually a humanist and it was only Matteo's blinkered confidence that enabled the soldier act out his part. This aide saw a man of steel. He wouldn't have given his devotion to any less a mortal.

Gerard Jorden had spent several sleepless nights since occupying Via La Rosa and quickly fell asleep. His dreams spiralled down into the dimension that reflected reality in a distorting glass. He was no longer a General, but Knight Templar. With a red cross emblazoned on a flowing white tabard, he sat on his favourite mare and looked across a ravaged Holy Land. Refugees eyed him with terror as they fled.

Jorden tried to wake from the familiar nightmare and suddenly he was back in the sunlit glade.

Something was wrong.

The sun had not risen high enough to give off such an intense light. Sitting on the branch above him was a large golden bird with soft brown eyes peering benignly down. The General desperately attempted to wake up. The apparition remained there, looking as though it wanted to strike up a conversation.

'What are you?' he murmured in the hope the sound of his own voice would send him crashing back to reality. Does too much alcohol make you talk to your own hallucinations?

The bird dipped its beak and replied with a soft warbling note. Were hallucinations meant to answer the person having them?

'What are you doing here?'

The bird's crest fanned open in a cascade of glittering gold and, unable to help himself, Jorden reached up and touched its feathers. They were soft, warm and very real. Surely he shouldn't be able to feel an illusion?

The bird couldn't have come from his brain. There was too much wine still swilling about it to dream up anything but nightmares. The apparition fluttered its wings.

'Don't go. Come again when I'm not sleeping and tell me you're real.'

The bird fixed its penetrating gaze on Jorden and he rapidly slipped into a deep sleep.

The next visitor to interrupt his dreams was very real, gaunt, battle scarred and dressed in black.

'Matteo...' As he woke, the General wondered why he was sprawled on a bed of fern and nettle.

Matteo didn't offer to help him up.

'I had a strange dream.'

'You drank rather heavily last night, General.'

'Did I do anything I should remember?'

'You called the chief magistrate a pimp and pit of corruption, their patron saint a sodomite who mistook masturbation for divine ecstasy, the keeper of the largest brothel the only honest woman in Via La Rosa, and their Fra Filippo a sanctimonious parasite who wouldn't bless a sick orphan unless they bled with the stigmata.'

The General groaned. 'Why didn't you stop me?'

'There didn't seem much point after you had told the town's elders that they were more interested in the dowries and ducats they had saved by selling their daughters than in freeing their town.'

'Why did I do that?'

'You summoned their council when the eldest daughter of a lawyer told you about Via La Rosa's trade of forced marriages.'

Jorden suddenly remembered the other victims she had brought with her. 'Dear Jesus! Are they still in my office?'

'No General. As you instructed, I took a detachment of men and broke into the town's coffers. We supplied the women with enough to start new lives and escorted them away from Via La Rosa under cover of darkness.'

'You did remember to pay the men guarding them as well?'

'Naturally, so I doubt if they will be back either.'

Jorden laughed. 'How this town must hate me.'

'You have managed to stamp on some tender sensibilities since we've been here. I hardly think it wise you should wander about without any armour or a sword.'

He knew that, but had to get away from the town before his brain boiled. It contained such carping, mean-minded people, he couldn't understand why the Duke wanted the town.

'What good can come out of a place like this, Matteo?'

'They make excellent wine.'

Jorden couldn't deny it. 'After last night you'll have to keep me away from it.'

Matteo raised an eyebrow. He knew that would put even his resolve to the test. He lifted Jorden's sword and scabbard from his shoulder and handed them to him.

The General reluctantly took the weapon. 'Why must you think I'm always ready to slay something? You're far more efficient with a blade than I am.'

'But I haven't your courage.'

'Killing doesn't require courage, Matteo. Dying does.'

'That I know you will do with honour as well.'

'I wasn't planning on it just yet, and then it will probably be from poisoned mushrooms.'

'Not wine?'

'That I forswear.'

Matteo's hard features cracked a cynical smile. 'What was this dream you had, General?'

'It was of a bird, a large golden bird.'

Matteo's face froze.

'What's the matter?'

'Two guards claimed they saw a golden bird circling Via La Rosa this morning.'

'Morning?' interrupted Jorden. 'How long have I been here?'

'It's well past midday.'

Jorden rubbed his head. 'That's not possible.'

'I've been searching for you for over three hours.'

The General leapt to his feet. 'But why...?'

'Why what, General?'

'Why would that bird send me to sleep for so long?'

Matteo cast him a circumspect glance.

'What was this bird doing?' Jorden demanded.

'The guards claimed that it was spying on the town.' Matteo shrugged. 'A Frenchman and Englishman. Not the most reliable.'

'We have to get back.'

Before Matteo could say any more, the General strode off.

CHAPTER 36

Via La Rosa was deserted at a time when it would have normally been bustling with its drab inhabitants.

Jorden and Matteo ran to the central piazza and merchant hall where they had made their barracks. Waiting for them was the first lieutenant and a soldier with the General's armour.

The officer was very agitated. 'Where have you been General?'

'In a drunken stupor, Menzies.' Jorden pulled on his pourpoint and Matteo fastened his breastplate over it; there was no time to buckle on the rest. 'Why is the place deserted?'

'A large golden vulture has been swooping down on our men.'

'Anyone hurt?'

Knowing the General's logical mind and sarcastic tongue, Menzies was surprised that he accepted the story. 'They ran off and hid in the barracks.'

'Call the rabble out and muster them in the piazza.'

'Very well General.' Menzies and the soldier left.

'If Via La Rosa is staying inside, shouldn't we do the same?' suggested Matteo.

'The people must see that the Duke's army cannot be intimidated by a bird.'

Matteo deferred to his superior's common sense.

The mercenaries were more intimidated by General Jorden than any harpy, and allowed themselves to be herded into the town's piazza. The townspeople looked on from behind their shutters. In his determination to show the resolve of his men, Jorden didn't pay any attention to the pile of wood near an olive tree in the centre of the piazza until it obstructed the formation his men.

'What's that doing there?'

'Two hours ago an old woman told the people to build a pyre,' explained Menzies. 'She was wittering something about it being for the firebird.'

'Wasn't carrying a basket of mushrooms was she?'

'General?'

'Forget it.'

'Everyone is out now, General.'

'Good.' Jorden knew that something was going to happen. His mercenary rabble would be unreliable when it did, even if the Duke had sent their wages. He turned to Matteo. 'Go inside and change into something less conspicuous. Try to look like a lawyer.'

'I should stay with you, General. I'm a better a fighter than any man here."

Jorden clasped Matteo's shoulders. 'Look you old fool, twenty years ago we could have controlled this town between us. Now I'm ordering you to leave Via La Rosa at the first sign of trouble.'

'What about you General? You could be killed.'

'Then don't stay around to see how well I die.'

'Very good General.' Matteo reluctantly went into the rotunda Jorden had made his HQ.

Through the curtain of silence, Via La Rosa's deep loathing was almost tangible from behind each balcony shutter. Jorden shuddered inside at the thought that his mangy, mercenary men were the only things between him and the resentful population.

Suddenly the air was filled with lightning.

Jorden shielded his eyes and looked up.

His lieutenant was alarmed. 'What is it General?'

The lightning hammered down like the bolts from crossbows and encircled the wide piazza in a blazing hoop of fire. Above it a winged shape was silhouetted against the dazzling sky.

The General drew his sword. 'That bloody bird!'

His troops weren't so keen to tackle magical entities, especially ones that could spit lightning. As they tried to escape the cauldron of flame, their lines broke up. Jorden turned to tell Menzies to sort them out, but he had gone.

When the golden bird swooped down on him, he knew it was pointless trying to rally his troops. Too enraged to remember the touch of the soft plumage or expression in the large brown eyes, the General slashed ineffectively at it with his sword.

Having made its point, the bird settled in the olive tree where it fluffed out its gleaming feathers and looked provokingly pleased with itself. His soldier's instinct told Jorden to destroy the creature, but his heart wouldn't allow him to cut down a beautiful dream. As he gazed at it, his sword slipped from his grasp. He gazed so intently he glimpsed a figure with carved jade features out of the corner of his eye.

Now the sky no longer spat lightning, the townspeople filtered from their houses to surround the General and the strange entity.

After looking down at Jorden for some time, the bird warbled a few notes.

He reached up to touch it.

As his troops had fled, the mob pounced.

The bird gave a whistle of alarm and fluttered its wings.

Many of the General's attackers received lasting impressions of his gauntlets before sheer weight of numbers overcame him.

A young man nursed a blow to his jaw. 'What shall we do with our General then?'

'Feed him to the bird!' screamed the miller's wife.

'Ask it if it likes serpent meat,' jeered her daughter.

Despite the crowd trying to sit on him, Jorden forced himself to his feet. 'If it lived off civilised reasoning, it would soon starve in this place.'

Someone struck him a blow in the kidneys with the shaft of a hoe and he crumpled to the ground.

As soon as it was safe enough, one of the magistrates appeared from the crowd. 'Oh look, our dreaded General has forgotten where his knees are. What a pity we can't say the same for his tongue.'

More magistrates and lawyers arrived. They were a deathly looking bunch. Over years of near isolation they had evolved a predatory appearance, close-capped and close-shaven with bottle green gowns and lacking the dull finery that was the only thing to redeem Count Paolo's court. If one spoke, he represented all of them, like a many-headed hydra with legal training. They may not have been as deadly, though few worked so hard at looking venomous.

Jorden sneered. 'I suppose you virtuous upholders of the law have crawled from under your stones to see justice done? Am I to be condemned because you never managed to catch those daughters you sold into slavery?'

Someone seized his hair and wrenched his head back. 'They'll be no law watching here until that self satisfied expression is nailed over the town gates.'

'The head off my shoulders would be a better advertisement for Via La Rosa than all your magistrates still able to use theirs. And where is your holy Fra Filippo? Still trying to confess all those honest women who chose a brothel sooner than marry?'

A sweet, bell like voice ascended above the melee. 'What is he talking about dear?'

'Go home woman!' boomed the magistrate. 'This is no place for an honourable lady.'

'Stay Signora, and learn a good reason for your divorce.' But Jorden had never had any influence over dutiful wives and she left.

A more familiar voice rose above the hubbub. 'You? Advise honest women?' Fra Filippo picked his way through the throng like a wading bird, shoulders hunched, and piercing gaze ready to skewer anything that could spell heresy. His mincing, sanctimonious manner was the opposite of Jorden's nonchalant stride that gave the impression he could step over anyone who didn't move out of the way. Unfortunately the General was in no position to demonstrate it.

'Ah, Fra Filippo. For a moment I thought the bird might have mistaken you for dry bread.'

The friar tried to tower over the General with virtuous indignation. He only managed to resemble a desiccated spider that had lost an argument with Matteo's knives. 'There is a cure for the immoral.'

'Cut anything from my body you want and I'll still be a better man than you. I've always been more honest in my dealings with women than these married lawyers.'

'Barbarian!'

'Having fair hair does not automatically consign a man to Hell.'

The friar knew what he wanted to do with him before that happened. 'You do realise the fate of heretics don't you?'

In reply a cacophony of gruesome suggestions filled the air.

While the crowd bickered amongst themselves, a boy retrieved the General's sword and wended his way to him. Unsure what to think, the crowd fell silent and allowed Gerard Jorden to take the weapon.

'Are you mad!?' raged the chief magistrate.

The boy was not intimidated. 'Even the Duke's henchman must be allowed his honour, Signore.'

Jorden hadn't been expecting this escape route. He quickly turned the sword, but Matteo had fastened his breastplate so well he couldn't release it. The boy tried to help him as jeers started to echo through the crowd.

As the mob once again closed in, Jorden thrust the sword back into the boy's hands. 'Get away quickly. Find a more deserving cause to risk your life for.'

The boy left and the General disappeared under a barrage of blows.

'Wait!' screeched the cracked voice of the old herbalist. She was clutching a torch and standing by the pile of wood. 'He's of no consequence.' She pointed to the golden bird. 'This creature saved Via La Rosa, now you don't even bother to look at it.'

'Vengeance can be too sweet to wait for,' called the candle maker.

The herbalist thrust the torch into the pyre and the dry kindling crackling into life. As the crowd watched the flames catch the branches and logs, she went to the battered General.

'Why didn't you use your sword, gentian eyes?'

'You sent the boy?'

'My grandson.'

'You understand that bird?'

'More successfully than I read your eyes.'

'I told you not to make a prophecy. You should have gone home and cooked your mushrooms.'

'If you had guarded your tongue better, it might have occurred to some lawyer to ransom you.'

'Duke Vittorio would have only returned my commission. He's not one to throw money after a lost cause. You saw how his army ran. There was no hope of them raising a sword without being paid first. The hatred now consuming your revered leaders was caused solely by my own sweet tongue. Words cut deeper than the sword when they're the truth.'

'May God forgive you for seeing so much truth.'

'I wish I could forgive myself for repeating it.'

'You are but human.'

'I'd give my soul to remain iron for one hour longer.'

She laid a rough hand on his head. 'It will help if you forget your honour. When you are dead, it won't matter to you what other people thought of the way you died.'

'Please go. This mob is so volatile it could turn on you.'

The herbalist looked back at the fire that was now well alight. 'Goodbye General.' She melted through the crowd after her grandson.

As the orange flames rose, the golden bird left its perch. Whistling and warbling, it swooped about the fire, fanning with its wings until it blazed higher than the surrounding roof tops, and the heat was so intense the onlookers had to move back.

The golden bird hovered, stationing itself above the inferno. It folded its wings and fell from the sky like a thunderbolt. The entity struck the fire with such force it exploded in an eye numbing flash.

When the crowd was able to see again, the piazza had been transformed. All that was left of the fire was a circle of fine ash. Inside it a huge dome of light glowed like an illuminated bubble of milk. It slowly cleared to reveal a slightly built brown man. He was dressed in a white robe from waist to ankle and more jewellery than the latest papal edict on the matter allowed. On his forehead, just above his closed eyes, was a disc of gold.

Jorden marvelled. Was this the true form of his immortal foe? He could have reached out and crumpled the strange creature with one hand.

The townspeople hesitated, wondering whether the Pope would approve of their deity. Even Fra Filippo, having long nursed the vision of donating his beatification to posterity, quailed at the sudden arrival of this pagan priest. The mangiest curs held their bark and the rabid crowd momentarily forgot they were lusting after General Jorden's blood. If it had occurred to him to crawl away to where Matteo and the few remaining regular soldiers were hiding, he would have found them also stricken by the same lack of battlefield wits.

When Ahmose eventually opened his eyes, he wondered why he had this effect on people.

The chief magistrate was nudged by his wife.

'What are you?' the trembling man waffled.

Ahmose replied in a civilised enough tone lacking any trace of exotic accent. 'A priest.'

Fra Filippo gave a nasty frown.

Ahmose tried to take in what was happening. 'I hope I wasn't interrupting anything?'

'No, no,' the chief magistrate explained agreeably. 'We were merely about to lynch the General here.'

He may have only possessed the brain of a bird at the time, but that hadn't been the Egyptian's intention. 'Is that necessary? Now his troops have gone, surely he is no longer any danger to you?'

Another magistrate smiled smugly. 'Ah, you must be foreign. This is a matter of vengeance. I've no doubt he would break every bone in your body for scattering his troops if we were to let him.'

Having already experienced a similar fate, Ahmose's mouth became so dry his tongue wouldn't leave its roof.

'It is just retribution for a heretic,' added Fra Filippo.

'I didn't realise...' After three thousand years Ahmose still couldn't think real evil of human beings. 'I never meant this to happen.'

'He is a heretic. This is what we do to them!' The friar raised his hand in a gesture a little too warlike for a holy man, and the crowd bayed like a many-headed banshee.

At any other time, the townspeople would have demanded the Church declare Ahmose's presence a miracle and Via La Rosa a place of pilgrimage. For all the splendour of his arrival, he didn't appear to be a Christian, and their determination to avenge themselves on General Jorden would have blinded them to a guest appearance by Mary, Mother of Christ. Not that she would have been inclined to attend the lynching of a libidinous non-believer.

Peasants, apprentices, shopkeepers, housewives, and matrons who had previously not even known how to box a child's ears, descended on Jorden like a deluge of ravenous rats, ripping off his breastplate and outer clothing. Blows and abuse rained down as he was dragged from one side of the piazza to the other until eventually felled in a pool of his own blood.

Ahmose was horrified. His wits were frozen, so he snatched off his crippling sandals in case he had to think with his feet.

As Jorden raised his arm to ward off the lash of a barber's strop, he could see another pyre being built against the olive tree. What the previous indignities had been unable to do, the thought of being burned alive could.

In panic, he thrust away the apprentices trying to seize him, only to have several farmers and peasants take their place. They overpowered the General and dragged him to the scorched olive tree where his legs were pinned against its trunk with logs and the blacksmith chained his arms to the lower branches. As Ahmose's arrival had obliterated the first blaze, the baker and his brother brought out a flaming log from their oven and placed it before Fra Filippo.

'Well, fire your torches,' ordered the holy man.

Numb with horror, Gerard Jorden watched as several young men obeyed the friar. One of them held his flame to the General's arm. The remaining shreds of his cream shirtsleeve blackened and ignited, his fair skin erupting into angry blisters. As the pain hit his brain, Jorden screamed. The youth lowered the fire, satisfied that the condemned was aware of the agony waiting for him. For the first time in his life the iron General experienced true terror and wept.

Fra Filippo gave a laugh that must have risen from the dungeons of Hell. 'Ah look, our proud General does have tears after all.'

'But not enough to put out this fire,' added a magistrate.

'Satan take all of you!' Jorden cursed.

Fra Filippo leaned as close to the soldier as he dared. 'No General, he's going to take you.' He turned to some peasants. 'Put more kindling under those logs.'

'Why not throw your bible on it as well, you shrivelled gargoyle!'

'You have a strange way of pleading for your life General, or perhaps I misunderstood you?' The friar's manner was so dangerous Jorden dare not answer. 'Well, is your pride worth burning for?'

Sense told Jorden that Fra Filippo was only tormenting him, but the terror of the flames made him realise that his honour and dignity were lying with the discarded armour on the other side of the piazza.

'Don't burn me...' he choked.

'Who are you talking to General? The pigeons?'

'Don't burn me!' This time the crowd heard him.

Was that an order?'

The rabble began to cackle in derision. Jorden hesitated. 'I beg you not to burn me!'

At last Fra Filippo had achieved something that justified his mean existence. 'Such fine honour! The General is begging us not to burn him!'

The townspeople hooted with laughter.

Jorden desperately strained against the chains.

'Stop those tears General, you'll only dampen the wood and die more slowly.'

The mob gloated, relishing the humiliation of the mighty man who had been sent to subdue them. When they had jeered themselves hoarse, Fra Filippo sardonically gave Jorden the last rites.

Torches were put to the ramshackle pyre and the twigs crackled into spiteful flame.

Suddenly something barged through the crowd like a demented hare. With one clumsy bound, Ahmose leapt onto the bonfire, scattering ignited twigs. Though they believed the deity was fireproof, the apprentices withdrew their torches. The Egyptian stood, back against the towering General, defying the mob like a squirrel defending its oak.

'What are you trying to do little 'priest'?' Fra Filippo asked as mockingly as he dare.

'You must not kill this man!'

'Why not?'

Ahmose wasn't quite sure. 'Are his crimes against you so terrible?'

Given the gravity of the situation, Fra Filippo daren't admit that they wanted to burn the man to death for being sarcastic.

'It is the natural order of things,' a lawyer said unsurely. 'Duke Vittorio executed the deputation we sent, so we shall execute the General he sent. He's a soldier, so should be prepared to die.'

'Why like this?'

The friar was becoming annoyed at the deity's attempt to steal his moment of glory. 'Who are you to interfere? What sort of priest are you anyway?'

'I'm a heretic. I believe in the Aton.'

The word heretic Fra Filippo knew only too well, though not what Atons had to do with them. 'So?'

'The Aton is compassion, the source of all light and enlightenment.'

'So is Jesus Christ! He is the only true saviour, not some obscure pagan fairy!'

The crowd held their breath. They may not have known what the Aton was, but its priest had a pretty dramatic way of making an entrance.

'Then the compassion of your Christ is very strange if you have to burn this man in his name.'

Defeated by logic, Fra Filippo resorted to cant. 'Christ is the only true saviour! He is the Son of God! Nothing is more powerful than the Holy Trinity!'

'The Aton is the sun! Isis, Hor and Osiris the Trinity!'

The friar paused, though not for long. 'Move aside heretic! This argument has gone on for long enough! Fire the wood!'

'They will not listen,' Jorden whispered desperately to Ahmose. 'If you aren't a demon able to save me, then save yourself!'

Jorden's plea only strengthened the animal priest's perverse resolve. Ahmose felt the flames rising on either side of him and wondered what would happen if he stayed where he was. He wished he could be as sure about his indestructibility as the crowd - That was the answer!

Not knowing where the authority in his voice came from, Ahmose raised his hand. 'Extinguish the fire or I shall bring down the wrath of the Aton on this miserable town and its cruel people!' The crowd fell silent. 'I shall lay a curse on everything you touch and eat and your women will be struck barren for generations to come.' He paused at the illogicality of generations to come springing from barren ancestors. Fortunately the mob seemed used to such inanities. 'You will draw only foul water from your wells and your cattle will drink from springs of blood.' It was getting hot and Ahmose was running out of threats. Something in his nature made them difficult to come by. 'The walls of Via La Rosa will crumble, and the lord who sent this General will plough your bones into the ground, the lakes will boil, your terraces be washed away in a deluge -' Though they were scared, Ahmose hadn't yet hit their Achilles heel, '- and very man here shall be struck impotent!'

Water hurtled from every direction.

The blacksmith released Jorden and he crumpled onto the wood. While he still had the power over the superstitious townspeople, Ahmose told them to carry the General to the rotunda requisitioned as his HQ.

Once inside, Ahmose ordered everyone out, then bolted all the doors he could find.

CHAPTER 37

Ahmose's head throbbed with the exhilaration of knowing he wasn't a powerless piece of mythological flotsam after all.

Then he looked down at Gerard Jorden who was feebly delirious and bleeding from an ugly tapestry of wounds.

The animal priest found the clean linen held in store as bandages for the troops and, although the butt of water in the basement kitchen looked clean, he boiled some in the cauldron on the still lit stove, threw in a cupful of salt, then left a bowl to cool. As it would have been impossible to drag the towering soldier up the twisting staircase to a bed, he pulled a straw mattress from the servants' quarters to the hall where the patient lay.

After cleaning and dressing Jorden's wounds, Ahmose covered him with a long russet coloured robe he had found. It was only then that he recalled what the magistrate had said about the soldier wanting to break every bone in his body. The Egyptian priest was used to ministering to large dangerous animals, but hoped that this one would remain unconscious.

Suddenly Ahmose didn't feel so clever after all. In his haste, he had locked himself inside a deserted building with a colossus who would probably have designs on his life as soon as he came to. If the priest fled back outside, the town would no longer believe in his magical powers and probably burn his patient anyway.

Although Jorden looked peaceful enough, Ahmose spent a couple of hours hunting for weapons and hiding them as a precaution.

When he returned to the hall the General and the russet robe had gone. From the basement stairs cold, grey eyes watched Ahmose with motionless madness. As the General slowly ascended, the priest marvelled at the man's power and height and the reluctance of the thought to reach his feet. He may have hidden all the weapons he believed fit for a soldier, but forgotten the collection of lethal kitchen implements below. Jorden was clutching one of the blackened spits used to roast the carcasses of animals. This was no time to try and interest him in a diet of cabbage.

Ahmose was unsure whether the man knew who either of them was. 'General...?'

'Demon!'

He obviously didn't.

The priest backed away. 'My name is Ahmose.'

'Offspring of Satan! Warlock!'

'I'm not really...' Ahmose thought he was sounding reasonable enough. Then the blackened iron lashed out from nowhere, surprising the air it cut through and removing some skin from the Egyptian's chest. The priest knew that not even bleeding would persuade the man of his mortality. He fled up the rotunda's staircase in the hope of reaching the roof and finding a trap door to bolt.

Insanity must have been a good suppresser of pain. Despite his injuries, Jorden was faster. Ahmose barely managed to reach the top floor where he hastily locked himself inside the General's quarters.

Jorden's room was still tidy, as though expecting his more orthodox return. The large bed had been made and there was a trimmed candle on some despatches beside it. Ahmose went to the window and looked out over the red and yellow roofs of the jumbled town and green hills beyond. In a distant valley, storm clouds were rising to unload the deluge he had threatened to bring down on the region's terraces. The priest poured some wine and swallowed it to stop himself shaking, then realised how cold it was.

Suddenly the lock was sheared from the door, and it clattered across the room after its key.

With a curious detachment, Ahmose watched it come to rest by the desk.

Then the door crashed open.

A distant flash of lightning briefly illuminated the demon hunter.

The spit had been bent by the General's novel way of picking the lock. It now looked even more menacing.

Ahmose gulped down some wine, hoping it would dull the pain of whatever was about to happen. As his eyes grew wider with fear, the more Gerard Jorden could see the Devil blaze in their depths.

Nimbly, Ahmose avoided two blows. The third buried the spit in a bedpost. Seeing his chance, he darted for the door. Jorden seized the priest as he passed, picking him up and shaking him like a half-full sack of sawdust.

The soldier's tone was harsh and manic. 'Curse me demon! Put your evil eye on me!'

For all the good it was, Ahmose suddenly realised that the General believed this pagan priest was indestructible. In his madness he was trying to provoke him into meting out some mystical punishment to purge his fevered brain.

Ahmose looked down from where he was suspended. 'I can't harm you. Please put me down,' he said firmly. The voice of authority had no effect.

Suddenly the priest was flying.

His head collided with something hard.

CHAPTER 38

Rain hammered against the shutters.

By a candle's glow, Ahmose could see the spit still impaled in the bedpost. A bandaged hand reached out to remove the blackened implement with one tug and tossed it to the floor. A bruised, haggard face looked down at him.

Ahmose pulled the bedclothes over his head.

Then there was a remarkably mellow voice. 'It's all right, the madness has gone.'

The priest cautiously lowered the sheets.

Jorden lamely flicked his russet robe. 'It's now safe to look at the headless chicken plucked from the armour which made it believe it was invulnerable.' Ahmose daren't say anything. 'Would you prefer me to go mad again?'

'No!' He would have pulled the bedclothes back, but Jorden clutched them before he could.

'I think, with a little more practise, I might even manage to frighten a few hens.'

'You terrified me!'

'I'm sorry, little pigeon. I've never had this problem with birds before.'

Ahmose was still apprehensive. 'Are you sure you're all right?'

'Oh yes. Only, instead of spitting venom, I'm now swallowing self-esteem.'

'I don't understand you?'

'Yes ... I'm foreign as well.'

'So am I.' As the conversation limped to a halt, Ahmose gazed at the rain trickling through the shutters.

Without his brain fever, Jorden was weak and had to perch on the bed. 'I thought you were immortal?'

'Only the bird. The man bleeds and breathes like everyone else. It can cause confusion.'

'You struck your head on the desk.' Jorden applied a cold compress to Ahmose's wound. 'Trying to kill you made me regain some of my wits. I don't know where the rest went to.'

'Can you escape?'

'There is no way out. If the mob try to take me again I will go down to join them from the window. It's a woman's way to die, but even Jezebel had more honour than this spineless insect ... and I can't find a sword to fall on.'

'I hid all the weapons.'

'Why did you risk your life to save a headless chicken?'

Ahmose was surprised he needed to ask. It would have been a horrible way to die. How could he have been expected to accept such a fate calmly?

The priest's humility refused to let him acknowledge his own valour. 'I really have no courage.'

'Then I'm the world's bravest man, a Hector, a Ulysses! I should be invited to Mount Olympus.'

'Mount Olympus?'

'Home of the Greek gods. I'm probably too Teutonic for them anyway.'

'Oh? They're nothing to do with the Aton?'

'The Aton?'

'The source of all compassion. The mighty orb of Ra Harakhte, Ra Atum, Khepri, Amon Ra...'

'You're as mad as I am, aren't you?' Jorden touched the disc gleaming on Ahmose's forehead, wondering what manner of creature he was. 'Why did you come to this witch's cauldron?'

'I'm looking for an alchemist and her companion.'

'A fierce Greek woman and large, placid man?'

'Yes. After so many centuries I thought I would never see them-' Ahmose cut his words short, but it was too late.

'What? You mean that they are under the same spell as you?'

'Not the same. They don't have to grow feathers to become immortal.' Ahmose carefully clasped Jorden's damaged hands. 'Please don't betray them. I shouldn't have said anything.'

He laughed. 'Betray them? Rabbits don't have much say in the intrigues of dukes, counts and Fra Filippo, and that Greek can devour with her gaze in the same way your's could melt mountains.' Now the world knew he was a coward Jorden could admit to himself that she frightened him more than the Grim Reaper.

'You're not a rabbit, merely human.'

'Don't contradict me, it's the only thing I'm sure of.' Jorden leaned back against a bedpost and gazed at the coarse fringing of the canopy. 'Why did I try to kill you?'

'You were confused? I seem to confuse most people.' But there was one who was certain about the Aton bird's appearance. 'Is Fra Filippo powerful?'

'These mean-minded people believe in him. The magistrates are spineless and govern from under the table. He's probably still out there, praying that we're both consumed by hellfire.' Jorden added quickly, 'They'll not harm you though.'

Ahmose smiled weakly. His short lives were proving that such common sense statements applied to another planet.

Jorden sipped some wine to clear his thoughts. 'We'll have to find you clothes. A necklace and bangles will be no protection against this weather.' Ahmose suddenly missed his jewellery. 'I put them in a safe place. There are minds in this town that start plotting the moment they see gold. I soaked your robe in cold water; it was splashed with blood.'

'I'm not used to clothes. As for shoes...'

Jorden laughed so much at his odd companion he became giddy and Ahmose had to steady him.

'Your wounds will take weeks to heal.'

'The mob will not wait weeks for me.'

'How can we escape?'

The General looked at the shuttered window.

'Neither of us can fly,' Ahmose reminded him.

'Escape ... Yes. Now I know its meaning - but honour ... I've never understood that word before, only spelt it in despatches.' Jorden's eyelids flickered as he tried to stay awake. 'Words are such irrational things - they always interfere with what you mean...'

Jorden toppled into an exhausted sleep.

The storm had brought freezing air with it. The priest rummaged through a clothes chest and pulled out a shift and sheet large enough to wear as a toga. The next imperative was food so he went down to the kitchen. By the time Ahmose had brought back some dry bread, sour milk and dubious looking cheese, Jorden was delirious again.

The rain had stopped. The priest opened the shutters a little to let in the chill fresh air then found some warm blankets and curled up on the floor to sleep.

The coldness of his feet and a stream of sunlight eventually woke Ahmose - or was it someone crossing the patterned floor cloth?

He leapt up, expecting to find the General looking down at him with murder in his eyes, but he was still fitfully sleeping. A pleasant smell dawdled its way to the priest's nostrils. The aroma was being wafted from the desk where a large bowl of soup and fresh bread had been placed.

Too hungry to bother whether they were being haunted by a culinary phantom, Ahmose ladled some of the spiced lentil soup into a goblet and drank most of it before suspicion overruled his appetite. He put down the soup and warily descended the stairs.

The outside doors were securely bolted and the grilles over the windows still intact; even a mouse would have needed an appointment to get into the rotunda.

Baffled, and a little frightened, Ahmose noticed a pile of neatly folded clothes on a chest. Placed on top of them were his hateful jewelled sandals. His feet were so numb with cold he was grateful to see them. Beside the clothes, looking clumsy and very comfortable, were a pair of fabric slippers. He pulled them on and found instant warmth in their oversize depths. He shook out the other garments that must have been intended for him. They would never have fitted the General. However well the animal priest could understand the language, this mode of dress was a mystery to him and he had no idea how to put them on.

Ahmose snatched up the clothes before some poltergeist could reclaim them and scuttled back up the stairs.

Jorden had stopped trying to fight off zealous friars, magistrates and mobs and lay in a peaceful doze.

Ahmose filled a goblet with soup and its smell revived the soldier. Between them they finished the food and drank enough wine to make them wonder what they had to worry about. The voices of the townspeople far below soon reminded them.

'How easily can you change back into a bird?'

'It's never been easy.'

'Why not?'

'I have to die first.'

Gerard Jorden frowned. 'Die? Isn't that inconvenient?'

'You nearly gave me wings when you threw me across the floor.'

'I wasn't trying to make you fly. Forgive me.'

'The last time I felt pain like your's I could have hit someone as well.'

'Why didn't you?'

'They'd broken every bone in my body.'

Jorden hesitated. 'Do you have trouble with fortune tellers as well?'

'No, I was already expecting something like that to happen.'

'I was cursed by a child.'

'Children often regret their cruelty. They probably took it back.'

'She didn't have time. She was dead within the hour.'

The once optimistic Ahmose was now beginning to expect nothing better of life. 'I'm not superstitious.'

'You don't have to be. You're some sort of godling.'

'You should rest. You still look very wan.'

Jorden didn't believe he deserved to. He had never been humiliated before. Once pushed through the door to that universe, there was no stepping back. Vulnerability took some getting used to.

The priest laughed. 'There's no benefit in being a deity – I wonder why people worship them, and these people hardly deserve their "Christ" after what they were going to do to you.'

'Don't laugh like that.'

'Why not?'

Ahmose's sympathy was unfathomable. 'It might reassure me. If I'm fated to die horribly, I want to be prepared for it this time.'

'I should redress your wounds.'

Once again the priest descended the stairs to the hall.

A figure in black stepped from the shadows. Alarmed, the priest stumbled back up the stairs and hid in the guards' dormitory for a short while before cautiously venturing down again. The phantom had gone. A pitcher of water and clean linen was on a table.

Before Ahmose could take them back up to Jorden, somebody pushed a letter under the main door. It was addressed in a florid hand to "The Bird Deity". The priest now realised he would have been better off not understanding their strange language and stood contemplating the hard wax seal like a hypnotised chicken. Someone else was more impatient. A sinewy hand reached over his shoulder and took the letter from him. It was the intruder in black.

Ahmose fell to his knees in fright. He would have crawled away, leaving the letter with the phantom, but its very real heel had pinned his shift to the floor. A row of iron fingers lifted him to his feet. The priest looked up into the rugged features of a clean-shaven man with weather beaten skin and short, steely grey hair. He had probably been a soldier - by the number of scars on his face and neck, quite a bold one - yet his penetrating gaze was not threatening.

Feeling foolish, Ahmose pulled his absurd costume about him in an attempt to look reasonably adult if not very dignified.

'You are not wearing the clothes I left?'

Ahmose saw no shame in admitting, 'I don't know how to put them on.'

The severe features cracked into a smile. 'What's your name, little sparrow?'

The intruder's derision possessed a brittle good nature, though Ahmose wasn't sure how his other manifestation would have taken to being called a sparrow.

'Ahmose. Who are you?'

'Matteo.'

'Does the General know you?'

'Very well.'

'You aren't going to harm him?'

'Merely return his sword.'

'His sword?'

'The instrument any honourable man would have used.'

Ahmose had difficulty understanding this world's idea of honour. 'For what?'

'Do you mind if I read your letter?' Matteo's dagger split the letter's seal and he quickly scanned its contents. 'The magistrates are demanding custody of General Jorden.'

Ahmose had expected as much so Matteo's presence gave him hope. 'You can rescue him?'

Matteo paused guiltily. 'That's not why I came.'

'You know they will burn him?'

'I know.'

'Couldn't you take him out of here?'

'Yes.'

'Then why don't you?'

'Honour. He must be given the chance to redeem his honour.'

By Ahmose's baffled expression, it was obvious he came from a different world.

'I have served the General for many years. I know his likes, dislikes, pet names of his mistresses, and his thoughts as well as he knows them himself. Unfortunately, neither of us realised that he was a coward.'

Ahmose stepped back. 'Coward? How can you accuse him of that?'

'He pleaded for his life.'

This place was more surreal than the Egyptian pantheon. 'There is no cowardice in being afraid. Why did you come here?' Ahmose snatched Jorden's sword from Matteo's belt.

The General's aide laughed at his absurd attempt to be threatening and took the sword from the priest before he cut himself. 'I came to rescue you.'

Ahmose was suspicious. 'Why?'

'Because of your courage.'

Something told the priest he was being mocked, and it showed in his dark brown eyes.

Matteo tried to explain. 'Those of us who remained in Via La Rosa went into hiding, and decided to leave the General to redeem his honour-'

'If the General doesn't come with us, you can rescue the kitchen rats instead!' stormed Ahmose.

'Fra Filippo is plotting with some lawyers to have you condemned as a creature of the Devil.'

'I believe you.'

'Do not underestimate the cleverness of lawyers. Every province in this land teems with them. Training men in the law is a major industry here. Don't doubt that these sharks and vultures will rapidly put together the argument that will have you burnt.'

This made Ahmose pause. 'I fear the flames as much as the General.' He sat on a chest. 'I can fly into a fire when a bird and not feel a thing, yet when a man...'

'We were right. You aren't immortal.'

'I have been afflicted with cosmic confusion and lost track of the only woman who could help me. The longer I stay here, the less chance there is of finding her.'

Matteo smiled. 'You mean that Greek alchemist? I know where she is.' Ahmose looked up. 'The General gave her the address of Bianca, his mistress. Come with me and I'll take you to her.'

'Not without the General.'

'You are a stubborn-!'

'Hippopotamus.'

'I could rescue you whether you want me to or not.'

That would have been a novelty for Ahmose. 'What would this Bianca say when she learns that we left her lover to burn?'

'We would tell her that he died an hon-' Ahmose glowered. 'He died a brave death. A disgraced General would have no currency as a client in her position.'

'I won't leave him.' The priest rose and, toga flapping defiantly, stomped up the stairs. When he looked back, Matteo had gone as silently as he had arrived.

After his wounds had been dressed, Jorden sat at his desk and sorted through despatches as though they were still relevant to some campaign or other.

Ahmose watched the flames of a bonfire sparking against the sky. About the blaze danced an unworldly mixture of carnival masks and wedding apparel. Via La Rosa had dug deep into its clothes chest and rescued the best costumes from the moths to celebrate the coming execution. The animal priest shuddered; there was something demonic about the ecstatic display. Those prancing silhouettes splashed by fierce flamelight might well have risen from the hell Fra Filippo wanted to drag Gerard Jorden down to.

Ahmose poured some wine and thrust the goblet into the soldier's hands. 'Drink this, it will help you sleep.'

The General caught his wrist instead. 'Let me see your eyes.' He looked into the dark brown irises that had halos speckled with flame. There were no flowers or petals; instead a living gem of the sun sparkled in each. Another entity existed in their soft, dark depths; a parasite with fiery tendrils reaching into Ahmose's mind.

The priest turned away. 'Drink your wine.'

'Why this urgency to make me sleep?'

There was a familiar voice from the shadows. 'Because of me.'

'Matteo!' Jorden gave a wry smile. 'I thought I heard you applaud my speech to the good people of this town.'

'Have you no shame?'

'Has it ever occurred to you what it would be like to be burned alive?'

'No.'

'Well it suddenly occurred to me. Now I know why martyrs deserve statues.'

'There is no excuse you can make-'

'Leave him alone!'

Ahmose would have tried to drive Matteo out if Jorden hadn't gripped his arm. 'It's all right.'

Matteo contemptuously tossed the General's sword onto the bed.

Jorden looked at it for some while. 'I used to have a weapon just like that before my tongue taught my soul humility.'

'Humiliation, General,' his aide corrected. 'You laughed when that girl cursed you.'

'She was only another fortune-teller. I seem to attract them.'

'She died bravely. So did Tommaso.'

'No - Not our gentle scholar...'

'He was poisoned. I would have told you yesterday morning if I had found you sooner.'

'I should have made my peace with him.'

'Where you're going, you'll probably get another chance.'

'Oh no, I'm going to some heavenly poultry farm.'

'Are you in your right mind?'

'Ahmose can turn into a firebird, and I will end up as roasted fowl.'

'That is Fra Filippo's intention.'

'How long do I have?'

'Until dawn.'

Ahmose had no intention of letting it happen. He continued to insist that he escape with Matteo and him, but Jorden was now ready to face the inevitable.

'I must stay. Surely you understand that?'

'No, he doesn't' said Matteo. 'His mind is full of summer sunbeams. Don't try to explain.'

'You must go with Matteo, Ahmose. He will take you to Bianca. She can tell you where your Greek alchemist is. Have you ever known a beautiful woman, little priest? Or is that something your church forbids as well?'

Ahmose had met several beautiful women. 'Many came to inspect the animals in the menagerie.'

'Menagerie?'

'Yes, I was the second keeper of the sacred animals of the temple of Amon Ra.'

'I thought your god was called the Aton?'

'That's why I'm a heretic.'

'It's a shame we'll not have the chance to go mad together.' Jorden turned to his aide. 'Look after my little Icarus.'

'I will take him away tonight.'

Jorden returned to the desk.

'You must come with us,' Ahmose persisted.

'Matteo never carries excess baggage.'

After Matteo dressed Ahmose in his new clothes, the priest had never felt so uncomfortable in his lives.

Jorden sealed the letter he had just written. He handed it to his aide and asked him to fasten his silver doublet.

'Why must you wear that? It's good material.'

'I want to look like a bridegroom.'

'Tommaso died in scholar's black.'

'Tommaso wouldn't have begrudged me one last self deception.'

Ahmose tried to wriggle his clothes into a more comfortable position. 'I'll do it if you won't.'

Matteo sighed. 'You couldn't even dress yourself.'

'My little priest has dressed a hippopotamus before.'

'A what?' The only way he could put an end to their madness was to agree. 'All right.'

'Don't forget to take Ahmose's jewellery with you. It's in the money trunk. Please let Bianca have the other gold.'

Matteo nodded.

CHAPTER 39

At dawn the same crowd that had been demonically carousing the night before had gathered in smug silence like the angels of some underworld judge, dark in their religious weeds. The chief magistrate rapped his staff on the main door of the rotunda. No one knew what to expect, so a few discreetly carried swords and pikes.

The door was already unlocked. It creaked open and allowed sunlight to stream into the building and illuminate the figure sitting in the centre of the hall. The apparition was immaculate in silver velvet with gold tracery on its gloves and boots. A plumed hat hung from the back of the chair and a sword lay on the floor before it.

For a moment the crowd thought that the fire deity had transformed itself into a shimmering phantom. The magistrates were just relieved that the General was well enough to execute. As they were lawyers, they had been considering the complications of putting an invalid to death.

Gerard Jorden looked up at the angels of unspeakable death. 'Fra Filippo?' The owner of that dusty habit bustled forward. 'You should have a word with that gown about the way it wears you.'

The friar tucked his hands in his sleeves and scowled. 'You are in no position to be sarcastic, heretic.'

'I didn't realise there were rules.'

'This is no time for frivolity either.'

'I'll be frivolous about my own death if I want to. You can call on the wrath of God and spout virtuous steam all you like.'

'Not so long ago someone was spouting tears over the prospect of his own death.'

'I've no doubt you've dried out the wood?'

But Fra Filippo had something else on his mind. 'Where is that creature?'

'Our little Egyptian?'

'Who else?'

The General shook his head. 'Perhaps he didn't want to make his nest here after all.'

The friar turned triumphantly to the crowd waiting outside. 'There is no other way out of this place! He must be a demon!'

'Isn't it enough that you have me to burn, holy crocodile?'

'Burn?' said the chief magistrate. 'Who said anything about burning you?'

'Not so long ago you gave me that impression.'

'No, no,' chided the elderly man. 'You must realise how people get excited. We've a much better idea.'

'I'm going to be drawn and quartered so that mangy friar can read my entrails?'

Now Fra Filippo had discovered a pagan entity to persecute, Jorden had become irrelevant. 'You are going back to Settimo. Duke Vittorio has agreed to our autonomy in exchange for your return. Damaged, deranged or disgraced, it doesn't matter so long as you get there alive.'

Having been prepared for death, the General was no longer sure he could live with dishonour. 'Why?'

'Because he is more interested in capturing our Egyptian. He wants that demon more than sovereignty over Via La Rosa.'

'I wonder he didn't surrender your miserable collection of hovels for a bale of rat skins. The amount you have in the treasury coffers wouldn't have covered the wages of that rabble he made me recruit.'

A predatory looking lawyer slowly circled the soldier. 'Don't think you have escaped. The Duke will want to know the whereabouts of this heathen entity.'

'To you bigots, a sheep that didn't bleat in tune with its flock would be a heretic.'

'Defending the priest of Beelzebub is a dangerous business.'

'Beelzebub? What have you blood suckers been telling Duke Vittorio?'

'Enough to make sure there is still the chance of you-'

'Dying horribly,' interrupted Jorden. 'The way people mobilise to fulfil my destiny is quite touching.'

Fra Filippo had a spontaneous burst of religious fervour. 'Beware the wrath of God!'

'Oh no,' groaned Jorden. 'I'd sooner be put to death now than have to listen to another prophecy.'

'Do not mock God's disciple,' warned the chief magistrate.

'It's just that the women do it so much better.' Jorden tried to rise but slumped down again. 'All right, so the trip to Hell is going to take a little longer. I can wait.'

Jorden's occupying troops had excavated the secret passage that had facilitated Matteo's ghostly comings and goings. It led to the barracks next to the rotunda from where its access was concealed by a large flagstone in the kitchen floor. Given the commotion going on in the town, and number of people wearing masks, it was a simple matter for the remaining regular soldiers to don disguises and come and go as they pleased.

The golden disc on his forehead concealed by a scarf and hat, and the rest of him in those tight, pricking, grey garments, Ahmose looked safely unexotic as he tried to keep up with Matteo. Once on the road sloping through the terraces and away from Via La Rosa, Ahmose threw down his bundle.

Matteo seized his coat to stop him dashing back. 'Where do you think you're going?'

The priest wriggled from his grasp and sat by the roadside, looking up at him with an expression that could have grilled bacon.

It took more that that to intimidate Matteo. He loomed over Ahmose like a huge raven. 'It is too late for the General. They must be putting the torch to the fire now and, when they have finished with him, they will start searching for you. We've a three-day walk ahead of us. Do you think I can whistle down a couple of wild horses to take us?'

'I could.' Ahmose added peevishly, 'But I'm not going to.'

That ruffled the raven's feathers. 'What?'

'Why should they stop grazing just to save us?'

'I don't believe you.'

The priest tucked his knees under his chin and prepared to take root. 'I understand animals better than I do people.'

Matteo began to weaken. It was worth being proved wrong to acquire a couple of willing steeds. 'I've got a family you know. I want to see them again.'

'What about the General's family?'

'Illegitimate and oblivious he's their father.'

Ahmose was indignant. 'I don't believe you!'

'You can ask Bianca. Why else would he have put a large dowry in trust for her daughter? He's not the saintly warrior you believe. If I thought he was worth canonisation I would run all the way to Avignon and tell the Pope of his martyrdom.'

Ahmose fidgeted uneasily. 'How many dependants do you have?'

'Four orphaned grandchildren, a loving wife and frail old father.'

Matteo looked ancient; his father must have boarded the Ark with Utnapishtim.

'How frail?'

'Near to death for want of medicine.'

'No mistresses?'

'I'm a religious man.'

'Wasn't the General?'

'He's a German.'

Ahmose pondered for a little while. 'All right.' He tossed his bundle to Matteo and jogged into the valley as fast as his oversize shoes would allow.

Several nervous horses, mainly escapees from the battlefield, were watching from the uncultivated slopes. Anticipating hunters, most of the herd bolted but two bolder mares and a stallion observed him in curiosity. Ahmose put his hands to his mouth and gave a long whinny. The stallion threw back its head and galloped off. The mares warmed to the sound and cautiously came down.

Matteo joined him.

'You can ride without a bridle and saddle?' Ahmose asked.

'Of course. Just how tame are these animals?'

'I'll have to talk to them. Leave us alone.'

Matteo stood off a short way and watched the conversation of whispers and whinnies in wonder and disbelief. Then he heard a two-wheeled carriage flanked by armed riders coming from Via La Rosa.

'Damn! Get down!'

Ahmose and Matteo jumped into a ditch while the mares

looked on with casual interest. The outriders were more concerned about ambushes than bird deities, and the carriage rattled past at a dangerous lick.

Ahmose was first to break cover. 'What was that?'

Matteo had a horrible suspicion and wasn't prepared to share it. 'Call back the horses.'

The animal priest renewed his dialogue with the mares.

'They will take us to the pasture nearest Settimo.'

'What do they want for it?'

'Want for it? They aren't human beings.'

Matteo was somewhat disconcerted to find that, however absurd Ahmose may have been on his own feet, he was a far better rider than he was. They easily reached Settimo's capital as dusk began to fall.

The city clustered round a steep hill on which perched a palace that looked like the Devil's saltcellar in the setting sun.

Ahmose made a great fuss of the two mares, and then they galloped off to rejoin their herd.

'What did they say?'

'They would rather carry holy travellers to sanctuary than soldiers into battle.'

'Sanctuary?'

'You said you were religious and I need sanctuary.'

Matteo sighed. 'Well, you should be safe enough here as long as you don't start talking to the rats.'

'Rats are very intelligent you know.'

Matteo put both their bundles on Ahmose's back. 'Try to look beaten and lame.'

'Why?'

'Because most people your colour are slaves. And wipe that wise expression off your face. Only lawyers and the clergy are allowed intelligence. Someone might think I've been educating you.'

'But you have.'

'Oh no. That off-white lily, Signora Bianca, is going to do that.'

Matteo and Ahmose reached the gates just as they were about to close and were allowed into the walled city.

Away from the main thoroughfare was a maze of roads, intertwining canals and strange odours. Matteo led his wondering slave through crowds of traders packing their wares and past porticoes where richly dressed merchants discussed ships and florins. A long path beside a canal took them into a quiet world of tall apartments, and squares overhung by wrought iron balconies. Even the rats seemed more discriminating as they sorted their food from the detritus in the gutters.

Matteo rapped out a complex signal with an ornate knocker on a door discreetly concealed in a deep porch. A young trim servant unbolted it and let them in. As they entered, a statuesque woman dressed in a gown embroidered with flowers slowly descended a wide staircase. She sent the servant girl back to her chores.

Bianca had the regal bearing of a Byzantine Empress and enough shrewdness to survive the intrigues of a murmuring court. She was darkly beautiful, like a Phoenician. Her hands, the only part to betray her true age, had the power of an eagle's talons and a small, fine scar outlined her chin, adding to its strength. If life had not always dealt her a fair hand, she had apparently learnt how to shuffle the cards.

'Out so late Matteo? It will soon be dark.'

'I have no reason to fear brigands.'

Bianca laughed. 'How well I know that. One day you will have to let me pay you for the service of those daggers.'

'My blades have never demanded money from a woman.' Matteo took the General's letter from his doublet and handed it to her.

'Your servant looks lame. Where did you buy him?'

Ahmose tried to hide in the shadows.

Having read, Bianca lowered the letter. 'Gerard Jorden dead?'

'By now, most probably.'

'It was expected when he didn't return with his lieutenants.' Heartbreak quickly over, she turned to Ahmose. 'Are you this remarkable paragon?'

Matteo pulled off the priest's hat and scarf. 'You will

respect his secret?'

'What a strange little man.'

'He was a dear friend of the General's.'

Bianca lightly touched the golden disc on his forehead then ran a finger round his face. 'Yes, I will take care of him.'

'The Greek and African have gone then?'

'There was no reason for them to stay since the scholar was given poison.'

'Poor Tommaso.'

'Life had become a burden for him. The silly girl couldn't have known the price he would pay for her gallantry.'

'She did love him.'

'Laura should have kept a parrot instead.'

'That's what the General-' Matteo stopped.

Bianca smiled. 'We sometimes had the same thoughts. He was a calculating stallion with a cruel wit, but I shall miss him.'

Ahmose had difficulty recognising the man from his short friendship. 'The General, cruel?'

It would take hours for the courtesan to explain the complexities of the soldier's character. 'While Matteo tries to discover the road your alchemist took, you must stay here with me.' Fascinated by Ahmose, Bianca gently pulled him into the light where the disc on his forehead sparkled as though it had a life on its own. 'You must be tired after walking so far?'

Ahmose was on the verge of telling her about the horses.

Matteo jabbed him in the back. 'Egyptians can walk very long distances without stopping.'

'You're an Egyptian? I thought such creatures were a myth?'

Ahmose gave a weak smile. 'Only some of us.'

Matteo discreetly placed the purse of gold Jorden had entrusted to him on a table and turned to go. 'How long can you keep the priest?'

'It doesn't matter,' purred Bianca. 'I've always wanted an Egyptian.'

A plump, pinkish woman bustled across the reception

chamber.

'Maria, bring Signore Matteo a lamp.'

Without replying, Maria somewhat ungraciously dumped the bundle she was carrying and waddled off towards the back porch.

Bianca smiled. 'Don't let Maria worry you, Ahmose. She is like a caravel under full sail. She keeps the house and will probably take you in hand after she has managed to make you out.'

Maria bustled back with a lighted lantern. Matteo took it and silently left.

The rooms of Bianca's house were not heavily furnished, though their tapestries, carved chairs, chests and glass ornaments were opulent. Overlooking the courtyard where a fountain cascaded from two marble dolphins was a well-lit room containing several valuable volumes. The maps might have been the General's, though Ahmose wasn't sure about the treatises by the Greek philosophers. The writing desk, inkwell and golden quill no doubt belonged to Bianca as well.

Ahmose shuddered.

There could be no mistaking that feather. Why hadn't Helen seen it? He pushed the thought away. The priest realised that this world was even more unfair than the ones in his previous incarnations.

Several days passed.

Bianca taught the priest how to use a fork, play cards and add up columns of complex figures - for some reason these people were obsessed with money and accounts.

Matteo eventually returned to tell them that the alchemist and her companion had left for a villa in the south. Ahmose went to his room to watch the firelight fill the wall with flickering demons. Would he at last be allowed to escape immortality?

CHAPTER 41

That night, in his dreams, Ahmose floated on thermals over secret oceans. Glass dragons were born from the waves that created funnels of surf, others rolled into foaming serpents on coral beaches. Island pinnacles of volcanoes soared from the steaming spume to touch the powder blue sky. Resembling molten candle wax, castles of alabaster crested even higher peaks. They were supported by natural flying buttresses, fretted, fantastic shapes clinging to sheer walls of limestone like massive butterfly wings.

Ahmose woke early the next morning, reminded of the freedom mortality was robbing him of.

Everything in the house was silent, apart from the cooing of a dove. He pulled on a robe and silently descended the stairs.

Voices were coming from the reception room: Bianca, Maria and Matteo were in secret conversation.

Ahmose listened at the door.

Maria sounded even more bad tempered than usual. 'Can they make him admit where the Egyptian is?'

Matteo sounded exhausted. 'They will do anything to make the General confess. I saw the device Stefano Nogaret is forging. It's an evil contrivance. I've never known the like before.'

Maria gasped. 'Dear Jesus! What if he does confess? What will become of us?'

'He is a powerful man. He will protect his firebird friend. They will not break him.'

Bianca wondered how well she had known Duke Vittorio and her German lover after all. 'Would the Duke really have Gerard Jorden tortured?'

'The bird did route the Duke's troops, so it's small wonder he would like to get his hands on the pagan priest. If his advisors could persuade him to part with his only daughter, they could persuade him to torture the General, especially now Tommaso is no longer here to reason with him.'

'We must get Ahmose away before he's discovered,' Bianca decided.

Matteo hesitated. 'Aren't you concerned about the General's fate, Signora?'

'Don't be such a hypocrite, Matteo. You could have rescued him yourself if you had wanted to.'

'That was different.'

'No Matteo, your reasons were just as mercenary as mine. You helped delude the man into thinking he was something he wasn't, and I can't afford to have my name associated with his any more. My only concern is that Ahmose might try and save him.'

'Then he mustn't know I'm here.'

Ahmose silently went back up to his room. He took his jewellery, sandals and robe from their chest and put them on. Then he covered his forehead with a scarf and hat. From another chest he selected a long cloak that concealed him from head to toe.

When the priest came back down the stairs the others were still talking. He silently drew the bolt of the street door and slipped out into the chill morning air.

Traders were assembling their stalls. He asked a fishmonger where the road to the Duke's palace started. She was too sleepy to think the question odd and pointed to the straight thoroughfare that led to the ornate building overlooking Settimo. Ahmose left the market's smell of sweet decomposition and walked up the steep road.

The sentry at the palace gates was impressed by the foreign visitor's dignified demeanour and passed his request for an audience to the Duke's attendants who led him inside.

The palace was not a fortress like Count Paolo's. It had been built on the highest point in the region where it caught the light that made it shine like confectionery. Long halls with balconies overlooking Settimo surrounded spacious courtyards, and even the smallest rooms had arched windows, sometimes set with precious panes of coloured glass. Statues of creamy marble had been installed where shafts of sunlight illuminated their subtle, soapy contours and, away from the bleaching rays, hung millefleurs tapestries of traditional allegories.

Ahmose was awed. How could a monster live in a palace filled with such delicate glassware, enamelled vases and gorgeous furnishings?

He waited in the warmth of the early morning sunlight streaming into the audience chamber. When Duke Vittorio had dressed he entered with a secretary, servant and advisor.

The noble was an amiable man. Though the corners of his mouth were down-turned, his face occasionally lit up with a smile that could have persuaded the angels to forgive him anything. His thinning hair was fine and white, the sort that would survive the death of his mortal body. Were he to be disinterred in centuries to come, all they would probably find of him would be a grinning parody of that charismatic smile and a poll of silver white hair.

Ahmose was reassured by the Duke's friendly manner, and wondered how the man could have had anyone tortured. Perhaps that was his naiveté rearing its pointed head once again.

Duke Vittorio flopped into his chair like a large tired rodent. 'Well stranger, how much do you want for this information?'

'Merely the release of General Jorden.'

The Duke could hardly conceal his relief. 'Friend of his, are you?'

'Yes.'

The noble waved away the servant trying to fasten his shoes. 'There aren't many who would admit to that now.'

Trying not to choke on the "h" word, Ahmose made an effort to sound convincing. 'He is an honourable man.'

'I've always believed it myself. It's those other swine I can't persuade.'

'He's already injured. Why should he be harmed any more?'

'It was all my chaplain's idea. Great believers in torture, these zealots. Claim it purges the soul. This state's run by lawyers and the clergy. Have to let them prosecute and burn the occasional Jew, you know. Unfortunately, virtually everything I have is now collateral against their loans, so this pagan would come in handy. I don't have any qualms about seeing him burnt after what he did to my troops, especially after I paid them.'

Though he knew that their wages were still in the Duke's coffers, Ahmose had not come to argue with the man about his financial irregularities. The noble had set his sights on an exotic deity, so exotic deity he would have.

'Of course.'

'Now you look a reasonable sort of fellow. Strange colour perhaps, but you wouldn't be the first offspring of a slave to prosper. You must see that I have to put this bird creature back into the fire it supposedly walked from?'

'Has it been decided?'

'Oh yes, lawyers here work fast. We've already had the trial. No point in expecting it to turn up and take part. Might have had something interesting to chirp in its defence I suppose.'

'There is no alternative execution?'

'Church I'm afraid. Have to keep them happy. They proved it was a familiar of the Devil, you see.'

Ahmose faltered as he realised the full horror of what he was letting himself in for. 'When will you release the General?'

'As soon as I have the bird creature. I'll even pay his passage back to his misty forests. I don't want to see the man crushed in that contraption my jailer devised. Nogaret hasn't been able to torture anyone for months and was determined to make the most of the opportunity. Hates Gerard for turning his fiancée's head. The marriage was abandoned because of it. Girl soon found someone her own age who wasn't after the dowry. She was far too young for Gerard to be interested, but you know how it is when a man's jealous.' Ahmose looked innocently blank. 'The first part of the General's anatomy Nogaret intended to crush wasn't his heart.' Ahmose now looked uncomfortable. 'Ah well, no need for Signora Bianca to worry about that any more,' Duke Vittorio turned to his secretary. 'Make out an order of release. I can see that our friend only half trusts us.'

The secretary wrote the letter in an ornate hand and the Duke put his seal to it. The secretary handed it to Ahmose.

'You seem an amiable sort of fellow, African. What's your name?' Duke Vittorio asked.

'Ahmose.'

That sounded exotic enough to impress the Duke. 'Stopping long?'

'I think I will be.'

'I like your face. There's something honest in those eyes.' The Duke's advisor whispered in his ear. 'Oh yes, of course. You were going to tell me where this bird creature is?'

Ahmose dipped his head. His hat fell to the floor. Then he pulled off his scarf. He unfastened his cloak and it slipped off to reveal the fine pleated gown and jewels of a pharaoh.

The Duke was crestfallen. 'Oh no. Why does it always have to be this way?'

'I'm sorry.'

'I've just had my only child murdered, my precious scholar assassinated, my General dishonoured, and now you turn up to ruin my morning meal.'

'I'm sorry.'

Involuntarily Duke Vittorio held out his hand to take back the order of release. 'You can change your mind.'

Ahmose hesitated, trying to convince himself that the noble wouldn't really have a man tortured to tell him something that he already knew, but this was a different zoo to the one he had been familiar with. The humans here were unpredictable and twice as savage as any river horse.

'The General must not learn of our agreement,' Ahmose insisted.

'I'd never be able to handle him if he found out. You really believe the man is worth the sacrifice?' Ahmose nodded. 'Is there anything you want of me?'

'I would like to see the General.'

'Very well, you can take the order of release to him. I'll have no more part in it.'

'I'm sorry.'

CHAPTER 42

A soldier unbolted the door to allow the captain of the guard in.

As the prisoner rose, the captain looked up at his disgraced superior with begrudging deference. 'The order for your release has arrived Signore.'

'Release?' Gerard Jorden had been expecting all the torments of Hell to descend on him. 'Why?'

The captain said nothing. Instead he turned and beckoned to someone.

'Ahmose! Who betrayed you? Tell me? I'll kill them!'

The priest's smile was serene and strangely secretive. 'Will you swear to that General?'

'I swear it!'

'The Duke has your sword. Ask him for it when you are ready to do the deed.'

'I promise. First I have to stop them burning you.'

'That is impossible. Everyone seems set on the idea. I think they want to sacrifice me to their "Christ".'

'No, these same people murdered the Son of God so they could create a church without being bound by his teachings.'

'That is blasphemy,' the captain dutifully reminded Jorden.

'Against whom? The swarms of self righteous prelates who drink his blood, make soup of his words and pass it around in their hypocritical ladle.'

'You are distraught, Signore.'

'Of course I'm distraught! Do I still have to pretend I'm invulnerable? Did you feel secure because you believed your General was made of iron?'

'Yes, Signore. All soldiers wish they were made of iron. Because we aren't, our best hope is to hide behind someone who is.'

'Then beware old women picking mushrooms.'

Though the sun had not set, the shutters of the study had been closed as if in anticipation of another bereavement. Or perhaps Duke Vittorio thought that his companion would be less likely to kill him if his noble contours were softened by candlelight.

Gerard Jorden had long since given up contemplating murder. His injured hands may have still been capable, but his battered senses no longer possessed the determination.

The air was not cold, but a large fire blazed in the grate. In its reflection the embroidery of the Duke's cotehardie gleamed, a filigree web of flowery stars floating over a haze of maroon velvet. Gerard Jorden should have cursed the man for bewitching him into being his mindless hired hand. Instead, being a victim had given him an irrational compassion.

From the sanctuary of his winged, brocade chair the Duke looked guiltily into Jorden's ashen features. 'Well of course I have to pay you. A contract is a contract. However much you're willing to surrender for Ahmose's life, there is no way I can reverse the court's decision. I was the one who first demanded that it be implemented.' He handed Jorden's commission back to him. 'Go home Gerard. This land is no place for a man of your burgeoning morality. If it helps, I know I've been dishonest with you.'

'Dishonest?' Jorden thought he was referring to his troop's lack of wages.

'I've always known you're not a soldier at heart. You couldn't wring the neck of a chicken in cold blood, even if you were starving.'

At last the General could admit it to himself. Why had he allowed himself to be encouraged in the delusion? If Via La Rosa had believed he was capable of putting it to the sword, that rabble would never have had such contempt for him. General Jorden was a porcupine in a tiger's skin. He'd never known himself for what he was. The Duke had helped delude him because it was convenient. He had more enemies in the guilds, Church and his own family than those abroad. The occasional sight of Jorden and that assassin, Matteo, striding through Settimo no doubt made him more secure than he deserved.

'I owe you much, and will never be able to repay it,' the Duke admitted.

'Save Ahmose.'

Duke Vittorio remained silent and reached forward to fasten one of the bandages unravelling from Jorden's hand.

The German shook his head. 'The forests of my home are gloomy enough to hide the gates of Hell. Small wonder they produce so many barbarians. You're a little nearer the sun. Why aren't you more compassionate?'

The Duke knew Jorden too well to bend to his argument. He didn't blame him for being unable to die honourably - there was nothing in his commission that said he should.

'Would you burn in Ahmose's place, Gerard?'

Jorden grew even paler. 'Yes, or be slowly crushed, publicly, in the machine Nogaret took great pleasure in showing me. At least there would be some entertainment in that.'

The Duke believed he would go through with it, but the Church would not trade an exotic pagan priest for a dishonoured, damaged mercenary.

'What else can we do but burn him?'

'You don't believe he changed from a bird?'

'If he walked out of a fire, why this desperation to stop him going back into one? Think rationally man.'

'Must he burn?'

Duke Vittorio resented the way Jorden towered over him like a mighty tree blasted by a gale. 'What can I do about it? Have him poisoned in his cell?'

'Why not? You did as much for Tommaso.' The Duke glowered. 'I'm sorry. Can I see Ahmose?'

'No. Don't try to get a stay of execution either. That would only prolong the wretched business.'

Jorden sat down and contemplated the fire for some time. 'Who betrayed him?'

'Must you know?'

'Ahmose made me swear to kill them.'

The Duke gave a thin smile. 'Would you do it?'

'I gave my oath, even if it were Bianca or Matteo.'

'No, it was neither of them.'

'Tell me?'

A sudden shiver convulsed Duke Vittorio as though the Grim Reaper had tapped his shoulder. 'Leave tomorrow morning Gerard and never return.'

'Tell me?'

The Duke rose from his chair. Hesitantly, as though approaching a wounded eagle, he put his hand on Jorden's shoulder. 'Ahmose betrayed himself to save you.'

Settimo lay far below, encircling the palace. The main piazza and the streets radiating from it made the capital resemble an embroidered flag, its edges crimped by the irregular city wall and network of alleyways surrounding its border. Though Duke Vittorio's province didn't have so many feuding families as Count Paolo's, their houses were tall enough to act as sundials for the rest of the city; the shadows they cast fell over everyone at some time or another.

The palace piazza was decked out as though ready for a tourney. Instead of the tilt, was a pyre and, where the knights should have struck their banners above it, sat several rows of stern faced lawyers. Facing them across the piazza was a large crucifix pointing up towards the glowering red sun; the representatives of the all-powerful Church seated beneath it. Only lawyers, the clergy, the Duke's household, and those merchants and bankers he owed money to, had been invited to attend the burning of a creature too exotic for the proletariat gaze. Everyone was so intent on the spectacle about to take place, few thought to look heavenward, though many astrologers in the land did notice the change in the sun.

Duke Vittorio sat back on his throne and wondered why he hadn't inherited the firm set of his father's chin. Apart from his title, all that man had passed on to him was a city full of vengeful clergy, avaricious merchants, uncompromising money lenders, predatory lawyers, and a province filled with rebellious towns. That sharp pain once again clenched the noble's stomach and, sooner than call a doctor who would only make it worse, he tightened the muscles in his abdomen. As he noticed a tall, dishevelled figure standing in the cover of an archway the pain slowly eased.

The ladies of the Duke's family, seated comfortably on a platform before the loggia, delved into their sleeves for perfumed kerchiefs to protect their noses from the impending stench, and he managed a cynical smile at his retinue of bloodthirsty harpies.

Ahmose was hustled up from the cells and the murmur of

anticipation slowly died. The nearer the priest was dragged
to the pyre, the harder he pulled back. Because the crowd
was intent on the uneven tussle, they didn't notice the lofty,
unkempt individual dressed in a silver velvet doublet dart
from the shadow of the loggia and kneel before Duke Vittorio.
The noble pulled the General's sword from the scabbard
beside his throne and handed it to him.

Gerard Jorden strode to the execution detail.

'Let me talk to the prisoner,' he commanded.

Despite the disapproval of the priest hoping to confess the
heretic before he burnt, the soldiers obeyed out of habit and
stepped back to form a semi circle behind Ahmose.

Ahmose toppled towards Jorden. 'General!'

'Don't be alarmed little priest.'

Jorden plunged his sword through the prisoner's chest
with the speed of a surgeon.

The guards didn't realise what had happened until the
blade clattered to the flagstones and blood spurted from the
severed aorta. Immediately the slender cord that had held
Ahmose to his incarnation snapped.

Clergy, lawyers, and ladies rose in protest at the
premature death of their sacrifice.

His silver velvet doublet and cream shirt saturated in
blood, Jorden lifted Ahmose's body above his head like an
offering to the setting sun. The soldier's sleeves fell back and
scarlet rivulets spiralled down his arms.

The reddening sun became livid, bathing everything in a
gory hue.

Those preparing to revel in a fiery execution now thought
they were being drowned in blood.

Silhouetted against the red mattress of the sky, Ahmose's
body started to glow. A pulsating halo engulfed him and
Gerard Jorden. There was a faint rustling above the
General's head and he could feel soft feathers between his
fingers. Petal like, a large golden bird was unfurling. It
spread huge fiery wings and left his outstretched arms to
soar into the scarlet sky.

Like a needle of gold threading its way through a field of
red silk, the bird flew towards the angry sunset. As the entity

disappeared, the sun's normal rosy hue returned and the air was purged of its leaden rage. All that lingered were the eerie notes of a song spun about the palace in a ghostly noose.

Jorden sank to the ground beside his sword, hardly aware that the sticky saturation of Ahmose's blood had vanished.

The clergy, lawyers, ladies and courtiers fled in panic until Jorden was the only one left in the piazza. He sat on the cool comforting flagstones watching the sun set, then became aware of a gaunt figure dressed in black.

'Your honour, General? Where is your honour?' it rasped.

'There is no such thing as honour, Matteo, only life, sensation, and death.'

'Your mind has become addled.'

'We were wrong. We were both wrong. Ahmose always knew that. Why didn't we understand?'

'Why did you betray him?'

Jorden nearly toppled over at the accusation. 'Betray him?'

'No one but the Duke's agents could have spirited him away from Signora Bianca's house so efficiently. You were the only other person with a key to the courtyard gate.'

'Kill me and pray my soul goes to Hell, but don't believe I betrayed him!'

'What did they do to make you confess?'

'I'm only a coward once, Matteo. They could have tortured me witless. Nothing would have induced me to betray Ahmose.'

'Now they believe you have consorted with the Devil, Stefano Nogaret will get his wish.'

'Is that what they think?'

'And a great deal more besides.'

'That sounds like a lot of pain.'

Matteo kicked the hilt of Jorden's sword towards him. 'Here is the cure. Even the Duke cannot help you now.'

'Would you watch while I fought the Devil with one hand and God with the other?'

'Don't be a fool!'

'Killing myself would eliminate no one's contempt of me, especially my own.'

At last Matteo started to have doubts. 'Then be a coward and escape while the palace guards are still hiding.'

'You don't really want me to die horribly, do you old friend?'

Matteo's frustration got the better of his carefully engineered disdain. 'Damn you General! For pity's sake do something!'

'Does it bother you that I proved to be a mere mortal after all?'

'A mere mortal would not be able to cope with what Nogaret has planned for you.' Matteo's resolve snapped. 'Must I plead with you to leave?'

'Do you remember Laura, Tommaso... Ahmose..?'

'There is no time for this.'

'Go Matteo. Tell Bianca to renounce me, then take your family to the alchemist.'

'Please General! Your sword!' Matteo reluctantly backed away and was lost in the shadows of the descending darkness.

A slender phantom rose up before Jorden. The scholar's gown billowed like black wings and its beak was a large, triangular cap. For a man who had always been kind, gentle, and unassuming in life, Tommaso made a splendid ghost.

His words echoed in the soldier's bewildered thoughts. 'Follow Matteo, Gerard.'

'Tommaso..?'

'It is unfortunate that mortals cannot see what fools they have been until they are dead.'

'Why are you here?'

Tommaso raised his long hands to the indigo sky spangled with infinity's lamps. 'There is more to eternity than Heaven and Hell.'

'Why did you come back?'

'I came to see you, Gerard.'

'Was the sight worth leaving Paradise for?'

'Despite your sharp tongue and hasty manners, I have always held you in high regard. Like me, you have been used.'

'Then why not materialise in the Duke's bedchamber and

give him a fright for both of us.'

'Please follow Matteo. The alchemist will give you her protection.'

Jorden laughed. 'Her? Protect me?'

'Your humility comes and goes like the Venetian tide. I don't want to rob you of an honourable death if that is what you've set your mind on. When the sun rises and you no longer have the choice, that prospect may not seem so noble.'

'Laura never retracted her curse.'

'Because she was not given the time. It does not mean you have to fulfil it.'

Jorden looked down at the flagstones, now a dull silver that merged with his doublet in the moonlight. 'If I were to donate this body to the amusement of Stefano Nogaret, could Ahmose's phantom save me?'

'Leave miracles to the alchemist or you will pay a dreadful price.'

But Jorden's irrational state of mind had fired his curiosity. 'Tell me Tommaso, what sort of creatures are Ahmose and his friends? What is the meaning of their existence?'

'If you ever had one ounce of regard for me Gerard, please do as I ask and leave now.'

'I must know.'

'They are going to close the gates.'

'I've always respected you Tommaso. I owe you and Laura my death.'

'The scorpions are crawling from their holes. I can see lamps. Fall on your sword and follow me.' Tommaso's phantom faded away, arms extended in ghostly welcome.

'Tell me Tommaso, tell me!?' But the shade had gone.

Suddenly lights surrounded the piazza. Renewed courage had brought out the palace to gawp. The General realised that he was the only thing left to gawp at. Like a millipede with a face glowing on every segment, the circle slowly closed in.

Gerard Jorden reached for his sword.

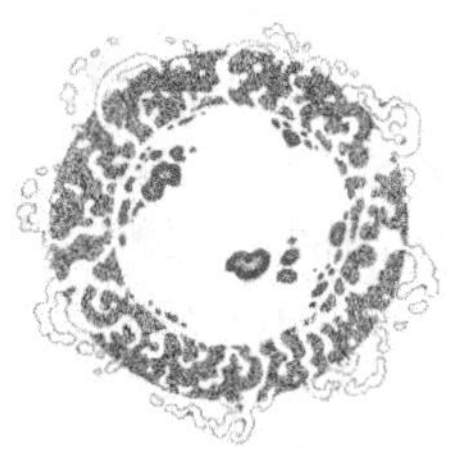

THE LETTER

CHAPTER 45

Dinan poured himself another tankard of sour wine. Through a drunken haze he once again reached for the letter Matteo had brought from Bianca. After swallowing a long draught, he flicked the paper and it fell open like a limp butterfly.

'Dear Signora and Signore,' it began, 'Please forgive my writing, this page has been drafted with much stealth.

'I hope Matteo and his family have reached you safely. I fear for their lives, and know you will help them.

'Though I was Gerard Jorden's mistress, I now have the protection of Duke Vittorio's brother. To earn this I had to do something for which I should live in eternal shame. Unlike Matteo, I have no family to share the dishonour as my daughter is far from here. If you do not want to remember me with contempt, please consign this letter to the flames before you read on. I would not write it at all, but you have the right to know the truth Matteo cannot bear to speak of.

'He may have mentioned that shortly before you left me, a friend of your's came to Via La Rosa, the town Gerard's troops had occupied. This small Egyptian, called Ahmose, saved Gerard's life after his troops had deserted him. Matteo helped Ahmose escape and Duke Vittorio traded Gerard's return for Via La Rosa's freedom. A terrible machine was constructed to make Gerard confess to your friend's whereabouts. I thought the Egyptian was safely lodged with me. Somehow learning of Gerard's danger, he gave himself up to be burnt. Before they could put Ahmose on the pyre, Gerard plunged a sword through his heart.

'Then the miracle to transcend all miracles happened. The setting sun changed and boiled like a cauldron of blood. As Gerard lifted Ahmose to the sky, the small Egyptian turned into a large golden bird that circled the palace like a shimmering dart, and then disappeared.

'Please do not speak to Matteo of what happened next.

'Gerard may have intended to fall on his sword, but was prevented. Once their courage had returned, Church and lawyers alike, in the absence of your Egyptian to blame, accused Gerard of being in league with Satan, plus a catalogue of crimes I will not list here. The Duke tried to intercede, but he is a weak man and satisfied to reap the harvest as long as he does not have to turn the soil.

'Gossip circulating the court claimed that Gerard had allowed himself to be taken because he knew Duke Vittorio would suffer by having to watch him die. The Duke did allow Tommaso to be poisoned and put Gerard in danger by not paying his troops. However, the idea seemed absurd to me. But then, perhaps I never knew the German as well as I thought. And the Duke did suffer torments. He has since taken to his bed and the doctors say he will not recover.

'At the prospect of seeing the man they once feared put to death, families embroiled in generations of vendetta with Duke Vittorio's house left their country estates and came, disguised, into the city. Even those relatives who hated his allegiance to the Church put on crucifixes so they could gawp from the front rows. Settimo was so packed not even a rat could have scuttled across its main piazza.

'Without a trial, or lawyer to speak for him, Gerard was brought down and clamped into that infernal machine Stefano Nogaret had forged. Every hour the glass was turned and the question put to him, "Was he in league with the Devil?" For as long as he was able, Gerard answered as brutally as he had been asked, then some levers were given a half turn. By degrees his body was crushed. Because of Nogaret's skill and Gerard's stubbornness this went on for two days. The Duke begged me to persuade Gerard to confess to their accusations. But my German no longer recognised me. So I renounced him, as did two former mistresses of his.

'Before the third day's interrogation could begin, the dawn sky changed colour. Daggers of fire fell about the piazza. Everyone fled, leaving Gerard to face the wrath of the sun. A brilliant light engulfed him. When it lifted, the sky had returned to normal, and he had gone.

'I hope Gerard is now with the blessed dead. He was a good man, and only wore armour about his heart because it was so vulnerable. Please light a candle to his memory.

'May God, or whatever deity protects you, attend you both,

Bianca.'

Dinan's large fist crumpled the letter and hurled it to the floor. 'The stupid man! Too proud to let us help him! Served him right!'

Helen laid a hand on Dinan's shoulder and discretely confiscated his flask of wine. 'You know you don't mean that. Get some sleep, it's late.'

'You never sleep.'

'I have things to think about.'

'You're always thinking. Your brain never stops. It's like a water wheel in a torrent.' Dinan brushed some drunken tears away. He resented the way she found it so easy to cope with her interminable life. 'You have no soul. Doesn't the thought of this miserable man being crushed because some petty tyrant is in debt bother you? I admired the sheer stubborn strength of the General. Perhaps you didn't, but he never deserved the fate of a common criminal.'

Helen was practical to the last. 'He never managed to save Ahmose.' She sat beside Dinan.

However drunk, he always knew when something was wrong. 'What's the matter?'

'Why did the sun want Gerard Jorden?'

'What?'

'While you've been sitting here drinking, I've been wondering whether Ahmose's monster was really responsible.'

'What then?'

'Another ghost perhaps?'

Dinan shook his large head. 'The one fighting the solar deity?'

'It would be more likely to end Jorden's suffering.'

'Then why allow him to suffer at all?'

'Perhaps it thought the experience was good for his soul. Anyway, it obviously wanted him for something.'

'Like it wanted us to keep Ahmose company?'

Helen looked at him sharply. 'Get some sleep, Dinan.'

'What are you going to do?'

'I want to study the charts Tommaso sent me.'

Dinan grunted. 'At least the stars are too far away to meddle with us - aren't they?' There was no answer, so he blundered off to bed.

Helen tucked a chart under her arm and went out into the garden with a lamp.

The moon was full and its light dimmed the surrounding stars. She placed the lamp on the head of the double faced Janus stonily guarding the front of the villa, and examined the symbols and inscriptions made by Tommaso's meticulous hand by its light.

The crackling parchment was the only sound to disturb the still night air. A pack of wolves had been taking livestock, so Matteo had gone out with some shepherds the previous night and given them a demonstration with his throwing knives. The survivors were not expected to return in a hurry.

Helen noticed a figure silhouetted against the ruins of the nearby temple. It was Anna, Matteo's wife. Usually as jovial as Matteo was stern, she was silent and didn't remove her veil until the alchemist beckoned her down.

'Won't Matteo miss you?'

'He's asleep and I have my eldest grandson with me.' Anna pointed to a young man by the crumbling temple wall.

'Why are you out at this time of night?'

Anna gave a conspiratorial smile. 'Gossip.'

For one cold, clammy moment Helen wondered if she had learnt of General Jorden's fate. Matteo had been determined to keep the details of it from her.

'Gossip that can only be passed on in the middle of the night often brings down empires.'

'In the harbour market I met some Oriental travellers who had recently come from Cappadocia.' Anna lifted an envelope of cotton from the belt pouch of her cotehardie. 'Matteo can bear no mention of General Jorden or golden birds, and I am afraid he might discover this.'

'What is it?'

There was an odd yellow glow emanating through the cotton. It lit up the blue velvet of Anna's cloak, giving it a greenish tinge.

'I couldn't resist buying this from them. Bianca and Tommaso had one like it. The travellers wouldn't have sold it but they needed the money towards their passage back to Cathay, and I had some set by from my lace. I think it should be yours.' Anna opened the cotton. Inside it was a large golden feather. 'When they were in the Aegean it fell to the deck of their ship.'

The alchemist momentarily froze. 'Now you want to be rid of it?'

'Fortunately none of the crew saw it. The travellers say that Greek crews are very superstitious.'

'What did they believe it came from?'

'In Cathay there is a bird called the Phoenix, a fabulous creature that brings happiness.'

That meant the bird must have been heading East. Helen automatically delved into her pouch.

'If what I heard is true...?' Anna stopped unsurely.

Helen gave a tight smile. 'Then why didn't it come back to rescue Gerard Jorden?'

Anna nodded and her eyes filled with tears. 'He was such a kind, thoughtful man. The real tragedy is that he would let no one know it.'

'The bird could have done nothing.'

'What manner of deity is it?'

Helen took the feather from her. 'The entity that controls it can subvert time, cloak the sky with its bloody veil, and curse you with immortality, whether you want it or not.' She pushed some ducats into Anna's hand. 'I'll look after your feather for you.'

Anna tried to hand the money back. 'This is ten times more than I paid.'

Helen refused to accept it. She had more gold than she needed, enough to travel the Orient for centuries.

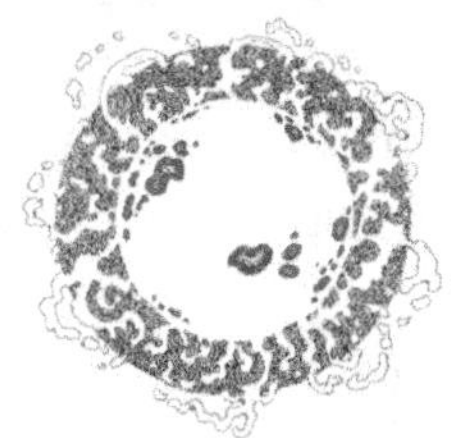

THE BUDDHIST

CHAPTER 46

On a gleaming gold dome under a luminous sky, huge painted eyes peered down at two travellers. The motionless pupils showed more curiosity than the worshippers turning prayer wheels and prostrating themselves before the large round idol laughing in its alcove.

The intense devotions were all too much for Dinan. 'For simple belief in the Middle Way, there seems to be a hell of a lot of worship going on.'

Helen half heard him. She knew that humans needed to feel enslaved by something, if only their own thoughts. The teaching of Jesus Christ was subverted in the same way. He was probably talking it over with Buddha at that moment.

Dinan brushed away some flies. 'So how long do we have to wait before this priest sends for us?'

'She's not a priest.'

'Nun then.'

'They say she is enlightened.'

After all the time they'd spent blundering about the world, Dinan believed that was where they should be, but the only thing he experienced after meditation was the craving for strong liquor and oblivion. It certainly did nothing for his intellect.

Helen was becoming peevish. 'It's all a state of mind at best, time wasting self indulgence at the worst.'

Dinan frowned. His state of mind had been through many twists and turns over the centuries, usually induced by alcohol and nasty frights. Perhaps Helen understood because she was still an alchemist at heart. They were a mad, mystical lot.

'How can we be sure that this creature which visits her is our Ahmose and not their Phoenix?'

'We can't until we see it.'

Dinan found a perch in the huge roots of a banyan. He sat there like a discontented outcrop blistered from the ancient temple the tree was undermining.

* * *

The small clearing became spangled with light reflected from golden feathers.

The enlightened didn't need to open her eyes to know the deity was there.

The Aton Bird warbled at the bald pate beneath its branch as though wanting conversation.

Realising that the Buddhist wasn't there to chat, the entity bounced from its perch and landed on the ground before her.

At last their gazes met.

In the depths of the bird's eyes blazed the demon that had parasitized its spirit. It was challenging the mystic to unravel it from its victim's soul – if she dare!

The Buddhist feared nothing. There were no such thing as demons, gods, good, or evil, only existence and enlightenment. Her thoughts delved into the dungeons of the phantom realm and summoned the only creature that could attempt the deed. For a brief moment something inside the bird struggled to push out the malevolent cosmic force pinning it to immortality, and a warm yellow halo emanated from its shining feathers.

The bird uttered a disconcerted 'Caw!' then threw its wings wide and reared like a rather plump cobra. Stretched to its full height, the shape began to ripple. Quivering feathers became fingers, a head as bald as the Buddhist's formed below its glittering crest, the bright ruff was a golden necklace and the tail fell into the soft folds of a white ankle length robe.

The phantom that had stage-managed the transformation briefly stood behind the metamorphosis, then filtered away.

The second keeper of the sacred animals of the temple of Amon Ra gazed at the dimensions reflected in the eyes of the old Buddhist. She intended that the Egyptian should meditate on his dilemma. Ahmose had endured too many centuries with the brain of a bird to think very deeply about anything at that moment and didn't comprehend what was happening. Despite having spent less time than the Aton bird in one incarnation, the Buddhist did understand, and wasn't intimidated by the knowledge.

She raised her hand.

Ahmose's thoughts stopped tumbling like thistledown in a whirlwind. There was a sinister halo about to the Buddhist's body. She closed her eyelids, slowed down her heartbeat, and then absorbed the aura. When the enlightened eventually opened her eyes they swam with the milkiness of the moon. Within her emaciated shell a cosmic battle was taking place. Like a tree trying to capture the lightning repeatedly striking it, the Buddhist radiated an internal glow.

As an envelope of heat struck Ahmose, he realised just how dangerous the entity controlling him was. 'Stop! Release the monster! It will kill you!'

'There is no such thing as death.'

To an immortal, this wasn't very reassuring. 'Do you want to end up flying the world as a golden bird? It can become tedious after the first thousand years.'

'Eternity is nothing.'

Ahmose wished he had enough of the same steely resolve to give the malevolent sun entity indigestion.

The Buddhist lowered her hand. 'Know your own demons before you can see anyone else's.'

Ahmose had lived long enough to house train his demons. The Buddhist must have known she was trying to help a born loser. But then, where was the point in trying to save someone who could help themselves?

'How long does this monster intend to control me?' asked Ahmose.

'The Universe can exist in the palm of Buddha's hand and flow for eternity.'

'Eternity!'

'There is no such thing as time. If you can fly to the moon, you can fly to the stars.'

'I don't really want to.'

'The answer is in the stars.'

Ahmose had trouble with metaphors. 'How far away are they?'

'As far as a thought.'

As the sun demon tried to consume her, the ground about the Buddhist began to ripple.

Ahmose watched, horrified.

'There is no such thing as time...' As the monster slipped from her psyche, her words drifted away like gossamer threads.

Ahmose tried to reach out and touch one. His fingers could no longer grasp.

The Buddhist's contract with life melted away, and the friendly phantom that had helped faded back to the dungeon of the Universe's subconscious.

The Aton bird flapped its wings and soared into the air. Below, the clearing revolved as though overlapped by another dimension. A cauldron of parasitical demons that drank the sun entity's power, scurried about inside it like the undigested meal of a cosmic ogre.

The monster once again attempted to devour the Buddhist. Her spirit was too tough. The world within the sun entity's stomach turned once again and a familiar figure went around inside it like an alien morsel. The phantom of the High Priest raised his Anubis-headed staff as though trying to plug some leak in the fabric of time.

Slowly the fantastic spectacle folded in on itself, leaving the mortal husk of the Enlightened.

With a downbeat of its huge wings, the bird took to the sky. Perhaps it should try to map the stars, but was now convinced that it was far safer to map the Earth.

CHAPTER 47

When Dinan and Helen Maat arrived with the Buddhist's small pupil, all they found was the old woman's husk. Like a fragile scroll of papyrus, Dinan carefully laid her out so the ten-year-old could perform a brief ritual. When she had finished, he wrapped her mentor in his cloak, and carried it back to her order. There the novice remained in contemplation as her mentor's remains were taken to a niche that had been prepared for her body decades ago.

Drowsy from the heady incense, Dinan yawned. 'Reassuring some people can be so certain about death. What do you think happened?'

Helen guided him outside before he disgraced himself by fainting in a mountainous heap. 'Like Kleopatra, the Buddhist decided to take on the creature. Finding out the truth killed her as well.'

'Wonder why she did it?'

'Buddhists don't think in those terms. They believe in evolution, not conflict.'

'So that means they're right?'

'Probably makes living a lot easier.'

Dinan took a deep breath of the scorching air. 'All this seems pretty pointless to me.'

'You're probably feeling your age. At least two others have taken on this entity and almost won.'

'Pity they never survived to tell us how they did it.'

'Now the West has woken up to science, we'll soon have the means to discover an explanation.'

'And be burnt as witches again.'

Helen wasn't listening. She needed an excuse to return to Europe. The East's gentle acceptance of whatever life had to throw at them was beginning to get on her nerves.

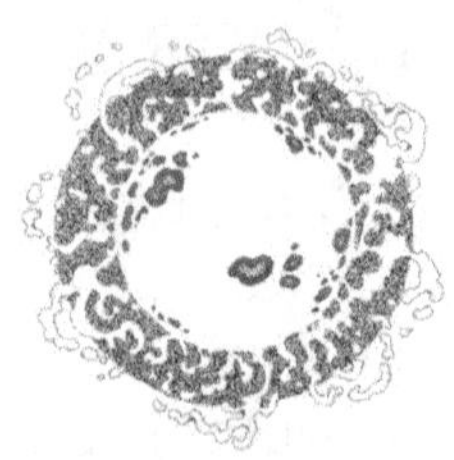

THE SMUGGLER

CHAPTER 48

Ned scraped the pitch from his hands and threw it back into the bucket. He would rather have been ashore filling kegs with fresh water than sitting just above the barnacle line, plastering the mouldering wood of the Red Jude. The job should have been easier with the ship careened over, but their carpenter insisted that the ancient timbers wouldn't take the strain. So there Ned sat on his bosun's chair, knocking off barnacles and filling in the cracks between the warped wood.

Beyond the blackened hull, he saw something sparkle on the island shore.

Also having a keen eye for anything that glittered, Captain Newthrap pounded down the powder and ball into her musket. She wended her way past the Red Jude's contraband littering the beach to the rock to where it perched.

Several residents apprehensively peered from their tents of sail canvas. Though the woman was a friend, she could be quite clumsy with loaded muskets.

As Olive Newthrap came closer to her quarry she tipped the barrel of her firearm skyward for fear of accidentally shooting the small brown man perched on a coral outcrop. He was holding a conversation with several dolphins as politely as a countess displaying her new tea caddy. The African couldn't have been an escaped slave because he was wearing more jewellery than clothes. Despite the goods and food Captain Newthrap brought the maroons in return for provisioning her ships, many still wore the rags they had

228

escaped in.

'Well, well, pretty fellow. Where did you swim from?'

Ahmose slid from the coral in surprise at the suddenness of the cracked voice. The dolphins splashed about in annoyance then swam off. Half expecting to be shot, the priest silently gazed at the mischief-lined features of a woman who could have been anything between fifty and embalming. Her trousers were secured by some Spanish ambassador's golden belt and the once white shirt under her tarpaulin jerkin glittered with an unnecessary amount of jewellery. Ahmose assumed her arrival to herald nothing more than a simple case of theft.

'Aren't you the African dandy then,' Newthrap cackled.

Ahmose reached up to unfasten his necklace.

'Oh no, I don't want your jewellery, albatross eyes.' She pinched his cheek like an affectionate crab. I want you.'

He hastily withdrew before any other part of his anatomy could come under attack from this ageing sea skua.

Captain Newthrap was prevented from committing any sort of robbery by the arrival of a tall, intimidating woman.

'He is not for touching.'

The black woman wore the unfathomable expression of a hungry polar bear.

Newthrap backed off. 'I wasn't going to so much as brush a sunbeam from that bald pate.' She sidled up to her friend. 'Come on Annie, where d'you get him? Some Eastern ship been out here?'

'He arrive two days ago.' Annie raised two fingers in more of a threat than desire to educate.

'What's he doing here?'

'Looking, he say.'

'What for? Talking dolphins?'

'You ask.' Still keeping her gaze on them, Annie stepped back.

'Thanks.' Ahmose had taken cover under a coral ledge so Newthrap had to stoop down. 'You know something, passion eyes? I had a mate once.' Ahmose wondered what sort of man would have had the constitution to court this crow of indeterminate colour. 'Collecting mother-of-pearl on a beach just like this. That and turtle shell brings in a good price on the mainland. Crawled under a ledge just like that. Put his foot in the water - about as deep as your's is now - then snap! Clam bit it off.'

Ahmose felt a crustacean brush against his leg. He leapt from his shelter and straight into the smuggler's arms. She tossed the musket aside to catch him. The flint sparked and there was a loud report as it was discharged in the direction of the ship. Ned ducked. Fortunately the shot lost its momentum and ricocheted harmlessly off the bowsprit.

After the smell of cordite, Ahmose was enveloped by the odour of stale tobacco and damp gabardine.

Newthrap was more pleasantly surprised. 'Now, there's a fragrant smell. Just like crushed camomile.'

Annie had always assumed the Captain's olfactory senses to be impaired. They had to be for anyone to live on the Red Jude. 'He smell of cedar.'

Newthrap was more interested in Ahmose than carpentry. 'Aren't you going to speak to me, pretty fellow?'

It hadn't taken Ahmose long to work out the nature of the world he had landed in. 'Are you going to sell me?'

'Sell you?' Newthrap was genuinely indignant and looked to Annie.

'Captain not slaver,' Annie conceded.

So she was interested in his body after all. Ahmose didn't know whether to be flattered or disgusted. He had never believed himself attractive but this smuggler obviously couldn't afford to be fussy. Though she probably wouldn't have been so enthusiastic with what was left after she had removed his jewellery.

'Amo look for wealthy Greek woman.'

'She arrived in a four-masted, square-rigged ship,' added Ahmose.

'Like mine?' asked Newthrap.

The priest cast a circumspect glance at the three masted hulk sitting with its hull low enough in the water to collect oysters. 'No. It was much cleaner and cut through the water like a dhow.'

'Dhow? What's a dhow?' sneered the smuggler.

'And it came from Bristol.'

Olive Newthrap's ship would have had trouble crossing the Florida Straights let alone the Atlantic. Most of her smuggled goods were supplied by visiting Moors, Indians and Spaniards who, for various reasons, didn't want to berth at the ports where their trade would be most in demand. They stopped to clean their hulls and take on provisions from keys and small islands while Newthrap's pinnaces dodged the pirates and Navy to ferry contraband to and fro.

'I think the ship and its consorts had names like jewels.' Ahmose had been unable to fly low enough to read them without attracting attention. Many superstitious crews, seeing a huge golden bird swooping down on them, tended to jump overboard. 'And guns. The largest had forty at least and the others thirty each.'

Newthrap nodded. So it was the Topaz. How she wished for a ship capable of carrying that firepower. She might have been able to bribe off pirates, though would have still preferred to blow them out of the water.

'Didn't have this tall, sweet-mannered navigator as captain, did it?'

'I don't know, I was too far up-' Ahmose stopped. 'I was only told that there was a Greek woman on the ship.'

The effect on Captain Newthrap was electric. 'I knew he'd come back! The Crown must have given him his trading rights.' She roared with laughter. 'That'll scupper the Navy.'

'Why?' Ahmose asked innocently.

'It means that they can't sneeze in his direction without signed authorisation, let alone go on board and check his cargo.' The smuggler noticed Annie's dour expression light up. 'Fancy some Maltese lace to trim that jacket of yours?'

'I not look like man then.'

Ahmose thought that the imposing dark woman was already intimidating enough. 'Look like a man?'

'Comes in handy when Annie's out on business. If you see her anywhere else but here, her name's Alexander.'

'Will you take me to this ship?'

'Have you got the fare?'

'You said you didn't want my jewels. What else can I give you?'

Before Newthrap's imagination could go into overdrive, Annie told her, 'Amo can draw islands and coastlines. He made map for us.'

'A cartographer?'

Ahmose was anxious to avoid paying in any other way the smuggler had in mind. 'I'll draw you maps.'

Newthrap was suspicious. 'How could you know what the coast looks like. You a bird or something?'

Ahmose said nothing.

'Come on Annie, where did you find him?'

'Three nights ago lookout lit large fire for our sloop. When he went back in morning, Amo was sitting in ashes.'

'He looks too clean.'

'Everyone is clean near you.'

'Sea cow.'

Ahmose was afraid this could lead to violence. 'What's a sea cow?'

'Like a hippopotamus. Don't talk to them as well, do you?'

'Oh yes.'

The women glanced at each other.

Newthrap shouldered her musket. 'Come on ash baby. I'll find you some clothes and a pen.'

The cream of Rupert Bullen's fine cotton shirt was ghostly against the Red Jude's decaying timbers. The few European members of the smuggler's crew wondered how he managed to keep his hair in place without tar. The Africans were more interested in whether there were any vacancies on the Topaz, Opal and Malachite.

The merchant captain placed a critical finger between a gap in the Red Jude's warped timbers. 'Your ship's foul, Olive. It's only kept together by the barnacles holding hands.'

She ignored him. The abuse her ship received had become a ritual. 'You've got something to offer?'

Bullen lowered his voice as though there were a man-of-war at his shoulder. 'Two Spaniards taken by pirates were impounded in Florida. They've been put up for auction.'

'How are they fitted?'

'Thirty guns each. Fully rigged. Main mast on one sheered off. Any carpenter who can keep this hulk afloat would have no problem with that.'

Newthrap was wary. 'I'm not so sure it'd be a good idea to put to sea in a couple of galleons until the peace is settled.'

'Nobody else is likely to take them because of that.' Bullen could tell that she was hooked on the idea. 'Give me the money and a percentage, Olive, and I'll send out the Malachite with crews for them. If they carry my authority, they'll be no problems.'

'I'm not sure. They're just the sort of prize a privateer would take, and I don't know how many people Annie can supply.'

'The only reason pirates leave this hulk of your's alone is because the damn thing would sink while they were plundering it.'

Newthrap waved a callused hand. 'I'll think about it, I'll think about it.'

'So what have you got for me?'

Newthrap became secretive. 'Below.'

No ship interior had yet been designed to accommodate

Bullen's inconvenient height so he had to duck most of his way down to the aft cabins. Newthrap scuttled ahead like a mongoose invading someone else's burrow, making him wonder what amazing find could have induced such girlish enthusiasm in an accomplished reprobate like her. Perhaps the smuggler had caught a merman and wanted a translator.

The Red Jude's captain pushed open the door of a cramped cabin with more window than was wise for a ship that sat so low on the high seas. It was decorated with the best fabrics from her contraband and, guttered out the night before, the remains of perfumed candles lay in their pools of expensive wax.

On a cot covered with chintz and brocade slept a small, bald man dressed in a calico shirt and knee breeches. Maps were scattered over the table. As he examined a couple, Bullen understood the reason for her gleeful excitement. The merchant had circumnavigated the world, yet had never set eyes on such detailed charts or anyone as strange as the small African with a golden disc on his forehead.

Inexplicably, Bullen felt a chill tingle of apprehension. 'Who did you steal him from Olive?'

'Steal! Steal! You know I'll steal anything but people.'

'He must belong to someone?'

'Probably the Greek woman you brought over.'

He tried not to look surprised. 'She's gone ashore. Can't be aware he's here.'

Olive Newthrap read calculation behind the amiable features. 'What're you thinking, lily eyes?'

'How much do you want for him?'

'Aren't you going to ask his name first?'

'What is it?'

'Ahmose.' She sidled up to him in devilment. 'Didn't think you dealt in slaves?'

'You know I don't. These maps are so detailed the Navy would pay a fortune for him.'

At the mention of the Navy, Newthrap drew back. 'You'd tell them?'

'Name your price?'

'No, he's not for sale.'

'Then why show him to me?'

She snatched the maps from Bullen. 'I thought you'd be more interested in these.'

'Oh Olive, you don't really believe you can flood the Caribbean with charts of that quality and keep him a secret? At least I could protect him.'

'You wouldn't show anyone else the charts, you well fed gannet.'

Bullen was silent for a moment. 'How does he manage it?' The merchant pointed to a map of the Southern continent with a wide river wending its serpentine way across it. 'Only a bird could know the course of a feature like this. If these charts are accurate, I could throw all my silver, gold, sugar, indigo and tobacco overboard and build an empire instead.'

The greed imperative peeped over the castelations of Olive Newthrap's principals to see if it was safe to come out. 'How much will you give me for them then?'

That inexplicable foreboding started to give Bullen second thoughts. 'I'm no conquistador.'

'What's the matter?'

He stood watching Ahmose for some while, unable to place where he had seen him before. 'I think you've landed an albatross, Olive.'

'I know, his eyes have that same look.'

Bullen asked suddenly, 'Let me return him to the Greek?'

'What?'

'Or take him back to where you found him.'

'You? Superstitious? What is the matter with you man?'

'I'm sure I know him.'

'How?'

'I don't know.' There was an edge of terror in his voice. 'I can't remember.'

Although Rupert Bullen's past may not have been so murky as some, it was certainly cloudy. Rumour said that he had made his fortune by plundering a Spanish galleon sunk in a storm. Given what else went on in the Caribbean that was hardly a crime. Then again, perhaps he had genuinely lost his memory and the small African had been part of it.

Newthrap had never known him so fearful before. 'Calm down. If the crew see you like this they'll begin to appreciate me.'

Bullen turned to go. 'Get rid of him Olive. Get rid of him.'

Newthrap hadn't expected this reaction to her find. Accurate charts were bought with blood and gold and could make the difference between a profit and lingering death to navigators like Rupert Bullen.

The Red Jude's Captain rolled up a map and pushed it into his hand. 'Remember me and Annie when you've got a cargo you can't get through customs.'

Bullen smiled. 'Old magpie. Let me know whether you want those galleons - and remember what I said about the Egyptian.'

'Egyptian? How d'you know he's Egyptian?'

Rupert Bullen said nothing and went above.

CHAPTER 50

The only stone building on Royal Haven was the fort. The rest of the town clustered about the harbour and up the steep hillside like a nest of old ship timbers made by a confused roc. The intention of the last hurricane had probably been to purge the once picturesque shoreline of humans and their litter. The location of Royal Haven was crucial to the Crown's control of the other islands in the group. So, up it sprang once again in all its ramshackle glory, ready for the next hurricane or careless torch to burn it down.

Although the coral bar provided a sheltered road for vessels to drop anchor outside the harbour, they were still within range of the fort's cannon. The customs house just below it kept an eye on the harbour while well-armed sloops patrolled the less accessible parts of the coast. The authorities here would have hanged their own grandfather for marking the pages of the Bible with smuggled lace. This didn't deter brazen rogues like Olive Newthrap from landing contraband, or stealthy night warriors like Annie from picking up slaves escaping from other island and mainland plantations.

The commander of Royal Haven hated the sight of Bullen, and the only reason the wealthy merchant set down there was to let his Greek passenger disembark. Also, his crew occasionally needed to get drunk on filthy ale and brave the caress of women wilder than the Topaz's macaw which could bite through belaying pins.

This time the telescope on the roof of the fort was trained on another ship. Captain Newthrap was getting too bold for her own good.

CHAPTER 51

'All right, all right!' Helen gave up. 'But next time someone asks you where you escaped from, don't upend them in a cask of molasses!'

Dinan stubbornly folded his arms. He would have wrecked the tavern if the molasses hadn't been handy.

The alchemist delved into a chest and pulled out a lens wrapped in muslin. 'Help me with this or I'll have to hire a servant.'

'Why not buy a slave.'

'Don't start that again.'

'I'll crack skulls or burst into tears whenever I feel like it!'

'Well don't cry over the tea, that's going to pay our rent.'

'Tea?'

'While you were in the throws of melancholia, I packed the lenses in tea.'

'That's smuggling.'

'Don't start being virtuous as well as bloody-minded.'

'Who on this island of riffraff wants to drink tea?'

'I've got a buyer in Jamaica. The plantation owners there have more money than morals and need something to stir all that sugar into.'

'Given the number of people they're murdering just to grow a crop that rots the teeth, these British don't only lack morals, they're mindless criminals!'

'I know. Just keep your mouth shut when they're in earshot. Whether they're running plantations, on the account, or in the Navy, they own this place.'

'I'll speak in Greek.'

'Do that, and remember that we no longer have the funds to start revolutions.'

Making those investments had been Helen's idea. Their remaining wealth was in Spain and Italy - if they ever managed to get back there.

Dinan sullenly watched her unpack. To him, the voyage seemed a waste of their eternity. 'Will it work this time?'

'Probably not, but Bullen's here for a reason.'

'You are sure?'

'Oh yes. Olive Newthrap's already picked up Ahmose. The Navy are watching her ship, so we can't collect him yet.'

After searching for so many centuries, it was odd that the news didn't fill Dinan with elation. There wasn't even a flicker of relief. Despite Helen's persistence, he knew it always ended the same way. He wondered Ahmose had been thinking about for the last five centuries. He must have changed. They certainly had, but couldn't grow wings.

Dinan pulled a mirror from its linen wrappings and studied his distorted reflection. 'You'll never be able to exorcise the creature with this equipment - or have you got something different in mind?'

'Nothing you need worry about.'

Neither of them had yet learnt how to be honest with the other.

'Bottled sunbeams?'

'Something like that?'

Dinan gave his companion an objective glare. 'You've changed.'

'Have I?'

'You're twice as mad.'

'You've become melancholy.'

'Why shouldn't I? I'm a one thousand-year-old eunuch.'

Being smugglers, not privateers, the Red Jude was unable to repel large boarding parties. The King's Navy could have easily impounded the ship's cargo of cochineal, bolts of silk, hogsheads of sugar, bales of cotton, chests of ducatoons, casks of port, benzin and dragon's blood. This time they were searching for something else.

Not expecting a raid in daylight, Olive Newthrap only had time to hide the maps. Unfortunately her first mate had been so anxious to get the crew away in the pinnaces, he forgot about Ahmose.

The rocking of the ship and another hard day's work as a cartographer had made the animal priest drowsy. Half asleep, he took the sound of the marines boarding the Red Jude as yet another movement of its rotten timbers. Had he been given time, the Egyptian would have worked out their official status. Uniforms to him represented the tyrannical precision of the Roman legion, not a motley collection of thugs with only their red jackets and tin buttons in common.

Still unsure whether he was dreaming, Ahmose was hustled above and dropped into a waiting longboat as marines combed the ship from stern to bow. They found some very disagreeable smells, puzzled rats and enough contraband to have Newthrap hanged, yet no maps.

Ahmose was taken ashore and handed up the harbour wall to another group of men a little smarter in appearance.

Dusk was falling and the stench of decaying fish permeated the air. In the shadow of the customs house stood a familiar figure. The remains of the braid on its jacket glittered in the lantern light and the buckles on the belt and shoes flashed like cutting metal. Annie was in her hunting gear.

The priest was bustled into the fort and an upper room where an avuncular man with cheeks flushed by years of imbibing port, greeted him. Ahmose noticed a map on his desk; it was one of the first he had drawn. There was only one way out of this, so he stared stupidly at the

Commander's splendid moustache and square beard like a half-wit.

After planting the cartographer in a chair before his desk, the escort stepped back to guard the doorway.

Given the way Ahmose had been manhandled, the King's representative sounded disconcertingly reasonable. 'What's your name?'

'Ahmose.'

'Where did you escape from?'

'Escape from?'

'All Newthrap's crews escape from somewhere.'

'I come from a menagerie.'

'Don't be insolent!' a voice behind him snapped.

They obviously weren't going to believe that he was only a simple zookeeper.

The King's officer topped up his glass of port. 'My name's Commander Pearce. I represent the Crown on Royal Haven.' He took a swig of his drink. 'That means I am the law. I can hang any pirate who refuses the King's Proclamation, imprison smugglers and flog escaped slaves.'

'I'm not an escaped slave.'

Despite Ahmose's act, Pearce knew he wasn't dealing with the island's usual riffraff. 'Oh, you're a sharp fellow all right. No doubt some wealthy plantation owner lavished an expensive education on you. But true gentlemen know how to fasten their shirt and wear shoes.'

'I was asleep.'

Pearce put down his glass and examined Ahmose's hands. His palms were stained with sepia ink. 'Where did you learn to write?'

'Egypt.'

'Egypt?'

'On papyrus and damp clay.'

Someone fetched Ahmose such a blow round the ear he wished he had said something to deserve it.

'Where did you learn to draw maps?' the Commander persisted.

'I change into a bird every so often.' The priest ducked before the next blow could land.

Pearce waved the guard away. 'If you decide to be reasonable, slave, you might not get a flogging.' He swallowed the rest of his port. 'We know you can draw an accurate chart and have been to regions the Spanish can't reach. The Crown could do with your services.'

'Why? Haven't you invaded enough lands already?'

This educated savage was more than Pearce had bargained for. He didn't expect minor human flotsam to have a grasp of politics, let alone express an opinion about it. 'Invaded? We're at war with Spain!'

'Why don't you go to Spain and fight then?'

'Would you really prefer a flogging?'

'Do you think that would persuade me to help you?'

'You're a stubborn little sprat. Got more gall than the pirate I hanged last week. Decked himself in ribbons and lace just to dance on the end of a rope.'

'So hang me. I might even wear a pair of shoes.'

Commander Pearce was finding it difficult to believe his own ears and couldn't afford to be sent up like this in front of his own men. 'No, I'll put you in a cell for the night. I reckon you're used to comfort. Might do you good to see what can happen to slaves.'

The cell Ahmose was thrown into would have stank if the high tide hadn't regularly washed away most of the filth. The full moon shining through the floor to ceiling grille, the only barrier to the sea, illuminated the adjoining cell.

There seemed to be a large body huddled against its far wall, out of reach of the water. Gradually the priest could make out two or three families, men, women, children and babies. Immobile and silent, their faces gaunt with hunger, they gazed back at Ahmose like dark waxen puppets, skins glistening with condensation. The Egyptian now understood the facetious Pearce. It was an education he preferred not to have, and the Commander had misjudged just how perverse the priest could be.

By morning, after hearing the treatment these fugitives from slavery had received, the normally benign Ahmose felt as murderous as a barracuda.

CHAPTER 53

As he wrote up the log of the Topaz, Rupert Bullen ignored the rapping at his cabin window. Gulls often fought to perch on its narrow sill. It was only when glass shattered that he turned to see a robber harpy pointing the barrel of a musket at his head. He instinctively glanced back at his desk. The map Captain Newthrap had given him was missing.

'Olive!' He leapt up and struck his skull on a beam.

'You always needed to be a foot shorter. Without a head, that should make it just right.'

Too stunned by the collision with the timber to wonder if it was advisable, Bullen pushed the window open wide enough for the scrawny smuggler to clamber inside.

She kept the musket trained on him. 'Where did they take Ahmose?'

'Who?'

'The King's vermin! Who else!'

Bullen was amazed that the thought could cross even her mercenary mind. 'That was nothing to do with me Olive, I swear it! We didn't know what was happening until we saw the marines mustering on the dock. I assumed they were after you.'

'You'll have to try harder than that, lily eyes, or I'll put some punctuation through those amiable features and you can log that!'

'I only just noticed that the map you gave me is missing.'

'So who gave it to Pearce?'

Suddenly Bullen realised. 'I signed on a naval midshipman in Bristol. I should have known he couldn't be trusted and tossed him over the side.'

Newthrap was heartened to hear that the virtuous merchant was capable of murder. 'Ginger-haired fellow? Looks as though he was weaned on vinegar?'

'Yes.'

She lowered the musket. 'He's ashore. Probably promoted by now. By the time I realised Ahmose wasn't in a pinnace with us it was too late. Lazy tyke must have been asleep when the marines came.'

'You're always mislaying things, Olive. If your cartographer's in the fort, you've lost him for good.'

'What makes you so sure?'

'How can we prove he's a free citizen?'

'What about your Greek? If she owns him, she could claim him back.'

'Of course - The Greek.'

* * *

The tall, dark figure watching the house had been there on and off for two days.

Dinan was curious; he found it a change from melancholia. He put on his jacket and hat and patiently waited for the spy to move off, then followed.

CHAPTER 54

Once again Ahmose was hauled into Pearce's study and dumped into a chair. A cacophony of voices echoed up the stairs as the Commander remonstrated with the high pitched complaints of a Portuguese woman. The Senhora flounced in with her maid, equally high pitched and covered in black lace. Commander Pearce, who looked as though every diplomatic hound was after his jugular, hotly followed them.

'Senhora, Senhora,' he blustered. 'How could we have known? This Newthrap has never carried off slaves before.'

'He was not carried off!' the Senhora shrieked. 'He run away!' Without introduction or apology she descended on Ahmose and belaboured him with her ivory fan. 'He is stubborn! The more we teach, the more stubborn he becomes!'

'But, the maps...?'

'He remembers things. My father was ambassador to Trinidad. Ahmose was taught to copy charts for English merchants because he knows the language well. Then we catch him inventing maps!' Her embroidered cuffs fluttered like angry butterflies as she gave him another hefty thwack on the head, then pointed to his feet. 'Where are his shoes?'

'Probably on Newthrap's ship. I should send out a party to arrest her.' Pearce glanced apprehensively at the empty port bottle. He would never see anything of that quality again if he did.

'You shall have maps, any maps you need.'

'Thank you Senhora.' Pearce hesitated. 'Tell me, Senhora, what is that golden disc on his forehead?'

'We put it there to stop his brains falling out.'

If the Commander had a sense of humour, he would have been able to tell the difference between a Portuguese joke and reason to be suspicious. He gave a diplomatic smile just in case.

The woman and her companion seized Ahmose's arms and lifted him from the chair.

'I will take him now.'

'I'll send a man with you.'

'There is no need. I have escort. He will not run away again.' the Senhora once more struck Ahmose with her fan. 'I flatten his head first!'

And so, his bald pate smarting, the priest was released into the custody of a fiery tornado who had enough strength beneath those flounces of lace and satin to restrain a drunken marine.

As they left the fort, a tall dark figure fell in some distance behind.

Ahmose was escorted through the harbour, up roughly paved streets and planked passages until they eventually reached a rickety building overlooking ships loading and unloading cargo.

'Were we followed?' The Senhora's accent had disappeared.

'No,' said their rear guard.

'Get inside you.'

Ahmose was bundled down some steps into a large room filled with fragrant and acrid aromas. In the half-light, he had trouble working out where he was, then found himself surrounded by several women in various stages of undress. There was nothing high class about this brothel.

'Hester used to be actor,' the tall, dark figure announced as the door was closed.

'Annie!' At the risk of being impaled on her buckle, Ahmose threw his arms about the braided jacket.

'Alexander,' she reminded him. 'You will be safe here.'

'But I have to go out again.'

Hester laughed. 'When they discover that there's no Portuguese galleon standing off the harbour, sweetheart, they will be searching for all of us. They'll never guess who I am, but there aren't many escaped slaves with golden discs on their forehead in Royal Haven.'

'But the people in the cell next to mine - Some were children!'

'You're going to rescue them?'

'Yes.'

The women laughed.

'He can do it.' Annie's tone didn't invite contradiction.

'Then why didn't he rescue himself?'

Ahmose shrugged. 'There didn't seem any point.'

'You're a rum one.'

'Who were those people An- Alexander?'

'Some slaves escaped on rafts with families from Jamaica. They are only ones to survive.'

'They won't last long in that place.'

'You get them out of fort. I have longboat waiting.'

'When?'

'Tonight, after evening gun.'

The woman who had played the Portuguese maid was beginning to wonder why she had bothered. 'But you can't leave here.'

Hester was rummaging in a large chest. 'Perhaps he can. Take those clothes off him.'

The priest protested but was soon undressed. He darted under the nearest blankets as though he had been modest all his life.

Annie remained indifferent and waited for the giggling to die down. 'Where?'

'Bring the longboat to the sea gates below the fort,' Ahmose called from the bed.

Annie nodded, then silently left.

Two women climbed under the bedclothes with Ahmose while Hester sorted out a wig and armful of clothes.

Suddenly another tall, dark figure was standing in the doorway, its moon features frozen with disbelief.

The two men gazed at each other.

The priest's bedfellows felt his flesh grow cold.

'Dinan!'

The large man quickly left.

Hester had to catch Ahmose before he could sprint after him. 'You won't get very far like that. Who was your friend? Never seen a creature like him before.'

Ahmose started to shake. 'Just a ghost.'

'You're terrified?'

'He just reminded me of who I am.'

'Who are you Ahmose?'

'I wanted to forget.'

'Don't we all have that feeling at some time. You should see the harbour rats that crawl up here.'

'Why work in a brothel?'

'Women stranded in places like Royal Haven don't have a choice unless they're wealthy.'

'Annie and Captain Newthrap?'

'What they never had in looks, they make up for in cunning.' Hester started to dress the priest. 'You've got a brain as well, haven't you.'

Ahmose was beginning to wonder. 'Have I?'

There were several urgent taps at the veranda doors. As Dinan had gone absent without leave, Helen was expecting him to lurch through them in a drunken stupor. She also wouldn't have been surprised to see Olive Newthrap or Rupert Bullen - but not both together.

The smuggler quickly darted inside. 'I mustn't be seen.'

Ducking to avoid the lintel, Bullen followed.

'What's the matter? I haven't unwrapped everything from the tea yet.'

Bullen pretended that he hadn't already guessed she was smuggling, and feigned indignation. 'So that was what your equipment was packed in.'

His holier-than-thou attitude annoyed Newthrap. 'Shut-up man!' She turned to the alchemist. 'Do you know where Ahmose is?'

Helen froze. 'I thought you had him?'

'Pearce arrested him last night.'

'He escaped with some women this morning,' added Bullen.

'Should I know where he is?' Helen evaded.

'He is your slave, isn't he?'

'Not exactly.'

'Then what?'

'A friend.'

'Like that mobile coffin pretending to be a servant?' asked Newthrap.

'You've seen Dinan?'

Bullen was suspicious. 'How could you manage to lose him?'

'He wanders off sometimes.' At that moment Dinan could have wandered off the end of the dock for all she cared.

'We have to find Ahmose before the Commander does. Pearce isn't a man to let a fish off the hook, and this island is crawling with vermin who'd sell their children for a glance of Spanish gold. You do want him back, don't you?'

'That's why we came here.'

Bullen understood the intrigues of rogues and authority.

This Greek baffled him. 'What?'

'To find Ahmose.'

'I don't understand. How did you know he would be here?'

'Didn't you feel something strange when you saw him?'

Rupert Bullen would have lied if Newthrap's memory had been as pickled as her morals.

'What's going on between you two that I don't know about?' she demanded.

Bullen turned to the door and left without a word.

'Tell me for pity's sake?'

'Stay here,' warned Helen. 'He'll find Ahmose.'

'Are you sure?'

'That's why he's here.'

'You a voodoo sorceress or something?'

'No, just an ancient Greek.'

As dusk fell, Newthrap left to round up her crew.

* * *

When Dinan returned he was bleary with drink and would have crept up to his room.

'Dinan.' Helen had been sitting in the dark, waiting for him.

He hesitated, then pulled off his hat and let it drop to the floor.

'What happened?' She struck a spark to a brimstone match and lit a candle.

Dinan had obviously drunk enough of the town's filthy ale to kill a basilisk.

'Why are you upset?'

He watched the shadows flickering on the floor for some time. 'I saw Ahmose.'

Helen started. 'Where?'

His gaze never moved from the mat. 'In a brothel.'

Not realising she was supposed to be shocked, Helen gave a small giggle. 'Where?'

'Doesn't it bother you?'

'Was he all right?'

'Fit enough to bed two women at once.'

Helen managed to choke back a laugh. Dinan upset over

that? He obviously expected the priest to be a saint as well as immortal? Poor Ahmose, he now had to wear Dinan's delusions as well as his own.

'He was never interested in women before,' he complained.

'He spent his life in a temple menagerie,' Helen told Dinan. 'It probably never occurred to him.'

'But his conviction was so powerful?'

'And you're upset because he's been corrupted?'

'Why would some cosmic force bother making him immortal if he was corruptible?'

There was no point in arguing, Dinan was so drunk she decided to go along with it. 'Vengeance. Ra is punishing him for being a devotee of the Aton.'

'That was centuries ago.'

'Time is nothing to a god, but Ahmose is still part human. Don't condemn him for that. After what he's been through it's not surprising he needs to satisfy the odd whim.'

'Dumb Egyptian ... Shall I fetch him?'

'No. Leave it to Bullen.'

'Does the man know why he's here?'

Helen paused. 'I don't know. He's been gone too long.'

A figure carrying a lantern, dressed in flounced red calico, and a large headscarf wended its way along the quayside. Several carousing men, too drunk to bother about what they were trying to catch, made snatches at her. She avoided them to go past the harbour wall and onto the line of breakers half submerged by the incoming tide. She swung the lantern over the waves lapping the rotting timbers and softly whistled. Locks of hair that had escaped the headscarf became damp with spray as her sepia stained fingers stroked the surface of the water.

The clicks of a dolphin eventually chattered beneath the waves. A long scarred beak, shining in the moonlight, stabbed the water's surface.

'Is that you, Sharkilla?' Ahmose asked.

'Who else has a beak like mine? What do you want?'

'A favour.'

'Kill a shark?'

'No, just rescue one or two people.'

'You mean humans?'

'Yes. They have been captured by the sharks that shoot at your pod when it rides on the bow waves of their ships.'

'All right. You want me to drown them?'

'No Sharkilla, I don't want you to drown anyone.'

'What then?'

'The sea gates on the fort's cells have corroded hinges. No human could break them without making a lot of noise. A few blows under water with that iron beak of your's wouldn't attract attention.'

'All right. I'll do it.'

'Not now!'

But Sharkilla had gone. Ahmose blew out his lantern and sped back to the harbour through the snatching hands of the drunks. To his horror, several marines took a fancy to this dark female in red flounces. He ducked and weaved to escape their advances until several other women diverted their attention. In a flurry of calico he dropped over the harbour wall and dashed along the tide line.

Annie's sloop was standing off the mouth of the harbour.
There was no sign of its longboat.

Ahmose heard a dull thud come from the fort wall.
Unfortunately it also reached the ears of a sober sentry who
looked down from a cannon port. Hoping Sharkilla hadn't
been deafened by his own endeavours, Ahmose whistled as
loudly as he dare. The thuds ceased. Then the sentry began
to wonder about the person below whistling. There was the
report of the evening gun from just above him. He covered
his ears and ducked back inside.

Annie's longboat came into view. Oars muffled and sail
down, it sped noiselessly towards the fort. There were two
more thuds, then silence.

As time passed, Ahmose was afraid that the imprisoned
slaves were no longer there, or refusing to move. Then the
moonlight silhouetted Annie's longboat pulling out towards
the sloop; it was carrying several figures. A splash of silver
broke the surface of the water as Sharkilla gave a victory
flip, then the sea was quiet again.

Ahmose climbed back onto the harbour wall, and walked
straight into the owner of a port complexion and square
beard.

'Well, well,' growled Commander Pearce with none of the
avuncularity of their first meeting. 'So the fellow was right.
What were you doing down there on the beach my beauty?
Looking for pearls?'

No doubt one of the marines had taken exception to being
spurned by the animal priest. Ahmose daren't say anything.
Instead he turned and fled, only to run into some more of
the sharks his dolphin friend wanted an excuse to drown.

'Speak up woman! You know whores aren't allowed near
the beach. I'm not having any of you sneaking onto the
King's ships again.'

Although Ahmose hadn't been recognised, his new
identity had hardly improved his status in the eyes of the
Navy. Someone gripped his arm so tightly it brought tears
to his eyes.

'Give her a thrashing,' Pearce casually ordered and would
have walked away if a tall figure hadn't blocked his path.

'Excuse me Commander, I believe you are maltreating a friend of mine.'

'That trash! Your woman, Bullen? I would have thought you could come by something better.'

'Whatever your opinion, I am not going to see her beaten.'

Unable to believe his eyes, Ahmose stared at the merchant captain. Then he viciously pinched the inside thigh of his captor. The stab of embarrassing pain made the man release the prisoner who immediately sprang into the arms of Bullen.

'General!'

Pearce sneered. 'General indeed? Do you teach all your whores to call you that?'

'She's confused.'

'She won't be after my men have knocked some sense into her.'

The Commander's order sounded final.

Without quite knowing why, Rupert Bullen drew his sword. Immediately there was a chorus of metal being unsheathed.

'Don't be a fool Sir,' the sergeant of marines tried to reason. 'You can't fight all of us.'

'Then the man who kills me will have to explain to the Crown why they did it.'

Pearce roared with laughter. 'You'd risk your life for a prostitute?'

'For this one, yes.'

'King's charter or not, I'll have you sent back in chains.'

'They'll be no need. After I've killed some of your men you'll have me hanged, then you can send me back in a barrel of brine.'

The noisy confrontation had attracted a crowd. It wasn't often that the harbour witnessed a dual between the King's Navy and a wealthy merchant captain.

'General, General! You'll be killed! Let me go!'

Bullen kept his free arm tight about the priest and whispered urgently, 'If they find out who you are, you'll be hanged. Don't do anything stupid.'

To test his readiness, a marine's cutlass flashed towards

the Captain. Bullen easily parried it, but half a dozen more were now willing to try their luck. As he didn't put it past the King's men to stab either of them in the back, he took cover against the careened over hull of a half built pink, and pushed Ahmose behind him.

Pearce sighed in tedium. 'Put your sword up Bullen, I'm only going to have the harlot shown the strap. The bruises won't notice on her skin.'

'She's done nothing to warrant it.'

'She's a whore.'

Bullen raised his sword. 'I say she's cleaner than any man here.'

The marines didn't like that. He was attacking their right to blame prostitutes for the syphilis they passed from port to port. Steel struck steel. Marine blood was drawn, though only enough for a moment's pause.

'You must leave me General!' pleaded Ahmose.

'Do you want to die?'

'It doesn't matter.'

The merchant captain turned to look at him and the glimmer of a dreadful memory paralysed his reflexes.

Rupert Bullen felt a blade pierce his ribs.

At the sight of blood pouring through his shirt, the onlooking crowd erupted, and the report of a musket sent Pearce's men running for cover.

Captain Newthrap tossed the musket aside and drew the pistols from her belt. 'That's the last port you'll have from me you old octopus! Get your filth back into the fort or this town will burn - Again!'

A rag tag mob behind her bellowed agreement.

Ahmose pulled Bullen down out of the firing line and two women appeared from nowhere to staunch his wound with their scarves.

Bullen winced. 'It's not deep, only ruined a good shirt.'

Two more people arrived. The large African lifted the overturned pink and supported it with a shipwright's sawhorse so the others could shelter underneath.

'Get these women out of here Dinan, if Pearce recognises them they'll be hanged,' ordered Helen. 'Let me see the wound.'

The two prostitutes were ushered to safety. The one in the red calico dress fought and bit so hard Dinan left her alone. As several explosions rocked the quay he decided they were better off where they were anyway.

'What's that lunatic, Newthrap, doing?' demanded Helen.

Dinan snatched a glance out of the hull. 'Her crew are throwing grenades.'

'They'll be a massacre,' warned Bullen. 'Get out of here, I'll be safe enough. Take your friend with you.'

Dinan glowered at the strange woman. 'No chance, she nearly took my finger off.'

'Don't you know who it is?'

'Probably one of the women Ahmose leapt into bed with.'

Helen assumed he was still addled by drink. Considering the centuries he'd had to learn better, Dinan could be dull-witted when it really mattered.

A burst of flame lit up their hiding place. Dinan crawled out on his knees and elbows.

Warehouses, the barracks and customs house were burning and Newthrap's crew, swollen by an opportunistic mob, was preventing the marines from tackling the flames.

'We're cut off. The only way out is by the beach.'

'We left one of the Topaz's yawls on the other side of the breaker,' said Bullen. 'But the men that rowed me in are probably in the middle of that riot and I'm in no fit state to handle an oar, even if we could get out of range of the fort's cannon in time.'

Helen had no intention of staying where she was, even if it meant leaving the precious lenses she had intended to perform her experiment with. 'Dinan knows how to use oars, and they've got other things on their mind. Let's go while we've got the chance. If Pearce wins his argument with Newthrap, at least two of us will be at the top of his hanging list. 'Can you walk?'

'I think so.'

Helen darted down to the beach to make sure it was clear. Nearby rioters took the Greek to be some unfortunate housewife caught in the crossfire and ignored her.

At her signal, Dinan helped Bullen from the cover of the pink. The Captain's cream shirt and Ahmose's red calico dress were like beacons against the backdrop of flame.

Olive Newthrap, standing on some barrels to incite the mob, saw them. To distract the musketmen's attention, she set fire to several barrels of pitch and sent them rolling lopsidedly into their frayed formation. By the time they had reloaded and were in position to take aim, Helen's party had made the beach and clambered into the yawl.

Dinan pushed out the small boat then jumped aboard and took up a pair of oars. With Helen and Ahmose hauling on the others, they bounced over the incoming swell and out onto the inky water.

The skeleton crew on the Red Jude, realising what their captain was doing, had lit every lantern on the vessel in celebration, and pique, at not being able to join in. Rupert Bullen's men had more sense. The Topaz and Opal were like black skuas against the starlit horizon as his officers-in-charge upped anchors to take them beyond the range of the fort's cannon.

Wanting no part of the fracas, a pinnace decided to put off taking on supplies and was cutting across the harbour to safety.

Bullen tried to light the yawl's prow lantern. There was too much spray and the match wouldn't take the spark from the tinderbox. 'We'll have to leave the harbour to reach my ships.'

'That means going under the fort,' warned Dinan.

'I'm prepared to take the risk but I've no right to endanger you.'

Helen gave a hard laugh.

'What's the matter?'

Without warning, there was a report from the fort cannon and hollow splash ahead of them.

Dinan glanced at the harbour. 'Looks like they've got the fires under control. We have to keep going whether we want to or not.'

'They've got us in range,' warned Bullen. 'Turn back. Pearce hasn't got any argument with you two.'

'Better tell that to his gunners.'

'Turn back!'

'You know he'll hang your little firecat as well, don't you?' warned Dinan.

In exasperation, Helen snatched the scarf and wig from Ahmose's head. The golden disc flashed in the munitions flame. Despite the roar of cannon raining shots between them and the Red Jude, Dinan dropped his oars and gawped at the priest.

'You!'

'Shut-up Dinan and carry on rowing! It makes no difference where any of us end up now.'

The yawl lifted on the swell made by another near miss.

Some sensation deep in Bullen started to make him doubt his very identity. 'What do you mean?'

Helen's gaze was unnerving. 'Because we're all immortal.'

Bullen clutched his wound like a piece of precious evidence against the madwoman's assertion.

'It's true General,' Ahmose added. He only convinced the man that he was stuck in a small boat with three dangerous lunatics.

Then the logjam of thoughts from his previous life broke. The fictitious memories of his seafaring existence dissolved and the brutal truth burst into his mind. 'How can I be immortal?'

Despite the rocking of the yawl, Helen's gaze never flickered. 'Can you remember where you originally came from?'

Rupert Bullen didn't want those memories back.

'You recognised Ahmose, isn't that proof enough?'

The Captain didn't want proof. The instincts of a sea rover had steeled him to the prospect of death long ago. Now here he was, about to be pulverised, with three immortals telling him that he wasn't able to die after all. That he couldn't take.

'We have to make the Red Jude!'

Dinan gave a moonish smile. 'There's no point.'

This time return cannon fire from the Red Jude nearly

hit them, but the battle seemed distant.

Bullen felt his soul retreat. 'You don't understand-'

'You cannot die!' Helen thought she was reassuring him.

A stray musket ball grazed the merchant's shoulder. He ignored it. 'I don't want to be immortal. What would become of me?'

Helen hesitated. 'I don't know.'

'If I can't die, where will I go? What will I change into?'

Aware that his well-meaning phantom guardian had cursed all three of his companions just to save him, Ahmose remained guiltily quiet. With the chance of Helen completing her experiment to rescue Ahmose during this incarnation gone, Rupert Bullen would have been better off not knowing his true identity.

Dinan sensed her misgivings. 'Don't pay any attention to Helen Maat. She's as mad as a dog,' he told Bullen.

It was too late. The merchant's mind was already swamped by the hideous memories of an earlier century. 'Dear God! What happened to me? What am I doing here?'

'Give us time,' Helen remonstrated. 'All we need is time.'

The cannonball that might have been intended for the Red Jude, or come from it, landed in the centre of the yawl and snapped its keel. The craft jack-knifed and catapulted its occupants into the water.

Ahmose, Dinan and Helen disappeared from sight. Bullen clung to some wreckage with the instincts of a sailor. He had never been so determined to stay alive.

The harbour battle became more spasmodic. The government buildings outside the fort gutted, the rioters were filtering away.

Olive Newthrap took stock of the situation and decided to call it a good night's work. She was no longer a mere smuggler. With the ships Rupert Bullen had purchased for her, she could now be a true menace of the high seas. The marines watched her crew tumble over the harbour wall into their longboats and decided not to pursue them. The fort cannon were low on ammunition and the smugglers easily made the Red Jude.

Captain Newthrap assumed Bullen's party had reached

the safety of the Topaz so didn't bother to look for wreckage. The harbour was always full of rubbish and it wasn't possible to tell the recent detritus from the ancient in the light of two lanterns and the moonlight. They even rowed past the cream shirt of Rupert Bullen, thinking it to be the belly of some sea creature killed in the crossfire.

Commander Pearce took his last bottle of port to the top of the fort and looked through the telescope at the burnt out buildings that had been his little empire, and the lights sparkling triumphantly on the Red Jude.

He glanced at the list of casualties his lieutenant held. 'She'll hang for it!'

'There's hardly any dry powder and shot left Sir. We can't give chase without leaving the town open to attack.'

'What about the Topaz and Opal?'

'Out of the harbour. Neither of our sloops are in position to cut them off.'

Pearce gave a surly nod. The Red Jude was making ready to sail. 'I can blow that hulk out of the water at any time.'

'I doubt she'll be back.'

Pearce glowered down at the sea. Dolphins were sporting with a few fragments of timber, nosing them into the air and letting them fall with a splash. The Commander became aware of an eerie glow beneath the water. It lit up a tall figure in a cream shirt laying on its surface, face down. Pearce adjusted the telescope. There could be no doubt; the body belonged to Rupert Bullen. Briefly - very briefly - he felt a pang at seeing the man dead in such an ignominious manner. Though he loathed the merchant Captain, Pearce had always expected him to have a more glorious end. He would have been quite willing to provide it himself. Being drowned like a common sailor somehow wasn't his style.

Then the water started to bubble like boiling milk. The dolphins swam when a globe of light rose to engulf Bullen. The foam turned yellow, then fiery gold. A huge clear bubble formed on the surface of the sea, glowing as intensely as a munitions fire. There was a shape inside it, flapping like an albatross trying to escape the water.

Then the bubble burst and the sea rushed back into the well it had made.

A glittering golden bird hung in the air for a brief moment, illuminating everything below it.

Rupert Bullen's body was nowhere to be seen. Pearce assumed it had been consumed by the firebird. With the downbeat of huge wings, the entity launched itself into the sky. Up and up it soared until the Red Jude was once again the only light visible on the night horizon.

Olive Newthrap was as baffled as Pearce. Perhaps Rupert Bullen's instincts about Ahmose were right after all. She went below to check his cabin. Amongst all the valuables the smuggler had accumulated over the years, she could find no trace of the Egyptian's necklace, earring, amulets, jewelled sandals or white robe. At least Helen's tea was safely in the hold. As long as the wind stayed in their favour she could trade that in Florida, collect the two Spanish galleons, then make a bonfire of the Red Jude.

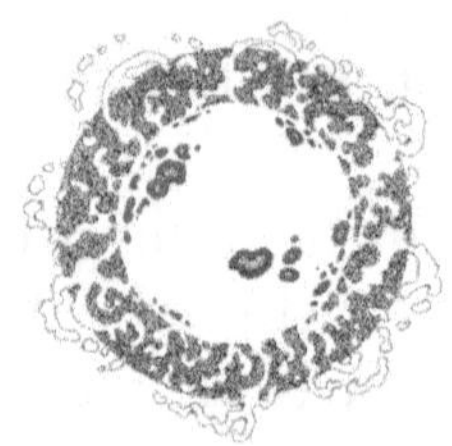

THE OWL AND THE PUSSYCAT

CHAPTER 57

As Laser's eyesight had been given the astronaut's mandatory three monthly check, she increased the polarisation of her helmet. 'There seems to be a departure from plausible causation, here.'

Her control link needed a break. 'Why won't you speak our language, you daft woman?'

'But Earwig, there is something out here. A flickering image is exacerbating my peripheral vision.'

'It's probably only a reflection, Laser.'

'It can't be. It's night-time on this hemisphere of the satellite. All lights are on a time dimmer.'

'Check your torch.'

'It's off. All my exploratory investigations are being executed with the sound scanner. I find it impossible to read the display with extraneous illumination.'

Earwig covered his mouthpiece and called across to the unit supervisor. 'We've got a flickering peripheral image of unidentifiable illumination on the dead side, Super.'

The gruff woman looked up. 'You what?' As her chin was always tucked in her huge uniform collar, it sounded as though her voice was coming through a thick beard.

'Laser's either auditioning for Zic Merton's Magic Show or seeing LGM which glow in the dark.'

'Well she'd better cut it out. She's on double time and the firm only pays her to find the cracks in that antique space station. She can have all the wobblies she wants when she comes off duty.'

'Want me to reel her in?' asked Earwig.

'Has she started speaking English then?'

'Thought she was about to relapse, then seemed to recover.'

'Tell her that if she sees it again to take a picture. She is jigged up with a helmet camera, isn't she?'

'Oh yeah.'

* * *

As the Super filled in the shift's operational hours, she reached over to take the sheets being printed by the processor without looking. They could wait. She'd discovered that two of her crew had decided to change suits and ended up with the wrong tabs. Cursing softly, she instructed the computer to sort out the mess.

She then took a cursory glance at the printouts that had fallen into her hand.

Suddenly, the machinations of her bumbling crew didn't seem so important. The Super found herself looking at the impossible. It was just as well that Laser hadn't seen what the lens on the side of her helmet was pointing at. That would have catapulted her into the verbally impenetrable heights without a parachute.

On the first picture it was only a speck. In the second, the wings were visible. The remaining exposures revealed the feathers, crest and inquisitive eyes of a huge golden bird.

CHAPTER 58

The human race thought that they had all the solutions to Earth's mysteries. Now they were in the wide open reaches of the solar system trying to solve the ones out there. So what was that fabulous golden bird doing, swooping through the stilts supporting maglev railways, roosting on the concrete ruins of 21st century cities and chasing automated cars at 300mph? Only two people could answer that. Unfortunately, they were so eccentric no one would have believed them.

High in a skyscraper's wall-less penthouse suite swept clean of mouldering furniture by the wind, two unearthly creatures met. One perched on a twisted balcony railing. The other lurked in the shadows like a stalking cat, its brown linen robe motionless in the whistling wind.

The bird thought it recognised the cat and dipped its beak several times before jumping to the floor and cautiously circling the ghost, its long tail describing a shimmering circle about the phantom.

The sky changed colour and stabbed the shadows with shafts of angry red sunlight.

The apparition stepped back.

The bird thought the jade cat had said, 'Soon, Ahmose, quite soon.'

The monstrous entity that controlled the Aton bird was not going to release the animal priest that easily.

So many battles had made the monster wise to the wiles of the High Priest.

There was one person the entity didn't yet suspect. The only person the bird could approach without him paying the same price as a Graeco-Roman alchemist and ancient Buddhist. And he would soon arrive, bewildered and annoyed, in this squeaky clean slice of impossible human future.

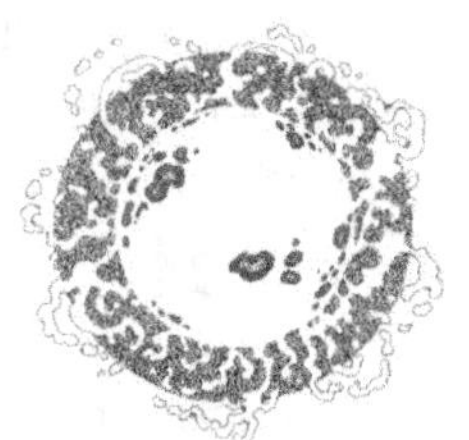

GHOSTS

CHAPTER 59

Ponderously, the man liveried in maroon and scarlet paced through the forecourt colonnade like a huge discontented ladybird. The hair on his temples, tinged by fatigued orange, was at last beginning to grey. Great age and the avoidance of sunlight had faded the African's complexion. Making a close companion of alcohol for so many centuries hadn't helped. Passive and massive, his appearance could still turn the heads of the curious and silence squalling brats; dogs and petty officials had long since ceased to pay any attention to him.

He entered the large gates and pushed his identification tab under the beam of the nearest security officer's scanner as though she didn't recognise him.

She smiled. 'All right Dinan. We know nobody could disguise themselves as you.'

'I'm really a two-thousand-year old genie escaped from the seal of Solomon, you know.'

'Where's your bottle then?'

'Our beloved dictator won't let me near them any more.'

'Well, you did scare the shit out of everyone when you fell from that balcony. You could have been killed.'

'Ah, but all jinn can fly.'

She preferred not to deal with the demonstrations. Security had enough trouble with what was crawling about down there.

The guard reset the surveillance beam. 'Oh - By the way, they're resurfacing the shuttle's tractor path, so try to avoid it.'

Dinan nodded. She was really saying that there was a strong possibility he could fall into one of the flooded grooves made by the excavators and still be trying to clamber out of it when the dogs picked up the exotic scent of his latest hair oil.

Dinan ambled off into the wooded area surrounding the research complex, following the path of the buried photon accelerator, until he reached the doors of the experimental bunker. He stood before the painfully bright white dome for some while. Then he changed his mind and wandered back into the trees towards a conservatory containing a collection of plants most botanists believed extinct.

Dinan flashed a cynical smile at the security scanner and the door lurched open to release the warm smell of tomatoes and ripe mango. He stepped inside, only to be given a light dusting by an automatic insecticide spray. He mouthed abuse at the unseeing nozzle and, removing his jacket, descended into the hothouse lounge.

Stretched out in a chair was a slender woman. For someone over two thousand years old, she displayed remarkably little bone loss, though her features had crumpled and resembled a carefully moulded prune's. In a bizarre way she was attractive, like a well-worn leather armchair. At least Helen Maat fascinated the older of her research assistants. Dinan had become so used to the martinet he had long ceased to pay any attention to what she looked like. Before he was compelled to give up drink he seldom paid attention to anything. Oh, how he longed for a slice of that oblivion, preferably garnished with a few of the narcotic plants about him. Sobriety had brought with it the awareness that he was jealous of those ageing fogies who clustered round Helen. How dare they find the old harridan attractive? As he dare not, and could not, make himself a fool over her, why should they be allowed to?

'What's the matter with your jacket now?' asked Helen, her eyes still closed.

'I've just been sterilised, not that it bothered you the first time it happened.'

'Stop being peevish and come here.' She pointed to the

seat beside her. He sat down as though whatever he had on his mind had slipped to his knees. 'What's bothering you? Is that suit too tight?'

Dinan avoided eye contact. 'I don't like it any more. It makes me look an idiot.'

'The gold cloak and yellow boots were hardly an improvement.'

'Why does everything you wear suit you?'

'Because I don't care whether it does or not.'

Dinan rose to listlessly meander about the huge conservatory. He circled the small lake where carp of every hue and degree of ugliness peered, boggle eyed, back at him.

'Why can't you relax for five minutes?' called Helen.

'My watch stopped telling me the time,' Dinan muttered as though that was the reason for everything, then wandered back to her.

'For goodness sake tell me what's troubling you?'

Dinan slumped down moodily in the chair facing Helen. 'You're up to something.'

'After spending billions on this research establishment, I should hope I am.'

'I didn't mean increasing the efficiency of cold fusion, trying to discover perpetual motion, and ruining the love life of the tsetse fly. I meant, as in defeating sun demons and restoring the Universe to a steady state.'

'Now that would be ambitious.'

'What are you up to?'

'I thought you lost interest when you hit the bottle?'

'Ever since the bottle hit me back, bits of my brain started to slot into place.'

'You want to know whether I've found out how to destroy Ahmose's monster?'

'Well have you? I'm more sick of this existence than you are.'

Helen closed her book and pushed it aside.

'You've always known more than you've been willing to admit to me,' Dinan accused.

Helen took a deep breath. Now Dinan had mustered enough interest to ask, she couldn't keep it to herself any longer. 'To be able to deal with this entity, I had to work out what it is.'

'And now you know?'

'I think so.'

'What is it?'

'Not such a simple beast.' Helen hesitated. 'If I could dissipate the entity's energy field, I'm convinced everything would spring back to the way it was before our lives were tampered with.'

Dinan was becoming uneasy. 'That's not possible.'

Though science could now explain pulsars, reorganise atomic particles and fuse electrons the solution to time was like death. It was worth pondering on, but not important enough to experiment with unless you were tired of life. Especially when the only two people tired of life had no way of dying.

'The creature is not made up of atomic matter as we know it. It is a combination of positive and negative force fields held together by an incomprehensible energy.'

Dinan made that intellectual leap not usual in those who had recently suffered from the DTs. 'You mean, it's a ghost?'

'By our standards, probably.'

'Then why do the bird and Ahmose have mass?'

'There is an explanation. You won't like it.'

So Dinan decided not to ask. 'You know how to exorcise this entity controlling them?'

'Yes.'

'Then what are you sitting here for? Let's get on with it.'

Helen shook her head. 'Why must you always reason along tramlines? You know we have to wait for the bird's next appearance.'

'Then where is it for pity's sake? It must be overdue.'

Helen airily waved his enthusiasm aside. 'It's all right. Everything's in hand.'

'What do you mean?'

'I've discovered the nature of the force that allows Ahmose to materialise.'

Dinan became sullen. 'You never tell me anything.'

Helen was afraid she had told him too much but, with

the final deadline approaching, she had no choice.

Dinan glowered. 'So how can you destroy it?'

'Several years ago we developed a beam capable of firing negative ions at such velocity, some forms of matter fell apart.'

'Not possible.'

'It can rob energy of its electrical or cohesive charge.'

Dinan was even more suspicious. 'You're talking dimensions, aren't you?'

'Strings and strings of them.'

'Which dimension are we in then?'

'Not the one you think.'

'Negative ions could oxygenate a fire, not put it out.'

'We aren't dealing with fire any more than the sun is burning coal. It's a reaction of plasma and-'

'A ghost!' Dinan gave a large, bland smile to conceal the fact that his soul had sunk back down to the Universe's basement.

CHAPTER 60

Suspended like a hammock between two granite outcrops on the steep hillside of conifers, was an orchard. The blossoming cherry trees floated in an eiderdown of pink amongst a sea of grey. They, and a few crumbling walls of yellow brick, were all that remained of a 21st century entrepreneur's garden. She had made her fortune from forests of regimented fir. Now Nature was taking her revenge. The humans fled long before the foundations of the large house slipped from its precarious hillside perch, taking the swimming pool and heliport with it. Birds roosted in the cavities the accident had exposed and salmon had to leap the marble tiles of the swimming pool, now shattered in the gorge below.

A shadowy figure formed in the balmy air sprinkled with petals. If it had possessed colour, it would have been dusty brown, and if it had been the ghost of anything other than a human, it would have been a jade cat.

Sinister and thoughtful, it raised its elegant hands to conjure up another phantom under the pale, pink blossom. This spectre's gown resembled a dark pyramid with voluminous sleeves. A mane of soft, silvery hair haloed the clean-shaven features illuminated from within. Nesting birds took him to be part of nature's realm, skimming his hair as they swooped under the branches.

The High Priest vanished. His creation remained as peaceful as a tombstone, but the patient apparition hadn't come to witness a mortal's passing - quite the reverse.

An indentation appeared in the cushion of petals as though a large invisible foot had lightly touched the orchard floor. Under the benign gaze of the silver haired sphinx, the shape became suffused with a busy mist weaving the gleaming body of a powerful man from another dimension. In real life his fair skin had never been so flawless or his features so handsome.

Then he woke.

In the dappled sunlight, the illusion filtered away, the taut skin slackened and hair turned white.

The newcomer gingerly reached up to touch his face.

'Welcome back to destiny's damnation,' said a soft voice.

The man lay still, silently watching the sunlight play through the blossom above. 'How long has it been, Tommaso?'

'Seven hundred years.'

'What world is this?'

'A clean one. No smoke escapes into the atmosphere unless reduced to steam, every extinct species has its own memorial, and pitch on anything is banned.'

'How do their ships stay afloat?'

'They skim the surface of the sea like bloated jellyfish.'

'They can fly?'

'To the outer planets.'

Tommaso's ghost faded as though he had been a mere trick of the light.

Gerard Jorden sat up. He rubbed his arms and discovered he was wearing a suit of soft cream material that reflected the pale pink blossom surrounding him.

He rose and unsurely climbed up to the summit of the perilous hillside from where he saw an alien landscape sprawling as far as the horizon. Instead of hardened mud tracks rutted by wagon wheels, the roads were smooth and hard. A massive ovate shape thrummed overhead like a floating whale and the sky was from free from the smoke of oven fires.

Jorden shuddered. This antiseptic world worried him. Although he had been an immaculately clean person in his previous lives, chaos and filth had always surrounded him. Here no nettles, brambles, bandits or diseases lay in wait, and the trees gleamed so much, the bugs probably slipped off at the slightest breeze.

Jorden strode on to another ridge. He looked over meadows of wild spring flowers dotted with tastefully positioned copses and large mushroom shapes. The occasional horseless, noiseless and cornerless vehicle passed by on a seamless road. One stopped beside him. Its side window hummed down.

A large, well-fed face with luxuriant side-whiskers

appeared. 'Are you a walker?'

Jorden had the presence of mind to say, 'I seem to have lost my way,' and wondered why his language didn't sound as antique as his perceptions.

The driver beamed and turned to his dashboard of many coloured lights. 'Oh, one should never leave home without their teller. Where are you going?'

Jorden's mind was working frantically. He nevertheless managed to stay calm. 'To a friend. She said it was within walking distance and gave me instructions, but she does have a strange sense of humour.'

'Thought you were looking lost.'

Jorden couldn't believe that the small panel of pretty lights was capable of working out who he meant. He saw no harm in telling the man. 'Her name is Helen.'

'Helen.' The driver tapped something into the keyboard. 'Not a common name. What is her registration ID?'

'Registration ID?'

'Second name?'

Jorden was flustered for a second. 'Oh, she hardly even used it. I think it was something like Ma - at.'

'Ma what?'

'Egyptian I think.'

The man was wondering why he had stopped to help. 'Think you should give her a buzz at the next call point. 'Ain't no name like that listed for this sector.'

Jorden thanked the man who, as he drove off, keyed in a record of the encounter which was automatically transmitted to the register of waifs, strays and lost souls.

Now, if Jorden had said that his friend was a multi billionaire, had a large eccentric companion called Dinan and a secret scientific establishment complete with spaceport, the man would have known whom he meant. Sooner than feed that information into the delicate digestion of his computer, he would have probably left him standing.

As he had been allowed to retain the memory of his previous incarnations this time, Jorden should have found it easier to deal with this one, yet it would take him some while to become orientated to this bizarre, squeaky-clean world. The fact that no one had leapt out on him with pitchforks, cutlasses or fiery brands accusing him of heresy, cowardice or piracy, was a hopeful sign. Bitter experience told him that existence always had a sting in its tail. At least he now felt as though he was in command of his destiny, whether it had sharp corners or not.

Cautiously reassured, Jorden was on the point of striding out to meet this bland, benign world when a small golden speck appeared in the distant sky.

CHAPTER 61

To escape Dinan's burgeoning curiosity, Helen retreated to the bunker where she had been working on the beam gun.

She donned a protective suit, and then instructed the laboratory above to activate the cut-outs in case of a power surge. Helen may have been immortal, but had learnt to avoid raising suspicion with too many fatal accidents.

She adjusted her polarised eye shield as she went to a reinforced shutter and gently turned a switch on the console beside it. The metre thick steel rose to reveal a ribbon of intense light. It resembled a frozen bolt of lightning. As though recognising the alchemist, it became a spiral of devouring plasma that coiled its way about the crucible like a ravenous tiger stalking its cage. There was the dry howling of oxygen being greedily consumed and, seeing escape, the unearthly dragon opened its dazzling maw. Helen found herself looking into a gullet spangled with the tiny explosions of colliding charged particles.

Helen unlocked the firing mechanism of the negative beam gun, lifted it from its bracket and onto her shoulder, and aimed. She always ran the risk of being devoured by the monster by hesitating. The demon seemed so alive, it was murder by another name, but murder all the same.

She fired. The plasma dragon reeled like a serpent with its tail blown off and briefly increased in size to compensate. Suddenly the artificial lightning dissipated into harmless steam, its structure broken apart by a chain reaction only the alchemist understood.

CHAPTER 62

No sooner had the Aton bird appeared on the horizon than several gyroplanes descended from nowhere like dragonflies with maliciously glinting wings. As they touched down, surrounding Gerard Jorden, their long tails scrolled over, scorpion style, as though ready to strike. He wasn't to know that the weapons the crews carried only fired tranquillising darts.

From a safe distance, the person in charge of the kidnapping, a sour-faced woman who looked as though she had overdosed on nettle tea, told Jorden that he was being taken to a place of safety. For whose safety she omitted to mention. It would have been pointless in fighting back in this world. Things had slipped so rapidly out of his control he had no choice but to let them bundle him into the leading gyroplane.

Being airborne for the first time terrified even the steel willed Jorden and every muscle in his body froze in an attempt to keep his stomach from turning. He had heard that in the land of El Dorado people could leave the ground suspended from sacks of hot air, but the engines of these infernal contraptions made an ugly whirring sound and spat angrily every time they banked or cornered.

Jorden began to wonder if this was reality after all. He ventured a glance at the gleaming towers and homogenised landscape far below. By the time they had landed on a circular pad of white concrete, his old wit had totally deserted him. Without anything familiar to hang a comment on, what was there to say?

The sour faced woman and a dozen guards in uniforms that blended with the bright, bland corridors, ushered their prisoner out into the grounds of an estate Louis XIV would have envied. Before they reached the entrance to the main house, Jorden noticed a large man watching him with moon-faced disbelief.

Without warning, Jorden sprinted away from the guards. 'Dinan!'

The African hugged Jorden as though he were the World

Lottery Fairy. 'What are you doing here?'

'I thought I'd been arrested.'

'Helen! She said something about expecting you!' Dinan waved away the sour-faced woman and her uniforms.

'Then she must know that the bird's returned.' Jorden suddenly realised how much both of them had changed, though didn't understand why Dinan's expression dropped. 'Hadn't we better tell the old harpy?'

Dinan now knew it had been a mistake to desert the bottle after all. 'Let's take a walk.'

Still uneasy at the gleaming orderliness of this new world, Jorden strolled around the boundary of the vast estate with Dinan. A bolt of fiery energy rocketed skywards from Helen's laboratory. It was apparently a normal occurrence.

Dinan eventually admitted, 'Helen knows how to destroy Ahmose's monster.'

Jorden was unsure what to think and several emotions surged through his thoughts. 'You don't sound very enthusiastic?'

Dinan suddenly smiled. 'Perhaps I've got used to immortality.'

'That's not it. What's bothering you?'

The African hesitated. 'She claims that the entity controlling Ahmose is some sort of ghost.'

Jorden stopped in his tracks. 'What? Have you existed so long only to find out you could have exorcised the creature centuries ago?'

'It's no normal ghost, the thing's an immensely powerful entity consumed by vengeful energy, and it's the way in which she's going to exorcise it that bothers me.'

'Why?'

Dinan had lost the power to calculate decades ago, and couldn't understand the technology involved. 'It's much more than bell, book and candle.' His light voice suddenly took on a hard edge. 'And there's more...'

'What?'

'There's another entity.'

'Another?'

'The one that snatched you to protect Ahmose and, before that, Helen and me to save him.'

'I don't understand?'

Lack of comprehension no longer bothered Dinan. 'I believe that is the power controlling our time, and that we are made of the same intangible substance.'

Jorden hoped he hadn't understood. 'What do you mean?'

'Our natural life spans were extended for one reason only. When that reason ceases to exist - so will we.'

'Then that must mean we're...' Jorden stopped. The path he stood on was solid. He felt real enough. The idea was absurd.

Dinan turned to face him. 'We are ghosts. From the time we encountered so much as a feather of the Aton Bird, we became creatures of Ahmose's protecting phantom.'

Jorden reeled slightly. 'Then how can we exist in the lives of those about us?' He hesitated. 'Though that would explain why you don't age.'

It all made horrible sense. The entity trying to help Ahmose knew Helen Maat would eventually find the solution, and perhaps only had the power to keep those two materialised. It just brought Jorden back when he was needed.

'Then we're really the ones who need exorcising?'

The two men reached the ornamental gardens and sat on a stone seat.

'How did Ahmose become a bird deity, Dinan?'

'He denied a vengeful god.'

'That all?' Jorden looked up and saw a small golden speck against the cobalt sky. 'What do we do now?'

Dinan looked doleful. 'Keep out of Helen's way.'

They became aware of a slight, wiry figure dressed in orange overalls.

'So now you know.' Helen Maat's tone suggested that they should have worked it out for themselves long ago.

Dinan and Jorden looked at each other, unable to fathom how she had overheard their conversation.

The alchemist turned her critical gaze on Jorden. 'You've not worn well.'

'And you still sound like the harridan from Hades.'

She laughed. 'When I've finished, we'll all have a one way ticket there.'

'So I've heard. How did you find out that we're ghosts?'

'On.'

'On what?'

'The biblical name for Innu. I had a team excavate a tomb there.'

Dinan was indignant. 'You never mentioned anything to me!'

'At the time you were too drunk to know a pyramid from a papyrus scroll.'

'That site must have already been turned over a hundred times?'

'All the complexes the Egyptologists expected to find, yes. But I had an ancient scroll. Remember Kleopatra?'

Dinan riffled through his abused memory cells and remembered the old alchemist who had been transformed into a pillar of fire.

Jorden wondered, if he was a ghost, why couldn't he just drop out of sight? It was bad enough listening to them argue when he knew what they were talking about.

'She, or something, left me a parchment to decipher,' Helen reminded Dinan.

'It wasn't in hieroglyphs you could identify. I thought you gave up on that centuries ago?'

'It would have certainly defeated Champollion. The individual characters had so many alternative combinations it needed advanced computing power to translate them.'

Dinan tried not to sound interested. 'Why was the papyrus made so difficult if we were meant to understand it?'

'It could have fallen into the wrong hands.'

'What did it say then?'

'It gave the location of a secret burial at the bottom of a deep shaft.'

'How does that prove we're ghosts?'

'The coffin was lined with a text explaining how Ahmose had been transformed into a bird. Once I had translated that, everything began to make sense.'

There was a peevish rumble in Jorden's mellow tone. 'You've been wandering the Earth for so many centuries, it's about time you discovered something that made sense.'

Helen ignored him. 'Come with me.'

Dinan and Jorden followed the wiry alchemist to a vault that had been constructed to resemble an excavated tomb.

The High Priest's sarcophagus was no longer standing upright and its lid had been removed. The coffin inside was also open. The two men peered down into it. Having steeled himself to come face to face with someone's mortal remains, Dinan was relieved to find that it was empty.

Helen beckoned them into an antechamber. Inside a vacuum sealed cabinet the dead eyed cadaver gazed unseeingly down at them. It was still amazingly intact, and belonged to a man who had been gaunt featured before being embalmed. Above the upright mummy was a screen.

Helen mischievously noted that the men were bothered. They obviously believed she had managed to reanimate a four-thousand-year-old corpse. 'Would you like to see what he really looked like?'

Dinan said nothing, but the soldier in Jorden ordered him to reply, 'Show us.'

Helen pushed a button and the screen pulsed into life.

Dinan was still eyeing the mummy, expecting it at any moment to make flesh all the nightmares that come with the DTs.

A face appeared from the green depths of the screen.

Dinan couldn't resist looking. 'He's not Egyptian.' He stopped. 'I know him...'

'He looks Oriental,' Jorden added.

Helen wasn't surprised at the men's determination to be offhand. 'He was the High Priest of Amon Ra's temple at the time of Ahmose's metamorphosis. All mention of him was eradicated more thoroughly than any reference to the Aton.'

'You mean that he was the one responsible for what happened to Ahmose?'

'To save his temple and the local population from Pharaoh Eye's retribution, he was compelled to trade off

Ahmose.'

Jorden was reminded of his disasters in diplomacy. 'Suppose it must have been the logical thing to do at the time.'

'All senior priests had to be politicians. The animal keeper was his closest friend and had been tending the secret temple of the Aton ever since the cult's overthrow. Because they believed the gods had conferred immortality on Ahmose, the High Priest and temple mystics dedicated his spirit to the Phoenix without consulting the poor little sod. They had no way of realising that our sun is a binary star.'

Jorden only just comprehended that the world was in orbit about the sun. 'A what?'

'Sol has a twin star. It's a dark red dwarf beyond the Kuiper Belt, invisible unless you're looking for it.'

What's that got to do with the Aton?'

'Us Greeks called the Earth's intelligent manifestation Gaia. This twin of Sol is more of a stunted sibling. The Egyptians called it Ra, thinking it was the sun they knew.'

Dinan gasped. 'It's intelligent?'

'And very cunning and vengeful.'

Jorden had no interest in astronomy, however cunning or vengeful. 'Why did this "Ra" pick on Ahmose?'

'He was the last true believer in the Aton that briefly usurped his cult. Ra saw his chance to revenge himself on humanity and made the priest his creature instead of sending him to Duat with the blessed dead. It was only when the bird rose from the waters of the Nile that the High Priest realised the enormity of what he had done. There was no way to reverse the spell. Once adopted by Ra, you stay adopted. Ahmose became the entity's eyes on the world and, as his cult grew weaker, all the angry red twin of our sun had left was the bird.' Helen hesitated. 'Ahmose isn't a mere ghost, he's a manifestation created by thousands of years of human conviction.'

Jorden looked wan. It all sounded like magic to him.

'All right,' Dinan suddenly demanded. 'How did the High Priest manage to get himself turned into a ghost as well?'

'The only way he and the mystics of the inner sanctum could hope to retrieve Ahmose's spirit was by sending another one after it. The High Priest didn't have the same power as Ra, otherwise he would have rescued him, though he was able to subvert time - our time. That's why he,' she pointed to the mummy, 'made us immortal.'

Dinan raised an accusing finger but was unable to attach any sensible words to the action.

If Helen Maat managed to destroy the entity controlling the firebird, their time would snap back into place. Jorden understood that as well and was terrified. It would mean reliving the pain and ignominy of his original life. Dinan placed a large reassuring hand on his shoulder. He hardly felt it.

But they had no choice. The spirit of the High Priest was losing his power. Without him Helen and Dinan would face existence in their interminable ghostly dimension, while Jorden would probably dwindle away in some twilight limbo without feeling or thought.

Dinan was suspicious of her detailed knowledge concerning this strange dwarf star. She had obviously known about it for centuries. 'How did you find out about the sun's red twin? No spaceship has managed to get that far out and return.'

'You don't want to know,' Helen told him.

* * *

Avoiding her own security, Helen made sure that the negative beam gun was fully charged, then concealed it in a sports bag that was more likely to attract attention than a machine gun case. The only sports Helen Maat indulged in were life threatening and required heavy munitions.

Jorden reluctantly took the bag and followed Dinan, who was now wishing he had remained the neighbourhood drunk.

The certainties of Jorden's original lives had made him self-assured until brutal reality interrupted. The dread of going back there overwhelmed him. 'Is this necessary?'

'Do you want to spend eternity waiting to nursemaid a

281

psychically disturbed priest who never appears again?'

To Jorden, eternal boredom was preferable to the destiny he would have to repeat. Helen and Dinan had forgotten what true agony was thousands of years ago.

'What will happen when we disappear?' he asked.

'Everyone will assume we've gone missing, like the crew of the Marie Celeste.'

'Marie Celeste?'

'A ghost ship.'

Jorden tried hard not to recall anything more about ships, pirates, or mercenary soldiers. He wandered away to blankly gaze at the rhododendrons spilling their brilliant blooms onto the maze of paths zigzagging up a terrace. It was ironic he should start wondering at the beauty of this world just as he was about to be swallowed back into Hell.

'Does the bird understand anything?' asked Dinan.

'There's probably nothing much left of Ahmose by now.'

'Then where's the point in putting Gerard Jorden through that again?' demanded Dinan.

Helen gave him piercing glare. 'So you want to live forever.'

'I don't want to see Ahmose or him harmed any more.'

'Ahmose died thousands of years ago. Jorden will now die just once.'

Jorden rejoined them. 'Why did this high priest bring me here?'

'You're the only one the bird might approach. The entity knows what we're up to and is not going to let the Aton bird perch on our shoulders.' Helen indicated the terrace. 'Over there is a sunken garden. Try to attract the bird's attention and lure it down.'

'Shall I light a fire?' Dinan asked.

'No, it'd ruin the azaleas.' Helen took the gun from the bag then turned to Jorden. 'Get on with it.' Without waiting to see if he obeyed, she disappeared into the rhododendrons.

Dinan smiled weakly. 'I'm sorry, none of us have any choice.'

'I know. What are you going to do?'

'Wish I was drunk.'

Watching the sky, Jorden reluctantly wandered away, half hoping that the guards would arrest him. Unfortunately they now realised that he was with Helen.

After they had waited a small eternity, the plumage of the firebird traced dazzling ribbons in the thin cloud. Helen Maat was right; it was reluctant to come down.

Jorden hesitated as he remembered the small, good-natured Egyptian who could materialise from the ashes of a fire. After losing two lives on his account, it now seemed strange that Jorden should be the one to lure Ahmose to his annihilation. He raised an arm as though enticing a trained owl. The bird slowly spiralled down towards him. He retreated carefully towards the terrace. The bird followed. As he increased his pace a yellow halo surrounded the deity as though a vengeful hand were trying to hold it back.

Jorden started to run. Touched by the angry entity engulfing the bird, the azaleas wilted as it descended. On reaching the terrace, Jorden felt his skin scorch. He lost his footing and tumbled into the sunken garden.

The bird's parasitic halo ballooned out like a malevolent yellow sun and trapped Jorden. Dinan chased after Helen and tried to take the gun from her.

She snatched it back. 'You don't know how to operate it you fool! Go and help Jorden!'

The fiery globe now covered the garden like a lid. Dinan plunged down through the malevolent emanation and pulled Jorden to the ground.

Helen followed. Her head was seared as she tried to calculate the creature's weakest point. If it had been a reasoning mood, the entity might have taken Ahmose and disappeared then and there but, Ra's power had receded, so had the god's rationality. The entity was determined that the only threat to it would at last be destroyed, whatever the cost.

'Now Helen! Now!' Dinan whispered desperately, afraid the creature was working out how to inflict something more horrific than immortality on them.

The entity's fiery globe suddenly absorbed Helen.

Everything seemed to have ended in total failure.

Then there was a flurry of movement inside the monster's body. With his Anubis headed staff, the phantom High Priest was holding back a breach in the entity's halo, circling it with a blue flame. It was the target Helen had been looking for. Blistering away the soft tissue of the alchemist's body, Ra turned its attention to her immortality.

Dead or alive, Helen was too obsessed to forget the position of the beam gun's trigger.

Dinan and Jorden remained pressed to the ground, wondering whether to expect eternity or annihilation.

The monstrous sphere rapidly expanded again, searing the bushed to their roots. The entity pulsed as though frantically trying to catch its breath.

Without warning it shrank to a pinpoint of light, then flickered out.

Helen was nowhere to be seen. The beam gun lay blackened on the gravel path.

Dinan and Jorden leapt up.

The point of light went out.

When the estate's security reached the spot they found nothing but the beam gun and a lot of replanting to do.

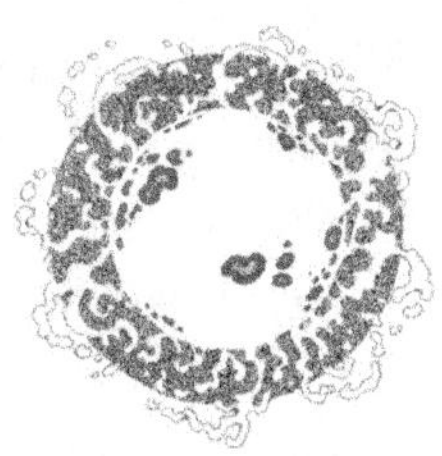

ENDINGS

CHAPTER 63

With one hand holding a huge wig, and the other pushing aside reeds, the small priest ran along the path only trodden by crocodiles. His pursuers, able to see the glint of jewellery and fluttering of his long robe, were gaining.

The deep pool in the menagerie filled with dangerous wild life was benign compared with the inky water beneath the matted reeds that could have drowned pharaoh's army. Near to the water's edge, Ahmose tried to find a tunnel in the stems to duck through. He was more afraid of being caught by Kahu's guards than any reptile that might have been laying in wait for its supper.

Something suddenly grabbed his ankle and pulled him into the water.

Ahmose threshed about in panic. A large hand closed over his mouth and another snatched the wig from his head. Seconds later he heard an impressive splash as the heavy hairpiece hit the river. There was a lot of snapping and snorting as the resident insomniacs tore it apart.

The footsteps of Ahmose's pursuers abruptly stopped.

'She's in the river!'

'Where?'

'Look! Look!'

'Get to the boat quickly!'

As they dashed off, the hand was withdrawn from Ahmose's mouth.

'Who is it? What's happening?'

'It's Goose. Keep your voice down. The High Priest told us to stop you.'

'You don't understand!' Ahmose desperately whispered. 'She must have time to get away!' He tried to struggle from the grasp of the High Priest's servant.

'No father, you're not throwing your life away for her,' Goose insisted.

'By the time they realise they've been fooled, she'll be well away,' the servant added. 'That fat toad, Kahu, will have you beaten to death if he finds out how you tricked him.'

The exertion on his insubstantial frame made Ahmose feel as though he was spinning through the midnight air and he clutched at the reeds to save himself.

'We have to get him out of the water. This has been too much for him.'

Goose shook the animal priest. 'Don't you dare faint.'

The young men hustled Ahmose to a small party of priests with the elderly Bast cat. Avoiding Kahu's men, they passed his barge lit up against the night sky.

Soldiers instead of the regular medjay guarded the temple's entrance, so the priests followed the Bast cat round the towering walls to a narrow tunnel leading down into the foundations. Ahmose was bundled through it and into the outer temple where the massive columns constructed to intimidate other mortals, made them feel secure. Now the animal priest could faint with a clear conscience if he wanted to.

As they entered the inner temple, the statues of animal deities seemed to dance in the light of their torches. The priests dropped back, allowing Goose to take Ahmose to the portal of the inner sanctum. There he waited while the High Priest escorted the animal keeper inside. The cult's six sinister mystics were waiting.

There was a reassuring mew from the Bast cat, so Goose went back to check on the menagerie. In case Kahu's guards felt like paying it a night-time visit, the apprentice had allowed the lion out of its pen to prowl the enclosure. It was too myopic and slow to catch anything that travelled faster than a basin of camel entrails, but they weren't to know that.

In the inner sanctum, Ahmose found himself surrounded by a circle of gaunt faces. Though he knew of the mysterious mystics, seeing their emaciated features in the light of flickering lamps made him wonder if they shouldn't have been in some necromantic menagerie as well.

The mystics silently drifted from the chamber like a formation of grounded vultures.

Ahmose looked up at the dancing shadows on the high ceiling and wondered what to give the animals for their morning meal. He lost his balance and toppled backwards.

A grip of iron steadied him. 'Will the queen take a small drink?'

'Queen?' Ahmose looked down at the jewelled amulets, necklace and robe he was wearing. He took the cup of ale from the High Priest. 'Should I be in here?'

'The inner sanctum is the only place Kahu would not dare send his men. You are lucky to have an apprentice with more sense than his master.' There was no annoyance in the High Priest's voice. He would have been more surprised if his friend ever managed to think with his head.

'Did she escape?'

The inscrutable expression on the hewn features softened. 'We believe so. You are now the problem. The Vizier's deputy has threatened us with terrible retribution if we try to hide you.'

'Then I must give myself up!' Ahmose was unable to escape the grasp powerful enough to hold back the bull of Merwer.

'Do you really believe I would surrender my dearest friend to a creature like Kahu?'

'You have no choice.'

'He believes you were devoured by a crocodile.'

'Not that one, he would know that they never get up until dawn.'

'Then he will have to face the wrath of the rising Aton.' It wasn't a heresy or a threat, merely a statement of probability.

Ahmose was always worried when his friend's voice resonated like the watcher in a tomb. 'What have you done?'

'This usurping pharaoh will not last long and his Vizier's deputy will never return to him.'

'What have you done?'

Faced with the only person who understood him, the High Priest couldn't remain inscrutable. 'For once in my life I am going to lay aside the welfare of the temple and all obligation to duty.'

* * *

The next morning Khepri pushed the brash copper sun disc into the rosy sky with its usual suddenness. Before there was enough breeze to flutter the temple's pennants, the shadow of its high walls reached out towards the river in a massive fist.

Ahmose and the High Priest looked out from the temple's highest point, while the mystics chanted incantations in its bowels. It gradually occurred to the animal keeper what the guardian vultures and his friend were up to. As the High Priest had no intention of admitting it, Ahmose could only protest with sullen silence.

Several of Kahu's men were loitering about the main jetty, awaiting orders. Others were still searching the smaller tributaries in reed boats. It was obvious that Queen Ankhesenamun had given them the slip and they now needed someone to blame and take back to Thebes.

Ahmose watched the concentration on the face of the High Priest. Knowing that whatever was about to happen would involve the breaking of every vow he had ever taken, not to mention cataclysm and sudden death. Ahmose was just a menial animal keeper. His aptitude with the miraculous only ran to feeding the crocodile of Sebek without donating any fingers. What was going to happen? Would ball lightning set the boat ablaze, leaving only the trace of the huge, oily Kahu in a murky slick? Or would a sea monster break the boat's keel and swallow the crew?

Ahmose involuntarily reached out and clutched his implacable friend's arm. 'Let them go.'

The High Priest half turned but didn't answer. He had rarely refused the menial animal priest anything. This was different.

Ahmose persisted. 'If Queen Ankhesenamun has escaped and the usurper is about to be deposed, where is the point in it?'

There could be no answer because there was no point in it. In his haste to protect his friend, the High Priest knew he was on the verge of committing a mortal sin. Calling on the gods to destroy an enemy would leave a stain on his soul that would follow him to his grave and beyond.

For all Kahu knew, crocodiles had devoured Ahmose, or even Queen Ankhesenamun, and Goose was quite capable of tending the menagerie while the animal keeper hid. The ruler who took the place of the usurping Pharaoh Eye was unlikely to be bothered with his predecessor's grudges.

'I will not allow you to risk eternal death for my sake!'

The High Priest turned to see his friend standing on the lip of the temple roof. As though hearing Ahmose, the six mystics in the depths of the temple stopped chanting.

In the distance the searching guards had returned to Kahu's barge and the crew were taking up their oars.

The High Priest pulled Ahmose away from the edge of the roof.

They watched as the boat's mooring ropes were released and it was rowed back to Thebes.

In the rising sun's glare, the High Priest briefly wondered what it would have been like to summon the wrath of Ra.

CHAPTER 64

Helen Maat looked up, then darted a glance back to the crucible. Just as they were reaching the climax of several years' work, a storm cloud had appeared in the south. The inundation had twice failed now. After months of drought, having to share her granary with the local farmers so they could save their seed, and losing her ferry to the baking mud, there was a promise of rain. She greeted this beneficence of nature with her customary stream of abuse. Dinan tried to look as though he never knew the woman.

It was a land that hardly ever saw rain, let alone a deluge. Women drawing muddy water all along the shallow river's bank threw off their robes and waved them at the large cloud bank and inside temples priests were shaving their bodies in preparation for the ceremonies of renewal.

As the heavens spat their first huge drops on the parched land, the effigy of Hapi was garlanded. Even the family of Ptolemy interrupted their thoughts of infanticide, fratricide, patricide, matricide, and assassination in general to watch the approaching downpour. Geese cackled, hippos bellowed, crocodiles grinned and Helen Maat swore hard enough to draw lightning.

The crucible sizzled with rainwater and rivulets ran down the polished surfaces of the lenses and mirrors.

'I don't think it would have worked anyway,' Dinan tried to console her from a safe distance. 'Look upon it as a warning from Amon.'

'You've spent so long with the Ptolemies, you're too riddled with superstition to know any better!' The alchemist tossed her tongs into the crucible. 'Let's get the equipment inside.' Dinan reached down to lift the crucible. 'Hay can take that, I don't want you coming apart again.'

Something large, furry and damp butted the back of his knees and he involuntarily obeyed. 'What's the matter, Ink?'

The panther gave a huge mew, then shook the water from her sleek fur.

'It's so long since she's seen rain she's forgotten she doesn't like it.'

'I thought she was trying to tell us something.'

Helen dismantled a mirror and tucked it under her arm. 'Until she learns Greek, she's not going to have much luck.'

Dinan watched Hay lug the crucible away. 'You know what?'

He sounded as though he was going to say something important.

The alchemist stopped trying to dismantle a tripod with one hand. 'What?'

'I think she knows where those tomb robbers hid their hoard.'

'If I thought that, I'd learn to purr her language.'

'Lilia understands her.'

'And who understands Lilia?'

Dinan had a mischievous glitter in his eye.

'Now what?' demanded Helen in a tone that suggested he could easily become Ptolemy's slave again.

'Let's go to Alexandria.'

'Why?'

'You'll not be happy until you've found people able to argue on your level. You said yourself that there was more knowledge to be gleaned from rational experiment than magic. This sort of tinkering only amuses the local peasants and their donkeys.'

As they reached the house, Helen brushed the water from her hair. 'But I know I'm right. Heat is the transformer of all matter.'

A green-eyed girl was ready with dry robes for Dinan and Helen.

'Thank you Lilia. Will you put some basins out to catch the rainwater.'

'There!' Dinan declared jubilantly.

'There what?'

'When the mistress thanks her servants, it means she's beginning to think rationally.'

'I knew it was a mistake to bring you back from the dead.'

'Why did you save me?'

'I needed a conscience.'

'All right then - give up these pointless experiments. Time is the only thing that can prove you right, and neither of us is immortal enough to see it.'

Helen looked into the mirror and saw yet another wrinkle. 'Yes, you're probably right.'

The southern Italian sun was cruel and had bleached Tommaso's shabby maroon gown. His scholar's black had long since fallen into tatters and only the charity of some nuns had saved him from starvation. The old velvet robe they gave him had outlived several owners and, in making him look a like pauper, probably saved him from many a thieving vagabond.

At least Tommaso had looked reasonably respectable when leaving Laura with her new husband. The young man came from a merchant family with attitudes as free as the trade winds, though the scholar did part more like a doting aunt then stern guardian. The marriage contract that had briefly bound tutor and pupil was easily annulled with a candle flame and carried off on the breeze that filled the sails of her new family's caravels.

Tommaso felt gratified at having saved the teenager from a wretched marriage and was also oddly satisfied at being compelled out into the world. Having spent a lifetime within the walls of some study or other, he used to believe that the universe beyond was wide and wicked and, whenever he travelled, it had been with a party. Now the blisters on his feet had stopped bleeding he no longer needed the comfort of company and, though the world was wide and wicked, notaries and scholars, even ones as shabby as himself, were given the respect he was sure they never quite deserved.

As he sat in the piazza of a small town an elderly Jew carrying an abacus and wine flask ambled from a doorway.

'Oh no,' Tommaso groaned to himself, 'not figures.'

The bearded worthy only wanted some intelligent gentile conversation and someone to listen to him bemoan the elopement of an errant offspring.

'Yes,' agreed Tommaso. 'Perhaps marriage is an overrated estate.'

The old man spun the beads of his abacus. 'But how would we generate without it?'

'In sin no doubt, in sin.'

Tommaso shared the Jew's wine, then spent his last coin on a frugal meal in the nearest tavern. When he had finished eating, a plump farmer approached the scholar. He hoped that this would be the fee to pay for a night's lodging. He straightened his cap, then took the bundle of letters the farmer offered. They were out of order, mostly undated and in some cases written before paper was manufactured.

It took Tommaso the rest of the day and half the night to unravel the complexities of the family's estate. Like most land, it had been divided and sub divided over generations until there was no plot large enough worth farming. Tommaso advised and commiserated as best as he could and was rewarded with enough ducats to keep him for a week.

The road to the next town passed through a canyon.

Tommaso shuffled along quickly, trying to look as destitute and imbecilic as possible. There was a clatter of a horse's hooves above. Someone was observing him. They eventually faded away and Tommaso could see the flat landscape beyond the walls of rock. He increased his pace. Before he could reach it, a gang of rough looking men surrounded him. They were probably dispossessed farmers and unemployed craftsmen, yet looked no less intimidating than genuine bandits.

'Where are you going?' asked the ringleader.

'It was my intention to follow the road.'

'Why?'

'Because I have no fear of it getting up and following me.'

The robber gave an ugly chuckle. 'We know you were well paid by Roberto's family.'

Tommaso tried to tell himself that having already travelled through the most dangerous provinces without being murdered, he should look at this as a down payment on fate's future benevolence. He reached inside his gown and pulled out his purse. The robber snatched it. The rogues didn't leave though.

'It's all I have, apart from my pen and some paper.'

'You could recognise us. People here don't think much of those who rob nuns or notaries.'

'I'm not returning to the town.'

Tommaso watched in horror as the robber raised his rusty sword. Attached to it was every intention of cutting his throat. There was nothing the scholar could do but cross his heart in preparation for the blade it was about to receive. He pushed himself to his full height and closed his eyes.

Suddenly there was a clatter of hooves and rapid crash of steel on steel.

Tommaso opened his eyes to find that he was in the middle of a bloody fracas. From nowhere, a giant of a man had leapt from his steed and with a sword in each hand easily driven off the bandits. The only evidence of their presence was Tommaso's split purse and several splashes of blood on the canyon wall.

The scholar crumpled to his knees as the saintly maniac wiped the gore from his swords and replaced them in their scabbards. Without looking up, Tommaso seized the frayed hem of the warrior's knee length tunic and kissed it, then his white mare ambled over and gave the scholar a nudge that unbalanced him.

There was a loud laugh. 'Herr Clerk! Fool! Don't you know me?'

Tommaso looked up at the fair, stubbly features, 'Gerard!' He flung his arms about the General's waist.

'Don't be an idiot, man.' Jorden lifted him with one hand. 'I've been following your trail for so long, I don't want to find a gibbering half-wit at the end of it.'

'But why?' Tommaso then noticed that his rescuer was as shabby and underfed as himself, though his horse seemed to have fared better. 'What happened to you, Gerard?'

'Duke Vittorio sent me packing in disgrace.'

'Because of what Laura and I did?'

'The knave had been using me. Expected me to put down an uprising in Via La Rosa with men who knew they wouldn't be paid. For years I was the only army he had. Me, Matteo and forty men.'

Tommaso blanched. 'You aren't thinking of becoming a condottiere are you?'

Jorden roared with laughter. 'The only army I could raise would be a vagabond one, and I seem to spend most of the time driving away my best recruits.'

Tommaso bandaged Jorden's slashed arm with some strips of linen he carried for emergencies. 'Then what do you do?'

'I'm bodyguard or labourer to anyone who'll pay me.'

The scholar pressed his purse into the soldier's hand. Jorden replaced the cap on Tommaso's head and tucked the purse back into the scholar's gown.

Jorden's voice mellowed. 'You're the only true hearted man I've ever known, Tommaso. Matteo may have been honourable, but he was a psychopath. Bianca was a good woman. To my shame, I never realised how good. She wanted to return all the jewels I had ever given her. But you! You gave up everything to save a girl from misery. There's more honour in that than fighting battles.' Jorden became uncharacteristically hesitant. 'Will you have me as a travelling companion, scholar? When we cease to be any use to each other, we can find a monastery where they might let you illuminate books and me dig the garden. We're no good for anything else in this mad, muddled world. Should we let it know we care though?'

'Will the horse mind?'

'As long as she's fed and watered she'd let the world go hang as well. Where were you heading?'

'I always wanted to visit the southern coast and dawdle through antiquity's ruins.'

Jorden pointed along the canyon to the far horizon. 'The sea is that way.'

THE END

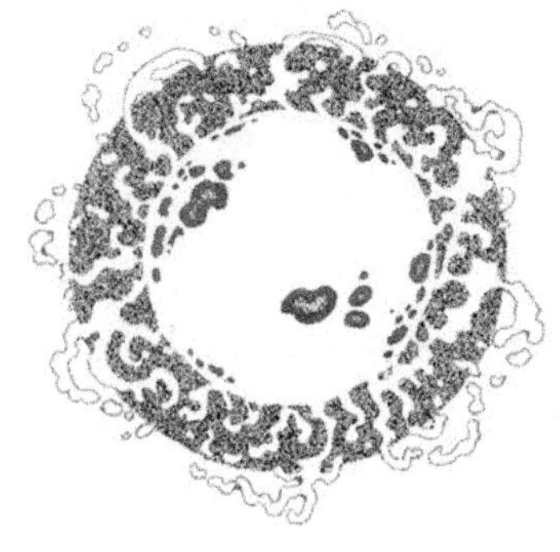